IMAGE PROBLEM

"I see it now. You are ... Naismith."

"Of course."

"Not Lord Vorkosigan."

"I am *annoyed* with Lord Vorkosigan."

So, the gulf that yawned between them was deeper than he'd truly realized. To her, it was Lord Vorkosigan who wasn't real. His fingers entwined around the back of her neck, and he breathed her breath as she asked, "Why do you let Barrayar screw you over?"

"It's the hand I was dealt."

"By whom? I don't get it."

"It's all right. It just happens to be very important to me to win with the hand I was dealt. So be it."

"Your funeral." Her lips were muffled on his mouth.

"Mmm."

She drew back a moment. "Can I still jump your bones? Carefully of course. You'll not go away mad, for turning you down? Turning Barrayar down, that is. Not you, never you . . ."

I'm getting used to it. Almost numb. . . . "Am I to sulk?" he inquired lightly. "Because I can't have it all, take none, and go off in a huff? I'd hope you'd bounce me down the corridor on my pointed head if I were so dense."

She laughed. It was all right, if he could still make her laugh. If Naismith was all she wanted, she could surely have him. Half a loaf for half a man.

Lois McMaster Bujold

A MILES VORKOSIGAN ADVENTURE

BROTHERS IN ARMS

BAEN BOOKS

A Baen Books Original

Baen Publishing Enterprises
P.O. Box 1403
Riverdale, NY 10471

ISBN: 0-671-69799-4

Cover art by Alan Gutierrez

First Printing, January 1989
Second Printing, July 1990
Third Printing, May 1992

Printed in the United States of America

Distributed by Simon & Schuster
1230 Avenue of the Americas
New York, NY 10020

For Martha and Andy

Chapter One

His combat drop shuttle crouched still and silent in the repairs docking bay—malevolent, to Miles's jaundiced eye. Its metal and fibreplas surface was scarred, pitted and burned. It had seemed such a proud, gleaming, efficient vessel when it was new. Perhaps it had undergone psychotic personality change from its traumas. It had been new such a short few months ago. . . .

Miles rubbed his face wearily, and blew out his breath. If there was any incipient psychosis floating around here, it wasn't contained in the machinery. In the eye of the beholder indeed. He took his booted foot off the bench he'd been draped over and straightened up, at least to the degree his crooked spine permitted. Commander Quinn, alert to his every move, fell in behind him.

"There," Miles limped down the length of the fuselage and pointed to the shuttle's portside lock, "is the design defect I'm chiefly concerned about."

1

He motioned the sales engineer from Kaymer Orbital Shipyards closer. "The ramp from this lock extends and retracts automatically, with a manual override—fine so far. But its recessed slot is inside the hatch, which means that if for any reason the ramp gets hung up, the door can't be sealed. The consequences of which I trust you can imagine." Miles didn't have to imagine them; they had burned in his memory for the last three months. Instant replay without an off switch.

"Did you find this out the hard way at Dagoola IV, Admiral Naismith?" the engineer inquired in a tone of genuine interest.

"Yeah. We lost . . . personnel. I was damn near one of them."

"I see," said the engineer respectfully. But his brows quirked.

How dare you be amused. . . . Fortunately for his health, the engineer did not smile. A thin man of slightly above average height, he reached up the side of the shuttle to run his hands along the slot in question, pull himself up chin-up fashion, peer about and mutter notes into his recorder. Miles resisted an urge to jump up and down like a frog and try to see what he was looking at. Undignified. With his own eye-level even with the engineer's chest, Miles would need about a one-meter stepladder even to reach the ramp slot on tiptoe. And he was too damn tired for calisthenics just now, nor was he about to ask Elli Quinn to give him a boost. He jerked his chin up in the old involuntary nervous tic, and waited in a posture of parade rest appropriate to his uniform, his hands clasped behind his back.

The engineer dropped back to the docking bay deck with a thump. "Yes, Admiral, I think Kaymer can take care of this for you all right. How many of these drop shuttles did you say you had?"

"Twelve." Fourteen minus two equalled twelve. Except in Dendarii Free Mercenary Fleet mathematics, where fourteen minus two shuttles equalled two hundred and seven dead. *Stop that*, Miles told the calculating jeerer in the back of his head firmly. *It does no one any good now.*

"Twelve." The engineer made a note. "What else?" He eyed the battered shuttle.

"My own engineering department will be handling the minor repairs, now that it looks like we'll actually be holding still in one place for a while. I wanted to see to this ramp problem personally, but my second in command, Commodore Jesek, is chief engineer for my fleet, and he wants to talk to your Jump tech people about re-calibrating some of our Necklin rods. I have a Jump pilot with a head wound, but Jumpset implant micro-neurosurgery is not one of Kaymer's specialities, I understand. Nor weapons systems?"

"No, indeed," the engineer agreed hastily. He touched a burn on the shuttle's scarred surface, perhaps fascinated by the violence it silently witnessed, for he added, "Kaymer Orbital mainly services merchant vessels. A mercenary fleet is something a bit unusual in this part of the wormhole nexus. Why did you come to us?"

"You were the lowest bidder."

"Oh—not Kaymer Corporation. Earth. I was wondering why you came to Earth? We're rather off the main trade routes, except for the tourists and historians. Er . . . peaceful."

He wonders if we have a contract here, Miles realized. Here, on a planet of nine billion souls, whose combined military forces would make pocket change of the Dendarii's five thousand—right. He thinks I'm out to make trouble on old mother Earth? Or that I'd break security and tell him even if I was. . . . "Peaceful, precisely," Miles said smoothly. "The Dendarii are in need of rest and refitting. A peaceful planet off the main nexus channels is just what the doctor ordered." He cringed inwardly, thinking of the doctor bill pending.

It hadn't been Dagoola. The rescue operation had been a tactical triumph, a military miracle almost. His own staff had assured him of this over and over, so perhaps he could begin to believe it true.

The break-out on Dagoola IV had been the third largest prisoner-of-war escape in history, Commodore Tung said. Military history being Tung's obsessive hobby, he ought to know. The Dendarii had snatched over ten thousand captured soldiers, an entire POW camp, from under the nose of the Cetagandan Empire, and made them into the nucleus of a new guerrilla army on a planet the Cetagandans had formerly counted on as an easy conquest. The costs had been so small, compared to the spectacular results—except for the individuals who'd paid for the triumph with their lives, for whom the price was something infinite, divided by zero.

It had been Dagoola's aftermath that had cost the Dendarii too much, the infuriated Cetagandans' vengeful pursuit. They had followed with ships till the Dendarii had slipped through political jurisdictions that Cetagandan military vessels could not traverse; hunted on with secret assassination and sabotage teams thereafter. Miles trusted they had outrun the assassination teams at last.

"Did you take all this fire at Dagoola IV?" the engineer went on, still intrigued by the shuttle.

"Dagoola was a covert operation," Miles said stiffly. "We don't discuss it."

"It made a big splash in the news a few months back," the Earthman assured him.

My head hurts. . . . Miles pressed his palm to his forehead, crossed his arms and rested his chin in his hand, twitching a smile at the engineer. "Wonderful," he muttered. Commander Quinn winced.

"Is it true the Cetagandans have put a price on your life?" the engineer asked cheerfully.

Miles sighed. "Yes."

"Oh," said the engineer. "Ah. I'd thought that was just a story." He moved away just slightly, as if embarrassed, or as if the air of morbid violence clinging to the mercenary were a contagion that could somehow rub off on him, if he got too close. He just might be right. He cleared his throat. "Now, about the payment schedule for the design modifications— what had you in mind?"

"Cash on delivery," said Miles promptly, "acceptance to follow my engineering staff's inspection and approval of the completed work. Those were the terms of your bid, I believe."

"Ah—yes. Hm." The Earthman tore his attention away from the machinery itself; Miles felt he could see him switching from technical to business mode. "Those are the terms we normally offer our established corporate customers."

"The Dendarii Free Mercenary Fleet is an established corporation. Registered out of Jackson's Whole."

"Mm, yes, but—how shall I put this—the most exotic risk our normal customers usually run is bankruptcy, for which we have assorted legal protections. Your mercenary fleet is, um . . ."

He's wondering how to collect payment from a corpse, Miles thought.

"—a lot riskier," the engineer finished candidly. He shrugged an apology.

An honest man, at least . . .

"We shall not raise our recorded bid. But I'm afraid we're going to have to ask for payment up front."

As long as we're down to trading insults . . . "But that gives us no protection against shoddy workmanship," said Miles.

"You can sue," remarked the engineer, "just like anybody else."

"I can blow your—" Miles's fingers drummed against his trouser seam where no holster was tied. Earth, old Earth, old civilized Earth. Commander Quinn, at his shoulder, touched his elbow in a fleeting gesture of restraint. He shot her a brief reassuring smile—no, he was not about to let himself get carried away by the—exotic—possibilities of Admiral Miles Naismith, Commanding, Dendarii Free Mercenary Fleet. He was merely tired, his smile said. A slight widening of her brilliant brown eyes replied, *Bullshit, sir*. But that was another argument, which they would not continue here, out loud, in public.

"You can look," said the engineer neutrally, "for a better offer if you wish."

"We have looked," said Miles shortly. *As you well know* . . . "Right. Um . . . what about . . . half up front and half on delivery?"

The Earthman frowned, shook his head. "Kaymer does not pad its estimates, Admiral Naismith. And our cost overruns are among the lowest in the business. That's a point of pride."

The term *cost overrun* made Miles's teeth hurt, in light of Dagoola. How much did these people really know about Dagoola, anyway?

"If you're truly worried about our workmanship, the monies could be placed in an escrow account in the control of a neutral third party, such as a bank, until you accept delivery. Not a very satisfactory compromise from Kaymer's point of view, but—that's as far as I can go."

A neutral third *Earther* party, thought Miles. If he hadn't checked up on Kaymer's workmanship, he wouldn't be here. It was his own cash flow Miles was thinking about. Which was definitely not Kaymer's business.

"You having cash flow problems, Admiral?" inquired the Earther with interest. Miles fancied he could see the price rising in his eyes.

"Not at all," Miles lied blandly. Rumors afloat about the Dendarii's liquidity difficulties could sabotage a lot more than just this repair deal. "Very well. Cash up front to be held in escrow." If he wasn't to have the use of his funds, neither should Kaymer. Beside him, Elli Quinn drew air in through her teeth. The Earther engineer and the mercenary leader shook hands solemnly.

Following the sales engineer back toward his own office, Miles paused a moment by a viewport that framed a fine view of Earth from orbit. The engineer smiled and waited politely, even proudly, watching his gaze.

Earth. Old, romantic, historic Earth, the big blue marble itself. Miles had always expected to travel here someday, although not, surely, under these conditions.

Earth was still the largest, richest, most varied and populous planet in scattered humanity's entire wormhole nexus of explored space. Its dearth of good exit points in solar local space and governmental disunity left it militarily and strategically minor from the greater galactic point of view. But Earth still reigned, if it did not rule, culturally supreme. More war-scarred than Barrayar, as technically advanced as Beta Colony, the end-point of all pilgrimages both religious and secular—in light of which, major embassies from every world that could afford one were collected here. Including, Miles reflected, nibbling gently on the side of his index finger, the Cetagandan. Admiral Naismith must use all means to avoid them.

"Sir?" Elli Quinn interrupted his meditations. He smiled briefly up at her sculptured face, the most beautiful his money had been able to buy after the plasma burn and yet, thanks to the genius of the surgeons, still unmistakably Elli. Would that every combat casualty taken in his service could be so redeemed. "Commodore Tung is on the comconsole for you," she went on.

His smile sagged. What now? He abandoned the view and marched off after her to take over the sales engineer's office with a polite, relentless, "Will you excuse us, please?"

His Eurasian third officer's bland, broad face formed above the vid plate.

"Yes, Ky?"

Ky Tung, already out of uniform and into civilian gear, gave him a brief nod in lieu of a salute. "I've just finished making arrangements at the rehab center for our nine severely-wounded. Prognoses are good, for the most part. And they think they will be able to retrieve four of the eight frozen dead, maybe five if they're lucky. The surgeons here even think they'll be able to repair Demmi's Jumpset, once the neural tissue itself has healed. For a price, of course . . ." Tung named the price in GSA Federal credits; Miles mentally converted it to Barrayaran Imperial marks, and made a small squeaking noise.

Tung grinned dry appreciation. "Yeah. Unless you want to give up on that repair. It's equal to all the rest put together."

Miles shook his head, grimacing. "There are a number of people in the universe I'd be willing to double-cross, but my own wounded aren't among 'em."

"Thank you," said Tung, "I agree. Now, I'm just about ready to leave this place. Last thing I have to do is sign a chit taking personal responsibility for the bill. Are you quite sure you're going to be able to collect the pay owed us for the Dagoola operation here?"

"I'm on my way to do that next," Miles promised. "Go ahead and sign, I'll make it right."

"Very good, sir," said Tung. "Am I released for my home leave after that?"

Tung the Earth man, the only Earther Miles had ever met—which probably accounted for the unconscious favorable feelings he had about this place, Miles reflected. "How much time off do we owe you by now, Ky, about a year and a half?" *With pay, alas,* a small voice added in his mind, and was suppressed as unworthy. "You can take all you want."

"Thank you." Tung's face softened. "I just talked to my daughter. I have a brand-new grandson!"

"Congratulations," said Miles. "Your first?"

"Yes."

"Go on, then. If anything comes up, we'll take care of it. You're only indispensable in combat, eh? Uh . . . where will you be?"

"My sister's home. Brazil. I have about four hundred cousins there."

"Brazil, right. All right." Where the devil was Brazil? "Have a good time."

"I shall." Tung's departing semi-salute was distinctly breezy. His face faded from the vid.

"Damn," Miles sighed, "I'm sorry to lose him even to a leave. Well, he deserves it."

Elli leaned over the back of his comconsole chair. Her breath barely stirred his dark hair, his dark thoughts. "May I suggest, Miles, that he's not the only senior officer who could use some time off? Even you need to dump stress sometimes. And you were wounded too."

"Wounded?" Tension clamped Miles's jaw. "Oh, the bones. Broken bones don't count. I've had the damn brittle bones all my life. I just have to learn to resist the temptation to play field officer. The place for my ass is in a nice padded tactics-room chair, not on the line. If I'd known in advance that Dagoola was going to get so—physical, I'd have sent somebody else in as the fake POW. Anyway, there you are. I had my leave in sickbay."

"And then spent a month wandering around like a cryo-corpse who'd been warmed up in the microwave. When you walked into a room it was like a visit from the Undead."

"I ran the Dagoola rig on pure hysteria. You can't be up that long and not pay for it after with a little down. At least, I can't."

"My impression was there was more to it than that."

He whirled the chair around to face her with a snarl. "Will you back off! Yes, we lost some good people. I don't like losing good people. I cry real tears—in private, if you don't mind!"

She recoiled, her face falling. He softened his voice, deeply ashamed of his outburst. "Sorry, Elli. I know I've been edgy. The death of that poor POW who fell from the shuttle shook me more than . . . more than I should have let it. I can't seem to . . ."

"I was out of line, sir."

The "sir" was like a needle through some voodoo doll she held of him. Miles winced. "Not at all."

Why, why, why, of all the idiotic things he'd done as Admiral Naismith, had he ever established as explicit policy not to seek physical intimacy with anyone in his own organization? It had seemed like a good idea at the time. Tung had approved. Tung was a grandfather, for God's sake, his gonads had probably withered years ago. Miles remembered how he had deflected the first pass Elli had ever made at him. "A good officer doesn't go shopping in the company store," he'd explained gently. Why hadn't she belted him in the jaw for that fatuousness? She had absorbed the unintended insult without comment, and never tried again. Had she ever realized he'd meant that to apply to himself, not her?

When he was with the fleet for extended periods, he usually tried to send her on detached duties, from which she invariably returned with superb results. She had headed the advance team to Earth, and had Kaymer and most of their other suppliers all lined up by the time the Dendarii fleet made orbit. A good officer; after Tung, probably his best. What would he not give to dive into that lithe body and lose himself now? Too late, he'd lost his option.

Her velvet mouth crimped quizzically. She gave him a—sisterly, perhaps—shrug. "I won't hassle you about it any more. But at least think about it. I don't think I've ever seen a human being who needed to get laid worse than you do now."

Oh, God, what a straight line—what did those words really mean? His chest tightened. Comradely comment, or invitation? If mere comment, and he mistook it for invitation, would she think he was leaning on her for sexual favors? If the reverse, would she be insulted again and not breathe on him for years to come? He grinned in panic. "Paid," he blurted. "What I need right now is paid, not laid.

After that—after that, um . . . maybe we could go see some of the sights. It seems practically criminal to come all this way and not see any of Old Earth, even if it was by accident. I'm supposed to have a bodyguard at all times downside anyway, we could double up."

She was sighing, straightening up. "Yes, duty first, of course."

Yes, duty first. And his next duty was to report in to Admiral Naismith's employers. After that, all his troubles would be vastly simplified.

Miles wished he could have changed to civilian clothes before embarking on this expedition. His crisp grey-and-white Dendarii admiral's uniform was conspicuous as hell in this shopping arcade. Or at least made Elli change—they could have pretended to be a soldier on leave and his girlfriend. But his civilian gear had been stashed in a crate several planets back—would he ever retrieve it? The clothes had been tailor-made and expensive, not so much as a mark of status as pure necessity.

Usually he could forget the peculiarities of his body—oversized head exaggerated by a short neck set on a twisted spine, all squashed down to a height of four-foot-nine, the legacy of a congenital accident—but nothing highlighted his defects in his own mind more sharply than trying to borrow clothes from someone of normal size and shape. *You sure it's the uniform that feels conspicuous, boy?* he thought to himself. *Or are you playing foolie-foolie games with your head again? Stop it.*

He returned his attention to his surroundings. The spaceport city of London, a jigsaw of nearly two millennia of clashing architectural styles, was a fascination. The sunlight falling through the arcade's pat-

terned glass arch was an astonishing rich color,
breathtaking. It alone might have led him to guess
his eye had been returned to its ancestral planet.
Perhaps later he'd have a chance to visit more historical sites, such as a submarine tour of Lake Los
Angeles, or New York behind the great dykes.

Elli made another nervous circuit of the bench
beneath the light-clock, scanning the crowd. This
seemed a most unlikely spot for Cetagandan hit squads
to pop up, but still he was glad of her alertness, that
allowed him to be tired. *You can come look for
assassins under my bed anytime, love. . . .*

"In a way, I'm glad we ended up here," he remarked to her. "This might prove an excellent opportunity for Admiral Naismith to disappear up his
own existence for a while. Take the heat off the
Dendarii. The Cetagandans are a lot like the Barrayarans,
really, they take a very personal view of command."

"You're pretty damn casual about it."

"Early conditioning. Total strangers trying to kill
me make me feel right at home." A thought struck
him with a certain macabre cheer. "You know, this is
the first time anybody has tried to kill me for myself,
and not because of who I'm related to? Have I ever
told you about what my grandfather really did when
I was . . ."

She cut off his babble with a lift of her chin. "I
think this is it. . . ."

He followed her gaze. He *was* tired, she'd spotted
their contact before he had. The man coming toward
them with the inquiring look on his face wore stylish
Earther clothes, but his hair was clipped in a
Barrayaran military burr. A non-com, perhaps. Officers favored a slightly less severe Roman patrician
style. *I need a haircut,* thought Miles, his collar
suddenly ticklish.

"My lord?" said the man.

"Sergeant Barth?" said Miles.

The man nodded, glanced at Elli. "Who is this?"

"My bodyguard."

"Ah."

So slight a compression of the lips, and widening of the eyes, to convey so much amusement and contempt. Miles could feel the muscles coil in his neck. "She is outstanding at her job."

"I'm sure, sir. Come this way, please." He turned and led off.

The bland face was laughing at him, he could feel it, tell by looking at the back of the head. Elli, aware only of the sudden increase of tension in the air, gave him a look of dismay. *It's all right,* he thought at her, tucking her hand in his arm.

They strolled after their guide, through a shop, down a lift tube and then some stairs, then picked up the pace. The underground utility level was a maze of tunnels, conduits, and power optics. They traversed, Miles guessed, a couple of blocks. Their guide opened a door with a palm-lock. Another short tunnel led to another door. This one had a live human guard by it, extremely neat in Barrayaran Imperial dress greens, who scrambled up from his comconsole seat where he monitored scanners to barely resist saluting their civilian-clothed guide.

"We dump our weapons here," Miles told Elli. "All of them. I mean really all."

Elli raised her brows at the sudden shift of Miles's accent, from the flat Betan twang of Admiral Naismith to the warm gutturals of his native Barrayar. She seldom heard his Barrayaran voice, at that—which one would seem put-on to her? There was no doubt which one would seem a put-on to the embassy personnel, though, and Miles cleared his throat, to be sure of fully disciplining his voice to the new order.

Miles's contributions to the pile on the guard's console were a pocket stunner and a long steel knife in a lizard-skin sheath. The guard scanned the knife, popped the silver cap off the end of its jewelled hilt to reveal a patterned seal, and handed it back carefully to Miles. Their guide raised his brows at the miniaturized technical arsenal Elli unloaded. *So there,* Miles thought to him. *Stuff that up your regulation nose.* He followed on feeling rather more serene.

Up a lift tube, and suddenly the ambience changed to a hushed, plush, understated dignity. "The Barrayaran Imperial Embassy," Miles whispered to Elli.

The ambassador's wife must have taste, Miles thought. But the building had a strange hermetically-sealed flavor to it, redolent to Miles's experienced nose as paranoid security in action. Ah, yes, a planet's embassy is that planet's soil. Feels just like home.

Their guide led them down another lift tube into what was clearly an office corridor—Miles spotted the sensor scanners in a carved arch as they passed—then through two sets of automatic doors into a small, quiet office.

"Lieutenant Lord Miles Vorkosigan, sir," their guide announced, standing at attention. "And—bodyguard."

Miles's hands twitched. Only a Barrayaran could convey such a delicate shade of insult in a half-second pause between two words. Home again.

"Thank you, Sergeant, dismissed," said the captain behind the comconsole desk. Imperial dress greens again—the embassy must maintain a formal tone.

Miles gazed curiously at the man who was to be, will or nill, his new commanding officer. The captain gazed back with equal intensity.

An arresting-looking man, though far from pretty.

Dark hair. Hooded, nutmeg-brown eyes. A hard, guarded mouth, fleshy blade of a nose sweeping down a Roman profile that matched his officer's haircut. His hands were blunt and clean, steepled now together in a still tension. In his early thirties, Miles guessed.

But why is this guy looking at me like I'm a puppy that just piddled on his carpet? Miles wondered. I just got here, I haven't had *time* to offend him yet. Oh, God, I hope he's not one of those rural Barrayaran hicks who see me as a mutant, a refugee from a botched abortion. . . .

"So," said the captain, leaning back in his chair with a sigh, "you're the Great Man's son, eh?"

Miles's smile became absolutely fixed. A red haze clouded his vision. He could hear his blood beating in his ears like a death march. Elli, watching him, stood quite still, barely breathing. Miles's lips moved; he swallowed. He tried again. "Yes, sir," he heard himself saying, as from a great distance. "And who are you?"

He managed, just barely, not to let it come out as "And whose son are you?" The fury bunching his stomach must not be allowed to show; he was going to have to work with this man. It might not even have been an intentional insult. Couldn't have been, how could this stranger know how much blood Miles had sweated fighting off charges of privilege, slurs on his competence? "The mutant's only here because his father got him in. . . ." He could hear his father's voice, countering, "For God's sake get your head out of your ass, boy!" He let the rage stream out on a long, calming breath, and cocked his head brightly.

"Oh," said the captain, "yes, you only talked to my aide, didn't you. I'm Captain Duv Galeni. Senior military attache for the embassy, and by default chief of Imperial Security, as well as Service Security, here. And, I confess, rather startled to have you appear in my chain of command. It is not entirely clear to me what I'm supposed to do with you."

Not a rural accent; the captain's voice was cool, educated, blandly urban. Miles could not place it in Barrayaran geography. "I'm not surprised, sir," said Miles. "I did not myself expect to be reporting in at Earth, nor so late. I was originally supposed to report back to Imperial Security Command at Sector Two HQ on Tau Ceti, over a month ago. But the Dendarii Free Mercenary Fleet was driven out of Mahata Solaris local space by a surprise Cetagandan attack. Since we were not being paid to make war directly on the Cetagandans, we ran, and ended up unable to get back by any shorter route. This is literally my first opportunity to report in anywhere since we delivered the refugees to their new base."

"I was not—" the captain paused, his mouth twitching, and began again, "I had not been aware that the extraordinary escape at Dagoola was a covert operation of Barrayaran Intelligence. Wasn't it perilously close to being an act of outright war on the Cetagandan Empire?"

"Precisely why the Dendarii mercenaries were used for it, sir. It was actually supposed to be a somewhat smaller operation, but things got a little out of hand. In the field, as it were." Beside him, Elli kept her eyes straight ahead, and didn't even choke. "I, uh . . . have a complete report."

The captain appeared to be having an internal struggle. "Just what is the relationship between the Dendarii Free Mercenary Fleet and Imperial Security, Lieutenant?" he finally said. There was something almost plaintive in his tone.

"Er . . . what do you know already, sir?"

Captain Galeni turned his hands palm-up. "I hadn't even heard of them, except peripherally, until you made contact by vid yesterday. My files—my Security files!—say exactly three things about the organization. They are not to be attacked, any requests for emergency assistance should be met with all due speed, and for further information I must apply to Sector Two Security Headquarters."

"Oh, yeah," said Miles, "that's right. This is only a Class III embassy, isn't it. Um, well, the relationship is fairly simple. The Dendarii are kept on retainer for highly covert operations which are either out of Imperial Security's range, or for which any direct, traceable connection with Barrayar would be politically embarrassing. Dagoola was both. Orders are passed from the General Staff, with the advice and consent of the Emperor, through Chief of Imperial Security Illyan to me. It's a very short chain of command. I'm the go-between, supposedly the sole connection. I leave Imperial HQ as Lieutenant Vorkosigan, and pop up—wherever—as Admiral Naismith, waving a new contract. We go do whatever we've been assigned to do, and then, from the Dendarii point of view, I vanish as mysteriously as I came. God knows what they think I do in my spare time."

"Do you really want to know?" Elli asked, her eyes alight.

"Later," he muttered out of the corner of his mouth.

The captain drummed his fingers on his desk console, and glanced down at a display. "None of this is in your official dossier. Twenty-four years old—aren't you a little young for your rank, ah—Admiral?" His tone was dry, his eyes passed mockingly over the Dendarii uniform.

Miles tried to ignore the tone. "It's a long story.

Commodore Tung, a very senior Dendarii officer, is the real brains of the outfit. I just play the part."

Elli's eyes widened in outrage; a severe glance from Miles tried to compel her to silence. "You do a lot more than that," she objected.

"If you're the sole connection," frowned Galeni, "who the devil is this woman?" His wording rendered her, if not a non-person, certainly a non-soldier.

"Yes, sir. Well, in case of emergencies, there are three Dendarii who know my real identity. Commander Quinn, who was in on the beginning of the whole scam, is one of them. I'm under orders from Illyan to maintain a bodyguard at all times, so Commander Quinn fills in whenever I have to change identities. I trust her implicitly." *You will respect my people, damn your mocking eyes, whatever you think of me. . . .*

"How long has this been going on, Lieutenant?"

"Ah," Miles glanced at Elli, "seven years, isn't it?"

Elli's bright eyes glinted. "It seems like only yesterday," she cooed blandly. It seemed she was finding it hard to ignore the tone too, Miles trusted she would keep her edged sense of humor under control.

The captain regarded his fingernails, and then stared at Miles sharply. "Well, I'm going to apply to Sector Two Security, Lieutenant. And if I find out that this is another Vor lordling's idea of a practical joke, I shall do my level best to see that you are brought up on charges for it. No matter who your father is."

"It's all true, sir. My word as Vorkosigan."

"Just so," said Captain Galeni through his teeth.

Miles, infuriated, drew breath—then placed Galeni's regional accent at last. He jerked up his chin. "Are you—Komarran, sir?"

Galeni gave him a wary nod. Miles returned it

gravely, rather frozen. Elli nudged him, whispering, "What the hell—?"

"Later," Miles muttered back. "Barrayaran internal politics."

"Will I need to take notes?"

"Probably." He raised his voice. "I must get in touch with my actual superiors, Captain Galeni. I have no idea what my next orders even are."

Galeni pursed his lips, and remarked mildly, "I am actually a superior of yours, Lieutenant Vorkosigan."

And chapped as hell, Miles judged, to be cut out of his own command chain—and who could blame him? Softly, now . . . "Of course, sir. What are my orders?"

Galeni's hands clenched briefly in frustration, his mouth set in irony. "I will have to add you to my staff, I suppose, while we all await clarification. Third assistant military attache."

"Ideal, sir, thank you," said Miles. "Admiral Naismith needs very much to vanish just now. The Cetagandans put a price on his—my—head after Dagoola. I've been lucky twice."

It was Galeni's turn to freeze. "Are you joking?"

"I had four dead and sixteen wounded Dendarii because of it," said Miles stiffly. "I don't find it amusing at all."

"In that case," said Galeni grimly, "you may consider yourself confined to the Embassy compound."

And miss Earth? Miles sighed reluctance. "Yes, sir," he agreed in a dull tone. "As long as Commander Quinn here can be my go-between to the Dendarii."

"Why do you need further contact with the Dendarii?"

"They're my people, sir."

"I thought you said this Commodore Tung ran the show."

"He's on home leave right now. But all I really need before Admiral Naismith departs into the woodwork is to pay some bills. If you could advance me their immediate expenses, I could wrap up this mission."

Galeni sighed; his fingers danced over his comconsole, and paused. "Assistance with all due speed. Right. Just how much do they require?"

"Roughly eighteen million marks, sir."

Galeni's fingers hung paralyzed. "Lieutenant," he said carefully, "that is more than ten times the budget for this entire embassy for a year. Several tens of times the budget for this department!"

Miles spread his hands. "Operating expenses for 5000 troops and techs and eleven ships for over six months, plus equipment losses—we lost a hell of a lot of gear at Dagoola—payroll, food, clothing, fuel, medical expenses, ammunition, repairs—I can show you the spreadsheets, sir."

Galeni sat back. "No doubt. But Sector Security Headquarters is going to have to handle this one. Funds in that amount don't even exist here."

Miles chewed on the side of his index finger. "Oh." Oh, indeed. He would not panic. . . . "In that case, sir, may I request you send to Sector HQ as soon as possible?"

"Believe me, Lieutenant, I consider getting you transferred to someone else's command an object of the highest priority." He rose. "Excuse me. Wait here." He exited the office shaking his head.

"What the hell?" prodded Elli. "I thought you were about to try and dismantle the guy, captain or no captain—and then you just stopped. What's so magic about being Komarran, and where can I get some?"

"Not magic," said Miles. "Definitely not magic. But very important."

"More important than being a Vor lord?"

"In a weird way, yes, right now. Look, you know the planet Komarr was Barrayar's first interstellar Imperial conquest, right?"

"I thought you called it an annexation."

"A rose by any other name. We took it for its wormholes, because it sat across our only nexus connection, because it was strangling our trade, and most of all because it accepted a bribe to let the Cetagandan fleet pass through it when Cetaganda first tried to annex *us*. You may also recall who was the chief conquistador."

"Your dad. Back when he was only Admiral Lord Vorkosigan, before he became regent. It made his reputation."

"Yeah, well, it made more than one reputation for him. You ever want to see smoke come out of his ears, whisper, 'the Butcher of Komarr' in his hearing. They actually called him that."

"Thirty years ago, Miles." She paused. "Was there any truth to it?"

Miles sighed. "There was something. I've never been able to get the whole story out of him, but I'm damn sure what's in the history books isn't it. Anyway, the conquest of Komarr got messy. As a result, in the fourth year he was Imperial Regent came the Komarr Revolt, and that got really messy. Komarran terrorists have been a Security nightmare for the Imperium ever since. It was pretty repressive there, I guess.

"Anyway, so time's gone on, things have calmed down a bit, anyone from either planet with energy to spare is off settling newly-opened Sergyar. There's been a movement among the liberals—spearheaded by my father—to fully integrate Komarr into the Empire. It's not a real popular idea with the Barrayaran right. It's a bit of an obsession with the old man— 'Between justice and genocide there is, in the long run, no middle ground,'" Miles intoned. "He gets real eloquent about it. So, all right, the route to the top on dear old caste-conscious, army-mad Barrayar was and always has been through the Imperial Military Service. It was opened to Komarrans for the first time just eight years ago.

"That means any Komarran in the Service now is on the spot. They have to prove their loyalty the way I have to prove my—" he faltered, "prove myself. It also follows that if I'm working with or under any Komarran, and I turn up unusually dead one day, that Komarran is dog meat. Because my father was the Butcher, and no one will believe it wasn't some sort of revenge.

"And not just that Komarran. Every other Komarran in the Imperial Service would be shadowed by the same cloud. It'd put things back years in Barrayaran politics. If I got assassinated now," he shrugged helplessly, "my father would kill me."

"I trust you weren't planning on it," she choked.

"So now we come to Galeni," Miles went on hastily. "He's in the Service—an officer—has a post in Security itself. Must have worked his tail off to get here. Highly trusted—for a Komarran. But not at a major or strategic post; certain critical kinds of Security information are deliberately withheld from him; and here I come along and rub his nose in it. And if he did have any relatives in the Komarr Revolt—well . . . here I am again. I doubt if he loves me, but he's going to have to guard me like the apple of his eye. And I, God help me, am going to have to let him. It's a real tricky situation."

She patted him on the arm. "You can handle it."

"Hm," he grunted glumly. "Oh, God, Elli," he wailed suddenly, letting his forehead fall against her shoulder, "and I didn't get the money for the Dendarii—can't, till God knows when—what will I tell Ky? I gave him my word . . . !"

She patted him on the head, this time. But she didn't say anything.

Chapter Two

He let his head rest against the crisp cloth of her uniform jacket a moment longer. She shifted, her arms reaching toward him. Was she about to hug him? If she did, Miles decided, he was going to grab her and kiss her right there. And then see what happened—

Behind him, Galeni's office doors swished open. Elli and he both flinched away from each other, Elli coming to parade rest with a toss of her short dark curls, Miles just standing and cursing inwardly at the interruption.

He heard and knew the familiar, drawling voice before he turned.

"—brilliant, sure, but hyper as hell. You think he's going to slip his flywheel any second. Watch out when he starts talking too fast. Oh, yeah, that's him all right. . . ."

"Ivan," Miles breathed, closing his eyes. "How, God, have I sinned against You, that You have given me Ivan—*here*. . . ."

God not deigning to answer, Miles smiled crookedly, and turned. Elli had her head tilted, frowning, and listening in sudden concentration.

Galeni had returned with a tall young lieutenant in tow. Indolent as he was, Ivan Vorpatril had obviously been keeping in shape, for his athletic physique set off his dress greens to perfection. His affable, open face was even-featured, framed by wavy dark hair in a neat patrician clip. Miles could not help glancing at Elli, covertly alert for her reaction. With her face and figure Elli tended to make anyone standing next to her look grubby, but Ivan might actually play the stem to her rose and not be overshadowed.

"Hi, Miles," said Ivan. "What are you doing here?"

"I might ask you the same thing," said Miles.

"I'm second assistant military attache. They assigned me here to get cultured, I guess. Earth, y'know."

"Oh," said Galeni, one corner of his mouth twitching upward, "is that what you're here for. I'd wondered."

Ivan grinned sheepishly. "How's life with the irregulars these days?" he asked Miles. "You still getting away with your Admiral Naismith scam?"

"Just barely," said Miles. "The Dendarii are with me now. They're in orbit," he jabbed his finger skyward, "eating their heads off even as we speak."

Galeni looked as if he'd bitten into something sour. "Does everybody know about this covert operation but me? You, Vorpatril—I know your Security clearance is no higher than my own!"

Ivan shrugged. "A previous encounter. It was in the family."

"Damned Vor power network," muttered Galeni.

"Oh," said Elli Quinn in a tone of sudden enlightenment, "this is your *cousin* Ivan! I'd always wondered what he looked like."

Ivan, who had been sneaking little peeks at her ever since he'd entered the room, came to attention with all the quivering alertness of a bird dog pointing. He smiled blindingly and bowed over Elli's hand. "Delighted to meet you, m'lady. The Dendarii must be improving, if you are a fair sample. The fairest, surely."

Elli repossessed her hand. "We've met."

"Surely not. I couldn't forget that face."

"I didn't have this face. 'A head just like an onion' was the way you phrased it, as I recall." Her eyes glittered. "Since I was blinded at the time, I had no idea how bad the plastiskin prosthesis really looked. Until you told me. Miles never mentioned it."

Ivan's smile had gone limp. "Ah. The plasma-burn lady."

Miles smirked and edged closer to Elli, who put her hand possessively through the crook of his elbow and favored Ivan with a cold samurai smile. Ivan, trying to bleed with dignity, looked to Captain Galeni.

"Since you know each other, Lieutenant Vorkosigan, I've assigned Lieutenant Vorpatril here to take you in tow and orient you to the Embassy, and to your duties here," said Galeni. "Vor or no Vor, as long as you're on the Emperor's payroll, the Emperor might as well get some use of you. I trust some clarification of your status will arrive promptly."

"I trust the Dendarii payroll will arrive as promptly," said Miles.

"Your mercenary—bodyguard—can return to her outfit. If for any reason you need to leave the Embassy compound, I'll assign you one of my men."

"Yes, sir," sighed Miles. "But I still have to be

able to get in touch with the Dendarii, in case of emergencies."

"I'll see that Commander Quinn gets a secured comm link before she leaves. As a matter of fact," he touched his comconsole, "Sergeant Barth?" he spoke into it.

"Yes, sir?" a voice replied.

"Do you have that comm link ready yet?"

"Just finished encoding it, sir."

"Good, bring it to my office."

Barth, still in his civvies, appeared within moments. Galeni shepherded Elli out. "Sergeant Barth will escort you out of the Embassy compound, Commander Quinn." She glanced back over her shoulder at Miles, who sketched her a reassuring salute.

"What will I tell the Dendarii?" she asked.

"Tell them—tell them their funds are in transit," Miles called. The doors hissed shut, eclipsing her.

Galeni returned to his comconsole, which was blinking for his attention. "Vorpatril, please make getting your cousin out of that . . . costume, and into a correct uniform your first priority."

Does Admiral Naismith spook you—just a little . . . sir? Miles wondered irritably. "The Dendarii uniform is as real as your own, sir."

Galeni glowered at him, across his flickering desk. "I wouldn't know, Lieutenant. My father could only afford toy soldiers for me when I was a boy. You two are dismissed."

Miles, fuming, waited until the doors had closed behind them before tearing off his grey-and-white jacket and throwing it to the corridor floor. "Costume! Toy soldiers! I think I'm gonna kill that Komarran son-of-a-bitch!"

"Oooh," said Ivan. "Aren't we touchy today."

"You heard what he said!"

"Yeah, so . . . Galeni's all right. A bit regulation, maybe. There's a dozen little tin-pot mercenary outfits running around in oddball corners of the wormhole nexus. Some of them tread a real fine line between legal and illegal. How's he supposed to know your Dendarii aren't next door to being hijackers?"

Miles picked up his uniform jacket, shook it out, and folded it carefully over his arm. "Huh."

"Come on," said Ivan. "I'll take you down to Stores and get you a kit in a color more to his taste."

"They got anything in my size?"

"They make a laser-map of your body and produce the stuff one-off, computer controlled, just like that overpriced sartorial pirate you take yourself to in Vorbarr Sultana. This is Earth, son."

"My man on Barrayar's been doing my clothes for ten years. He has some tricks that aren't in the computer. . . . Well, I guess I can live with it. Can the embassy computer do civilian clothes?"

Ivan grimaced. "If your tastes are conservative. If you want something in style to wow the local girls, you have to go farther afield."

"With Galeni for a duenna, I have a feeling I'm not going to get a chance to go very far afield," Miles sighed. "It'll have to do."

Miles sighted down the forest-green sleeve of his Barrayaran dress uniform, adjusted the cuff, and jerked his chin up, the better to settle his head on the high collar. He'd half-forgotten just how uncomfortable that damn collar was, with his short neck. In front the red rectangles of his lieutenant's rank seemed to poke into his jaw; in back it pinched his still-uncut hair. And the boots were hot. The bone he'd broken in his left foot at Dagoola still twinged, even now after being re-broken, set straight, and treated with electra-stim.

Still, the green uniform was home. His true self. Maybe it was time for a vacation from Admiral Naismith and his intractable responsibilities, time to remember the more reasonable problems of Lieutenant Vorkosigan, whose sole task now was to learn the procedures of one small office and put up with Ivan Vorpatril. The Dendarii didn't need him to hold their hand for routine rest and refit, nor could he have arranged any more safe and thorough a disappearance for Admiral Naismith.

Ivan's particular charge was this tiny windowless room deep in the bowels of the embassy compound; his job, to feed hundreds of data disks to a secured computer that concentrated them into a weekly report on the status of Earth, to be sent back to Security Chief Illyan and the general staff on Barrayar. Where, Miles supposed, it was computer-collated with hundreds of other such reports to create Barrayar's vision of the universe. Miles hoped devoutly that Ivan wasn't adding kilowatts and megawatts in the same column.

"By far the bulk of this stuff is public statistics," Ivan was explaining, seated before his console and actually looking at ease in his dress greens. "Population shifts, agricultural and manufacturing production figures, the various political divisions' published military budgets. The computer adds 'em up sixteen different ways, and blinks for attention when things don't match. Since all the originators have computers too, this doesn't happen too often—all the lies are embedded before it ever gets to us, Galeni says. More important to Barrayar are records of ship movements in and out of Earth local space.

"Then we get to the more interesting stuff, real spy work. There's several hundred people on Earth this embassy tries to keep track of, for one security reason or another. One of the biggest groups is the Komarran rebel expatriates." A wave of Ivan's hand, and dozens of faces flickered one after another above the vid plate.

"Oh, yeah?" said Miles, interested in spite of himself. "Does Galeni have secret contacts and so on with them? Is that why he's assigned here? Double agent—triple agent . . ."

"I bet Illyan wishes," said Ivan. "As far as I know, they regard Galeni as a leper. Evil collaborator with the imperialist oppressors and all that."

"Surely they're no great threat to Barrayar at this late date and distance. Refugees . . ."

"Some of these were the smart refugees, though, the ones who got their money out before the boom dropped. Some were involved in financing the Komarr Revolt during the Regency—they're mostly a lot poorer now. They're aging, though. Another half generation, if your father's integration policies succeed, and they'll have totally lost momentum, Captain Galeni says."

Ivan picked up another data disk. "And then we come to the real hot stuff, which is keeping track of what the other embassies are doing. Such as the Cetagandan."

"I hope they're on the other side of the planet," said Miles sincerely.

"No, most of the galactic embassies and consuls are concentrated right here in London. Makes watching each other ever so much more convenient."

"Ye gods," moaned Miles, "don't tell me they're across the street or some damned thing."

Ivan grinned. "Almost. They're about two kilometers away. We go to each other's parties a lot, to practice being snide, and play I-know-you-know-I-know games."

Miles sat, hyperventilating slightly. "Oh, shit."

"What's up you, coz?"

"Those people are trying to kill me."

"No they're not. It'd start a war. We're at peace right now, sort of, remember?"

"Well, they're trying to kill Admiral Naismith, anyway."

"Who vanished yesterday."

"Yeah, but—one of the reasons this whole Dendarii scam has held up for so long is distance. Admiral Naismith and Lieutenant Vorkosigan never show up within hundreds of light years of each other. We've never been trapped on the same planet together, let alone the same city."

"As long as you leave your Dendarii uniform in my closet, what's to connect?"

"Ivan, how many four-foot-nine-inch black-haired grey-eyed hunchbacks can there be on this damn planet? D'you think you trip over twitchy dwarfs on every street corner?"

"On a planet of nine billion," said Ivan, "there's got to be at least six of everything. Calm down!" He paused. "Y'know, that's the first time I've ever heard you use that word."

"What word?"

"Hunchback. You're not really, you know." Ivan eyed him with friendly worry.

Miles's fist closed, opened in a sharp throw-away gesture. "Anyway, Cetagandans. If they have a counterpart doing what you're doing—"

Ivan nodded. "I've met him. His name's ghem-lieutenant Tabor."

"Then they know the Dendarii are here, and know

Admiral Naismith's been seen. They probably have a list of every purchase order we've put through the comm net, or will soon enough, when they turn their attention to it. They're tracking."

"They may be tracking, but they can't get orders from higher up any faster than we can," said Ivan reasonably. "And in any case they've got a manpower shortage. Our security staff's four times the size of theirs, on account of the Komarrans. I mean, this may be Earth, but it's still a minor embassy, even more so for them than us. Never fear," he struck a pose in his station chair, hand across his chest, "Cousin Ivan will protect you."

"That's so reassuring," Miles muttered.

Ivan grinned at the sarcasm, and turned back to his work.

The day wore on interminably in the quiet, changeless room. His claustrophobia, Miles discovered, was developed to a much higher pitch than it used to be. He absorbed lessons from Ivan, and paced from wall to wall between times.

"You could do that about twice as fast, you know," Miles observed to Ivan, plugging away at his data analysis.

"But then I'd be done right after lunch," said Ivan, "and then I wouldn't have anything to do at all."

"Surely Galeni could find something."

"That's what I'm afraid of," said Ivan. "Quitting time rolls around soon enough. Then we go party."

"No, then you go party. I go to my room, as ordered. Maybe I'll catch up on my sleep, finally."

"That's it, think positive," said Ivan. "I'll work out with you in the embassy gym, if you want. You don't look so good, you know. Pale and, um . . . pale."

Old, thought Miles, is the word you just edited.

He glanced at the distorted reflection of his face in a bit of chrome plating on the console. *That bad, eh?*

"Exercise," Ivan thumped his chest, "will be good for you."

"No doubt," muttered Miles.

The days fell quickly into a set pattern. Miles was awakened by Ivan in the room they shared, did a stint in the gym, showered, breakfasted, and went to work in the data room. He began to wonder if he would ever be permitted to see Earth's beautiful sunlight again. After three days Miles took the computer-stuffing job away from Ivan and started finishing it by noon, so that he might at least have the later hours for reading and study. He devoured embassy and security procedures, Earth history, galactic news. In the later afternoon they knocked off for another grueling workout in the gym. On the nights Ivan stayed in, Miles watched vid dramas with him; on the nights he went out, travelogues of all the sites of interest he wasn't allowed to go visit.

Elli reported in daily on the secured comm link on the status of the Dendarii fleet, still holding in orbit. Miles, closeting himself with the comm link, found himself increasingly hungry for that outside voice. Her reports were succinct. But afterwards they drifted off into inconsequential small talk, as Miles found it harder and harder to cut her off, and she never hung up on him. Miles fantasized about courting her in his own persona—would a commander accept a date from a mere lieutenant? Would she even like Lord Vorkosigan? Would Galeni ever let him leave the embassy to find out?

Ten days of clean living, exercise, and regular hours had been bad for him, Miles decided. His energy level was up. Up, and bottled in the immobilized persona of Lord Vorkosigan, while the list of chores facing Admiral Naismith piled up and up and up. . . .

"Will you stop fidgeting, Miles?" Ivan complained. "Sit down. Take a deep breath. Hold still for five minutes. You can do it if you try."

Miles made one more circuit of the computer room, then flung himself into a chair. "Why hasn't Galeni called me yet? The courier from Sector HQ got in an hour ago!"

"So, give the man time to go to the bathroom and get a cup of coffee. Give Galeni time to read his reports. This is peacetime, everybody's got lots of leisure to sit around writing reports. They'd be hurt if nobody read 'em."

"That's the trouble with your government-supported troops," said Miles, "you're spoiled. You get paid not to make war."

"Wasn't there a mercenary fleet that did that once? They'd show up in orbit somewhere, and get paid—to *not* make war. Worked, didn't it? You're just not a creative enough mercenary commander, Miles."

"Yeah, LaVarr's fleet. It worked real good till the Tau Cetan Navy caught up with 'em, and then LaVarr was sent to the disintegration chamber."

"No sense of humor, the Tau Cetans."

"None," Miles agreed. "Neither has my father."

"Too true. Well—"

The comconsole blinked. Ivan had to duck out of the way as Miles pounced on it. "Yes sir?" said Miles breathlessly.

"Come to my office, Lieutenant Vorkosigan," said Galeni. His face was saturnine as ever, no cues there.

"Yes, sir, thank you sir." Miles cut the com and

plunged for the door. "My eighteen million marks, at last!"

"Either that," said Ivan genially, "or he's found a job for you in inventory. Maybe you're going to get to count all the goldfish in the fountain in the main reception court."

"Sure, Ivan."

"Hey, it's a real challenge! They keep moving around, you know."

"How do you know?" Miles paused, his eyes lighting. "Ivan, did he actually make you do that?"

"It had to do with a suspected security breach," said Ivan. "It's a long story."

"I'll bet." Miles beat a brief tattoo on the desk, and vaulted around its corner. "Later. I'm gone."

Miles found Captain Galeni sitting staring dubiously at the display on his comconsole, as if it was still in code.

"Sir?"

"Hm." Galeni leaned back in his chair. "Well, your orders have arrived from Sector HQ, Lieutenant Vorkosigan."

"And?"

Galeni's mouth tightened. "And they confirm your temporary assignment to my staff. Officially and publicly. You may now draw your lieutenant's pay from my department as of ten days ago. As for the rest of your orders, they read the same as Vorpatril's—in fact, they could be templated from Vorpatril's orders with the name changed. You are to assist me as required, hold yourself at the disposal of the ambassador and his lady for escort duties, and as time permits take advantage of educational opportunities unique to Earth and appropriate to your status as an Imperial officer and lord of the Vor."

"What? This can't be right! What the devil are escort duties?" *Sounds like a call-girl.*

A slight smile turned one corner of Galeni's mouth. "Mostly, standing around in parade dress at official Embassy social functions and being Vor for the natives. There are a surprising number of people who find aristocrats—even off-planet aristocrats—peculiarly fascinating." Galeni's tone made it clear that he found this fascination peculiar indeed. "You will eat, drink, dance perhaps . . ." his tone grew doubtful for a second, "and generally be exquisitely polite to anyone the ambassador wants to, ah, impress. Sometimes, you will be asked to remember and report conversations. Vorpatril does it all very well, rather to my surprise. He can fill in the details for you."

I don't need to take social notes from Ivan, Miles thought. *And the Vor are a military caste, not an aristocracy.* What the hell was HQ thinking of? It seemed extraordinarily obtuse even for them.

Yet if they had no new project on line for the Dendarii, why not use the opportunity for Count Vorkosigan's son to acquire a little more diplomatic polish? No one doubted that he was destined for the most rarified levels of the Service—he would hardly be exposed to less varied experience than Ivan. It wasn't the content of the orders, it was only the lack of separation from his other persona that was so . . . unexpected.

Still . . . *report conversations.* Could this be the start of some special spy work? Perhaps further, clarifying details were en route.

He didn't even want to think about the possibility that HQ had decided it was finally time to shut down Dendarii covert ops altogether.

"Well . . ." said Miles grudgingly, "all right . . ."

"So glad," murmured Galeni, "you find your orders to your taste, Lieutenant."

Miles flushed, and closed his mouth tightly. But if only he could get his Dendarii taken care of, the rest didn't matter. "And my eighteen million marks, sir?" he asked, taking care to keep his tone humble this time.

Galeni drummed his fingers on his desk. "No such credit order arrived with this courier, Lieutenant. Nor any mention of one."

"What!" shrieked Miles. "There's got to be!" He almost lunged across Galeni's desk to examine the vid himself, caught himself up just in time. "I calculated ten days for all the . . ." His brain dumped unwanted data, streaming past his consciousness—fuel, orbital docking fees, re-supply, medical-dental-surgical, the depleted ordnance inventory, payroll, roll-over, liquidity, margin. . . . "Dammit, we bled for Barrayar! They can't—there must be some mistake!"

Galeni spread his hands helplessly. "No doubt. But not one in my power to repair."

"Send again—sir!"

"Oh, I shall."

"Better yet—let me go as courier. If I talked to HQ in person—"

"Hm." Galeni rubbed his lips. "A tempting idea . . . no, better not. Your orders, at least, were clear. Your Dendarii will simply have to wait for the next courier. If all is as you *say*," his emphasis was not lost on Miles, "I'm sure it will all be straightened out."

Miles waited an endless moment, but Galeni offered nothing more. "Yes, sir." He saluted and faced about. Ten days . . . ten more days . . . ten more days at least . . . They could wait out ten more days.

But he hoped HQ would get the oxygen back to its collective brain by then.

The highest-ranking female guest at the afternoon reception was the ambassador from Tau Ceti. She was a slender woman of indeterminate age, fascinating facial bone structure, and penetrating eyes. Miles suspected her conversation would be an education in itself, political, subtle, and scintillating. Alas, as the Barrayaran ambassador had monopolized her, Miles doubted he was going to get a chance to find out.

The dowager Miles had been assigned to squire about held her rank by virtue of her husband, who was the Lord Mayor of London and now being entertained by the ambassador's wife. The mayor's lady seemed able to chatter on interminably, mainly about the clothing worn by the other guests. A passing servant of rather military bearing (all the human servants in the embassy were members of Galeni's department) offered Miles a wine glass full of straw-pale liquid from a gold tray, which Miles accepted with alacrity. Yes, two or three of those, with his low tolerance for alcohol, and he would be numb enough to endure even this. Was this not exactly the constrained social scene he had sweated his way, despite his physical handicaps, into the Imperial Service to escape? Of course, more than three glasses, and he would be stretched out asleep on the inlaid floor with a silly smile on his face, and deep in trouble when he woke up.

Miles took a large sip, and almost choked. *Apple juice*. . . . Damn Galeni, he was thorough. A quick glance around confirmed that this was not the same beverage being served to the guests. Miles ran his thumb around the high collar of his uniform jacket, and smiled tightly.

"Something wrong with your wine, Lord Vorkosigan?" the dowager inquired with concern.

"The vintage is a trifle, ah . . . young," Miles murmured. "I may suggest to the ambassador that he keep this one in his cellars a little longer." *Like till I get off this planet. . . .*

The main reception court was a high-arched, skylighted, elegantly appointed chamber that looked as if it should echo cavernously, but was strangely hushed for the large crowd its levels and niches could enclose. Sound absorbers concealed somewhere, Miles thought—and, he bet, if you knew just where to stand, secure cones to baffle eavesdroppers both human and electronic. He noted where the Barrayaran and Tau Cetan ambassadors were standing, for future reference; yes, even their lip movements seemed shadowed and blurred somehow. Certain right-of-passage treaties through Tau Cetan local space were coming up for renegotiation soon.

Miles and his charge drifted toward the architectural center of the room, the fountain and its pool. It was a cool, trickling sort of sculptured thing, with color-coordinated ferns and mosses. Red-gold shapes moved mysteriously in the shadowed waters.

Miles stiffened, then forced his spine to relax. A young man in black Cetagandan dress uniform with the yellow and black face-paint markings of a ghem-lieutenant approached, smiling and watchful. They exchanged wary nods.

"Welcome to Earth, Lord Vorkosigan," murmured the Cetagandan. "Is this an official visit, or are you on a grand tour?"

"A little of both," Miles shrugged. "I've been assigned to the embassy for my, ah, education. But I believe you have the advantage of me, sir." He didn't, of course; both the two Cetagandans who were in uniform and the two who were not, plus three individuals suspected of being their covert jackals, had been pointed out to Miles first thing.

"Ghem-lieutenant Tabor, military attache, Cetagandan Embassy," Tabor recited politely. They exchanged nods again. "Will you be here long, my lord?"

"I don't expect so. And yourself?"

"I have taken up the art of bonsai for a hobby. The ancient Japanese are said to have worked on a single tree for as long as a hundred years. Or perhaps it only seemed like it."

Miles suspected Tabor of humor, but the lieutenant kept his face so straight it was hard to tell. Perhaps he feared cracking his paint job.

A trill of laughter, mellow like bells, drew their attention toward the far end of the fountain. Ivan Vorpatril was leaning against the chrome railing down there, dark head bent close to a blonde confection. She wore something in salmon pink and silver that seemed to waft even when she was standing still, as now. Artfully artless golden hair cascaded across one white shoulder. Her fingernails flashed silver-pink as she gestured animatedly.

Tabor hissed slightly, bowed exquisitely over the dowager's hand, and passed on. Miles next saw him on the other side of the fountain jockeying for position near Ivan—but somehow Miles felt it was not military secrets Tabor was prowling for. No wonder he'd seemed only marginally interested in Miles. But Tabor's stalk on the blonde was interrupted by a signal from his ambassador, and he perforce followed the dignitaries out.

"Such a nice young man, Lord Vorpatril," Miles's dowager cooed. "We like him very much here. The ambassador's lady tells me you two are related?" She cocked her head at him, brightly expectant.

"Cousins, of a sort," Miles explained. "Ah—who is the young lady with him?"

The dowager smiled proudly. "That's my daughter, Sylveth."

Daughter, of course. The ambassador and his lady had a keen Barrayaran appreciation of the nuances of social rank. Miles, being of the senior family line, not to mention the son of Prime Minister Count Vorkosigan, outranked Ivan socially if not militarily. Which meant, oh God, he was doomed. He'd be stuck with the VIP dowagers forever while Ivan— Ivan carried off *all* the daughters. . . .

"A lovely couple," said Miles thickly.

"Aren't they? Just what sort of cousins, Lord Vorkosigan?"

"Uh? Oh, Ivan and me, yes. Our grandmothers were sisters. My grandmother was Prince Xav Vorbarra's eldest child, Ivan's was his youngest."

"Princesses? How romantic."

Miles considered describing in detail how his grandmother, her brother, and most of their children had been blown into hamburger during Mad Emperor Yuri's reign of terror. No, the mayor's lady might find it merely a shivery and outré tale, or even worse, romantic. He doubted she'd grasp the true violent stupidity of Yuri's affairs, with their consequences escaping in all directions to warp Barrayaran history to this day.

"Does Lord Vorpatril own a castle?" she inquired archly.

"Ah, no. His mother, my Aunt Vorpatril," *who is a social barracuda who would eat you alive,* "has a very nice flat in the capital city of Vorbarr Sultana." Miles paused. "We used to have a castle. But it was burned down at the end of the Time of Isolation."

"A ruined castle. That's almost as good."

"Picturesque as hell," Miles assured her.

Someone had left a small plate with the remains of their hors d'oeuvres sitting on the railing by the fountain. Miles took the roll and started breaking off bits for the goldfish. They glided up to snap at the crumbs with a brief gurgle.

One refused to rise to the bait, lurking in the depths. How interesting, a goldfish that did not eat—now, there was a solution to Ivan's fish-inventory problem. Perhaps the stubborn one was a fiendish Cetagandan construct, whose cold scales glittered like gold because they were.

He might pluck it out with a feline pounce, stamping it underfoot with a mechanical crunch and electric sizzle, then hold it up with a triumphal cry—"Ah! Through my quick wits and reflexes, I have discovered the spy among you!"

But if his guess were wrong, ah. The *squish!* under his boot, the dowager's recoil, and the Barrayaran prime minister's son would have acquired an instant reputation as a young man with *serious* emotional difficulties. . . . "Ah ha!" he pictured himself cackling to the horrified woman as the fish guts slithered underfoot, "You should see what I do to kittens!"

The big goldfish rose lazily at last, and took a crumb with a splash that marred Miles's polished boots. *Thank you, fish,* Miles thought to it. *You have just saved me from considerable social embarrassment.* Of course, if the Cetagandan artificers were really clever, they might have designed a mechanical fish that really ate, and excreted little . . .

The mayor's lady had just asked another leading question about Ivan, which Miles in his absorption failed to completely catch. "Yes, most unfortunate about his disease," Miles purred, and prepared to launch a monologue maligning Ivan's genes involving inbred aristocracies, radiation areas left from the First Cetagandan War, and Mad Emperor Yuri, when the secured comm link in his pocket beeped.

"Excuse me, ma'am. I'm being paged." *Bless you, Elli,* he thought as he fled the dowager to find a quiet corner to answer it. No Cetagandans in sight. He found an unoccupied niche on the second level made private by green plants, and opened the channel.

"Yes, Commander Quinn?"

"Miles, thank God." Her voice was hurried. "We seem to have us a Situation down there, and you're the closest Dendarii officer."

"What sort of situation?" He didn't care for situations that came capitalized. Elli was not normally inclined to panicky exaggerations. His stomach tightened nervously.

"I haven't been able to get details I can trust, but it appears that four or five of our soldiers on downside leave in London have barricaded themselves in some sort of shop with a hostage, holding off the police. They're armed."

"Our guys, or the police?"

"Both, unfortunately. The police commander I talked to sounded like he was prepared for blood on the walls. Very soon."

"Worse and worse. What the hell do they think they're doing?"

"Damned if I know. I'm in orbit right now, preparing to leave, but it'll be forty-five minutes to an hour before I can get down there. Tung's in worse position, it'd be a two-hour suborbital flight from Brazil. But I think you could be there in about ten minutes. Here, I'll key the address into your comm link."

"How were our guys permitted to take Dendarii weaponry off-ship?"

"A good question, but I'm afraid we'll have to save it for the post-mortem. So to speak," she said grimly. "Can you find the place?"

Miles glanced at the address on his readout. "I think so. I'll meet you there." Somehow . . .

"Right. Quinn out." The channel snapped closed.

Chapter Three

Miles pocketed the comm link, and gazed around the main reception court. The reception had peaked. There were perhaps a hundred people present, in a blinding variety of Earth and galactic fashions, and a fair sprinkling of uniforms besides Barrayaran. A few of the earlier arrivals were cutting out already, ushered past security by their Barrayaran escorts. The Cetagandans appeared to be truly gone, along with their friends. His escape must be opportune rather than clever, it appeared.

Ivan was still chatting with his beautiful charge down at the end of the fountain. Miles bore down upon him ruthlessly.

"Ivan. Meet me by the main doors in five minutes."

"What?"

"It's an emergency. I'll explain later."

"What sort of—?" Ivan began, but Miles was already slipping out of the room and making his way toward the back lift tubes. He had to force himself not to run.

When the door to his and Ivan's room slid shut behind him he peeled out of his dress greens, tore off the boots, and catapulted for the closet. He yanked on the black T-shirt and grey trousers of his Dendarii uniform. Barrayaran boots were descended from a cavalry tradition; Dendarii had evolved from foot-soldiers' gear. In the presence of a horse the Barrayaran were the more practical, although Miles had never been able to explain that to Elli. It would take two hours or so in the saddle on heavy cross-country terrain, and her calves rubbed to bleeding blisters, to convince her that the design had a purpose besides looks. No horses here.

He sealed the Dendarii combat boots and adjusted the grey-and-white jacket in midair, tumbling back down the lift tube at max drop. He paused at the bottom to pull down his jacket, jerk up his chin, and take a deep breath. One could not saunter inconspicuously while gasping. He took an alternate corridor, around the main court to the front entrance. Still no Cetagandans, thank God.

Ivan's eyes widened as he saw Miles approach. He flashed a smile at the blonde, excusing himself, and backed Miles against a potted plant as if to hide him from view. "What the hell—?" he hissed.

"You've got to walk me out of here. Past the guards."

"Oh, no I don't! Galeni will have your hide for a doormat if he sees you in that get-up."

"Ivan, I don't have time to argue and I don't have time to explain, which is precisely why I'm sidestepping Galeni. Quinn wouldn't have called me if she didn't need me. I've got to go *now*."

"You'll be AWOL!"

"Not if I'm not missed. Tell them—tell them I retired to our room due to excruciating pain in my bones."

"Is that osteo-joint thing of yours acting up again? I bet the embassy physician could get that anti-inflammatory med for you— "

"No, no—no more than usual, anyway—but at least it's something real. There's a chance they'll believe it. Come on. Bring her." Miles gestured with his chin toward Sylveth, waiting out of earshot for Ivan with an inquiring look on her flower-petal face.

"What for?"

"Camouflage." Smiling through his teeth, Miles propelled Ivan by his elbow toward the main doors.

"How do you do?" Miles nattered to Sylveth, capturing her hand and tucking it through his arm. "So nice to meet you. Are you enjoying the party? Wonderful town, London. . . ."

He and Sylveth made a lovely couple too, Miles decided. He glanced at the guards from the corner of his eye as they passed. They noticed her. With any luck, he would be a short grey blur in their memories.

Sylveth glanced in bewilderment at Ivan, but by this time they had stepped into the sunlight.

"You don't have a bodyguard," Ivan objected.

"I'll be meeting Quinn in a short time."

"How are you going to get back in the embassy?"

Miles paused. "You'll have until I get back to figure that out."

"Ngh! When's that?"

"I don't know."

The outside guards' attention was drawn to a ground car hissing up to the embassy entrance. Abandoning Ivan, Miles darted across the street and dove into the entrance to the tubeway system.

Ten minutes and two connections later, he emerged

to find himself in a very much older section of town, restored 22nd-century architecture. He didn't have to check for street numbers to spot his destination. The crowd, the barricades, the flashing lights, the police hovercars, fire equipment, ambulance . . . "Damnation," Miles muttered, and started down that side street. He rolled the words back through his mouth, switching gears, to Admiral Naismith's flat Betan accent, "Aw, *shit* . . ."

Miles guessed the policeman in charge was the one with the amplifier comm, and not one of the half-dozen in body armor toting plasma rifles. He pushed his way through the crowd and hopped over the barricade. "Are you the officer in charge?"

The constable's head snapped around in bewilderment, then he looked down. At first purely startled, he frowned as he took in Miles's uniform. "Are you one of those psychopaths?" he demanded.

Miles rocked back on his heels, wondering how to answer that one. He suppressed all three of the initial retorts that came to his mind, and chose instead, "I'm Admiral Miles Naismith, commanding, Dendarii Free Mercenary Fleet. What's happened here?" He interrupted himself to slowly and delicately extend one index finger and push skyward the muzzle of a plasma rifle being held on him by an armored woman. "Please, dear, I'm on your side, really." Her eyes flashed mistrustfully at him through her faceplate, but the police commander jerked his head, and she faded back a few paces.

"Attempted robbery," said the constable. "When the clerk tried to foil it, they attacked her."

"Robbery?" said Miles. "Excuse me, but that makes no sense. I thought all transactions were by computer credit transfer here. There's no cash to rob. There must be some misunderstanding."

"Not cash," said the constable. "Stock."

The store, Miles noticed out of the corner of his eye, was a wineshop. A display window was cracked and starred. He suppressed a queasy feeling of unease, and plunged on, keeping his voice light. "In any case, I fail to understand this stand-off with deadly weapons over a case of shoplifting. Aren't you overreacting a trifle? Where are your stunners?"

"They hold the woman hostage," said the constable grimly.

"So? Stun them all, God will recognize his own."

The constable gave Miles a peculiar look. He didn't read his own history, Miles guessed—the source of that quote was just across the water from here, for pity's sake.

"They claim to have arranged some sort of deadman switch. They claim this whole block will go up in flames." The constable paused. "Is this possible?"

Miles paused too. "Have you got ID's on any of these guys yet?"

"No."

"How are you communicating with them?"

"Through the comconsole. At least, we were—they appear to have destroyed it a few minutes ago."

"We will, of course, pay damages," Miles choked.

"That's not all you'll pay," growled the constable.

"Well . . ." Out of the corner of his eye Miles saw a hovercar labeled EURONEWS NETWORK dropping down to the street. "I think it's time to break this up."

He started toward the wineshop.

"What are you going to do?" asked the constable.

"Arrest them. They face Dendarii charges for taking ordnance off-ship."

"All by yourself? They'll shoot you. They're crazy-drunk."

"I don't think so. If I were going to be shot by my own troops, they've had much better opportunities than this."

The constable frowned, but did not stop him.

The autodoors were not working. Miles stood baffled before the glass a moment, then pounded on it. There was shadowy movement behind the iridescent shimmer. A very long pause, and the doors slid open about a third of a meter; Miles turned sideways and slipped through. A man inside shoved them shut again by hand and jammed a metal brace in their slot.

The interior of the wineshop was a shambles. Miles gasped at the fumes in the air, aromatic vapors from shattered bottles. *You could get plastered just from breathing*. . . . The carpeting squished underfoot.

Miles glanced around, to determine who he wanted to murder first. The one who'd unblocked the door stood out, as he was wearing only underwear.

" 'S Admiral Naismith," the doorman hissed. He came to a tilted attention, and saluted.

"Whose army are you in, soldier?" Miles growled at him. The man's hands made little waving motions, as if to offer explanations by mime. Miles couldn't dredge up his name.

Another Dendarii, in uniform this time, was sitting on the floor with his back to a pillar. Miles squatted down, considering hauling him to his feet, or at least his knees, by his jacket and bracing him. Miles stared into his face. Little red eyes like coals in the caverns of his eye-sockets stared back without recognition. "Eugh," muttered Miles, and rose without further attempt to communicate. That one's consciousness was somewhere in wormhole space.

"Who cares?" came a hoarse voice from the floor

behind a display rack, one of the few that hadn't been violently upended. "Who t'hell cares?"

Oh, we've got the best and brightest here today, don't we? Miles thought sourly. An upright person emerged around the end of the display rack, saying, "Can't be, he's disappeared again . . ."

At last, someone Miles knew by name. All too well. Further explanation for the scene was almost redundant. "Ah, Private Danio. Fancy meeting you here."

Danio shambled to a species of attention, towering over Miles. An antique pistol, its grip defaced with notches, dangled menacingly from his ham hand. Miles nodded toward it. "Is that the deadly weapon I was called away from my affairs to come collect? They talked like you had half our bleeding arsenal down here."

"No, sir!" said Danio. "That would be against regs." He patted the gun fondly. "Jus' my personal property. Because you never know. The crazies are everywhere."

"Are you carrying any other weapons among you?"

"Yalen has his bowie knife."

Miles controlled a twinge of relief as premature. Still, if these morons were on their own, the Dendarii fleet might not have to get officially sucked into their morass after all. "Did you know that carrying any weapon is a criminal offense in this jurisdiction?"

Danio thought this over. "Wimps," he said at last.

"Nevertheless," said Miles firmly, "I'm going to have to collect them and take them back to the flagship." Miles peered around the display rack. The one on the floor—Yalen, presumably—lay clutching an unsheathed hunk of steel suitable for butchering an entire steer, should he encounter one mooing down the metalled streets and skyways of London.

Miles thought it through, and pointed. "Bring me that knife, Private Danio."

Danio pried the weapon from his comrade's grip. "Nooo . . ." said the horizontal one.

Miles breathed easier when he had both weapons in his possession. "Now, Danio—quickly, because they're getting nervous out there—exactly what happened here?"

"Well, sir, we were having a party. We'd rented a room." He jerked his head toward the demi-naked doorman who hovered listening. "We ran out of supplies, and came here to buy more, 'cause it was close by. Got everything all picked out and piled up, and then the bitch wouldn't take our credit! Good Dendarii credit!"

"The bitch . . . ?" Miles looked around, stepping over the disarmed Yalen. *Oh, ye gods. . . .* The store clerk, a plump, middle-aged woman, lay on her side on the floor at the other end of the display rack, gagged, trussed up in the naked soldier's twisted jacket and pants by way of makeshift restraints.

Miles pulled the bowie knife out of his belt and headed for her. She made hysterical gurgling noises down in her throat.

"I wouldn't let her loose if I were you," said the naked soldier warningly. "She makes a lot of noise."

Miles paused and studied the woman. Her greying hair stuck out wildly, except where it was plastered to her forehead and neck by sweat. Her terrorized eyes rolled whitely; she bucked against her bonds.

"Mm." Miles thrust the knife back in his belt temporarily. He caught the naked soldier's name off his uniform at last, and made an unwelcome mental connection. "Xaveria. Yes, I remember you now. You did well at Dagoola." Xaveria stood straighter.

Damn. So much for his nascent plan of throwing the entire lot to the local authorities, and praying they were all still incarcerated when the fleet broke orbit. Could Xaveria be detached from his worthless comrades somehow? Alas, it looked like they were all in this together.

"So she wouldn't take your credit cards. You, Xaveria—what happened next?"

"Er—insults were exchanged, sir."

"And?"

"And tempers kind of got out of hand. Bottles were thrown, and thrown on the floor. The police were called. She was punched out." Xaveria eyed Danio warily.

Miles contemplated the sudden absence of actors from all this action, in Xaveria's syntax. "And?"

"And the police got here. And we told them we'd blow the place up if they tried to come in."

"And do you actually have the means to carry out that threat, Private Xaveria?"

"No, sir. It was pure bluff. I was trying to think—well—what you would do in the situation, sir."

This one is too damned observant. Even when he's potted, Miles thought dryly. He sighed, and ran his hands through his hair. "Why wouldn't she take your credit cards? Aren't they the Earth Universals you were issued at the shuttleport? You weren't trying to use the ones left over from Mahata Solaris, were you?"

"No, sir," said Xaveria. He produced his card by way of evidence. It looked all right. Miles turned, to test it in the comconsole at the checkout, only to discover that the comconsole had been shot. The final bullet hole in the holovid plate was precisely centered, must have been intended as the coup de grace, although the console still emitted little wheezing popping noises now and then. He added the price of it to the running tally in his head, and winced.

"Actually," Xaveria cleared his throat, "it was the machine that spat it up, sir."

"It shouldn't have done that," Miles began, "unless—" *Unless there's something wrong with the central account,* his thought finished. The pit of his stomach felt suddenly very cold. "I'll check it out," he promised. "Meanwhile we have to wrap this up and get you out of here without your being fried by the local constables."

Danio nodded excitedly toward the pistol in Miles's hand. "We could blast our way out the back. Make a run for the nearest tubeway."

Miles, momentarily bereft of speech, envisioned plugging Danio with his own pistol. Danio was saved only by Miles's reflection that the recoil might break his arm. He'd smashed his right hand at Dagoola, and the memory of the pain was still fresh.

"No, Danio," Miles said when he could command his voice. "We are going to walk quietly— very quietly—out the front door and surrender."

"But the Dendarii never surrender," said Xaveria.

"This is not a firebase," said Miles patiently. "It is a wineshop. Or at any rate, it was. Furthermore, it is not even our wineshop." *Though I shall no doubt be compelled to buy it.* "Think of the London police not as your enemies, but as your dearest friends. They are, you know. Because," he fixed Xaveria with a cold eye, "until they get done with you, I can't start."

"Ah," said Xaveria, quelled at last. He touched Danio on the arm. "Yeah. Maybe—maybe we better let the Admiral take us home, eh, Danio?"

Xaveria hauled the ex-bowie knife owner to his

feet. After a moment's thought, Miles walked quietly behind red-eye, pulled out his pocket stunner, and placed a light blast to the base of his skull. Red-eye toppled sideways. Miles sent up a short prayer that this final stimulus wouldn't send him into trauma-shock. God alone knew what chemical cocktail it chased, except that it clearly wasn't alcohol alone.

"You take his head," Miles directed Danio, "and you, Yalen, take his feet." There, that effectively immobilized all three of them. "Xaveria, open the door, place your hands on top of your head, and walk, do not run, to where you will submit quietly to arrest. Danio, you follow. That's an order."

"Wish we had the rest of the troops," muttered Danio.

"The only troop you need is a troop of legal experts," said Miles. He eyed Xaveria, and sighed. "I'll send you one."

"Thank you, sir," said Xaveria, and lurched gravely forward. Miles brought up the rear, gritting his teeth.

Miles blinked in the sunlight of the street. His little patrol fell into the arms of the waiting police. Danio did not fight when they started to frisk him, though Miles only relaxed when he saw the tangle-field finally turned on. The constable commander approached, inhaling for speech.

A soft *foomp!* broke from the door of the wine-shop. Blue flames licked out over the slidewalk.

Miles cried out, wheeled, and sprinted explosively from his standing start, gulping a huge breath and holding it. He hurtled through the wineshop doors, into darkness shot through with twisting heat, around the display case. The alcohol-soaked carpeting was growing flames, like stands of golden wheat running in a crazy pattern following concentrations of fumes. Fire was advancing on the bound woman on the floor; in a moment, her hair would be a terrible halo. . . .

Miles dove for her, wriggled his shoulder under her, grunted to his feet. He swore he could feel his bones bend. She kicked unhelpfully. Miles staggered for the door, bright like the mouth of a tunnel, like the gate of life. His lungs pulsed, straining for oxygen against his tightly-closed lips. Total elapsed time, eleven seconds.

In the twelfth second, the room behind them brightened, roaring. Miles and his burden fell to the slidewalk, rolling—he rolled her over and over—flames were lapping over their clothing. People were screaming and yelling at an unintelligible distance. His Dendarii uniform cloth, combat-rated, would neither melt nor burn, but still made a dandy wick for the volatile liquids splashed on it. The effect was bloody spectacular. But the poor clerk's clothing offered no such protection—

He choked on a faceful of foam, sprayed on them by the fireman who had rushed forward. He must have been standing at the ready all this time. The frightened-looking policewoman hovered anxiously clutching her thoroughly redundant plasma-rifle. The fire extinguisher foam was like being rolled in beer suds, only not so tasty—Miles spat vile chemicals, and lay a moment gasping. God, air was good. Nobody praised air enough.

"A bomb!" cried the constable commander.

Miles wriggled onto his back, appreciating the blue slice of sky seen through eyes miraculously unglazed, unburst, unslagged. "No," he panted sadly, "brandy. Lots and lots of very expensive brandy. And cheap grain alcohol. Prob'ly set off by a short circuit in the comconsole."

He rolled out of the way as firemen in white protective garments bearing the tools of their trade stampeded forward. A fireman pulled him to his feet, farther away from the now-blazing building. He came up staring at a person pointing a piece of equipment at him resembling, for a disoriented moment, a microwave cannon. The adrenalin rush washed over him without effect, there was no response left in him. The person was babbling at him. Miles blinked dizzily, and the microwave cannon fell into more sensible focus as a holovid camera.

He wished it had been a microwave cannon. . . .

The clerk, released at last, was pointing at him and crying and screaming. For someone he'd just saved from a horrible death, she didn't sound very grateful. The holovid swung her way for a moment, until she was led away by the ambulance personnel. He hoped they'd supply her with a sedative. He pictured her arriving home that night, to husband and children—"And how was the shop today, dear . . . ?" He wondered if she'd accept hush-money, and if so, how much it would be.

Money, oh God . . .

"Miles!" Elli Quinn's voice over his shoulder made him jump. "Do you have everything under control?"

They collected stares, on the tubeway ride to the London shuttleport. Miles, catching a glimpse of himself in a mirrored wall while Elli credited their tokens, was not surprised. The sleek, polished Lord Vorkosigan he'd last seen looking back at him before the embassy reception has been transmuted, werewolf-like, into a most degraded little monster. His scorched, damp, bedraggled uniform was flecked with little fluffy bits of drying foam. The white placket down the jacket front was filthy. His face was smudged, his voice a croak, his eyes red and feral from smoke irritation. He reeked of smoke and sweat and drink, especially drink. He'd been rolling in it, after all. People near them in line caught one whiff and started edging away. The constables, thank God, had relieved him of knife and pistol, impounded as evidence. Still he and Elli had their end of the bubble-car all to themselves.

Miles sank into his seat with a groan. "Some bodyguard you are," he said to Elli. "Why didn't you protect me from that interviewer?"

"She wasn't trying to shoot you. Besides, I'd just got there. I couldn't tell her what had been going on."

"But you're far more photogenic. It would have improved the image of the Dendarii Fleet."

"Holovids make me tongue-tied. But you sounded calm enough."

"I was trying to downplay it all. 'Boys will be boys' chuckles Admiral Naismith, while in the background his troops burn down London. . . ."

Elli grinned. " 'Sides, they weren't interested in me. I wasn't the hero who'd dashed into a burning building—by the gods, when you came rolling out all on fire—"

"You saw that?" Miles was vaguely cheered. "Did it look good in the long shots? Maybe it'll make up for Danio and his jolly crew, in the minds of our host city."

"It looked properly terrifying." She shuddered appreciation. "I'm surprised you're not more badly burned."

Miles twitched singed eyebrows, and tucked his blistered left hand unobtrusively under his right arm. "It was nothing. Protective clothing. I'm glad not all our equipment design is faulty."

"I don't know. To tell the truth, I've been shy of fire ever since . . ." her hand touched her face.

"As well you should be. The whole thing was carried out by my spinal reflexes. When my brain finally caught up with my body, it was all over, and then I had the shakes. I've seen a few fires, in combat. The only thing I could think of was speed, because when fires hit that certain point, they expand *fast*."

Miles bit back confiding his further worries about the security aspects of that damned interview. It was too late now, though his imagination played with the idea of a secret Dendarii raid on Euronews Network to destroy the vid disk. Maybe war would break out, or a shuttle would crash, or the government would fall in a major sex scandal, and the whole wineshop incident would be shelved in the rush of other news events. Besides, the Cetagandans surely already knew Admiral Naismith had been seen on Earth. He would disappear back into Lord Vorkosigan soon enough, perhaps permanently this time.

Miles staggered off the tubeway clutching his back.

"Bones?" said Elli worriedly. "Did you do something to your spine?"

"I'm not sure." He stomped along beside her, rather bent. "Muscle spasms—that poor woman must have been fatter than I thought. Adrenalin'll fool you. . . ."

It was no better by the time their little personnel shuttle docked at the *Triumph*, the Dendarii flagship in orbit. Elli insisted on a detour to sickbay.

"Pulled muscles," said his fleet surgeon unsympathetically after scanning him. "Go lie down for a week."

Miles made false promises, and exited clutching a packet of pills in his bandaged hand. He was pretty sure the surgeon's diagnosis was correct, for the pain was easing, now that he was aboard his own flagship. He could feel the tension uncoiling in his neck at least, and hoped it would continue all the way down. He was coming down off his adrenalin-induced high, too—better finish his business here while he could still walk and talk at the same time.

He straightened his jacket, brushing rather futilely at the white flecks, and jerked up his chin, before marching into his fleet finance officer's inner sanctum.

It was evening, ship-time, only an hour skewed from London downside time, but the mercenary accountant was still at her post. Vicki Bone was a precise, middle-aged woman, heavy-set, definitely a tech not a troop, whose normal tone of voice was a calming drawl. Now she spun in her station chair and squealed at him, "Oh, sir! Do you have the credit transfer . . . ?" She took in his appearance and her voice dropped to a more usual timbre. "Good God, what happened to you?" As an afterthought, she saluted.

"That's what I'm here to find out, Lieutenant Bone." He hooked a second seat into its floor brackets and swung it around to sit backwards, his arms draped over its back. As an afterthought, he returned her salute. "I thought you reported yesterday that all our resupply orders not essential for orbital life-support were on hold, and that our Earthside credit was under control."

"Temporarily under control," she replied. "Fourteen days ago you told me we'd have a credit transfer in ten days. I tried to time as many expenses as possible to come in after that. Four days ago you told me it would be another ten days—"

"At least," Miles confirmed glumly.

"I've put off as much stuff as I can again, but some

of it had to be paid off, in order to get credit extended another week. We've dipped dangerously far into reserve funds since Mahata Solaris."

Miles rubbed a finger tiredly over the seat back. "Yeah, maybe we should have pushed on straight to Tau Ceti." Too late now. If only he were dealing with Sector II Security Headquarters directly . . .

"We would have had to drop three-fourths of the fleet at Earth anyway, sir."

"And I didn't want to break up the set, I know. We stay here much longer, and none of us will be able to leave—a financial black hole. . . . Look, tap your programs and tell me what happened to the downside personnel credit account about 1600 London time tonight."

"Hm?" Her fingers conjured up arcane and colorful data displays from her holovid console. "Oh, dear. It shouldn't have done that. Now where did the money go . . . ? Ah, direct override. That explains it."

"Explain it to me," Miles prodded.

"Well," she turned to him, "of course when the fleet is on station for long at any place with any kind of financial net at all, we don't just leave our liquid assets sitting around."

"We don't?"

"No, no. Anything that isn't actually outgoing is held for as long as possible in some sort of short-term, interest-generating investment. So all our credit accounts are set to ride along at the legal minimum; when a bill comes due, I cycle it through the computer and shoot just enough to cover it from the investment account into the credit account."

"Is this, er, worth the risk?"

"Risk? It's basic good practice! We made over four thousand GSA federal credits on interest and dividends last week, until we fell out of the minimum amount bracket."

"Oh," said Miles. He had a momentary flash about giving up war and playing the stock market instead. The Dendarii Free Mercenary Holding Company? Alas, the Emperor might have a word or two to say about that. . . .

"But these morons," Lieutenant Bone gestured at the schematic representing her version of Danio's adventures that afternoon, "attempted to tap the account directly through its number, instead of through Fleet Central Accounting as everyone has been told and told to do. And because we're riding so low at the moment, it bounced. Sometimes I think I'm talking to the deaf." More lurid bar graphs fountained up at her fingertips. "But I can only run it round and round for so long, sir! The investment account is now empty, so of course it's generating no extra money. I'm not sure we can even make it six more days. And if the credit transfer doesn't arrive then . . ." she flung up her hands, "the whole Dendarii fleet could start to slide, piecemeal, into receivership!"

"Oh." Miles rubbed his neck. He'd been mistaken, his headache wasn't waning. "Isn't there some way you can shift the stuff around from account to account to create, er . . . virtual money? Temporarily?"

"Virtual money?" Her lips curled in loathing.

"To save the fleet. Just like in combat. Mercenary accounting. . . ." he clasped his hands together, between his knees, and smiled up at her hopefully. "Of course, if it's beyond your abilities . . ."

Her nostrils flared. "Of course it's not. But the kind of thing you're talking about relies mostly on time lags. Earth's financial network is totally integrated; there are no time lags unless you want to start working it interstellar. I'll tell you what would work, though . . ." her voice trailed off. "Well, maybe not. . . ."

"What?"

"Go to a major bank and get a short-term loan against, say, some major capital equipment." Her eyes, glancing around by implication through the walls to the *Triumph,* revealed what order of capital equipment she had in mind. "We might have to conceal certain other outstanding liens from them, and the extent of depreciation, not to mention certain ambiguities about what is and is not owned by the Fleet corporation versus the Captain-owners—but at least it would be real money."

And what would Commodore Tung say when he found out that Miles had mortgaged his command ship? But Tung wasn't here. Tung was on leave. It could be all over by the time Tung got back.

"We'd have to ask for two or three times the amount we really needed, to be sure of getting enough," Lieutenant Bone went on. "You would have to sign for it, as senior corporation officer."

Admiral Naismith would have to sign for it, Miles reflected. A man whose legal existence was strictly— virtual, not that an Earth bank could be expected to find that out. The Dendarii fleet propped his identity most convincingly. This could be almost the safest thing he'd ever done. "Go ahead and set it up, Lieutenant Bone. Um . . . use the *Triumph,* it's the biggest thing we've got."

She nodded, her shoulders straightening, as she regained some of her accustomed serenity. "Yes, sir. Thank you, sir."

Miles sighed, and shoved to his feet. Sitting down had been a mistake; his tired muscles were seizing up. Her nostrils wrinkled as he passed upwind of her. Perhaps he'd better take a few minutes to clean up. It would be hard enough to explain his disappearance, when he returned to the embassy, without explaining his remarkable appearance as well.

"Virtual money," he heard Lieutenant Bone mutter disapprovingly to her comconsole as he exited. "Good God."

Chapter Four

By the time Miles had showered, groomed, and donned a fresh uniform and glossy spare boots, his pills had cut in and he was feeling no pain at all. When he caught himself whistling as he splashed on after-shave and adjusted a rather flashy and only demi-regulation black silk scarf around his neck, tucked into his grey-and-white jacket, he decided he'd better cut the dosage in half next round. He was feeling much too good.

Too bad the Dendarii uniform did not include a beret one could tilt at a suitably rakish angle, though. He might order one added. Tung would probably approve; Tung had theories about how spiffy uniforms helped recruiting and morale. Miles was not entirely sure this wouldn't just result in acquiring a lot of recruits who wanted to play dress-up. Private Danio might like a beret . . . Miles abandoned the notion.

Elli Quinn was waiting patiently for him in the

Triumph's number six shuttle hatch corridor. She swung gracefully to her feet and ahead of him into their shuttle, remarking, "We'd better hustle. How long do you think your cousin can cover for you at the embassy?"

"I suspect it's already a lost cause," Miles said, strapping himself in beside her. In light of the warnings on the pain pill packet about operating equipment, he let her take the pilot's seat again. The little shuttle broke smoothly away from the side of the flagship and began to drop through its orbital clearance pattern.

Miles meditated morosely on his probable reception when he showed up back at the embassy. Confined-to-quarters was the least he might expect, though he plead mitigating circumstances for all he was worth. He did not feel at all like hustling back to that doom. Here he was on Earth on a warm summer night, with a glamorous, brilliant woman friend. It was only—he glanced at his chronometer—2300. Night life should just be getting rolling. London, with its huge population, was an around-the-clock town. His heart rose inexplicably.

Yet what might they do? Drinking was out; God knew what would happen if he dropped alcohol on top of his current pharmaceutical load, with his peculiar physiology, except that it could be guaranteed not to improve his coordination. A show? It would immobilize them for a rather long time in one spot, security-wise. Better to do something that kept them moving.

To hell with the Cetagandans. He was damned if he would become hostage to the mere fear of them. Let Admiral Naismith have one last fling, before being hung back in the closet. The lights of the shuttleport flashed beneath them, reached up to pull them in. As they rolled into their rented hardstand (140 GSA federals per diem) with its waiting Dendarii guard, Miles blurted, "Hey, Elli. Let's go—let's go window shopping."

And so it was they found themselves strolling in a fashionable arcade at midnight. Not just Earth's but the galaxy's wares were spread out for the visitor with funds. The passers-by were a parade worth watching in their own right, for the student of fad and fashion. Feathers were in this year, and synthetic silk, leather, and fur, in revival of primitive natural fabrics from the past. And Earth had such a lot of past to revive. The young lady in the—the Aztec-Viking outfit, Miles guessed—leaning on the arm of the young man in faintly 24th-century boots and plumes particularly caught his eye. Perhaps a Dendarii beret wouldn't be too unprofessionally archaic after all.

Elli, Miles observed sadly, was not relaxing and enjoying this. Her attention on the passers-by was more in the nature of a hunt for concealed weapons and sudden movements. But she paused at last in real intrigue before a shop discreetly labeled, CULTURED FURS: A DIVISION OF GALACTECH BIOENGINEERING. Miles eased her inside.

The display area was spacious, a sure tip-off to the price range they were operating in. Red fox coats, white tiger carpets, extinct leopard jackets, gaudy Tau Cetan beaded lizard bags and boots and belts, black and white macaque monkey vests—a holovid display ran a continuous program explaining the stock's origins not in the slaughter of live animals, but in the test tubes and vats of GalacTech's R&D division. Nineteen extinct species were offered in natural colors. Coming up for the fall line, the vid assured them, were rainbow rhino leather and triple-length white fox in designer pastels. Elli buried her hands to the wrists in something that looked like an explosion of apricot Persian cat.

"Does it shed?" Miles inquired bemusedly.

"Not at all," the salesman assured them. "GalacTech cultured furs are guaranteed not to shed, fade, or discolor. They are also soil-resistant."

An enormous width of silky black fur poured through Elli's arms. "What is this? Not a coat. . . ."

"Ah, that's a very popular new item," said the salesman. "The very latest in biomechanical feedback systems. Most of the fur items you see here are ordinary tanned leathers—but this is a live fur. This model is suitable for a blanket, spread, or throw rug. Various sorts of outerwear are upcoming from R&D next year."

"A live fur?" Her eyebrows rose enchantingly. The salesman rose on his toes in unconscious echo—Elli's face was having its usual effect on the unintiated.

"A live fur," the salesman nodded, "but with none of the defects of a live animal. It neither sheds nor eats nor," he coughed discreetly, "requires a litter box."

"Hold on," said Miles. "How can you advertise it as living, then? Where's it getting its energy from, if not the chemical breakdown of food?"

"An electromagnetic net in the cellular level passively gathers energy from the environment. Holovid carrier waves and the like. And every month or so, if it seems to be running down, you can give it a boost by placing it in your microwave for a few minutes on the lowest setting. Cultured Furs cannot be responsible, however, for the results if the owner accidently sets it on high."

"That still doesn't make it alive," Miles objected.

"I assure you," said the salesman, "this blanket

was blended from the very finest assortment of *felis domesticus* genes. We also have the white Persian and the chocolate-point Siamese stripe in stock, in the natural colors, and I have samples of decorator colors that can be ordered in any size."

"They did *that* to a cat?" Miles choked as Elli gathered up the whole huge boneless double-armful.

"Pet it," the salesman instructed Elli eagerly.

She did so, and laughed. "It purrs!"

"Yes. It also has programmable thermotaxic orientation—in other words, it snuggles up."

Elli wrapped it around herself completely, black fur cascading over her feet like the train of a queen's robe, and rubbed her cheek into the silky shimmer. "What won't they think of next? Oh, my. You want to rub it all over your skin."

"You do?" muttered Miles dubiously. Then his eyes widened as he pictured Elli, in all her lovely skin, lolling on the hairy thing. "You do?" he said in an entirely changed tone. His lips peeled back in a hungry grin. He turned to the salesman. "We'll take it."

The embarrassment came when he pulled out his credit card, stared at it, and realized he couldn't use it. It was Lieutenant Vorkosigan's, chock full of his embassy pay and utterly compromising to his present cover. Quinn, beside him, glanced over his shoulder at his hesitation. He tilted the card toward her to see, shielded in his palm, and their eyes met.

"Ah . . . no," she agreed. "No, no." She reached for her wallet.

I should have asked the price first, Miles thought to himself as they exited the shop carting the unwieldy bundle in its elegant silver plastic wrappings. The package, the salesman had finally convinced them, did not require air-holes. Well, the fur had delighted

Elli, and a chance to delight Elli was not to be lost for mere imprudence—or pride—on his part. He wanted to delight her. He would pay her back later.

But now, where could they go to try it out? He tried to think, as they exited the arcade and made their way to the nearest tubeway access port. He didn't want the night to end. He didn't know what he did want. No, he knew perfectly well what he wanted, he just didn't know if he could have it.

Elli, he suspected, didn't know how far his thought had taken him either. A little romance on the side was one thing; the change of career he was thinking of proposing to her—nice turn of phrase, that—would overturn her existence. Elli the space-born, who called all downsiders dirtsuckers in careless moments, Elli with a career agenda of her own. Elli who walked on land with all the dubious distaste of a mermaid out of water. Elli was an independent country. Elli was an island. And he was an idiot and this couldn't go on unresolved much longer or he would burst.

A view of Earth's famous moon, Miles figured, was what they needed, preferably shining on water. The town's old river, unfortunately, went underground in this sector, absorbed into arterial pipes below the 23rd-century building boom that had domed the half of the landscape not occupied by dizzily soaring spires and preserved historic architecture. Quietude, some fine and private place, was not easy to come by in a city of roiling millions.

The grave's a fine and private place, but none, I think, do there embrace. . . . The deathly flashbacks to Dagoola had faded of late weeks, but this one took him unawares in an ordinary public lift tube descending to the bubble-car system. Elli was falling, torn out of his numb grip by a vicious vortex—

design defect in the anti-grav system—swallowed by darkness—

"Miles, ow!" Elli objected. "Let go of my arm! What's the matter?"

"Falling," Miles gasped.

"Of course we're falling, this is the down-tube. Are you all right? Let me see the pupils of your eyes." She grabbed a hand-grip and pulled them to the side of the tube, out of the central fast traffic zone. Midnight Londoners continued to flow past them. Hell had been modernized, Miles decided wildly, and this was a river of lost souls gurgling down some cosmic drain, faster and faster.

The pupils of *her* eyes were large and dark. . . .

"Do your eyes get dilated or constricted when you get one of your weird drug reactions?" she demanded worriedly, her face centimeters from his.

"What are they doing now?"

"Pulsing."

"I'm all right." Miles swallowed. "The surgeon double-checks anything she puts me on, now. It may make me a little dizzy, she told me that." He had not loosed his grip.

In the lift tube, Miles realized suddenly, their height difference was voided. They hung face to face, his boots dangling above her ankles—he didn't even need to hunt up a box to stand on, nor risk a twist in his neck—impulsively, his lips dove onto hers. There was a split-second wail of terror in his mind, like the moment after he'd plunged from the rocks into thirty meters of clear green water that he knew was icy cold, after he'd surrendered all choice to gravity but before the consequences engulfed him.

The water was warm, warm. . . . Her eyes widened in surprise. He hesitated, losing his precious forward momentum, and began to withdraw. Her lips parted for him, and her arm clamped around the back of his neck. She was an athletic woman; the grip was a non-regulation but effective immobilization. Surely the first time his being pinned to the mat had meant *he'd* won. He devoured her lips ravenously, kissed her cheeks, eyelids, brow, nose, chin—where was the sweet well of her mouth? there, yes. . . .

The bulky package containing the live fur began to drift, bumping down the lift tube. They were jostled by a descending woman who frowned at them, a teenage boy shooting down the center of the tube hooted and made rude, explicit gestures, and the beeper in Elli's pocket went off.

Awkwardly, they recaptured the fur and scrambled off the first exit they came to, and fled the tube's field through an archway onto a bubble-car platform. They staggered into the open and stared at each other, shaken. In one lunatic moment, Miles realized, he'd upended their carefully-balanced working relationship, and what were they now? Officer and subordinate? Man and woman? Friend and friend, lover and lover? It could be a fatal error.

It could also be fatal without the error; Dagoola had thrust that lesson home. The person inside the uniform was larger than the soldier, the man more complex than his role. Death could take not just him but her tomorrow, and a universe of possibilities, not just a military officer, would be extinguished. He would kiss her again—damn, he could only reach her ivory throat now—

The ivory throat emitted a dismayed growl, and she keyed open the channel on the secure comm link, saying, "What the hell . . . ? It can't be you, you're here. Quinn here!"

"Commander Quinn?" Ivan Vorpatril's voice came small but clear. "Is Miles with you?"

Miles's lips rippled in a snarl of frustration. Ivan's timing was supernatural, as ever.

"Yes, why?" said Quinn to the comm link.

"Well, tell him to get his ass back here. I'm holding a hole in the Security net for him, but I can't hold it much longer. Hell, I can't stay awake much longer." A long gasp that Miles interpreted as a yawn wheezed from the comm link.

"My God, I didn't think he could really do it," Miles muttered. He grabbed the comm link. "Ivan? Can you really get me back in without being seen?"

"For about fifteen more minutes. And I had to bend regs all to hell and gone to do it, too. I'm holding down the guard post on the third sub-level, where the municipal power and sewer connections come through. I can loop the vid record and cut out the shot of your entry, but only if you get back here before Corporal Veli does. I don't mind putting my tail on the line for you, but I object to putting my tail on the line for nothing, you copy?"

Elli was studying the colorful holovid display mapping the tubeway system. "You can just make it, I think."

"It won't do any good—"

She grabbed his elbow and marched him toward the bubble cars, the firm gleam of duty crowding out the softer light in her eyes. "We'll have ten more minutes together on the way."

Miles massaged his face, as she went to credit their tokens, trying to rub his escaping rationality back through his skin by force. He looked up to see his own dim reflection staring back at him from the mirrored wall, shadowed by a pillar, face suffused with frustration and terror. He squeezed his eyes shut and looked again, moving in front of the pillar and staring. Most unpleasant—for a second, he had

seen himself wearing his green Barrayaran uniform.
Damn the pain pills. Was his subconscious trying to
tell him something? Well, he didn't suppose he was
in real trouble until a brain scan taken of him in his
two different uniforms produced two different patterns.

Upon reflection, the idea was suddenly not funny.

He embraced Quinn upon her return with more
complicated feelings than sexual desire alone. They
stole kisses in the bubble car—more pain than pleasure; by the time they reached their destination Miles
was in the most physically uncomfortable state of
arousal he could ever recall. Surely all his blood had
departed his brains to engorge his loins, rendering
him moronic by hypoxia and lust.

She left him on the platform in the embassy district with an anguished whisper of "Later . . . !" It
was only after the tubeway had swallowed her that
Miles realized she'd left him holding the bag, which
was vibrating with a rhythmic purr.

"Nice kitty." Miles hoisted it with a sigh, and
began walking—hobbling—home.

He awoke blearily the next morning engulfed in
rumbling black fur.

"Friendly thing, isn't it?" remarked Ivan.

Miles fought his way clear, spitting fuzz. The salesman had lied: clearly the near-beast ate people, not
radiation. It enveloped them secretly in the night
and ingested them like an amoeba—he'd left it on
the foot of his bed, dammit. Thousands of little kids,
sliding under their blankets to protect them from the
monsters in their closets, were in for a shocking
surprise. The cultured fur salesman was clearly a
Cetagandan agent-provocateur assassin. . . .

Ivan, wearing his underwear and with his toothbrush sticking jauntily out between gleaming inci-

sors, paused to run his hands through the black silk. It rippled, as if trying to arch into the strokes. " 'At's amazing," Ivan's unshaven jaw worked, shifting the toothbrush around. "You want to rub it all over your skin."

Miles pictured Ivan, lolling. . . . "Yech," he shuddered. "God. Where'sa coffee?"

"Downstairs. After you're dressed all nice and regulation. Try to at least look as if you'd been in bed since yesterday afternoon."

Miles smelled trouble instantly when Galeni called him, alone, into his office a half hour after their work-shift started.

"Good morning, Lieutenant Vorkosigan," Galeni smiled, falsely affable. Galeni's false smile was as horrendous as his rare real one was charming.

"Morning, sir," Miles nodded warily.

"All over your acute osteo-inflammatory attack, I see."

"Yes, sir."

"Do sit down."

"Thank you, sir." Miles sat, gingerly—no pain pills this morning. After last night's adventure, topped by that unsettling hallucination in the tubeway, Miles had flushed them, and made a mental note to tell his fleet surgeon that there was yet another med she could cross off his list. Galeni's eyebrows drew down in a flash of doubt. Then his eye fell on Miles's bandaged right hand. Miles shifted in his seat, and tried to be casual about tucking it behind the small of his back. Galeni grimaced sourly, and keyed up his holovid display.

"I picked up a fascinating item on the local news this morning," said Galeni. "I thought you'd like to see it too."

I think I'd rather drop dead on your carpet, sir.

Miles had no doubt about what was coming. Damn, and he'd only worried about the Cetagandan embassy picking it up.

The journalist from Euronews Network began her introduction—clearly, this part had been made a little later, for the wineshop fire was dying down in the background. When the cut with Admiral Naismith's smudged, strained face came on, it was still burning merrily. ". . . unfortunate misunderstanding," Miles heard his own Betan voice coughing. "—I promise a full investigation . . ." The long shot of himself and the unhappy clerk rolling out the front door on fire was only moderately spectacular. Too bad it couldn't have been nighttime, to bring out the full splendor of the pyrotechnics. The frightened fury in the holovid Naismith's face was faintly echoed in Galeni's. Miles felt a certain sympathy. It was no pleasure commanding subordinates who failed to follow orders and sprang dangerous idiocies on you. Galeni was not going to be happy about this.

The news clip ended at last, and Galeni flipped the off-switch. He leaned back in his chair and regarded Miles steadily. "Well?"

This was not, Miles's instincts warned him, the time to get cute. "Sir, Commander Quinn called me away from the embassy yesterday afternoon to handle this situation because I was the closest ranking Dendarii officer. In the event, her fears proved fully justified. My prompt intervention did prevent unnecessary injuries, perhaps deaths. I must apologize for absenting myself without leave. I cannot regret it, however."

"Apologize?" purred Galeni, suppressing fury. "You were out, AWOL, unguarded in direct defiance of standing orders. I missed the pleasure, evidently by seconds, of making my next report to Security HQ a query of where to ship your broiled body. Most interesting of all you managed to, apparently, teleport in and out of the embassy without leaving a ripple in my security records. And you plan to wave it all off with an apology? I think not, Lieutenant."

Miles stood the only ground he had. "I was not without a bodyguard, sir. Commander Quinn was present. I wave off nothing."

"Then you can begin by explaining precisely how you passed out, and back in, through my security net without anyone noticing you." Galeni leaned back in his chair with his arms folded, frowning fiercely.

"I . . ." here was the fork of the thing. Confession might be good for his soul, but should he rat on Ivan? "I left in a group of guests departing the reception through the main public entrance. Since I was wearing my Dendarii uniform, the guards assumed I was one of them."

"And your return?"

Miles fell silent. Galeni ought to be put in full possession of the facts, in order to repair his net, but among other things Miles didn't know himself exactly how Ivan had diddled the vid scanners, not to mention the guard corporal. He'd fallen into bed without asking the details.

"You cannot protect Vorpatril, Lieutenant," remarked Galeni. "He's my meat next after you."

"What makes you think Ivan was involved?" Miles's mouth went on, buying time to think. No, he should have thought first.

Galeni looked disgusted. "Get serious, Vorkosigan."

Miles took a breath. "Everything Ivan did, he did at my command. The responsibility is entirely mine. If you'll agree that no charges will fall upon him, I'll ask him to give you a complete report on how he created the temporary hole in the net."

"You will, eh?" Galeni's lips twisted. "Has it occurred to you yet that Lieutenant Vorpatril is *above* you in this chain of command?"

"No, sir," gulped Miles. "It, er . . . slipped my mind."

"His too, it appears."

"Sir. I had originally planned to be gone only a short time, and arranging my return was the least of my worries. As the situation extended itself, it was apparent to me that I should return openly, but when I did get back it was two in the morning and he'd gone to a great deal of trouble—it seemed ungrateful—"

"And besides," Galeni interpolated *sotto voce*, "it looked like it might work. . . ."

Miles suppressed an involuntary grin. "Ivan is an innocent party. Charge me as you wish, sir."

"Thank you, Lieutenant, for your kind permission."

Goaded, Miles snapped, "Dammit, sir, what would you have of me? The Dendarii are as much Barrayaran troops as any who wear the Emperor's uniform, even if they don't know it. They are my assigned charge. I cannot neglect their urgent needs even to play the part of Lieutenant Vorkosigan."

Galeni rocked back in his chair, his eyebrows shooting up. "*Play the part* of Lieutenant Vorkosigan? Who do you think you *are*?"

"I'm . . ." Miles fell silent, seized by a sudden vertigo, like falling down a defective lift tube. For a dizzy moment, he could not even make sense of the question. The silence lengthened.

Galeni folded his hands on his desk with an unsettled frown. His voice went mild. "Lose track, did you?"

"I'm . . ." Miles's hands opened helplessly. "It's my duty, when I'm Admiral Naismith, to be Admiral

Naismith as hard as I can. I don't usually have to switch back and forth like this."

Galeni cocked his head. "But Naismith isn't real. You said so yourself."

"Uh . . . right, sir. Naismith isn't real." Miles inhaled. "But his duties are. We must set up some more rational arrangement for me to be able to carry them out."

Galeni did not seem to realize that when Miles had, however inadvertantly, entered his chain of command, it had expanded not by one but by five thousand. Yet if he did awake to the fact, might he start messing with the Dendarii? Miles's teeth closed on the impulse to point out this possibility in any way. A hot flash of—jealousy?—shot through him. Let Galeni continue, please God, to think of the Dendarii as Miles's personal affair. . . .

"Hm." Galeni rubbed his forehead. "Yes, well—in the meantime, when Admiral Naismith's duties call, you come to me first, Lieutenant Vorkosigan." He sighed. "Consider yourself on probation. I would order you confined to quarters, but the ambassador has specifically requested your presence for escort duties this afternoon. But be aware that I could have made serious charges. Disobeying a direct order, for instance."

"I'm . . . keenly aware of that, sir. Uh . . . and Ivan?"

"We'll see about Ivan." Galeni shook his head, apparently contemplating Ivan. Miles couldn't blame him.

"Yes, sir," said Miles, deciding he'd pushed as hard as he dared, for now.

"Dismissed."

Great, thought Miles sardonically, exiting Galeni's

office. First he thought I was insubordinate. Now he just thinks I'm crazy.

Whoever I am.

The afternoon's political-social event was a reception and dinner in honor of a visit to Earth of the Baba of Lairouba. The Baba, hereditary head-of-state of his planet, was combining political and religious duties. After completing his pilgrimage to Mecca he had come to London for participation in the right-of-passage talks for the Western Orion Arm group of planets. Tau Ceti was the hub of this nexus, and Komarr connected to it through two routes, hence Barrayar's interest.

Miles's duties were the usual. In this case he found himself partnering one of the Baba's four wives. He wasn't sure whether to classify her as a dread dowager or not—her bright brown eyes and smooth chocolate hands were pretty enough, but the rest of her was swathed in yards of creamy silk edged with gold embroidery that suggested a zaftig pulchritude, like a very enticing mattress.

Her wit he could not gauge, as she spoke neither English, French, Russian nor Greek, in their Barrayaran dialects or any other, and he spoke neither Lairouban nor Arabic. The box of keyed translator earbugs had unfortunately been mis-delivered to an unknown address on the other side of London, leaving half the diplomats present able only to stare at their counterparts and smile. Miles and the lady communicated basic needs by mime—salt, ma'am?—with good will through dinner, and he made her laugh twice. He wished he knew why.

Even more unfortunately, before the after-dinner speeches could be cancelled a box of replacement ear-bugs was delivered by a panting caterer's assistant. There followed several speeches in a variety of tongues for the benefit of the press corps. Things broke up, the zaftig lady was swept off Miles's hands by two of her co-wives, and he began to make his way across the room back to the Barrayaran ambassador's party. Rounding a soaring alabaster pillar holding up the arched ceiling, he came face to face with the lady journalist from Euronews Network.

"*Mon Dieu*, it's the little admiral," she said cheerfully. "What are you doing here?"

Ignoring the anguished scream inside his skull, Miles schooled his features to an—exquisitely—polite blankness. "I beg your pardon, ma'am?"

"Admiral Naismith Or . . ." She took in his uniform, her eyes lighting with interest. "Is this some mercenary covert operation, Admiral?"

A beat passed. Miles allowed his eyes to widen, his hand to stray to his weaponless trouser seam and twitch there. "My God," he choked in a voice of horror—not hard, that—"Do you mean to tell me Admiral Naismith has been seen on Earth?"

Her chin lifted, and her lips parted in a little half-smile of disbelief. "In your mirror, surely."

Were his eyebrows visibly singed? His right hand was still bandaged. *Not a burn, ma'am*, Miles thought wildly. *I cut it shaving. . . .*

Miles came to full attention, snapping his polished boot heels together, and favored her with a small, formal bow. In a proud, hard, and thickly Barrayaran-accented voice, he said, "You are mistaken, ma'am. I am Lord Miles Vorkosigan of Barrayar. Lieutenant in the Imperial Service. Not that I don't aspire to the rank you name, but it's a trifle premature."

She smiled sweetly. "Are you entirely recovered from your burns, sir?"

Miles's eyebrows rose—no, he shouldn't have drawn

attention to them—"Naismith's been burned? You have seen him? When? Can we speak of this? The man you name is of the greatest interest to Barrayaran Imperial Security."

She looked him up and down. "So I would imagine, since you are one and the same."

"Come, come over here," and how was he going to get out of this one? He took her by the elbow and steered her toward a private corner. "Of course we are the same. Admiral Naismith of the Dendarii Mercenaries is my—" illegitimate twin brother? No, that didn't scan. Light didn't just dawn, it came like a nuclear flash at ground zero. "—clone," Miles finished smoothly.

"What?" Her certainty cracked; her attention riveted upon him.

"My clone," Miles repeated in a firmer voice. "He's an extraordinary creation. We think, though we've never been able to confirm it, that he was the result of an intended Cetagandan covert operation that went greatly awry. The Cetagandans are certainly capable of the medical end of it, anyway. The real facts of their military genetic experiments would horrify you." Miles paused. That last was true enough. "Who are you, by the way?"

"Lise Vallerie," she flashed her press cube at him, "Euronews Network."

The very fact she was willing to reintroduce herself confirmed he'd chosen the right tack. "Ah," he drew back from her slightly, "the news services. I didn't realize. Excuse me, ma'am. I should not be talking to you without permission from my superiors." He made to turn away.

"No, wait—ah—Lord Vorkosigan. Oh—you're not related to *that* Vorkosigan, are you?"

He jerked up his chin and tried to look stern. "My father."

"Oh," she breathed in a tone of enlightenment, "that explains it."

Thought it might, Miles thought smugly. He made a few more little escaping-motions. She clamped to him like a limpet. "No, please . . . if you don't tell me, I shall surely investigate it on my own."

"Well . . ." Miles paused. "It's all rather old data, from our point of view. I can tell you a few things, I suppose, since it impinges upon me so personally. But it is not for public dissemination. You must give me your word of that, first."

"A Barrayaran Vor lord's word is his bond, is it not?" she said. "I never reveal my sources."

"Very well," nodded Miles, pretending he was under the impression she'd promised, though her words in fact had said nothing of the sort. He nabbed a pair of chairs, and they settled themselves out of the way of the roboservers clearing the banquet debris. Miles cleared his throat, and launched himself.

"The biological construct who calls himself Admiral Naismith is . . . perhaps the most dangerous man in the galaxy. Cunning—resolute—both Cetagandan and Barrayaran Security have attempted, in the past, to assassinate him, without success. He's started to build himself a power-base, with his Dendarii Mercenaries. We still don't know what his long-range plans for this private army are, except that he must have some."

Vallerie's finger went to her lips doubtfully. "He seemed—pleasant enough, when I spoke with him. Allowing for the circumstance. A brave man, certainly."

"Aye, there's the genius and the wonder of the man," cried Miles, then decided he'd better tone it down a bit. "Charisma. Surely the Cetagandans, if it was the Cetagandans, must have intended something extraordinary for him. He's a military genius, you know."

"Wait a moment," she said. "He is a true clone, you say—not just an exterior copy? Then he must be even younger than yourself."

"Yes. His growth, his education, were artificially accelerated, apparently to the limits of the process. But where have you seen him?"

"Here in London," she answered, started to say more, and then stopped. "But you say Barrayar is trying to kill him?" She drew away from him slightly. "I think perhaps I'd better let you trace him yourselves."

"Oh, not anymore." Miles laughed shortly. "Now we just keep track of him. He'd dropped out of sight recently, you see, which makes my own security extremely nervous. Clearly, he must have been originally created for some sort of substitution plot aimed ultimately against my father. But seven years ago he went renegade, broke away from his captors-creators, and started working for himself. We—Barrayar—know too much about him now, and he and I have diverged too much, for him to attempt to replace me at this late date."

She eyed him. "He could. He really could."

"Almost." Miles smiled grimly. "But if you could ever get us in the same room, you'd see I was almost two centimeters taller than he is. Late growth, on my part. Hormone treatments . . ." His invention must give out soon—he babbled on. . . .

"The Cetagandans, however, are still trying to kill him. So far, that's the best proof we have that he's actually their creation. Clearly, he must know too much about something. We'd dearly love to know what." He favored her with an inviting canine smile, horribly false. She drew back slightly more.

Miles let his fists close angrily. "The most offensive thing about the man is his nerve. He might at least have picked another name for himself, but he flaunts mine. Perhaps he became used to it when he was training to be me, as he must have done once. He speaks with a Betan accent, and takes my mother's Betan maiden name for his surname, Betanstyle, and do you know why?"

Yeah, why, why . . . ?

She shook her head mutely, staring at him in repelled fascination.

"Because by Betan law regarding clones, he would actually be my legal brother, that's why! He attempts to gain a false legitimacy for himself. I'm not sure why. It may be a key to his weakness. He must have a weakness, somewhere, some chink in his armor—" besides hereditary insanity, of course— He broke off, panting slightly. Let her think it was from suppressed rage, and not suppressed terror.

The ambassador, thank God, was motioning at him from across the room, his party assembled to depart. "Pardon me, ma'am," Miles rose. "I must leave you. But, ah . . . if you encounter the false Naismith again, I should consider it a great service if you would get in touch with me at the Barrayaran embassy."

Pour quoi? her lips moved slightly. Rather warily, she rose too. Miles bowed over her hand, executed a neat about-face, and fled.

He had to restrain himself from skipping down the steps to the Palais de London in the ambassador's wake. Genius. He was a frigging genius. Why hadn't he thought of this cover story years ago? Imperial Security Chief Illyan was going to love it. Even Galeni might be slightly cheered.

Chapter Five

Miles camped in the corridor outside Captain Galeni's office the day the courier returned for the second time from Sector HQ. Exercising great restraint, Miles did not trample the man in the doorway as he exited, but he let him clear the frame before plunging within.

Miles came to parade rest before Galeni's desk. "Sir?"

"Yes, yes, Lieutenant, I know," said Galeni irritably, waving him to wait. Silence fell while screen after screen of data scrolled above Galeni's vid plate. At the end Galeni sat back, creases deepening between his eyes.

"Sir?" Miles reiterated urgently.

Galeni, still frowning, rose and motioned Miles to his station. "See for yourself."

Miles ran it through twice. "Sir—there's nothing *here*."

"So I noticed."

Miles spun to face him. "No credit chit—no orders—no explanation—no nothing. No reference to my affairs at all. We've waited here twenty bleeding days for nothing. We could have walked to Tau Ceti and back in that time. This is insane. This is *impossible*."

Galeni leaned thoughtfully on his desk on one splayed hand, staring at the silent vid plate. "Impossible? No. I've seen orders lost before. Bureaucratic screw-ups. Important data misaddressed. Urgent requests filled away while waiting for someone to return from leave. That sort of thing happens."

"It doesn't happen to me," hissed Miles through his teeth.

One of Galeni's eyebrows rose. "You are an arrogant little vorling." He straightened. "But I suspect you speak the truth. That sort of thing wouldn't happen to you. Anybody else, yes. Not you. Of course," he almost smiled, "there's a first time for everything."

"This is the second time," Miles pointed out. He glowered suspiciously at Galeni, wild accusations boiling behind his lips. Was this some bourgeois Komarran's idea of a practical joke? If the orders and credit chit weren't there, they had to have been intercepted. Unless the queries hadn't been sent at all. He had only Galeni's word that they had. But it was inconceivable that Galeni would risk his career merely to inconvenience an irritating subordinate. Not that a Barrayaran captain's pay was much loss, as Miles well knew.

Not like eighteen million marks.

Miles's eyes widened, and his teeth closed behind set lips. A poor man, a man whose family had lost all its great wealth in, say, the Conquest of Komarr, could conceivably find eighteen million marks tempting indeed. Worth risking—much for. It wasn't the way he would have read Galeni, but what, after all, did Miles really know about the man? Galeni hadn't spoken one word about his personal history in twenty days' acquaintance.

"What are you going to do now, sir?" Miles jerked out stiffly.

Galeni spread his hands. "Send again."

"Send again. That's all?"

"I can't pull your eighteen million marks out of my pocket, Lieutenant."

Oh, no? We'll just see about that. . . . He had to get out of here, out of the embassy and back to the Dendarii. The Dendarii, where he had left his own fully professional information-gathering experts gathering dust, while he'd wasted twenty days in immobilized paralysis. . . . If Galeni had indeed diddled him to that extent, Miles swore silently, there wasn't going to be a hole deep enough for him to hide in with his eighteen million stolen marks.

Galeni straightened and cocked his head, eyes narrowed and absent. "It's a mystery to me." He added lowly, almost to himself, ". . . and I don't like mysteries."

Nervy . . . cool . . . Miles was struck with admiration for an acting ability almost equal to his own. Yet if Galeni had embezzled his money, why was he not long gone? What was he waiting around for? Some signal Miles didn't know about? But he would find out, oh, yes he would. "Ten more days," said Miles. "Again."

"Sorry, Lieutenant," said Galeni, still abstracted.

You will be. . . . "Sir, I must have a day with the Dendarii. Admiral Naismith's duties are piling up. For one thing, thanks to this delay we're now absolutely forced to raise a temporary loan from commercial sources to stay current with our expenses. I have to arrange it."

"I regard your personal security with the Dendarii as totally insufficient, Vorkosigan."

"So add some from the embassy if you feel you have to. The clone story surely took some of the pressure off."

"The clone story was idiotic," snapped Galeni, coming out of himself.

"It was brilliant," said Miles, offended at this criticism of his creation. "It completely compartmentalizes Naismith and Vorkosigan at last. It disposes of the most dangerous ongoing weakness of the whole scam, my . . . unique and memorable appearance. Undercover operatives shouldn't be memorable."

"What makes you think that vid reporter will ever share her discoveries with the Cetagandans anyway?"

"We were seen together. By millions on the holovid, for God's sake. Oh, they'll be around to ask her questions, all right, one way or another." A slight twinge of fear—but surely the Cetagandans would send somebody to pump the woman subtly. Not just snatch, drain, and dispose of her, not a publicly prominent Earth citizen right here on Earth.

"In that case, why the hell did you pick the Cetagandans as Admiral Naismith's putative creators? The one thing they'll know for sure is that they didn't do it."

"Verisimilitude," explained Miles. "If even *we* don't know where the clone really came from, they might not be so surprised that they hadn't heard of him till now either."

"Your logic has a few glaring weaknesses," sneered Galeni. "It may help your long-term scam, possibly. But it doesn't help me. Having Admiral Naismith's corpse on my hands would be just as embarrassing as having Lord Vorkosigan's. Schizoid or no, not even you can compartmentalize yourself to that extent."

"I am not schizoid," Miles bit off. "A little manic-depressive, maybe," he admitted in afterthought.

Galeni's lips twitched. "Know thyself."

"We try, sir."

Galeni paused, then chose perhaps wisely to ignore that one. He snorted and went on. "Very well, Lieutenant Vorkosigan. I'll assign Sergeant Barth to supply you with a security perimeter. But I want you to report in no less than every eight hours by secured comm link. You may have twenty-four hours' leave."

Miles, drawing breath to marshall his next argument, was bereft of speech. "Oh," he managed. "Thank you, sir." And why the hell did Galeni just flip-flop like that? Miles would give blood and bone to know what was going on behind that deadpan Roman profile right now.

Miles withdrew in good order before Galeni could change his mind again.

The Dendarii had chosen the most distant hardstand of those available for rent at the London shuttleport for security, not economy. The fact that the distance also made it the cheapest was merely an added and delightful bonus. The hardstand was actually in the open, at the far end of the field, surrounded by lots of empty, naked tarmac. Nothing could sneak up on it without being seen. And if any—untoward activity—did happen to take place around it, Miles reflected, it was therefore less likely to fatally involve innocent civilian bystanders. The choice had been a logical one.

It was also a damned long walk. Miles tried to step out briskly, and not scurry like a spider across a kitchen floor. Was he getting a trifle paranoid, as well as schizoid and manic-depressive? Sergeant Barth, marching along beside him uncomfortably in civvies, had wanted to deliver him to the shuttle's hatch in the embassy's armored groundcar. With difficulty Miles had persuaded him that seven years of painfully careful subterfuge would go up in smoke if Admiral Naismith was ever seen getting out of a Barrayaran official vehicle. The good view from the shuttle hardstand was something that cut two ways, alas. Still, nothing could sneak up on them.

Unless it was psychologically disguised, of course. Take that big shuttleport maintenance float truck over there, for instance, speeding along busily, hugging the ground. They were all over the place; the eye quickly became used to their irregular passing. If he were going to launch an attack, Miles decided, one of those would definitely be the vehicle of choice. It was wonderfully doubtful. Until it fired first, no defending Dendarii could be sure he or she wasn't about to randomly murder some hapless stray shuttleport employee. Criminally embarrassing, that, the sort of mistake that wrecked careers.

The float truck shifted its route. Barth twitched and Miles stiffened. It looked awfully like an interception course. But dammit, no windows or doors were opening, no armed men were leaning out to take aim with so much as a slingshot. Miles and Barth both drew their legal stunners anyway. Miles tried to separate himself from Barth as Barth tried to step in front of him, another precious moment's confusion.

And then the now-hurtling float truck was upon them, rising into the air, blotting out the bright morning sky. Its smooth sealed surface offered no target a stunner would matter to. The method of his assassination was at last clear to Miles. It was to be death by squashing.

Miles squeaked and spun and scrambled, trying to get up a sprint. The float truck fell like a monstrous brick as its anti-grav was abruptly switched off. It seemed like overkill, somehow; didn't they know *his* bones could be shattered by an overloaded grocery pallet? There'd be nothing left of him but a revolting wet smear on the tarmac.

He dove, rolled—only the blast of displaced air as the truck boomed to the pavement saved him. He opened his eyes to find the skirt of the truck centimeters in front of his nose, and recoiled onto his feet as the maintenance vehicle rose again. Where was Barth? The useless stunner was still clutched convulsively in Miles's right hand, his knuckles scraped and bleeding.

Ladder handholds were recessed into a channel on the truck's gleaming side. If he were *on* it he couldn't be *under* it— Miles shook the stunner from his grip and sprang, almost too late, to cling to the handholds. The truck lurched sideways and flopped again, obliterating the spot where he'd just been lying. It rose and fell again with an angry crash. Like an hysterical giant trying to smash a spider with a slipper. The impact knocked Miles from his precarious perch, and he hit the pavement rolling, trying to save his bones. There was no crack in the floor here to scuttle into and hide.

A line of light widened under the truck as it rose again. Miles looked for a reddened lump on the tarmac, saw none. Barth? No, over there, crouched at a distance screaming into his wrist comm. Miles shot to his feet, zigged, zagged. His heart was pounding so hard it seemed his blood was about to burst from his ears on adrenalin overload, his breathing half-stopped despite his straining lungs. Sky and tarmac spun around him, he'd lost the shuttle—no, there—he started to sprint toward it. Running had never been his best sport. They'd been right, the people who'd wanted to disbar him from officer's training on the basis of his physicals. With a deep vile whine the maintenance truck clawed its way into the air behind him.

The violent white blast blew him forward onto his face, skidding over the tarmac. Shards of metal, glass, and boiling plastic spewed across him. Something glanced numbly across the back of his skull. He clapped his arms over his head and tried to melt a hole down into the pavement by heat of fear alone. His ears hammered but he could only hear a kind of roaring white noise.

A millisecond more, and he realized he was a stopped target. He jerked onto his side, glaring up and around for the falling truck. There was no more falling truck.

A shiny black aircar, however, was dropping swiftly and illegally through shuttleport traffic control space, no doubt lighting up boards and setting off alarms on the Londoners' control computers. Well, it was a lost cause now to try and be inconspicuous. Miles had it pegged as Barrayaran outer-perimeter backup even before he glimpsed the green uniforms within, by virtue of the fact that Barth was running toward it eagerly. No guarantee that the three Dendarii sprinting toward them from his personnel shuttle had drawn the same conclusions, though. Miles sprang to his—hands and knees. The abrupt if aborted movement rendered him dizzy and sick. On the second attempt he made it to his feet.

Barth was trying to drag him by the elbow toward

the settling aircar. "Back to the embassy, sir!" he urged.

A cursing grey-uniformed Dendarii skidded to a halt a few meters away and aimed his plasma arc at Barth. "Back off, you!" the Dendarii snarled.

Miles stepped hastily between the two as Barth's hand went to his jacket. "Friends, friends!" he cried, flipping his hands palm-out toward both combatants. The Dendarii paused, doubtful and suspicious, and Barth clenched his fists at his sides with an effort.

Elli Quinn cantered up, swinging a rocket-launcher one-handed, its stock nestled in her armpit, smoke still trickling from its five-centimeters-wide muzzle. She must have fired from the hip. Her face was flushed and terrorized.

Sergeant Barth eyed the rocket-launcher with suppressed fury. "That was a little close, don't you think?" he snapped at Elli. "You damn near blew him up with your target." Jealous, Miles realized, because he hadn't had a rocket launcher.

Elli's eyes widened in outrage. "It was better than nothing. Which was what you came equipped with, apparently!"

Miles raised his right hand—his left shoulder spasmed when he tried to raise the other arm—and dabbed gingerly at the back of his head. His hand came away red and wet. Scalp wound, bleeding like a stuck pig but not dangerous. Another clean uniform shot.

"It's awkward to carry major ordnance on the tubeway, Elli," Miles intervened mildly, "nor could we have gotten it through shuttleport security." He paused and eyed the smoking remnant of the float truck. "Even they couldn't get weapons through shuttleport security, it seems. Whoever they were."

He nodded significantly toward the second Dendarii who, taking the hint, went off to investigate.

"Come away, sir!" Barth urged anew. "You're injured. The police will be here. You shouldn't be mixed up in this."

Lieutenant Lord Vorkosigan shouldn't be mixed up in this, he meant, and he was absolutely right. "God, yes, Sergeant. Go. Take a circuitous route back to the embassy. Don't let anyone trace you."

"But sir—"

"My own security—which has just demonstrated its effectiveness, I think—will take over now. Go."

"Captain Galeni will have my head on a platter if—"

"Sergeant, Simon Illyan himself will have my head on a platter if my cover is blown. That's an order. Go!"

The dreaded Chief of Imperial Security was a name to conjure with. Torn and distressed, Barth allowed Miles to chivvy him toward the aircar. Miles breathed a sigh of relief as it streaked away. Galeni really would lock him in the basement forever if he went back now.

The Dendarii guard was returning, grim and a little green, from the scattered remains of the float truck. "Two men, sir," he reported. "At least, I think they were male, and there were at least two, judging from the number of, um, parts remaining."

Miles looked at Elli and sighed. "Nothing left to question, eh?"

She shrugged an insincere apology. "Oh—you're bleeding . . ." She closed on him fussily.

Damn. If there had been something left to question, Miles would have been in favor of shoveling it onto the shuttle and taking off, clearance or no clearance, to continue his investigation in the *Triumph's* sickbay unimpeded by the legal constraints that would doubtless delay the local authorities. The London constables could scarcely be more unhappy with him anyway. From the looks of things he'd be dealing with them again shortly. Fire equipment and shuttleport vehicles were converging on them even now.

Still, the London police employed some 60,000 individuals, an army much larger, if less heavily equipped, than his own. Maybe he could sic them on the Cetagandans, or whoever was behind this.

"Who were those guys?" asked the Dendarii guard, glancing in the direction the black aircar had gone.

"Never mind," said Miles. "They weren't here, you never saw 'em."

"Yes, sir."

He loved the Dendarii. They didn't *argue* with him. He submitted to Elli's first aid, and began mentally marshalling his story for the police. The police and he were doubtless going to be quite tired of each other before his visit to Earth was over.

Before the forensic lab team had even arrived on the tarmac, Miles turned to find Lise Vallerie at his elbow. He should have expected her. Since Lord Vorkosigan had exerted himself to repel her, Admiral Naismith now marshalled his charm, struggling to remember just which of his personas had told her what.

"Admiral Naismith. Trouble certainly seems to follow you!" she began.

"This did," he said affably, smiling up at her with what fragmented calm he could muster under the circumstances. The holovid man was off recording elsewhere on-site—she must be trying to set up something more than an off-the-cuff spot interview.

"Who were those men?"

"A very good question, now in the lap of the

London police. My personal theory is that they were Cetagandan, seeking revenge for certain Dendarii operations, ah, not against them, but in support of one of their victims. But you had better not quote that. No proof. You could be sued for defamation or something."

"Not if it's a quote. You don't think they were Barrayarans?"

"Barrayarans! What do you know of Barrayar?" He let startlement segue into bemusement.

"I've been looking into your past," she smiled.

"By asking the Barrayarans? I trust you don't believe everything they say of me."

"I didn't. *They* think you were created by the Cetagandans. I've been looking for independent corroboration, from my own private sources. I found an immigrant who used to work in a cloning laboratory. His memory was somewhat lacking in detail, unfortunately. He had been forcibly debriefed at the time he was fired. What he could remember was appalling. The Dendarii Free Mercenary Fleet is officially registered out of Jackson's Whole, is it not?"

"A legal convenience only. We're not connected in any other way, if that's what you're asking. You've been doing some homework, eh?" Miles craned his neck. Over by a police groundcar, Elli Quinn was gesticulating vividly to an earnest constable captain.

"Of course," said Vallerie. "I'd like, with your cooperation, to do an in-depth feature on you. I think it would be extremely interesting to our viewers."

"Ah . . . The Dendarii do not seek publicity. Quite the reverse. It could endanger our operations and operatives."

"You personally, then. Nothing current. How you came to this. Who had you cloned, and why—I already know from whom. Your early memories. I understand you underwent accelerated growth and hypnotic training. What was it like? And so on."

"It was unpleasant," he said shortly. Her offered feature was a tempting notion indeed, apart from the fact that after Galeni had him skinned, Illyan would have him stuffed and mounted. And he rather liked Vallerie. It was all very well to float a few useful fictions into the air through her, but too close an association with him just now—he glanced across the tarmac at the police lab team now arrived and poking about the remains of the float truck—could be bad for her health. "I have a better idea. Why don't you do an expose on the civilian illegal cloning business?"

"It's been done."

"Yet the practices still go on. Apparently not enough has been done."

She looked less than thrilled. "If you would work closely with me, Admiral Naismith, you would have some input into the feature. If you don't—well, you are news. Fair game."

He shook his head reluctantly. "Sorry. You're on your own." The scene by the police groundcar compelled his attention. "Excuse me," he said distractedly. She shrugged and went to catch up with her vid-man as Miles jogged off.

They were taking Elli away.

"Don't worry, Miles, I've been arrested before," she tried to reassure him. "It's no big deal."

"Commander Quinn is my personal bodyguard," Miles protested to the police captain, "and she was on duty. Manifestly. She still is. I need her!"

"Sh, Miles, calm down," Elli whispered to him, "or they could end up taking you too."

"Me! I'm the bloody victim! It's those two goons who tried to flatten me who should be under arrest."

"Well, they're taking them away too, as soon as the forensic guys get the bags filled. You can't expect the authorities to just take our word for it all. They'll check out the facts, they'll corroborate our story, then they'll release me." She twinkled a smile at the captain, who melted visibly. "Policemen are human too."

"Didn't your mother ever tell you never to get in a car with strangers?" Miles muttered. But she was right. If he kicked up much more fuss it might occur to the constables to order his shuttle grounded, or worse. He wondered if the Dendarii would ever get back the rocket-launcher, now impounded as the murder weapon. He wondered if getting his key bodyguard arrested was step one of a deep-laid plot against him. He wondered if his fleet surgeon had any psychoactive drugs to treat galloping paranoia. If she did, he'd probably be allergic to them. He ground his teeth and took a deep, calming breath.

A two-man Dendarii mini-shuttle was rolling up to the hardstand. What was this, now? Miles glanced at his wrist chrono, and realized he'd lost almost five hours out of his precious twenty-four fooling around here at the shuttleport. Knowing what time it was, he knew who had arrived, and swore in frustration under his breath. Elli used the new distraction to prod the police captain into motion, sketching Miles a breezy, reassuring salute by way of farewell. The reporter, thank God, had gone off to interview the shuttleport authorities.

Lieutenant Bone, squeaky-clean, polished, and striking in her best velvet dress greys, exited her shuttle and approached the remnant of men left at the foot of the larger shuttle's ramp. "Admiral Naismith, sir? Are you ready for our appointment . . . Oh, *dear* . . ."

He flashed her a toothy grin from his bruised and

dirt-smudged face, conscious of his hair, matted and sticky with drying blood, his blood-soaked collar and spattered jacket and ripped trouser knees. "Would you buy a used pocket dreadnought from this man?" he chirped at her.

"It won't do," she sighed. "The bank we're dealing with is *very* conservative."

"No sense of humor?"

"Not where their money is concerned."

"Right." He bit short further quips; they were too close to nervous-involuntary. He made to run his hands through his hair, winced, and changed the gesture to a gentle probing touch around the temporary plas dressing. "And all my spare uniforms are in orbit—and I'm not anxious to go carting around London without Quinn at my back. Not now, anyway. And I need to see the surgeon about this shoulder, there's something still not right—" throbbing agony, if you wanted to get technical about it—"and there are some new and serious doubts about just where our outstanding credit transfer went."

"Oh?" she said, alert to the essential point.

"Nasty doubts, which I need to check out. All right," he sighed, yielding to the inevitable, "cancel our appointment at the bank for today. Set up another one for tomorrow if you can."

"Yes, sir." She saluted and moved off.

"Ah," he called after her, "you needn't mention why I was unavoidably detained, eh?"

One corner of her mouth tugged upward. "I wouldn't dream of it," she assured him fervently.

Back in close Earth orbit aboard the *Triumph*, a visit to his fleet surgeon revealed a hairline crack in Miles's left scapula, a diagnosis which surprised him not at all. The surgeon treated it with electra-stim and put his left arm in an excessively annoying plastic immobilizer. Miles bitched until the surgeon threatened to put his entire body in a plastic immobilizer. He slunk out of sickbay as soon as she was done treating the gouge on the back of his head, before she got carried away with the obvious medical merit of the idea.

After getting cleaned up, Miles tracked down Captain Elena Bothari-Jesek, one of the triumvirate of Dendarii who knew his real identity, the other being her husband and Miles's fleet engineer, Commodore Baz Jesek. Elena in fact probably knew as much about Miles as he did himself. She was the daughter of his late bodyguard, and they had grown up together. She had become an officer of the Dendarii by Miles's fiat back when he'd created them, or found them lying around, or however one wanted to describe the chaotic beginnings of this whole hideously overextended covert op. Been named an officer, rather; she had become one since then by sweat and guts and fierce study. Her concentration was intense and her fidelity was absolute, and Miles was as proud of her as if he'd invented her himself. His other feelings about her were no one's business.

As he entered the wardroom, Elena sketched him a greeting that was halfway between a wave and a salute, and smiled her somber smile. Miles returned her a nod and slid into a seat at her table. "Hello, Elena. I've got a security mission for you."

Her long, lithe body was folded into her chair, her dark eyes luminous with curiosity. Her short black hair was a smooth cap framing her face; pale skin, features not beautiful yet elegant, sculptured like a hunting wolfhound. Miles regarded his own short square hands, folded on the table, lest he lose his eye in the subtle planes of that face. Still. Always.

"Ah . . ." Miles glanced around the room, and caught the eye of a couple of interested techs at a nearby table. "Sorry, fellows, not for you." He jerked his thumb, and they grinned and took the hint and their coffee and clattered out.

"What sort of security mission?" she said, biting into her sandwich.

"This one is to be sealed on both ends, from both the Dendarii point of view and that of the Barrayaran embassy here on Earth. Especially from the embassy. A courier job. I want you to get a ticket on the fastest available commercial transport to Tau Ceti, and take a message from Lieutenant Vorkosigan to the Imperial Security Sector Headquarters at the embassy there. My Barrayaran commanding officer here on Earth doesn't know I'm sending you, and I'd like to keep it that way."

"I'm . . . not anxious to deal with the Barrayaran command structure," she said mildly after a moment. Watching her own hands, she was.

"I know. But since this involves both my identities, it has to be either you, Baz, or Elli Quinn. The London police have Elli under arrest, and I can't very well send your husband; some confused underling on Tau Ceti might try to arrest him."

Elena glanced up from her hands at that. "Why were the desertion charges against Baz never dropped by Barrayar?"

"I tried. I thought I almost had them persuaded. But then Simon Illyan had a spasm of twitchiness and decided leaving the arrest warrant outstanding, if not actually pursued, gave him an extra handle on Baz in case of, er, emergencies. It also gives a little artistic depth to the Dendarii's cover as a truly independent outfit. I thought Illyan was wrong—in fact, I told him so, till he finally ordered me to shut up on the subject. Someday, when I'm giving the orders, I'll see that's changed."

Her eyebrow quirked. "It could be a long wait, at your present rate of promotion—Lieutenant."

"My Dad's sensitive to charges of nepotism. Captain." He picked up the sealed data disk he'd been pushing about one-handed on the table top. "I want you to give this into the hand of the senior military attache on Tau Ceti, Commodore Destang. Don't send it in via anyone else, because among my other suspicions is the nasty one that there may be a leak in the Barrayaran courier channel between here and there. I think the problem's on this end, but if I'm wrong . . . God, I hope it isn't Destang himself."

"Paranoid?" she inquired solicitously.

"Getting more so by the minute. Having Mad Emperor Yuri in my family tree doesn't help a bit. I'm always wondering if I'm starting to come down with his disease. Can you be paranoid about being paranoid?"

She smiled sweetly. "If anyone can, it's you."

"Hm. Well, this particular paranoia is a classic. I softened the language in the message to Destang—you better read it before you embark. After all, what would you think of a young officer who was convinced his superiors were out to get him?"

She tilted her head, winged eyebrows climbing.

"Quite." Miles nodded. He tapped the disk with one forefinger. "The purpose of your trip is to test a hypothesis—only a hypothesis, mind you—that the reason our eighteen million marks aren't here is that they disappeared en route. Just possibly into dear Captain Galeni's pockets. No corroborative evidence yet, such as Galeni's sudden and permanent disappearance, and it's not the sort of charge a young and ambitious officer had better make by mistake. I've embedded it in four other theories, in the report, but that's the one I'm hot about. You must find out if HQ ever dispatched our money."

"You don't sound hot. You sound unhappy."

"Yes, well, it's certainly the messiest possibility. It has a deal of forceful logic behind it."

"So what's the hook?"

"Galeni's a Komarran."

"Who cares? So much the more likely that you're right, then."

I care. Miles shook his head. What, after all, were Barrayaran internal politics to Elena, who had sworn passionately never to set foot on her hated home world again?

She shrugged, and uncoiled to her feet, pocketing the disk.

He did not attempt to capture her hands. He did not make a single move that might embarrass them both. Old friends were harder to come by than new lovers.

Oh, my oldest friend.

Still. Always.

Chapter Six

He ate a sandwich and slurped coffee for dinner in his cabin while he perused Dendarii fleet status reports. Repairs had been completed and approved on the *Triumph*'s surviving combat drop shuttles. And paid for, alas, the money now passed beyond recall. Refit chores were all caught up throughout the fleet, downside leaves used up, spit spat and polish polished off. Boredom was setting in. Boredom and bankruptcy.

The Cetagandans had it all wrong, Miles decided bitterly. It wasn't war that would destroy the Dendarii, it was peace. If their enemies would just stay their hands and wait patiently, the Dendarii, his creation, would collapse all on its own without any outside assistance.

His cabin buzzer blatted, a welcome interruption to the dark and winding chain of his thoughts. He keyed the comm on his desk. "Yes?"

"It's Elli."

His hand leapt eagerly to tap the lock control. "Enter! You're back before I'd expected. I was afraid you'd be stuck down there like Danio. Or worse, with Danio."

He wheeled his chair around, the room seeming suddenly brighter as the door hissed open, though a lumen-meter might not have registered it. Elli waved him a salute and hitched a hip over the edge of his desk. She smiled, but her eyes looked tired.

"Told you," she said. "In fact there was some talk of making me a permanent guest. I was sweet, I was cooperative, I was nearly prim, trying to convince them I wasn't a homicidal menace to society and they really could let me back out on the streets, but I was making no headway till their computers suddenly hit the jackpot. The lab came back with ID's on those two men I . . . killed, at the shuttleport."

Miles understood the little hesitation before her choice of terms. Someone else might have picked a breezier euphemism—*blew away*, or *offed*—distancing himself from the consequences of his action. Not Quinn.

"Interesting, I take it," he said encouragingly. He made his voice calm, drained of any hint of judgment. Would that the ghosts of your enemies only escorted you to hell. But no, they had to hang about your shoulder interminably, waiting until that service was called for. Maybe the notches Danio gouged in the hilts of his weapons weren't such a tasteless idea after all. Surely it was a greater sin to forget a single dead man in your tally. "Tell me about them."

"They turned out to be both known to and desired by the Eurolaw Net. They were—how shall I put this—soldiers of the sub-economy. Professional hit men. Locals."

Miles winced. "Good God, what have I ever done to them?"

"I doubt they were after you of their own accord. They were almost certainly hirelings, contracted by a third party or parties unknown, though I imagine we could both give it a good guess."

"Oh, no. The Cetagandan Embassy is sub-contracting my assassination now? I suppose it makes sense: Galeni said they were understaffed. But do you realize—" he rose and began to pace in his agitation, "this means I could be attacked again from any quarter. Anywhere, any time. By totally un-personally-motivated strangers."

"A security nightmare," she agreed.

"I don't suppose the police were able to trace their employer?"

"No such luck. Not yet, anyway. I did direct their attention to the Cetagandans, as candidates for the motive leg of any method-motive-opportunity triangle they may try to put together."

"Good. Can we make anything of the method and opportunity parts ourselves?" Miles wondered aloud. "The end results of their attempt would seem to indicate they were a trifle underprepared for their task."

"From my point of view their method looked like it came awfully damn close to working," she remarked. "It suggests, though, that opportunity might have been their limiting factor. I mean, Admiral Naismith doesn't just go into hiding when you go downside, tricky as it would be to find one man among nine billion. He literally ceases to exist anywhere, zip! There was evidence these guys had been hanging around the shuttleport for some days waiting for you."

"Ugh." His visit to Earth was quite spoiled. Admiral Naismith was, it appeared, a danger to himself and others. Earth was too congested. What if his assailants next tried to blow up a whole tubeway car or restaurant to reach their target? An escort to hell by the souls of his enemies was one thing, but what if he were standing beside a class of primary-school children next round?

"Oh, by the way, I did see Private Danio when I was downside," Elli added, examining a chipped fingernail. "His case is coming up for judicial review in a couple of days, and he asked me to ask you to come."

Miles snarled under his breath. "Oh, sure. A potentially unlimited number of total strangers are trying to off me, and he wants me to schedule a public appearance. For target practice, no doubt."

Elli grinned, and nibbled her fingernail off evenly. "He wants a character witness by someone who knows him."

"Character witness! I wish I knew where he hid his scalp collection; I'd bring it just to show the judge. Sociopath therapy was *invented* for people like him. No, no. The last person he wants for a character witness is someone who knows him." Miles sighed, subsiding. "Send Captain Thorne. Betan, got a lot of cosmopolitan *savoir faire*, should be able to lie well on the witness stand."

"Good choice," Elli applauded. "It's about time you started delegating some of your work load."

"I delegate all the time," he objected. "I am extremely glad, for instance, that I delegated my personal security to you."

She flipped up a hand, grimacing, as if to bat away the implied compliment before it could land. Did his words bite? "I was slow."

"You were fast enough." Miles wheeled and came

to face her, or at any rate her throat. She had folded back her jacket for comfort, and the arc of her black T-shirt intersected her collarbone in a kind of abstract, aesthetic sculpture. The scent of her—no perfume, just woman—rose warm from her skin.

"I think you were right," she said. "Officers shouldn't go shopping in the company store—"

Dammit, thought Miles, *I only said that back then because I was in love with Baz Jesek's wife and didn't want to say so—better to never say so—*

"—it really does distract from duty. I watched you, walking toward us across the shuttleport, and for a couple of minutes, critical minutes, security was the last thing on my mind."

"What was the first thing on your mind?" Miles asked hopefully, before his better sense could stop him. Wake up man, you could fumble your whole future in the next thirty seconds.

Her smile was rather pained. "I was wondering what you'd done with that stupid cat blanket, actually," she said lightly.

"I left it at the embassy. I was going to bring it," and what wouldn't he give to whip it out now, and invite her to sit with him on the edge of his bed? "but I had some other things on my mind. I haven't told you yet about the latest wrinkle in our tangled finances. I suspect—" dammit, business again, intruding into this personal moment, this would-be personal moment. "I'll tell you about that later. Right now I want to talk about us. I have to talk about us."

She moved back from him slightly; Miles amended his words hastily, "and about duty." She stopped retreating. His right hand touched her uniform collar, turned it over, slid over the smooth cool surface of her rank insignia. Nervous as lint-picking. He drew his hand back, clenched it over his breast to control it.

"I . . . have a lot of duties, you see. Sort of a double dose. There's Admiral Naismith's duties, and there's Lieutenant Vorkosigan's duties. And then there's Lord Vorkosigan's duties. A triple dose."

Her eyebrows were arched, her lips pursed, her eyes blandly inquiring; supernal patience, yes, she'd wait for him to make an ass of himself at his own pace. His pace was becoming headlong.

"You're familiar with Admiral Naismith's duties. But they're the least of my troubles, really. Admiral Naismith is subordinate to Lieutenant Vorkosigan, who exists only to serve Barrayaran Imperial Security, to which he has been posted by the wisdom and mercy of his Emperor. Well, his Emperor's advisors, anyway. In short, Dad. You know that story."

She nodded.

"That business about not getting personally involved with anyone on his staff may be true enough for Admiral Naismith . . ."

"I'd wondered, later, whether that . . . incident in the lift tube might have been some kind of test," she said reflectively.

This took a moment to sink in. "Eugh! No!" Miles yelped. "What a repulsively lowdown, mean and scurvy trick that would have been—no. No test. Quite real."

"Ah," she said, but failed to reassure him of her conviction with, say, a heartfelt hug. A heartfelt hug would be very reassuring just now. But she just stood there, regarding him, in a stance uncomfortably like parade rest.

"But you have to remember, Admiral Naismith isn't a real man. He's a construct. I invented him. With some important parts missing, in retrospect."

"Oh, rubbish, Miles." She touched his cheek lightly. "What is this, ectoplasm?"

"Let's get back, all the way back, to Lord Vorkosigan," Miles forged on desperately. He cleared his throat and with an effort dropped his voice back into his Barrayaran accent. "You've barely met Lord Vorkosigan."

She grinned at his change of voice. "I've heard you do his accent. It's charming if, um, rather incongruous."

"I don't do his accent, he does mine. That is—I think—" he stopped, tangled. "Barrayar is bred in my bones."

Her eyebrows lifted, their ironic tilt blunted by her clear good will. "Literally, as I understand it. I shouldn't think you'd thank them, for poisoning you before you'd even managed to get born."

"They weren't after me, they were after my father. My mother—" considering just where he was attempting to steer this conversation, it might be better to avoid expanding upon the misfired assassination attempts of the last twenty-five years. "Anyway, that kind of thing hardly ever happens any more."

"What was that out there on the shuttleport today, street ballet?"

"It wasn't a *Barrayaran* assassination."

"You don't know that," she remarked cheerfully.

Miles opened his mouth and hung, stunned by a new and even more horrible paranoia. Captain Galeni was a subtle man, if Miles had read him aright. Captain Galeni could be far ahead down any linked chain of logic of interest to him. Suppose he was indeed guilty of embezzlement. And suppose he had anticipated Miles's suspicions. And suppose he'd spotted a way to keep money and career both, by eliminating his accuser. Galeni, after all, had known just when Miles was to be at the shuttleport. Any local dealer in death that the Cetagandan embassy could hire, the Barrayaran embassy could hire just as readily, just as covertly. "We'll talk about that—later—too," he choked.

"Why not now?"

"BECAUSE I'M—" he stopped, took a deep breath, "trying to say something else," he continued in a small, tightly contained voice.

There was a pause. "Say on," Elli encouraged.

"Um, duties. Well, just as Lieutenant Vorkosigan contains all of Admiral Naismith's duties, plus others of his own, so Lord Vorkosigan contains all of Lieutenant Vorkosigan, plus duties of his own. Political duties separate from and overarching a lieutenant's military duties. And, um . . . family duties." His palm was damp; he rubbed it unobtrusively on the seam of his trousers. This was even harder than he'd thought it would be. But no harder, surely, than someone who'd had her face blown away once having to face plasma fire again.

"You make yourself sound like a Venn diagram. 'The set of all sets which are members of themselves' or something."

"I feel like it," he admitted. "But I've got to keep track somehow."

"What contains Lord Vorkosigan?" she asked curiously. "When you look in the mirror when you step out of the shower, what looks back? Do you say to yourself, Hi, Lord Vorkosigan?"

I avoid looking in mirrors. . . . "Miles, I guess. Just Miles."

"And what contains Miles?"

His right index finger traced over the back of his immobilized left hand. "This skin."

"And that's the last, outer perimeter?"

"I guess."

"Gods," she muttered. "I've fallen in love with a man who thinks he's an onion."

Miles snickered; he couldn't help it. But—"fallen in love?" His heart lifted in vast encouragement. "Better than my ancestress who was supposed to have thought herself—" no, better not bring that one up either.

But Elli's curiosity was insatiable; it was why he'd first assigned her to Dendarii Intelligence, after all, where she'd been so spectacularly successful. "What?"

Miles cleared his throat. "The fifth Countess Vorkosigan was said to suffer from the periodic delusion that she was made of glass."

"What finally happened to her?" asked Elli in a tone of fascination.

"One of her irritated relations eventually dropped and broke her."

"The delusion was that intense?"

"It was off a twenty-meter-tall turret. I don't know," he said impatiently. "I'm not responsible for my weird ancestors. Quite the reverse. Exactly the inverse." He swallowed. "You see, one of Lord Vorkosigan's non-military duties is to eventually, sometime, somewhere, come up with a Lady Vorkosigan. The eleventh Countess-Vorkosigan-to-be. It's rather expected from a man from a strictly patrilinear culture, y'see. You do know," his throat seemed to be stuffed with cotton, his accent wavered back and forth, "that these, uh, physical problems of mine," his hand swept vaguely down the length, or lack of it, of his body, "were teratogenic. Not genetic. My children should be normal. A fact which may have saved my life, in view of Barrayar's traditional ruthless attitude toward mutations. I don't think my grandfather was ever totally convinced of it, I've always wished he could have lived to see my children, just to prove it. . . ."

"Miles," Elli interrupted him gently.

"Yes?" he said breathlessly.

"You're babbling. Why are you babbling? I could listen by the hour, but it's worrisome when you get stuck on fast-forward."

"I'm nervous," he confessed. He smiled blindingly at her.

"Delayed reaction, from this afternoon?" She slipped closer to him, comfortingly. "I can understand that."

He eased his right arm around her waist. "No. Yes, well, maybe a little. Would you like to be Countess Vorkosigan?"

She grinned. "Made of glass? Not my style, thanks. Really, though, the title sounds more like something that would go with black leather and chromium studs."

The mental image of Elli so attired was so arresting, it took him a full half minute of silence to trace back to the wrong turn. "Let me rephrase that," he said at last. "Will you marry me?"

The silence this time was much longer.

"I thought you were working up to asking me to go to bed with you," she said finally, "and I was laughing. At your nerves." She wasn't laughing now.

"No," said Miles. "That would have been easy."

"You don't want much, do you? Just to completely rearrange the rest of my life."

"It's good that you understand that part. It's not just a marriage. There's a whole job description that goes with it."

"On Barrayar. Downside."

"Yes. Well, there might be some travel."

She was quiet for too long, then said, "I was born in space. Grew up on a deep-space transfer station. Worked most of my adult life aboard ships. The time I've spent with my feet on real dirt can be measured in months."

"It would be a change," Miles admitted uneasily.

"And what would happen to the future Admiral Quinn, free mercenary?"

"Presumably—hopefully—she would find the work of Lady Vorkosigan equally interesting."

"Let me guess. The work of Lady Vorkosigan would not include ship command."

"The security risks of allowing such a career would appall even me. My mother gave up a ship command —Betan Astronomical Survey—to go to Barrayar."

"Are you telling me you're looking for a girl just like Mom?"

"She has to be smart—she has to be fast—she has to be a determined survivor," Miles explained unhappily. "Anything less would be a slaughter of the innocent. Maybe for her, maybe for our children with her. Bodyguards, as you know, can only do so much."

Her breath blew out in a long, silent whistle, watching him watching her. The slippage between the distress in her eyes and the smile on her lips tore at him. *Didn't want to hurt you— the best I can offer shouldn't be pain to you—is it too much, too little . . . too awful?*

"Oh, love," she breathed sadly, "you aren't thinking."

"I think the world of you."

"And so you want to maroon me for the rest of my life on a, sorry, backwater dirtball that's just barely climbed out of feudalism, that treats women like chattel—or cattle—that would deny me the use of every military skill I've learned in the past twelve years from shuttle docking to interrogation chemistry . . . I'm sorry. I'm not an anthropologist, I'm not a saint, and I'm not crazy."

"You don't have to say no right away," said Miles in a small voice.

"Oh, yes I do," she said. "Before looking at you makes me any weaker in the knees. Or in the head."

And what am I to say to that? Miles wondered. If you really loved me, you'd be delighted to immolate your entire personal history on my behalf? Oh, sure. She's not into immolation. This makes her strong, her strength makes me want her, and so we come full circle. "It's Barrayar that's the problem, then."

"Of course. What female human in her right mind would voluntarily move to that planet? With the exception of your mother, apparently."

"She is exceptional. But . . . when she and Barrayar collide, it's Barrayar that changes. I've seen it. You could be a force of change like that."

Elli was shaking her head. "I know my limits."

"No one knows their limits till they've gone beyond them."

She eyed him. "You would naturally think so. What's with you and Barrayar, anyway? You let them push you around like . . . I've never understood why you've never just grabbed the Dendarii and taken off. You could make it go, better than Admiral Oser ever did, better than Tung even. You could end up emperor of your own rock by the time you were done."

"With you at my side?" He grinned strangely. "Are you seriously suggesting I embark on a plan of galactic conquest with five thousand guys?"

She chuckled. "At least I wouldn't have to give up fleet command. No, really seriously. If you're so obsessed with being a professional soldier, what do you need Barrayar for? A mercenary fleet sees ten times the action of a planetary one. A dirtball may see war once a generation, if it's lucky—"

"Or unlucky," Miles interpolated.

"A mercenary fleet follows it around."

"That statistical fact has been noted in the Barrayaran high command. It's one of the chief reasons I'm here. I've had more actual combat experience, albeit on a small scale, in the past four years than most other Imperial officers have seen in the last fourteen. Nepotism works in strange ways." He ran a finger along the clean line of her jaw. "I see it now. You are in love with Admiral Naismith."

"Of course."

"Not Lord Vorkosigan."

"I am *annoyed* with Lord Vorkosigan. He sells you short, love."

He let the double entendre pass. So, the gulf that yawned between them was deeper than he'd truly realized. To her, it was Lord Vorkosigan who wasn't real. His fingers entwined around the back of her neck, and he breathed her breath as she asked, "Why do you let Barrayar screw you over?"

"It's the hand I was dealt."

"By whom? I don't get it."

"It's all right. It just happens to be very important to me to win with the hand I was dealt. So be it."

"Your funeral." Her lips were muffled on his mouth. "Mmm."

She drew back a moment. "Can I still jump your bones? Carefully, of course. You'll not go away mad, for turning you down? Turning Barrayar down, that is. Not you, never you . . ."

I'm getting used to it. Almost numb . . . "Am I to sulk?" he inquired lightly. "Because I can't have it all, take none, and go off in a huff? I'd hope you'd bounce me down the corridor on my pointed head if I were so dense."

She laughed. It was all right, if he could still make her laugh. If Naismith was all she wanted, she could surely have him. Half a loaf for half a man. They tilted bedward, hungry-mouthed. It was easy, with Quinn; she made it so.

Pillow talk with Quinn turned out to be shop talk. Miles was unsurprised. Along with a sleepy body-rub that turned him to liquid in danger of pouring over the edge of the bed into a puddle on the deck, he absorbed the rest of her complete report on the activities and discoveries of the London police. He in turn brought her up to date on the events of the embassy, and the mission on which he'd dispatched Elena Bothari-Jesek. And all these years he'd thought he needed a conference room for debriefing. Clearly, he'd stumbled into an unsuspected universe of alternative command style. Sybaritic had it all over cybernetic.

"Ten more days," Miles complained smearily into his mattress, "until Elena can possibly return from Tau Ceti. And there's no guarantee she can bring the missing money with her even then. Particularly if it's already been sent once. While the Dendarii fleet hangs idly in orbit. You know what we need?"

"A contract."

"Damn straight. We've taken interim contracts before, in spite of Barrayaran Imperial Security having us on permanent retainer. They even like it; it gives their budget a break. After all, the less taxes they have to squeeze out of the peasantry, the easier Security gets on the domestic side. It's a wonder they've never tried to make the Dendarii Mercenaries a revenue-generating project. I'd have sent our contract people out hunting weeks ago if we weren't stuck in Earth orbit till this mess at the embassy gets straightened out."

"Too bad we can't put the fleet to work right here on Earth," said Elli. "Peace seems to have broken out all over the planet, unfortunately." Her hands unknotted the muscles in his calves, fiber by fiber. He wondered if he could persuade her to work on his feet next. He'd done hers a while ago, after all, albeit with higher goals in view. Oh, joy, he wasn't even going to have to persuade her . . . he wriggled his toes in delight. He'd never suspected that his toes were sexy until Elli'd pointed it out. In fact, his satisfaction with his entire pleasure-drenched body was at an all-time high.

"There's a blockage in my thinking," he decided. "I'm looking wrong at something. Let's see. The Dendarii fleet isn't tied to the embassy, though I am. I could send you all off . . ."

Elli whimpered. It was such an unlikely noise, coming from her, that he risked muscle spasm to twist his neck and look over his shoulder at her. "Brainstorming," he apologized.

"Well, don't stop with *that* one."

"And anyway, because of the mess at the embassy, I'm not anxious to strip myself of my private backup. It's—there's something very wrong going on there. Which means that any more sitting around waiting for the embassy to come through is dumber than rocks. Well. One problem at a time. The Dendarii. Money. Odd jobs . . . hey!"

"Hey?"

"What says I've got to contract out the entire fleet at a time? Work. Odd jobs. Interim cash flow. Divide and conquer! Security guards, computer techs, anything and everything anyone can come up with that will generate a little cash income—"

"Bank robberies?" said Elli in a tone of rising interest.

"And you say the police let you out? Don't get carried away. But I'm sitting on a labor pool of five thousand variously and highly trained people. Surely that's a resource of even greater value than the *Triumph*. Delegate! Let *them* spread out and go scare up some bloody cash!"

Elli, sitting cross-legged on the foot of his bed, remarked in aggravation, "I worked for an hour to get you relaxed, and now look! What are you, memory-plastic? Your whole body is coiling back up right before my eyes . . . Where are you going?"

"To put the idea into action, what else?"

"*Most* people go to *sleep* at this point. . . ." Yawning, she helped him sort through the pile of uniform bits on the floor nearby. The black T-shirts proved nearly interchangable. Elli's was distinguishable by the faint scent of her body lingering in it—Miles almost didn't want to give it back, but reflected that keeping his girlfriend's underwear to sniff probably wouldn't score him points in the savoir-faire department. The agreement was unspoken but plain: this phase of their relationship must stop discreetly at the bedroom door, if they were to disprove Admiral Naismith's fatuous dictum.

The initial Dendarii staff conference, at the start of a mission when Miles arrived on fleet station with a new contract in hand, always gave him the sense of seeing double. He was an interface, conscious of both halves, trying to be a one-way mirror between the Dendarii and their true employer the Emperor. This unpleasant sensation usually faded rapidly, as he concentrated his faculties around the mission in question, re-centering his personality; Admiral Naismith came very near to occupying his whole skin then. "Relaxing" wasn't quite the right term for this alpha-state, given Naismith's driving personality; "uncon-strained" came closer.

He had been with the Dendarii an unprecedented five months straight, and the sudden re-intrusion of Lieutenant Vorkosigan into his life had been unusually disruptive this time. Of course, it wasn't normally the *Barrayaran* side of things that was screwed up. He'd always counted on that command structure to be solid, the axiom from which all action flowed, the standard by which subsequent success or failure was measured. Not this time.

This night he stood in the *Triumph*'s briefing room before his hastily called department heads and ship captains, and was seized by a sudden, schizoid paralysis: what was he to say to them? *You're on your own, suckers. . . .*

"We're on our own for a while," Admiral Naismith began, emerging from whatever cave in Miles's brain he dwelt in, and he was off and running. The news, made public at last, that there was a glitch in their contract payment inspired the expected dismay; more baffling was their apparently serene reassurance when he told them, his voice heavy with menacing emphasis, that he was personally investigating it. Well, at least it accounted from the Dendarii point of view for all the time he'd spent stuffing the computers in the bowels of the Barrayaran embassy. God, thought Miles, I 'swear I could sell them all radioactive farmland.

But when challenged they unleashed an impressive flurry of ideas for short-term cash creation. Miles was intensely relieved, and left them to it. After all, nobody arrived on the Dendarii general staff by being dense. His own brain seemed drained. He hoped it was because its circuits were subconsciously working on the Barrayaran half of the problem, and not a symptom of premature senile decay.

*   *   *

He slept alone and badly, and woke tired and sore. He attended to some routine internal matters, and approved the seven least harebrained schemes for cash creation evolved by his people during the night. One officer had actually come up with a security guard contract for a squad of twenty, never mind that it was for the grand opening of a shopping mall in—where the hell was Xian?

He arrayed himself carefully in his best—grey velvet dress tunic with the silver buttons on the shoulders, trousers with the blinding white side trim, his shiniest boots—and accompanied Lieutenant Bone downside to the London bank. Elli Quinn backed him with two of his largest uniformed Dendarii and an unseen perimeter, before and behind, of civilian-dressed guards with scanners.

At the bank Admiral Naismith, quite polished and urbane for a man who didn't exist, signed away questionable rights to a warship he did not own to a financial organization who did not need or want it. As Lieutenant Bone pointed out, at least the money was real. Instead of a piecemeal collapse beginning that afternoon—the hour when Lieutenant Bone had calculated the first Dendarii payroll chits would start bouncing—it would be just one great crash at an undefined future date. Hooray.

He peeled off guards, as he approached the Barrayaran Embassy, until only Elli remained. They paused before a door in the underground utility tunnels marked DANGER: TOXIC: AUTHORIZED PERSONNEL ONLY.

"We're under the scanners now," Miles remarked warningly.

Elli touched her finger to her lips, considering. "On the other hand, you may go in there to find orders have arrived to spirit you off to Barrayar, and I won't see you for another year. Or ever."

"I would resist that—" he began, but she touched the finger to his lips now, bottling whatever stupidity he'd been about to utter, transferring the kiss. "Right." He smiled slightly. "I'll be in touch, Commander Quinn."

A straightening of her spine, a small ironic nod, an impressionistic version of a salute, and she was gone. He sighed and palmed open the intimidating door's lock.

On the other side of the second door, past the uniformed guard at the scanner console, Ivan Vorpatril was waiting for him. Shifting from foot to foot with a strained smile. *Oh, God, now what?* It was doubtless too much to hope that the man merely had to take a leak.

"Glad you're back, Miles," Ivan said. "Right on time."

"I didn't want to abuse the privilege. I might want it again. Not that I'm likely to get it—I was surprised that Galeni didn't just yank me back to the embassy permanently after that little episode at the shuttleport yesterday."

"Yes, well, there's a reason for that," said Ivan.

"Oh?" said Miles, in a voice drained to neutrality.

"Captain Galeni left the embassy about half an hour after you did yesterday. He hasn't been seen since."

Chapter Seven

The ambassador let them into Galeni's locked office. He concealed his nerves rather better than Ivan, merely remarking quietly, "Let me know what you find, Lieutenant Vorpatril. Some certain indication as to whether or not it's time to notify the local authorities would be particularly desirable." So, the ambassador, who had known Duv Galeni some two years, thought in terms of multiple possibilities too. A complex man, their missing captain.

Ivan sat at the desk console and ran through the routine files, searching for recent memos, while Miles wandered the perimeter of the room looking for—what? A message scrawled in blood on the wall at the level of his kneecap? Alien vegetable fiber on the carpet? A note of assignation on heavily perfumed paper? Any or all would have been preferable to the bland blankness he found.

Ivan threw up his hands. "Nothing here but the usual."

"Move over." Miles wriggled the back of Galeni's swivel chair to evict his big cousin and slid into his place. "I have a burning curiosity as to Captain Galeni's personal finances. This is a golden opportunity to check them out."

"Miles," said Ivan with trepidation, "isn't that a little, um, invasive?"

"You have the instincts of a gentleman, Ivan," said Miles, absorbed in breaking into the coded files. "How did you ever get into Security?"

"I don't know," said Ivan. "I wanted ship duty."

"Don't we all? Ah," said Miles as the holoscreen began to disgorge data. "I love these Earth Universal Credit Cards. So revealing."

"What do you expect to find in Galeni's charge account, for God's sake?"

"Well, first of all," Miles muttered, tapping keys, "let's check the totals for the last few months and find out if his outgo exceeds his income."

It was the work of a moment to answer that one. Miles frowned slight disappointment. The two were in balance; there was even a small end-of-month surplus, readily traceable to a modest personal savings fund. It proved nothing one way or another, alas. If Galeni were in some kind of serious money trouble he had both the wit and the know-how not to leave evidence against himself. Miles began going down the itemized list of purchases.

Ivan shifted impatiently. "Now what are you looking for?"

"Secret vices."

"How?"

"Easy. Or it would be, if . . . compare, for example, the records of Galeni's accounts with yours for the same three-month period." Miles split the screen and called up his cousin's data.

"Why not compare it with yours?" said Ivan, miffed.

Miles smiled in scientific virtue. "I haven't been here long enough for a comparable baseline. You make a much better control. For example—well, well. Look at this. A lace nightgown, Ivan? What a confection. It's totally non-regulation, y'know."

"That's none of your business," said Ivan grumpily.

"Just so. And you don't have a sister, and it's not your mother's style. Inherent in this purchase is either a girl in your life or transvestism."

"You will note it's not my size," said Ivan with dignity.

"Yes, it would look rather abbreviated on you. A sylph-like girl, then. Whom you know well enough to buy intimate presents. See how much I know about you already, from just that one purchase. Was it Sylveth, by chance?"

"It's Galeni you're supposed to be checking," Ivan reminded him.

"Yes. So what kind of presents does Galeni buy?" He scrolled on. It didn't take long; there wasn't that much.

"Wine," Ivan pointed out. "Beer."

Miles ran a cross check. "About one-third the amount you drank in the same period. But he buys book-discs in a ratio of thirty-five to—just two, Ivan?"

Ivan cleared his throat uncomfortably.

Miles sighed. "No girls here. No boys either, I don't think . . . eh? You've been working with him for a year."

"Mm," said Ivan. "I've run across one or two of that sort in the Service, but . . . they have ways of letting you know. Not Galeni, I don't think either."

Miles glanced up at his cousin's even profile. Yes, Ivan probably had collected passes from both sexes, by this time. Scratch off yet another lead. "Is the man a monk?" Miles muttered. "Not an android, judging from the music, books, and beer, but . . . terribly elusive."

He killed the file with an irritated tap on the controls. After a moment of thought he called up Galeni's Service records instead. "Huh. Now that's unusual. Did you know Captain Galeni had a doctorate in history before he ever joined the Imperial Service?"

"What? No, he never mentioned that. . . ." Ivan leaned over Miles's shoulder, gentlemanly instincts overcome by curiosity at last.

"A Ph.D. with honors in Modern History and Political Science from the Imperial University at Vorbarr Sultana. My God, look at the dates. At the age of twenty-six Dr. Duv Galeni gave up a brand-new faculty position at the College of Belgravia on Barrayar, to go back to the Imperial Service Academy with a bunch of eighteen-year-olds. On a cadet's pittance." *Not* the behavior of a man to whom money was an all-consuming object.

"Huh," said Ivan. "He must have been an upper-classman when we entered. He got out just two years ahead of us. And he's a captain already!"

"He must have been one of the first Komarrans permitted to enter the military. Within weeks of the ruling. And he's been on the fast track ever since. Extra training—languages, information analysis, a posting at the Imperial HQ—and then this plum of a post on Earth. Duvie is our darling, clearly." Miles could see why. A brilliant, educated, liberal officer—Galeni was a walking advertisement for the success of the New Order. An Example. Miles knew all about being an Example. He drew in his breath, a long, thoughtful inhalation hissing cold through his front teeth.

"What?" prodded Ivan.

"I'm beginning to get scared."

"Why?"

"Because this whole thing is acquiring a subtle political odor. And anyone who isn't alarmed when things Barrayaran start smelling political hasn't studied . . . history." He uttered the last word with a subsiding, ironic sibilant, hunching in the chair. After a moment he hit the file again, searching on.

"Jack. Pot."

"Eh?"

Miles pointed. "Sealed file. Nobody under the rank of an Imperial Staff officer can access this part."

"That lets us out."

"Not necessarily."

"Miles . . ." Ivan moaned.

"I'm not contemplating anything illegal," Miles reassured him. "Yet. Go get the ambassador."

The ambassador, upon arrival, pulled up a chair next to Miles. "Yes, I do have an emergency access code that will override that one," he admitted when Miles pressed him. "The emergency in mind was something on the order of war breaking out, however."

Miles nibbled the side of his index finger. "Captain Galeni's been with you two years now. What's your impression of him?"

"As an officer, or as a man?"

"Both, sir."

"Very conscientious in his duties. His unusual educational background—"

"Oh, you knew of it?"

"Of course. But it makes him an extraordinarily good pick for Earth. He's very good, very at ease on the social side, a brilliant conversationalist. The officer who preceded him in the post was a Security man of the old school. Competent, but dull. Almost . . . ahem! . . . boorish. Galeni accomplishes the same duties, but more smoothly. Smooth security is invisible security, invisible security does not disturb my diplomatic guests, and so my job becomes that much easier. That goes double for the, er, information-gathering activities. As an officer I'm extremely pleased with him."

"What's his fault as a man?"

" 'Fault' is perhaps too strong a term, Lieutenant Vorkosigan. He's rather . . . cool. In general I find this restful. I do notice that in any given conversation he will come away knowing a great deal more about you than you of him."

"Ha." What a very diplomatic way of putting it. And, Miles reflected, thinking back over his own brushes with the missing officer, dead-on.

The ambassador frowned. "Do you think some clue to his disappearance may be in that file, Lieutenant Vorkosigan?"

Miles shrugged unhappily. "It isn't anywhere else."

"I am reluctant . . ." the ambassador trailed off, eyeing the strongly worded access restrictions on the vid.

"We could wait a little longer," said Ivan. "Suppose he's just found a girlfriend. If you were so worried about that as to make that other suggestion, Miles, you ought to be glad for the man. He isn't going to be too happy, coming back from his first night out in years, to find we've turned his files inside out."

Miles recognized the singsong tone of Ivan playing dumb, playing devil's advocate, the ploy of a sharp but lazy intellect to get others to do its work. Right, Ivan.

"When you spend nights out, don't you leave notice where you'll be and when you'll return?" asked Miles.

"Well, yes."

"And don't you return on time?"

"I've been known to oversleep a time or two," Ivan admitted.

"What happens then?"

"They track me down. 'Good morning, Lieutenant Vorpatril, this is your wake-up call.' " Galeni's precise, sardonic accent came through clearly in Ivan's parody. It had to be a direct quote.

"D'you think Galeni's the sort to make one rule for subordinates and another for himself, then?"

"No," said Ivan and the ambassador in unison, and glanced sideways at each other.

Miles took a deep breath, jerked up his chin, and pointed at the holovid. "Open it."

The ambassador pursed his lips and did so.

"I'll be damned," whispered Ivan after a few minutes of scrolling. Miles elbowed into the center place and began speed-reading in earnest. The file was enormous: Galeni's missing family history at last.

David Galen had been the name to which he was born. *Those* Galens, owners of the Galon Orbital Transshipping Warehouse Cartel, strong among the oligarchy of powerful families who had run Komarr, straddling its important wormhole connections like ancient Rhine River robber barons. Its wormholes had made Komarr rich; it was from the power and wealth pouring through them that its jewel-like domed cities sprang, not grubbed up from the planet's dire, barren soil by sweaty labor.

Miles could hear his father's voice, ticking off the points that had made the conquest of Komarr Admiral Vorkosigan's textbook war. *A small population concentrated in climate-controlled cities; no place for guerillas to fall back and regroup. No allies; we had only to let it be known that we were dropping their twenty-five-percent cut of everything that passed through their wormhole nexus to fifteen percent and the neighbors that should have supported them fell into our pockets. They didn't even want to do their own fighting, till the mercenaries they'd hired saw what they were up against and turned tail. . . .*

Of course, the unspoken heart of the matter was the sins of the Komarran fathers a generation earlier, who had accepted the bribe to let the Cetagandan invasion fleet pass through for the quick and easy conquest of poor, newly rediscovered, semi-feudal Barrayar. Which had proved neither quick, nor easy, nor a conquest; twenty years and a river of blood later the last of the Cetagandan warships withdrew back the way they had come, through "neutral" Komarr.

Barrayarans might have been backward, but no one could accuse them of being slow learners. Among Miles's grandfather's generation, who came to power in the harsh school of the Cetagandan occupation, there grew an obsessed determination that such an invasion must never be permitted to happen again. It had fallen on Miles's father's generation to turn the obsession into fact, by taking absolute and final control of Barrayar's Komarran gateway.

The avowed aim of the Barrayaran invasion fleet, its lightning speed and painstaking strategic subtleties, was to take Komarr's wealth-generating economy intact, with minimal damage. Conquest, not revenge, was to be the Emperor's glory. Imperial Fleet Commander Admiral Lord Aral Vorkosigan had made that abundantly and explicitly clear, he'd thought.

The Komarran oligarchy, supple middlemen that they were, were brought into alignment with that aim, their surrender eased in every possible way.

Promises were made, guarantees given; subordinate life and reduced property were life and property still, calculatedly leavened with hope for future recovery. Living well was to be the best revenge all round.

Then came the Solstice Massacre.

An overeager subordinate, growled Admiral Lord Vorkosigan. Secret orders, cried the surviving families of the two hundred Komarran Counsellors gunned down in a gymnasium by Barrayaran Security forces. Truth, or at any rate certainty, lay among the victims. Miles himself was not sure any historian could resurrect it. Only Admiral Vorkosigan and the security commander knew for sure, and it was Admiral Vorkosigan's word that was on trial. The security commander lay dead without trial at the admiral's own furious hands. Justly executed, or killed to keep from talking, take your pick according to your prejudices.

In absolute terms Miles was disinclined to get excited about the Solstice Massacre. After all, Cetagandan atomics had taken out the entire city of Vorkosigan Vashnoi, killing not hundreds but thousands, and nobody rioted in the streets about *that*. Yet it was the Solstice Massacre that got the attention, captured an eager public imagination; it was the name of Vorkosigan that acquired the sobriquet "Butcher" with a capital letter, and the word of a Vorkosigan that was besmirched. And that made it all a very personal bit of ancient history indeed.

Thirty years ago. Miles hadn't even been born. David Galen had been four years old on the very day his aunt, Komarran Counsellor Rebecca Galen, had died in the gym at the domed city of Solstice.

The Barrayaran High Command had argued the matter of twenty-six-year-old Duv Galeni's admittance to the Imperial Service back and forth in the frankest personal terms.

". . . I can't recommend the choice," Imperial Security Chief Illyan wrote in a private memo to Prime Minister Count Aral Vorkosigan. "I suspect you're being quixotic about this one out of guilt. And guilt is a luxury you cannot afford. If you're acquiring a secret desire to be shot in the back, please let me know at least twenty-four hours in advance, so I can activate my retirement. —Simon."

The return memo was handwritten in the crabbed scrawl of a thick-fingered man for whom all pens were too tiny, a handwriting achingly familiar to Miles. ". . . guilt? Perhaps. I had a little tour of that damned gym, soon after, before the thickest blood had quite dried. Pudding-like. Some details burn themselves permanently in the memory. But I happen to remember Rebecca Galen particularly because of the way she'd been shot. She was one of the few who died facing her murderers. I doubt very much if it will ever be my back that's in danger from 'Duv Galeni.'

"The involvement of his father in the later Resistance worries me rather less. It wasn't just for us that the boy altered his name to the Barrayaran form.

"But if we can capture this one's true allegiance, it will be something like what I'd had in mind for Komarr in the first place. A generation late, true, and after a long and bloody detour, but—since you bring up these theological terms—a sort of redemption. Of course he has political ambitions, but I beg to suggest they are both more complex and more constructive than mere assassination.

"Put him back on the list, Simon, and leave him there this time. This issue tires me, and I don't want to be dragged over it again. Let him run, and prove himself—if he can."

The closing signature was the usual hasty scribble.

After that, Cadet Galeni became the concern of officers much lower in the Imperial hierarchy, his record the public and accessible one Miles had viewed earlier.

"The trouble with all this," Miles spoke aloud into the thick, ticking silence that had enveloped the room for the last thirty minutes, "fascinating as it all is, is that it doesn't narrow the possibilities. It multiplies them. Dammit."

Including, Miles reflected, his own pet theory of embezzlement and desertion. There was nothing here that actually disproved it, just rendered it more painful if true. And the shuttleport assassination idea took on new and sinister overtones.

"He might also," Ivan Vorpatril put in, "just be the victim of some perfectly ordinary accident."

The ambassador grunted, and pushed to his feet, shaking his head. "Most ambiguous. They were right to seal it. It could be very prejudicial to the man's career. I think, Lieutenant Vorpatril, I will have you go ahead and file a missing person report now with the local authorities. Seal that back up, Vorkosigan." Ivan followed the ambassador out.

Before he closed the console, Miles traced through the documents pertinent to the tantalizing reference to Galeni's father. After his sister was killed in the Solstice Massacre, the senior Galen had apparently become an active leader in the Komarran underground. What wealth the Barrayaran conquest had left to the once-proud family evaporated entirely at the time of the violent Revolt six years later. Old Barrayaran Security records explicitly traced some of it, transformed into smuggled weapons, payroll, and expenses of the terrorist army; later, bribes for exit visas and transport off-planet for the survivors. No transport off Komarr for Galeni's father, though; he was blown up with one of his own bombs during the last, futile, exhausted attack on a Barrayaran Security HQ. Along with Galeni's older brother, incidentally.

Thoughtfully, Miles ran a cross-check. Rather to his relief there were no more stray Galen relations among the Earthbound refugees listed in the embassy's Security files.

Of course, Galeni had had plenty of opportunity to edit those files, in the last two years.

Miles rubbed his aching head. Galeni had been fifteen when the last spasm of the Revolt had petered out. Was stamped out. Too young, Miles hoped, to have been actively involved. And whatever his involvement, Simon Illyan had apparently known of it and been willing to let it pass into history. A closed book. Miles resealed the file.

Miles permitted Ivan to do all the dealing with the local police. True, with the clone story now afloat he was in part protected from the chance of meeting the same people in both his personas, but there was no point in pushing it. The police could be expected to be more alert and suspicious than most others, and he hadn't counted on being a two-headed crime wave.

At least the police seemed to take the military attaché's disappearance with proper seriousness, promising cooperation even to the extent of honoring the ambassador's request that the matter not be given to the news media. The police, manned and equipped for such things, could take over the routine legwork such as checking the identities of any unexplained human body parts found in trash receptacles, etc. Miles appointed himself official detective for all matters inside the embassy walls. Ivan, as senior man now, suddenly found all of Galeni's normal routine dumped in his lap; Miles heartlessly left it there.

Twenty-four hours passed, for Miles mostly in a console station chair cross-checking embassy records on Komarran refugees. Unfortunately, the embassy had amassed huge quantities of such information. If there was something significant, it was well camouflaged in the tons of irrelevencies. It simply wasn't a one-man job.

At two in the morning, cross-eyed, Miles gave it up, called Elli Quinn, and dumped the whole problem on the Dendarii Mercenaries' Intelligence Department.

Dumped was the word for it: mass data transfer via comm link from the embassy's secured computers to the *Triumph* in orbit. Galeni would have had convulsions; screw Galeni, it was all his fault for disappearing in the first place. Miles thoughtfully didn't ask Ivan, either. Miles's legal position, if it came to that, was that the Dendarii were de facto Barrayaran troops and the data transfer therefore internal to the Imperial military. Technically. Miles included all of Galeni's personnel files too, in fully accessed form. Miles's legal position there was that the seal was only to protect Galeni from the prejudice of Barrayaran patriots, which the Dendarii clearly were not. One argument or the other had to work.

"Tell the spooks that finding Galeni is a contract," Miles told Elli, "part of the fleet-wide fund-raising drive. We only get paid for producing the man. That could actually be true, come to think of it."

He fell into bed hoping his subconscious would work it out during what was left of the night, but woke blank and bleary as before. He set Barth and a couple of the other non-coms to rechecking the movements of the courier officer, the other possible weak link in the chain. He sat tight, waiting for the police to call, his imagination weaving daisy chains of ever more gaudy and bizarre explanatory scenarios. Sat still as stone in a darkened room, one foot tapping uncontrollably, feeling like the top of his head was about to blow off.

On the third day Elli Quinn called in.

He snapped the comm link into place in the holovid, hungry for the pleasure of seeing her face. It bore a most peculiar smirk.

"I thought this might interest you," she purred. "Captain Thorne was just contacted with a *fascinating* contract offer for the Dendarii."

"Does it have a fascinating price?" Miles inquired. The gears in his head seemed to grind as he tried to switch back to Admiral Naismith's problems, which had been overwhelmed and forgotten in the past two days' uncertain tensions.

"A hundred thousand Betan dollars. In untraceable cash."

"Ah . . ." That came to close to half a million Imperial marks. "I thought I'd made it clear we weren't going to touch anything illegal this time. We're in enough trouble as it is."

"How does a kidnapping grab you?" She giggled inexplicably.

"Absolutely not!"

"Oh, you're going to make an exception in this case," she predicted with confidence, even verve.

"Elli . . ." he growled warningly.

She controlled her humor with a deep breath, though her eyes remained alight. "But Miles—our mysterious and wealthy strangers want to hire Admiral Naismith to kidnap Lord Miles Vorkosigan from the Barrayaran embassy."

*   *   *

"It's got to be a trap," Ivan jittered nervously, guiding the groundcar Elli had rented through the levels of the city. Midnight was scarcely less well lit than daytime, though the shadows of their faces shifted as the sources of illumination flitted by outside the bubble canopy.

The grey Dendarii sergeant's uniform Ivan wore flattered him no less than his Barrayaran dress greens, Miles noted glumly. The man just looked good in uniform, any uniform. Elli, sitting on Miles's other side, seemed Ivan's female twin. She simulated ease, lithe body stretched out, one arm flung carelessly and protectively across the back of the seat above Miles's head. But she had taken to biting her nails again, Miles noted. Miles sat between them in Lord Vorkosigan's Barrayaran dress greens, feeling like a piece of wilted watercress between two slices of moldy bread. Too damn tired for these late-night parties.

"Of course it's a trap," said Miles. "Who set it and why, is what we want to find out. And how much they know. Have they set this up because they believe Admiral Naismith and Lord Vorkosigan to be two separate people—or because they don't? If the latter, will it compromise Barrayar's covert connection with the Dendarii Mercenaries in future operations?"

Elli's sideways glance met Miles's. Indeed. And if the Naismith game were over, what future had they?

"Or maybe," said Ivan helpfully, "it's something totally unrelated, like local criminals looking for a spot of ransom. Or something really tortuous, like the Cetagandans trying to get Admiral Naismith in deep trouble with Barrayar, in hopes that we'd have better luck killing the little spook than they have. Or maybe—"

"Maybe you're the evil genius behind it all, Ivan,"

Miles suggested affably, "clearing the chain of command of competition so you can have the embassy all to yourself."

Elli glanced at him sharply, to be sure he was joking. Ivan just grinned. "Ooh, I like that one."

"The only thing we can be sure of is that it's not a Cetagandan assassination attempt," Miles sighed.

"I wish I was as sure as you seem to be," muttered Elli. It was late evening of the fourth day since Galeni's disappearance. The thirty-six hours since the Dendarii had been offered their peculiar contract had given Elli time for reflection; the initial charm had worn off for her even as Miles had become increasingly drawn in by the possibilities.

"Look at the logic of it," argued Miles. "The Cetagandans either still think I'm two separate people, or they don't. It's Admiral Naismith they want to kill, not the Barrayaran prime minister's son. Killing Lord Vorkosigan could restart a bloody war. In fact, we'll know my cover's been blown the day they stop trying to assassinate Naismith—and start making a great and embarrassing public flap about Dendarii operations against them instead. They wouldn't miss that diplomatic opportunity for anything. Particularly now, with the right-of-passage treaty through Tau Ceti up in the air. They could cripple our galactic trade in one move."

"They could be trying to prove your connection, as step one of just that plan," said Ivan, looking thoughtful.

"I didn't say it wasn't the Cetagandans," said Miles mildly. "I just said that if it was, this isn't an assassination."

Elli groaned.

Miles looked at his chrono. "Time for the last check."

Elli activated her wrist comm. "Are you still up there, Bel?"

Captain Thorne's alto voice lilted back, signalling from the aircar that followed with its troop of Dendarii soldiers. "I have you in my sights."

"All right, keep us that way. You watch the back from above, we'll watch the front. This will be the last voice contact till we invite you to drop in."

"We'll be waiting. Bel out."

Miles rubbed the back of his neck nervously. Quinn, watching the gesture, remarked, "I'm really not crazy about springing the trap by letting them take you."

"I have no intention of letting them take me. The moment they show their hand, Bel drops in and we take them instead. But if it doesn't look like they want to kill me outright, we could learn a lot by letting their operation run on a few steps further. In view of the, ah, Situation at the embassy, it could be worth a little risk."

She shook her head in mute disapproval.

The next few minutes passed in silence. Miles was about halfway through a mental review of all the branching possibilities they had hammered out for this evening's action when they pulled up in front of a row of ancient, three-story houses crammed together along a crescent street. They seemed very dark and quiet, unoccupied, apparently in process of condemnation or renovation.

Elli glanced at the numbers on the doors and swung up the bubble canopy. Miles slid out to stand beside her. From the groundcar, Ivan ran the scanners. "There's nobody home," he reported, squinting at his readouts.

"What? Not possible," said Elli.

"We could be early."

"Rats," said Elli. "As Miles is so fond of saying,

look at the logic. The people who want to buy Lord Vorkosigan didn't give us this rendezvous till the last second. Why? So we couldn't get here first and check it out. They have to be set up and waiting." She leaned back into the car's cockpit, reaching over Ivan's shoulder. He turned his hands palm-out in acquiescence as she ran the scan again. "You're right," she admitted, "but it still feels wrong."

Was it chance vandalism that a couple of street-lights were broken out, just here? Miles peered into the night. "Don't like it," Elli murmured. "Let's not tie your hands."

"Can you handle me, all by yourself?"

"You're drugged to the eyeballs."

Miles shrugged, and let his jaw hang slack and his eyes track randomly and not quite in unison. He shambled beside her as her hand pinched his upper arm, guiding him up the steps. She tried the door, an old-fashioned one hung on hinges. "It's open." It swung wide squeaking, revealing blackness.

Elli reluctantly reholstered her stunner and un-hooked a handlight from her belt, flashing it into the darkness. An entry hall; rickety-looking stairs ascended to the left, twin archways on either side led into empty, dirty front rooms. She sighed and stepped cautiously across the threshold. "Anybody here?" she called softly. Silence. They entered the left-hand room, the beam of the handlight darting from corner to corner.

"We're not early," she muttered, "not late, the address is right . . . where are they?"

He could not very well answer and stay in charac-ter. Elli released him, switched the light to her left hand and re-drew her stunner. "You're too tanked to wander far," she decided, as if talking to herself. "I'm going to take a look around."

One of Miles's eyelids shivered in acknowledgement. Until she finished checking for remote bugs and scanner beams, he had better keep playing Lord Vorkosigan in a convincingly kidnapped state. After a moment's hesitation, she took to the stairs. Taking the light with her, dammit.

He was still listening to the swift, faint creak of her footsteps overhead when the hand closed over his mouth and the back of his neck was kissed by a stunner on very light power, zero range.

He convulsed, kicking, trying to shout, trying to bite. His assailant hissed in pain and clutched harder. There were two—his hands were yanked up behind his back, a gag stuffed into his mouth before his teeth could snap closed on the hand that fed him. The gag was permeated with some sweet, penetrating drug; his nostrils flared wildly, but his vocal cords went involuntarily slack. He seemed out of touch with his body, as if it had moved leaving no forwarding address. Then a pale light came up.

Two large men, one younger, one older, dressed in Earther clothing, shifted in the shadows, faintly blurred. Scanner shields, dammit! And very, very good ones, to beat the Dendarii equipment. Miles spotted the boxes belted to their waists—a tenth the size of the latest thing his people had. Such tiny power packs—they looked new. The Barrayaran embassy was going to have to update its secured areas . . . He went cross-eyed, for a mad moment, trying to read the maker's mark on them, until he saw the third man.

Oh, the third. *I've lost it,* Miles's panicked thought gyrated. *Gone right over the edge.* The third man was himself.

The alter-Miles, neatly turned out in Barrayaran dress greens, stepped forward to stare long and strangely, hungrily, into his face as he was held up by the two younger men. He began emptying the contents of Miles's pockets into his own. Stunner . . . IDs . . . half a pack of clove breath mints . . . He frowned at the breath mints as if momentarily puzzled, then pocketed them with a shrug. He pointed to Miles's waist.

Miles's grandfather's dagger had been willed explicitly to him. The 300-year-old blade was still flexible as rubber, sharp as glass. Its jewelled hilt concealed the Vorkosigan seal. They took it from beneath his jacket. The alter-Miles shrugged the sheath-strap over his shoulder and refastened his tunic. Finally, he unhooked the scanner-shield belt from his own waist and slipped it swiftly around Miles.

The alter-Miles's eyes were hot with an exhilarated terror, as he paused to sweep one last glance over Miles. Miles had seen the look once before, in his own face in the mirrored wall of a tube station.

No.

He'd seen it on *this one's* face in the mirrored wall of a tube station.

He must have been standing feet away that night, behind Miles at an angle. In the wrong uniform. The green one, at a moment Miles was wearing his Dendarii greys.

Looks like they managed to get it right this time, though. . . .

"Perfect," growled the alter-Miles, freed of the scanner-shield's sonic muffling. "We didn't even have to stun the woman. She'll suspect nothing. Told you this would work." He inhaled, jerked up his chin, and smiled sardonically at Miles.

Posturing little martinet, Miles thought poisonously. *I'll get you for that.*

Well, I always was my own worst enemy.

The switch had taken only seconds. They carried Miles through the doorway at the back of the room. With a heroic twitch, he managed to bump his head on the frame, going through.

"What was that?" Elli's voice called instantly from upstairs.

"Me," the alter-Miles called back promptly. "I just checked around. There's nobody down here either. This is a wash-out."

"You think?" Miles heard her cantering down the stairs. "We could wait a while."

Elli's wristcom chimed. "Elli?" came Ivan's voice thinly. "I just got a funny blip in the scanners a minute ago."

Miles's heart lurched in hope.

"Check again." The alter-Miles's voice was cool.

"Nothing, now."

"Nothing here either. I'm afraid something's panicked them, and they've aborted. Pull in the perimeter and take me back to the embassy, Commander Quinn."

"So soon? You sure?"

"Now, yes. That's an order."

"You're the boss. Damn," said Elli regretfully, "I had my heart set on that hundred thousand Betan dollars."

Their syncopated footsteps echoed out the hallway and were muted by the closing door. The purr of a groundcar faded in the distance. Darkness, silence scored by breathing.

They dragged Miles along again, out a back door, through a narrow mews and into the back seat of a groundcar parked in the alley. They sat him up like a mannequin between them, while a third kidnapper drove. Miles's thoughts spun dizzily along the edge of consciousness. Goddamn scanners . . . five-year-old technology from the rim zone, which put it maybe ten years behind Earth's—they'd have to bite the budget bullet and scrap the Dendarii scanner system fleet-wide, now—if he lived to order it. . . . Scanners, hell. The fault didn't lie in the scanners. Wasn't the formerly-mythical unicorn hunted with mirrors, to fascinate the vainglorious beast while its killers circled for the strike? Must be a virgin around here somewhere. . . .

This was an ancient district. The tortuous route the groundcar was taking could be either to confuse him or merely the best shortcut local knowledge could supply. After about a quarter hour they dove into an underground parking garage and hissed to a halt. The garage was small, clearly private, with room for only a few vehicles.

They hauled him to a lift tube and ascended one level to a short hallway. One of the goons pulled off Miles's boots and scanner-shield belt. The stun was starting to wear off. His legs were rubbery, shot with pins and needles, but at least they propped him up. They released his wrists; clumsily, he tried to rub his aching arms. They popped the gag from his mouth. He emitted a wordless croak.

They unlocked a door in front of him and bundled him into a windowless room. The door closed behind with a click like trap jaws snapping. He staggered and stood, feet spread a little, panting.

A sealed light fixture in the ceiling illuminated a narrow room furnished only with two hard benches along the walls. To the left a doorframe with the door removed led to a tiny, windowless washroom.

A man, wearing only green trousers, cream shirt, and socks, lay curled on one of the benches, facing the wall. Stiffly, gingerly, he rolled over and sat up. One hand flung up automatically, as if to shield his reddened eyes from some too-bright light; the other pressed the bench to keep him from toppling. Dark hair mussed, a four-day beard stubble. His shirt collar hung open in a V, revealing a throat strangely vulnerable, in contrast to the usual turtle-armored effect of the high, closed Barrayaran tunic collar. His face was furrowed.

The impeccable Captain Galeni. Rather the worse for wear.

Chapter Eight

Galeni squinted at Miles. "Bloody hell," he said in a flattened voice.

"Same to you," Miles rasped back.

Galeni sat up straighter, bleary eyes narrowing with suspicion. "Or—is it you?"

"I don't know." Miles considered this. "Which me were you expecting?" He staggered over to the bench opposite before his knees gave way and sat, his back against the wall, feet not quite reaching the floor. They were both silent for a few minutes, taking in the details of the other.

"It would be pointless to throw us together in the same room unless it were monitored," said Miles at last.

For answer Galeni flipped an index finger up toward the light fixture.

"Ah. Visual too?"

"Yes."

Miles bared his teeth and smiled upward.

148

Galeni was still regarding him with wary, almost painful uncertainty.

Miles cleared his throat. There was a bitter tang lingering in his mouth. "I take it you've met my alter-ego?"

"Yesterday. I think it was yesterday." Galeni glanced at the light.

His kidnappers had relieved Miles of his own chrono, too. "It's now about one in the morning, of the start of the fifth day since you disappeared from the embassy," Miles supplied, answering Galeni's unspoken question. "Do they leave that light on all the time?"

"Yes."

"Ah." Miles fought down a queasy twinge of associative memory. Continuous illumination was a Cetagandan prison technique for inducing temporal disorientation. Admiral Naismith was intimately familiar with it.

"I saw him for just a few seconds," Miles went on, "when they made the switch." His hand touched the absence of a dagger, massaged the back of his neck. "Do I—really look like that?"

"I thought it was you. Till the end. He told me he was practicing. Testing."

"Did he pass?"

"He was in here for four or five hours."

Miles winced. "That's bad. That's very bad."

"I thought so."

"I see." A sticky silence filled the room. "Well, historian. And how do you tell a forgery from the real thing?"

Galeni shook his head, then touched his hand to his temple as though he wished he hadn't; blinding headache, apparently. Miles had one too. "I don't believe I know anymore." Galeni added reflectively, "He saluted."

A dry grin cracked one corner of Miles's mouth. "Of course, there could be just one of me, and all this a ploy to drive you crazy. . . ."

"Stop that!" Galeni almost shouted. A ghastly answering smile lit his face for a moment nonetheless.

Miles glanced up at the light. "Well, whoever I am, you should still be able to tell me who they are. Ah—I hope it's not the Cetagandans? I would find that just a little too weird for comfort, in light of my . . . duplicate. He's a surgical construct, I trust." *Not a clone—please, don't let him be my clone. . . .*

"He said he was a clone," said Galeni. "Of course, at least half of what he said was lies, whoever he was."

"Oh." Stronger exclamations seemed wholly inadequate.

"Yes. It made me rather wonder about you. The original you, that is."

"Ah . . . hem! Yes. I think I know now why I popped out with that . . . that story when the reporter cornered me. I'd seen him once before. In the tubeway, when I was out with Commander Quinn. Eight, ten days ago now. They must have been maneuvering in to make the switch. I thought I was seeing myself in the mirror. But he was wearing the wrong uniform, and they must have aborted."

Galeni glanced down at his own sleeve. "Didn't you notice?"

"I had a lot on my mind."

"You never reported this!"

"I was on some pain meds. I thought it might be a little hallucination. I was a bit stressed out. By the time I'd got back to the embassy I'd forgotten about it. And besides," he smirked weakly, "I didn't think our working relationship would benefit from planting serious doubts about my sanity."

Galeni's lips compressed with exasperation, then softened with something like despair. "Perhaps not."

It alarmed Miles, to see despair in Galeni's face. He babbled on, "Anyway, I was relieved to realize I hadn't suddenly become clairvoyant. I'm afraid my subconscious must be brighter than the rest of my brain. I just didn't get its message." He pointed upward again, "Not Cetagandans?"

"No." Galeni leaned back against the far wall, stone-faced. "Komarrans."

"Ah," Miles choked. "A Komarran plot. How . . . fraught."

Galeni's mouth twisted. "Quite."

"Well," said Miles thinly, "they haven't killed us yet. There must be some reason to keep us alive."

Galeni's lips drew back on a deathly grin, his eyes crinkling. "None whatsoever." The words came out in a *whee*ing chuckle, abruptly cut off. A private joke between Galeni and the light fixture, apparently. "He imagines he has reason," Galeni explained, "but he's very mistaken." The bitter thrust of those words was also directed upward.

"Well, don't tell *them*," said Miles through his teeth. He took a deep breath. "Come on, Galeni, spill it. What happened the morning you disappeared from the embassy?"

Galeni sighed, and seemed to compose himself. "I got a call that morning. From an old . . . Komarran acquaintance. Asking me to meet him."

"There was no log of a call. Ivan checked your comconsole."

"I erased it. That was a mistake, though I didn't realize it at the time. But something he'd said led me to think this might be a lead into the mystery of your peculiar orders."

"So I did convince you my orders had to have been screwed up."

"Oh, yes. But it was clear that if that were so, my embassy Security had been penetrated, compromised from the inside. It was probably through the courier. But I dared not lay such a charge without adducing objective evidence."

"The courier, yes," said Miles. "That was my second choice."

Galeni's brows lifted. "What was your first choice?"

"You, I'm afraid."

Galeni's sour smile said it all.

Miles shrugged in embarrassment. "I figured you'd made off with my eighteen million marks. Except if you had, why hadn't you absconded? And then you absconded."

"Oh," said Galeni in turn.

"All the facts fit, then," Miles explained. "I had you pegged as an embezzler, deserter, thief, and all-around Komarran son of a bitch."

"So what kept you from laying charges to that effect?"

"Nothing, unfortunately." Miles cleared his throat. "Sorry."

Galeni's face went faintly green, too dismayed even to get up a convincing glare, though he tried.

"Too right," said Miles. "If we don't get out of here, your name is going to be mud."

"All for nothing . . ." Galeni braced his back to the wall, his head tilting back against it for support, eyes closing as if in pain.

Miles contemplated the probable political consequences, should he and Galeni disappear now without further trace. Investigators must find his embezzlement theory even more exciting than he had, compounded now by kidnapping, murder, elopement, God knew what. The scandal could be guaranteed to rock the Komarran integration effort to its foundations, perhaps destroy it altogether. Miles glanced across the room at the man his father had chosen to take a chance on. *A kind of redemption . . .*

That alone could be enough reason for the Komarran underground to murder them both. But the existence of the—oh God, not a clone!—alter-Miles suggested that this slander upon Galeni's character, courtesy of Miles, was merely a happy bonus from the Komarran viewpoint. He wondered if they'd be properly grateful.

"So you went to meet this man," Miles prodded. "Without taking a beeper or a backup."

"Yes."

"And promptly got yourself kidnapped. And you criticize my Security techniques!"

"Yes." Galeni's eyes opened. "Well, no. We had lunch first."

"You sat down to lunch with this guy? Or—was she pretty?" Miles awoke to Galeni's choice of pronoun, back when he'd been addressing edged remarks to the light fixture. No, not a pretty.

"Hardly. But he did attempt to suborn me."

"Did he succeed?"

At Galeni's withering glare, Miles explained, "Making this entire conversation a play for my benefit, y'see."

Galeni grimaced, half irritation, half wry agreement. Forgeries and originals, truth and lies, how were they to be tested here?

"I told him to get stuffed." Galeni said this loudly enough that the light fixture couldn't possibly miss it. "I should have realized, in the course of our argument, that he had told me entirely too much about what was really going on to dare let me go. But we exchanged guarantees, I turned my back on him . . . let sentiment cloud my judgment. He did not. And so I ended up here." Galeni glanced around their narrow cell, "For a little time yet. Until he gets over his surge of sentiment. As he will, eventually." Defiance, glared at the light fixture.

Miles drew breath cold, cold through his teeth. "Must have been a pretty compelling old acquaintance."

"Oh yes." Galeni closed his eyes again, as if he contemplated escaping Miles, and this whole tangle, by retreating into sleep.

Galeni's stiff, halting movements hinted of torture. . . . "They been urging you to change your mind? Or interrogating you the old hard way?"

Galeni's eyes slitted open; he touched the purple splotch under the left one. "No, they have fast-penta for interrogation. No need to get physical. I've been round on it, three, four times. There's not much they don't know about embassy Security by now."

"Why the contusions, then?"

"I made a break for it . . . yesterday, I guess. The three fellows who tackled me look worse, I assure you. They must still be hoping I'll change my mind."

"Couldn't you have pretended to cooperate at least long enough to get away?" said Miles in exasperation.

Galeni's eyes snapped truculently. "Never," he hissed. The spasm of rage evaporated with a weary sigh. "I suppose I should have. Too late now."

Had they scrambled the captain's brains with their drugs? If old cold Galeni had let emotion ambush his reason to that extent, well—it must be a bloody strong emotion. The down-deep deadlies that IQ could do nothing about.

"I don't suppose they'd buy an offer to cooperate from me," Miles said glumly.

Galeni's voice returned to its original drawl. "Hardly."

"Right."

A few minutes later Miles remarked, "It can't be a clone, y'know."

"Why not?" said Galeni.

"Any clone of mine, grown from my body cells, ought to look—well, rather like Ivan. Six feet tall or so and not . . . distorted in his face and spine. With good bones, not these chalk-sticks. Unless," horrid thought, "the medics have been lying to me all my life about my genes."

"He must have been distorted to match," Galeni offered thoughtfully. "Chemically or surgically or both. No harder to do that to your clone than to any other surgical construct. Maybe easier."

"But what happened to me was so random an accident—even the repairs were experimental—my own doctors didn't know what they'd have till it was over."

"Getting the duplicate right must have been tricky. But obviously not impossible. Perhaps the . . . individual we saw represents the last in a series of trials."

"In that case, what have they done with the discards?" Miles asked wildly. A parade of clones passed through his imagination like a chart of evolution run in reverse, upright Ivanish Cro-Magnon devolving through missing links into chimpanzee-Miles.

"I imagine they were disposed of." Galeni's voice was high and mild, not so much denying as defying horror.

Miles's belly shivered. "Ruthless."

"Oh, yes," Galeni agreed in that same soft tone.

Miles groped for logic. "In that case, he—the

clone—" *my twin brother*, there, he had thought the thought flat out, "must be significantly younger than myself."

"Several years," agreed Galeni. "At a guess, six."

"Why six?"

"Arithmetic. You were about six when the Komarran revolt ended. That would have been the time this group would have been forced to turn its attention toward some other, less direct plan of attack on Barrayar. The idea would not have interested them earlier. Much later, and the clone would still be too young to replace you even with accelerated growth. Too young to carry off the act. It appears he must act as well as look like you, for a time."

"But why a clone at all? Why a clone of me?"

"I believe he's intended for some sabotage timed with an uprising on Komarr."

"Barrayar will never let Komarr go. Never. You're our front gate."

"I know," said Galeni tiredly. "But some people would rather drown our domes in blood than learn from history. Or learn anything at all." He glanced involuntarily at the light.

Miles swallowed, rallied his will, spoke into the silence. "How long have you known your father hadn't been blown up with that bomb?"

Galeni's eyes flashed back to him; his body froze, then relaxed, if so grating a motion could be called relaxation. But he said merely, "Five days." After a time he added, "How did you know?"

"We cracked open your personnel files. He was your only close relative with no morgue record."

"We believed he was dead." Galeni's voice was distant, level. "My brother certainly was. Barrayaran Security came and got my mother and me, to identify what was left. There wasn't much left. It was no effort to believe there was literally nothing left of my father, who'd been reported much closer to the center of the explosion."

The man was in knots, fraying before Miles's eyes. Miles found he did not relish the idea of watching Galeni come apart. Very wasteful of an officer, from the Imperium's viewpoint. Like an assassination. Or an abortion.

"My father spoke constantly of Komarr's freedom," Galeni went on softly. To Miles, to the light fixture, to himself? "Of the sacrifices we must all make for the freedom of Komarr. He was very big on sacrifices. Human or otherwise. But he never seemed to care much about the freedom of anyone *on* Komarr. It wasn't until the day the revolt died that I became a free man. The day he died. Free to look with my own eyes, make my own judgments, choose my own life. Or so I thought. Life," the lilt of Galeni's voice was infinitely sarcastic, "is full of surprises." He favored the light fixture with a vulpine smile.

Miles squeezed his eyes shut, trying to think straight. Not easy, with Galeni sitting two meters away emanating murderous tension on red-line overload. Miles had the unpleasant feeling that his nominal superior had lost sight of the larger strategic picture just now, locked in some private struggle with old ghosts. Or old non-ghosts. It was up to Miles.

Up to Miles to do—what? He rose, and prowled the room on shaky legs. Galeni watched him through slitted eyes without comment. No exit but the one. He scratched at the walls with his fingernails. They were impervious. The seams at floor and ceiling—he hopped up on the bench and reached dizzily—yielded not at all. He passed into the half-bath, relieved himself, washed his hands and face and sour mouth at the sink—cold water only—drank from his cupped hands. No glass, not even a plastic cup. The water sloshed nauseatingly in his stomach, his hands twitched from the aftereffects of the stun. He wondered what the result of stuffing the drain with his shirt and running the water might be. That seemed to be the maximum possible vandalism. He returned to his bench, wiping his hands on his trousers, and sat down before he fell down.

"Do they feed you?" he asked.

"Two or three times a day," said Galeni. "Some of whatever they're cooking upstairs. Several people seem to be living in this house."

"That would seem to be the one time you could make a break, then."

"It was," agreed Galeni.

Was, right. Their captors' guard would be redoubled now, after Galeni's attempt. Not an attempt that Miles dared duplicate; a beating like the one Galeni had taken would incapacitate him completely.

Galeni contemplated the locked door. "It does provide a certain amount of entertainment. You never know, when the door opens, if it's going to be dinner or death."

Miles got the impression Galeni was rather hoping for death. *Bloody kamikaze.* Miles knew the fey mood inside out. You could fall in love with that grave-narrow option—it was the enemy of creative strategic thought. It was the enemy, period.

But his resolve failed to find a practical form, though he spun it round and round inside his head. Surely Ivan must recognize the imposter immediately. Or would he just put down any mistakes the clone made to Miles having an off day? There was certainly precedent for that. And if the Komarrans had spent four days pumping Galeni dry on embassy procedures, it was quite possible the clone would be able to carry out Miles's routine duties error-free. After all, if the creature were truly a clone, he should be just as smart as Miles.

Or just as stupid . . . Miles hung on to that comforting thought. If Miles made mistakes, in his desperate dance through life, the clone could make just as many. Trouble was, would anyone be able to tell their mistakes apart?

But what about the Dendarii? His Dendarii, fallen into the hands of a—a what? What were the Komarrans' plans? How much did they know about the Dendarii? And how the hell could the clone duplicate both Lord Vorkosigan and Admiral Naismith, when Miles himself had to make them up as he went along?

And Elli—if Elli hadn't been able to tell the difference in the abandoned house, could she tell the difference in bed? Would that filthy little imposter dare swive Quinn? But what human being of any of the three sexes could possibly resist an invitation to cavort between the sheets with the brilliant and beautiful. . . ? Miles's imagination curdled with detailed pictures of the clone, out there, Doing Things to his Quinn, most of which Miles hadn't even had time to try yet himself. He found his hands writhing in a white knuckled grip on the edge of the bench, in danger of snapping his finger-bones.

He let up. Surely the clone must try to avoid intimate situations with people who knew Miles well, where he would be in most danger of getting tripped up. Unless he was a cocky little shit with a compulsive experimental bent, like the one Miles shaved daily in his mirror. Miles and Elli had just begun to get intimate—would she, wouldn't she know the difference? If she—Miles swallowed, and tried to bring his mind back to the larger political scenario.

The clone hadn't been created just to drive him crazy; that was merely a fringe benefit. The clone had been forged as a weapon, directed against Barrayar. Through Prime Minister Count Aral Vorkosigan against Barrayar, as if the two were one. Miles had no illusions; it wasn't for his own self's sake that this plot had been gotten up. He could think of a dozen ways a false Miles might be used against his father, ranging from relatively benign to horrifically cruel. He glanced across the cell at Galeni, sprawled coolly, waiting for his own father to kill him. Or using that very coolness to force his father to kill him, proving . . . what? Miles quietly dropped the benign scenarios off his list of possibilities.

In the end exhaustion overtook him, and he slept on the hard bench.

He slept badly, swimming up repeatedly out of some unpleasant dream only to re-encounter the even more unpleasant reality—cold bench, cramped muscles, Galeni flung across the bench opposite twisting in equal discomfort, his eyes gleaming through the fringe of his lashes not revealing whether he woke or dozed—then wavering back down to dreamland in self-defense. Miles's sense of the passage of time became totally distorted, though when he finally sat up his creaking muscles and the water-clock of his bladder suggested he'd slept long. By the time he made a trip to the washroom, splashed cold water on his now-stubbled face, and drank, his mind was churning back into high gear, rendering further sleep impossible. He wished he had his cat-blanket.

The door clicked. Galeni snapped from his apparent doze into a sitting position, feet under his center of gravity, face utterly closed. But this time it was dinner. Or breakfast, judging from the ingredients:

lukewarm scrambled eggs, sweet raisin bread, blessed coffee in a flimsy cup, one spoon each. It was delivered by one of the poker-faced young men Miles had seen the night before. Another hovered in the doorway, stunner at ready. Eyeing Galeni, the man set the food down on the end of one bench and backed quickly out.

Miles regarded the food warily. But Galeni collected his and ate without hesitation. Did he know it wasn't drugged or poisoned, or did he just not give a damn anymore? Miles shrugged and ate too.

Miles swallowed his last precious drops of coffee and asked, "Have you picked up any hint of what the purpose of this whole masquerade is? They must have gone to incredible lengths to produce this . . . duplicate me. It can't be a minor plot."

Galeni, looking a bit less pale by virtue of the decent food, rolled his cup carefully between his hands. "I know what they've told me. I don't know if what they've told me is the truth."

"Right, go on."

"You've got to understand, my father's group is a radical splinter of the main Komarran underground. The groups haven't spoken to each other in years, which is one of the reasons we—Barrayaran Security," a faint ironic smile played around his lips, "—missed them. The main body has been losing momentum over the last decade. The expatriates' children, with no memory of Komarr, have been growing up as citizens of other planets. And the older ones have been—well, growing old. Dying off. And with things becoming not so bad at home, they're not making new converts. It's a shrinking power base, critically shrinking."

"I can see that would make the radicals itchy to

make some move. While they still had a chance," Miles remarked.

"Yes. They're in a squeeze." Galeni crushed his cup slowly in his fist. "Reduced to wild gambles."

"This one seems pretty damned exotic, to bet— sixteen, eighteen years on? How the devil did they assemble the medical resources? Was your father a doctor?"

Galeni snorted. "Hardly. The medical half was the easy part, apparently, once they'd got hold of the stolen tissue sample from Barrayar. Though how they did that—"

"I spent the first six years of my life getting prodded, probed, biopsied, scanned, sampled, sliced and diced by doctors. There must have been kilograms of me floating around in various medical labs to choose from, a regular tissue smorgasbord. That was the easy part. But the actual cloning—"

"Was hired out. To some shady medical laboratory on the planet of Jackson's Whole, as I understand it, that would do anything for a price."

Miles's mouth, opening, gaped for a moment. "Oh. Them."

"Do you know about Jackson's Whole?"

"I've—encountered their work in another context. Damned if I can't name the lab most likely to have done it, too. They're experts at cloning. Among other things, they do the illegal brain-transfer operations— illegal anywhere but Jackson's Whole, that is—where the young clone is grown in a vat, and the old brain is transferred into it—the old rich brain, needless to say—and, um, they've done some bioengineering work that I can't talk about, and . . . yes. And all this time they had a copy of me in the back room—those sons of bitches, they're going to find out they're not as bloody untouchable as they think they are this time . . . !" Miles controlled incipient hyperventilation. Personal revenge upon Jackson's Whole must wait for some more propitious time. "So. The Komarran underground invested nothing except money in the project for the first ten or fifteen years. No wonder it was never traced."

"Yes," said Galeni. "So a few years ago, the decision was made to pull this card out of their sleeve. They picked up the completed clone, now a young teenager, from Jackson's Whole and began training him to be you."

"Why?"

"They're apparently going for the Imperium."

"What?!" Miles cried. "No! Not with *me*—!"

"That . . . individual . . . stood right there," Galeni pointed to a spot near the door, "two days ago and told me I was looking at the next Emperor of Barrayar."

"They would have to kill both Emperor Gregor and my father to mount anything of a sort—" Miles began frantically.

"I would imagine," said Galeni dryly, "they're looking forward to just that." He lay back on his bench, eyes glinting, hands locked behind his neck for a pillow, and purred, "Over my dead body, of course."

"Over both our dead bodies. They don't dare let us live. . . ."

"I believe I mentioned that yesterday."

"Still, if anything goes wrong," Miles's gaze flickered toward the light fixture, "it might be handy for them to have hostages." He enunciated this idea clearly, emphasizing the plural. Though he feared that from the Barrayaran point of view, only one of them had value as a hostage. Galeni was no fool; he knew who the goat was too.

Damn, damn, damn. Miles had walked into this

trap, knowing it was a trap, in hopes of gaining just the sort of information he now possessed. But he hadn't meant to stay trapped. He rubbed the back of his neck in utter frustration—what joy it would have been to call down a Dendarii strike force on this—this nest of rebels—right now—

The door clicked. It was too early for lunch. Miles whipped around, hoping for a wild instant to find Commander Quinn leading a patrol to his rescue—no. It was just the two goons again, and a third in the doorway with a stunner.

One gestured at Miles. "You. Come along."

"Where to?" Miles asked suspiciously. Could this be the end already—to be taken back down to the garage sub-level and shot or have his neck broken? He felt disinclined to walk voluntarily to his own execution.

Something like that must have been passing through Galeni's mind too, for as the pair grabbed Miles unceremoniously by the arms, Galeni lunged for them. The one with the stunner dropped him before he was halfway across the floor. Galeni convulsed, teeth bared, in desperate resistance, then lay still.

Numbly, Miles allowed himself to be bundled out the door. If his death were coming, he wanted to at least stay conscious, to spit in its eye one last time as it closed on him.

Chapter Nine

To Miles's temporary relief, they took him up, not down the lift tube. Not that they couldn't perfectly well kill him someplace other than the garage sub-level. Galeni, now, they might murder in the garage to avoid having to lug the body, but Miles's own dead weight, so to speak, would not present nearly the logistic load.

The room into which the two men now shoved him was some sort of study or private office, bright despite the polarized window. Library data files filled a transparent shelf on the wall; an ordinary comconsole desk occupied one corner. The comconsole vid was presently displaying a fish-eye view of Miles's cell. Galeni still lay stunned on the floor.

The older man who had seemed in charge of Miles's kidnapping the night before sat on a beige-padded chrome bench before the darkened window, examining a hypospray just taken from its case, which lay open beside him. So. Interrogation, not execution, was the plan. Or at any rate, interrogation before execution. Unless they simply contemplated poisoning him.

Miles tore his gaze from the glittering hypo as the man shifted, his head tilting to study Miles through narrowed blue eyes. A flick of his gaze checked the comconsole. It was a momentary accident of posture, a hand gripping the edge of the bench, that snapped Miles's realization into place, for the man did not greatly resemble Captain Galeni except perhaps in the paleness of his skin. He appeared to be about sixty. Clipped greying hair, lined face, body thickening with age, clearly not that of an outdoorsman or athlete. He wore conservative Earther clothes a generation removed from the historical fashions of the parading teenagers that Miles had enjoyed in the shopping arcade. He might have been a businessman or a teacher, anything but a hairy terrorist.

Except for the murderous tension. In that, in the coil of the hands, flare of the nostril, iron of the mouth, stiffness of the neck, Ser Galen and Duv Galeni were as one.

Galen rose, and stalked slowly around Miles with the air of a man studying a sculpture by an inferior artist. Miles stood very still, feeling smaller than usual in his sock feet, stubbled and grubby. He had come to the center at last, the secret source from which all his coiling troubles had been emanating these past weeks. And the center was this man, who orbited him staring back with hungry hate. Or perhaps he and Galen were both centers, like the twin foci of an ellipse, brought together and superimposed at last to create some diabolical perfect circle.

Miles felt very small and very brittle. Galen could very well begin by breaking Miles's arms with the same absent, nervous air that Elli Quinn bit her nails, just to release tension. *Does he see me at all? Or am I an object, a symbol representing the enemy— will he murder me for the sake of sheer allegory?*

"So," Ser Galen spoke. "This is the real thing at last. Not very impressive, to have seduced my son's loyalty. What can he see in you? Still, you represent Barrayar very well. The monster son of a monster father, Aral Vorkosigan's secret moral genotype made flesh for all to see. Perhaps there is some justice in the universe after all."

"Very poetic," choked Miles, "but biologically in- accurate, as you must know, having cloned me."

Galen smiled sourly. "I won't insist on it." He completed his circuit and faced Miles. "I suppose you couldn't help being born. But why have you never revolted from the monster? He made you what you are—" an expansive gesture of Galen's open hand summed up Miles's stunted and twisted frame. "What dictator's charisma does the man possess, that he's able to hypnotize not only his own son but everyone else's too?" The prone figure in the vid console seemed to pluck at Galen's eye. "Why do you follow him? Why does David? What corrupt kick can my son get out of crawling into a Barrayaran goon-uniform and marching behind *Vorkosigan?*" Ga- len's voice feigned light banter very badly; the un- dertones twisted with anguish.

Miles, glowering, clipped out, "For one thing, my father has never abandoned me in the presence of an enemy."

Galen's head jerked back, all pretense of banter extinguished. He turned abruptly away, and went to take up the hypospray from the bench.

Miles silently cursed his own tongue. But for that stupid impulse to grab the last word, to return the cut, he might have kept the man talking, and learned something. Now the talking, and the learning, would all be going the other way.

The two guards took him by the elbows. The one on the left pushed up his shirt sleeve. Here it came. Galen pressed the hypospray against the vein on the inside of Miles's elbow, a hiss, a prickling bite. "What is it?" Miles had just time to ask. His voice sounded unfortunately weak and nervous in his own ears.

"Fast-penta, of course," replied Galen easily.

Miles was not surprised, though he cringed inwardly, knowing what was to come. He had studied fast-penta's pharmacology, effects, and proper use in the Security course at the Barrayaran Imperial Academy. It was the drug of choice for interrogation, not only for the Imperial Service but galaxy-wide. The near-perfect truth serum, irresistible, harmless to the subject even with repeated doses. Irresistible and harmless, that is, except to the unfortunate few who had either a natural or artificially-induced allergic reaction to it. Miles had never even been considered as a candidate for this last conditioning, his person being judged more valuable than any secret information he might contain. Other espionage agents were less lucky. Anaphylactic shock was an even less heroic death than the disintegration chamber usually reserved for convicted spies.

Despairing, Miles waited to go ga-ga. Admiral Naismith had sat in on more than one real fast-penta interrogation. The drug washed all reason out to sea on a flood of benign good feeling and charitable cheer. Like a cat on catnip, it was highly amusing to watch—in somebody else. In moments he would be mellow to the point of drooling idiocy.

Ugly, to think of the resolute Captain Galeni having been so shamefully reduced. Four times running, he'd said. No wonder he was twitchy.

Miles could feel his heart racing, as though he'd overdosed on caffeine. His vision seemed to sharpen to an almost painful focus. The edge lines of every object in the room glowed, the masses they enclosed palpable to his exacerbated senses. Galen, standing back by the pulsing window, was a live-wiring diagram, electric and dangerous, loaded with deadly voltage awaiting some triggering discharge.

Mellow, this wasn't.

He had to be slipping into natural shock. Miles took his last breath. Would his interrogator ever be surprised. . . .

Rather to Miles's own surprise, he kept on panting. Not anaphylactic shock, then. Just another damned idiosyncratic drug reaction. He hoped the stuff wouldn't bring on those ghastly hallucinations like that bloody sedative he'd been given once by an unsuspecting surgeon. He wanted to scream. His eyes flashed white-edged to follow Galen's least motion.

One of the guards shoved a chair up behind him and sat him down. Miles fell into it gratefully, shivering uncontrollably. His thoughts seemed to explode in fragments and reform, like fireworks being run forward and then in reverse through a vid. Galen frowned down at him.

"Describe the security procedures for entry and exit from the Barrayaran embassy."

Surely they must have squeezed this basic information out of Captain Galeni already—it must merely be a question to check the effect of the fast-penta, ". . . of the fast-penta," Miles heard his own voice echoing his thoughts. Oh, hell. He'd hoped his odd reaction to the drug might have included the ability to resist spilling his mind out his mouth. "—what a repulsive image . . ." Head swaying, he stared down at the floor in front of his feet as if he might see a pile of bloody brains vomited there.

Ser Galen strode forward and yanked his head up by the hair, and repeated through his teeth, "Describe the security procedures for entry and exit from the Barrayaran embassy!"

"Sergeant Barth's in charge," Miles began impulsively. "Obnoxious bigot. No savoir faire at all, and a jock to boot—" Unable to stop himself, Miles poured out not only codes, passwords, scanner perimeters, but also personnel schedules, his private opinions of each and every individual, and a scathing critique of the Security net's defects. One thought triggered another and then the next in an explosive chain like a string of firecrackers. He couldn't stop; he babbled.

Not only could he not stop himself, Galen couldn't stop him either. Prisoners on fast-penta tended to wander by free association from the topic unless kept on track by frequent cues from their interrogators. Miles found himself doing the same on fast-forward. Normal victims could be brought up short by a word, but only when Galen struck him hard and repeatedly across the face, shouting him down, did Miles halt, and sit panting.

Torture was not a part of fast-penta interrogation because the happily drugged subjects were impervious to it. For Miles the pain pulsed in and out, at one moment detached and distant, the next flooding his body and whiting out his mind like a burst of static. To his own horror, he began to cry. Then stopped with a sudden hiccup.

Galen stood staring at him in repelled fascination.

"It's not right," muttered one of the guards. "He shouldn't be like that. Is he beating the fast-penta, some kind of new conditioning?"

"He's not beating it, though," Galen pointed out.

He glanced at his wrist chrono. "He's not withhold-ing information. He's giving more. Too much more."

The comconsole began chiming insistently.

"I'll get it," volunteered Miles. "It's probably for me." He surged up out of his seat, his knees gave way, and he fell flat on his face on the carpet. It prickled against his bruised cheek. The two guards dragged him off the floor and propped him back up in the chair. The room jerked in a slow circle around him. Galen answered the comconsole.

"Reporting in." Miles's own crisp voice in its Barrayaran-accented incarnation rang from the vid.

The clone's face seemed not quite as familiar as the one Miles shaved daily in his mirror. "His hair's parted on the wrong side if he wants to be me," Miles observed to no one in particular. "No, it's not . . ." No one was listening, anyway. Miles consid-ered angles of incidence and angles of reflection, his thoughts bouncing at the speed of light back and forth between the mirrored walls of his empty skull.

"How's it going?" Galen leaned anxiously across the comconsole.

"I nearly lost it all in the first five minutes last night. That big Dendarii sergeant-driver turned out to be the damned cousin." The clone's voice was low and tense. "Blind luck, I was able to carry off my first mistake as a joke. But they've got me rooming with the bastard. And he snores."

"Too true," Miles remarked, unasked. "For real entertainment, wait'll he starts making love in his sleep. Damn, I wish I had dreams like Ivan's. All I get are anxiety nightmares—playing polo naked against a lot of dead Cetagandans with Lieutenant Murka's severed head for the ball. It screamed every time I hit it toward the goal. Falling off and getting tram-

pled . . ." Miles's mutter trailed off as they continued to ignore him.

"You're going to have to deal with all kinds of
people who knew him, before this is done," said
Galen roughly to the vid. "But if you can fool Vorpatril,
you'll be able to carry it off anywhere—"

"You can fool all of the people some of the time,"
chirped Miles, "and some of the people all of the
time, but you can fool Ivan anytime. He doesn't pay
attention."

Galen glanced over at him in irritation. "The embassy is a perfect isolated test-microcosm," he went
on to the vid, "before you go on to the larger arena
of Barrayar itself. Vorpatril's presence makes it an
ideal practice opportunity. If he tumbles to you, we
can find some way to eliminate him."

"Mm." The clone seemed scarcely reassured. "Before we started, I thought you'd managed to stuff my
head with everything it was possible to know about
Miles Vorkosigan. Then at the last minute you find
out he's been leading a double life all this time—
what else have you missed?"

"Miles, we've been over that—"

Miles realized with a start that Galen was addressing the clone with his name. Had he been so thoroughly conditioned to his role that he had no name
of his own? Strange . . .

"We knew there'd be gaps over which you'd have
to improvise. But we'll never have a better opportunity than this chance visit of his to Earth has given
us. Better than waiting another six months and trying
to maneuver in on Barrayar. No. It's now or never."
Galen took a calming breath. "So. You got through
the night all right."

The clone snorted. "Yeah, if you don't count waking up being strangled by a damned animated fur coat."

"What? Oh, the live fur. Didn't he give it to his woman?"

"Evidently not. I nearly peed myself before I realized what it was. Woke up the cousin."

"Did he suspect anything?" Galen asked urgently.

"I passed it off as a nightmare. It seems Vorkosigan has them fairly often."

Miles nodded sagely. "That's what I told you. Severed heads . . . broken bones . . . mutilated relatives . . . unusual alterations to important parts of my body . . ." The drug seemed to be imparting some odd memory effects, part of what made fast-penta so effective for interrogation, no doubt. His recent dreams were coming back to him far more clearly than he'd ever consciously remembered them. All in all, he was glad he usually tended to forget them.

"Did Vorpatril say anything about it in the morning?" asked Galen.

"No. I'm not talking much."

"That's out of character," Miles observed helpfully.

"I'm pretending to have a mild episode of one of those depressions in his psyche report—who is that, anyway?" The clone craned his neck.

"Vorkosigan himself. We've got him on fast-penta."

"Ah, good. I've been getting calls all morning over a secured comm link from his mercenaries, asking for orders."

"We agreed you'd avoid the mercenaries."

"Fine, tell them."

"How soon can you get orders cut getting you out of the embassy and back to Barrayar?"

"Not soon enough to avoid the Dendarii completely. I broached it to the ambassador, but it appears Vorkosigan's in charge of the search for Captain Galeni. He seemed surprised I'd want to leave, so I backed off for now. Has the captain changed his mind about cooperating yet? If not, you'll have to generate my return-home orders from out there and slip them in with the courier or something."

Galen hesitated visibly. "I'll see what I can do. In the meantime, keep trying."

Doesn't Galen know we know the courier's compromised? Miles thought in a flash of near-normal clarity. He managed to keep the vocalization to a low mumble.

"Right. Well, you promised me you'd keep him alive for questions until I left, so here's one. Who is Lieutenant Bone, and what is she supposed to do about the surplusage from the *Triumph?* She didn't say what it was a surplus of."

One of the guards prodded Miles. "Answer the question."

Miles struggled for clarity of thought and expression. "She's my fleet accountant. I suppose she should dump it into her investment account and play with it as usual. It's a surplus of money," he felt compelled to explain, then cackled bitterly. "Temporary, I'm sure."

"Will that do?" asked Galen.

"I think so. I told her she was an experienced officer and to use her discretion, and she seemed to go off satisfied, but I sure wondered what I'd just ordered her to do. All right, next. Who is Rosalie Crew, and why is she suing Admiral Naismith for half a million GSA federal credits?"

"Who?" gaped Miles in genuine astonishment as the guard prodded him again. "What?" Miles was confusedly unable to convert half a million GSA credits to Barrayaran Imperial marks in his drug-scrambled head with any precision beyond "lots and lots and lots"; for a moment the association of the name remained blocked, then clicked in. "Ye gods, it's that poor clerk from the wine shop. I saved her from burning up. Why sue me? Why not sue Danio, he burned down her store—of course, he's broke . . ."

"But what do I do about it?" asked the clone.

"You wanted to be me," said Miles in a surly voice, "you figure it out." His mental processes clicked on anyway. "Slap her with a countersuit for medical damages. I think I threw my back out, lifting her. It still hurts . . ."

Galen overrode this. "Ignore it," he instructed. "You'll be out of there before anything can come of it."

"All right," said the Miles-clone doubtfully.

"And leave the Dendarii holding the bag?" said Miles angrily. He squeezed his eyes shut, trying desperately to think in the wavering room. "But of course, you don't care anything about the Dendarii, do you? You must care! They put their lives on the line for you—me—it's wrong—you'll betray them, casually, without even thinking about it, you scarcely know what they are—"

"Quite," sighed the clone, "and speaking of what they are, just what is his relationship with this Commander Quinn, anyway? Did you finally decide he was screwing her, or not?"

"We're just good friends," caroled Miles, and laughed hysterically. He lunged for the comconsole—the guards grabbed for him and missed—and climbing across the desk snarled into the vid, "Stay away from her, you little shit! She's mine, you hear, mine, mine, all mine—Quinn, Quinn, beautiful Quinn, Quinn of the evening, beautiful Quinn," he sang off-key as the guards dragged him back. Blows ran him down into silence.

"I thought you had him on fast-penta," said the clone to Galen.

"We do."

"It doesn't sound like fast-penta!"

"Yes. There's something wrong. Yet he's not supposed to have been conditioned. . . . I'm beginning to seriously doubt the utility of keeping him alive any longer as a data bank if we can't trust his answers."

"That's just great," scowled the clone. He glanced over his shoulder. "I've got to go. I'll report again tonight. If I'm still alive by then." He vanished with an irritated bleep.

Galen turned back to Miles with a list of questions, about Barrayaran Imperial Headquarters, about Emperor Gregor, about Miles's usual activities when quartered in Barrayar's capital city Vorbarr Sultana, and question after question about the Dendarii Mercenaries. Miles, writhing, answered and answered and answered, unable to stop his own rapid gabble. But partway through he hit on a line of poetry, and ended by reciting the whole sonnet. Galen's slaps could not derail him; the strings of association were too strong to break into. After that he managed to jump off the interrogation repeatedly. Works with strong meter and rhyme worked best, bad narrative verse, obscene Dendarii drinking songs, anything a chance word or phrase from his interrogators could trigger. His memory seemed phenomenal. Galen's face was darkening with frustration.

"At this rate we'll be here till next winter," said one of the guards in disgust.

Miles's bleeding lips peeled back in a maniacal grin. " 'Now is the winter of our discontent,' " he cried, " 'made glorious summer by this sun of York—' "

It had been years since he'd memorized the ancient play, but the vivid iambic pentameter carried him along relentlessly. Short of beating him into unconsciousness, there seemed nothing Galen could do to turn him off. Miles was not even to the end of Act I when the two guards dragged him back down the lift tube and threw him roughly back into his prison room.

Once there, his rapid-firing neurons drove him from wall to wall, pacing and reciting, jumping up and down off the bench at appropriate moments, doing all the women's parts in a high falsetto. He got all the way through to the last Amen! before he collapsed on the floor and lay gasping.

Captain Galeni, who had been scrunched into the corner on his bench with his arms wrapped protectively around his ears for the last hour, lifted his head cautiously from their circle. "Are you quite finished?" he said mildly.

Miles rolled over on his back and stared blankly up at the light. "Three cheers for literacy . . . I feel sick."

"I'm not surprised." Galen looked pale and ill himself, still shaky from the aftereffects of the stun. "What was that?"

"The play, or the drug?"

"I recognized the play, thank you. What drug?"

"Fast-penta."

"You're joking."

"Not joking. I have several weird drug reactions. There's a whole chemical class of sedatives I can't touch. Apparently this is related."

"What a piece of good fortune!"

I seriously doubt the utility of keeping him alive. . . .

"I don't think so," Miles said distantly. He lurched to his feet, ricocheted into the bathroom, threw up, and passed out.

He awoke with the unblinking glare of the overhead light needling his eyes, and flung an arm over his face to shut it out. Someone—Galeni?—had put him back on his bench. Galeni was asleep now across the room, breathing heavily. A meal, cold and congealed, sat on a plate at the end of Miles's bench. It must be deep night. Miles contemplated the food queasily, then put it down out of sight under his bench. Time stretched inexorably as he tossed, turned, sat up, lay down, aching and nauseous, escape even into sleep receding out of reach.

The next morning after breakfast they came and took not Miles but Galeni. The captain left with a look of grim distaste in his eyes. Sounds of a violent altercation came from the hallway, Galeni trying to get himself stunned, a draconian but surely effective way of avoiding interrogation. He did not succeed. Their captors returned him, giggling vacuously, after a marathon number of hours.

He lay limply on his bench giving vent to an occasional snicker for what might have been another hour before slipping into torpid sleep. Miles gallantly resisted taking advantage of the residual effects of the drug to get in a few questions of his own. Alas, fast-penta subjects remembered their experiences. Miles was fairly certain by now that one of Galeni's personal triggers was in the key word *betrayal*.

Galeni returned to a thick but cold consciousness at last, looking ill. Fast-penta hangover was a remarkably unpleasant experience; in that, Miles's response to the drug had not been at all idiosyncratic.

Miles winced in sympathy as Galeni made his own trip to the washroom.

Galeni returned to sit heavily on his bench. His eye fell on his cold dinner plate; he prodded it dubiously with an experimental forefinger. "You want this?" he asked Miles.

"No, thanks."

"Mm." Galeni shoved the plate out of sight under his bench and sat back rather nervelessly.

"What were they after," Miles jerked his head doorward, "in your interrogation?"

"Personal history, mostly, this time." Galeni contemplated his socks, which were getting stiff with grime; but Miles was not sure Galeni was seeing what he was looking at. "He seems to have this strange difficulty grasping that I actually mean what I say. He had apparently genuinely convinced himself that he had only to reveal himself, to whistle, to bring me to his heel as I had run when I was fourteen. As if the weight of my entire adult life counted for nothing. As if I'd put on this uniform for a joke, or out of despair or confusion—anything but a reasoned and principled decision."

No need to ask who "he" was. Miles grinned sourly. "What, it wasn't for the spiffy boots?"

"I'm just dazzled by the glittering tinsel of neo-fascism," Galeni informed him blandly.

"Is that how he phrased it? Anyway, it's feudalism, not fascism, apart maybe from some of the late Emperor Ezar Vorbarra's experiments in centralization. The glittering tinsel of neo-feudalism I will grant you."

"I am thoroughly familiar with the principles of Barrayaran government, thank you," remarked Dr. Galeni.

"Such as they are," muttered Miles. "It was all arrived at by improvisation, y'know."

"Yes, I do. Glad to know you aren't as historically illiterate as the average young officer coming up these days."

"So . . ." Miles said, "if it wasn't for the gold braid and the shiny boots, why *are* you with us?"

"Oh, of *course*," Galeni rolled his eyes toward the light fixture, "I get a sadistic psychosexual kick out of being a bully, goon, and thug. It's a power trip."

"Hi," Miles waved from across the room, "talk to me, not him, huh? He had his turn."

"Mm." Galeni crossed his arms glumly. "In a sense, it's true, I suppose. I am on a power trip. Or I was."

"For what it's worth, that's not a secret to the Barrayaran high command."

"Nor to any Barrayaran, though people from outside your society seem to miss it regularly. How do they imagine such an apparently caste-rigid society has survived the incredible stresses of the century since the end of the Time of Isolation without exploding? In a way, the Imperial Service has performed something of the same social function as the medieval church once did here on Earth, as a safety valve. Through it, anyone of talent can launder his caste origins. Twenty years of Imperial service, and they step out for all practical purposes an honorary Vor. The names may not have changed since Dorca Vorbarra's day, when the Vor were a closed caste of self-serving horse goons—"

Miles grinned at this description of his great-grandfather's generation.

"—but the substance has altered out of all recognition. And yet through it all the Vor have managed, however desperately, to hang on to certain vital principles of service and sacrifice. To the knowledge that it is possible for a man who would not stop and stoop to take, to yet run down the street for a chance to give. . . ." He stopped short, and cleared his throat, flushing. "My Ph.D. thesis, y'know. 'The Barrayaran Imperial Service, A Century of Change.' "

"I see."

"I wanted to serve Komarr—"

"As your father before you," Miles finished. Galeni glanced up sharply, suspecting sarcasm, but found, Miles trusted, only sympathetic irony in his eyes.

Galeni's hand opened in a brief gesture of agreement and understanding. "Yes. And no. None of the cadets who entered the service when I did have yet seen a shooting war. I saw one from street level—"

"I had suspected you were more intimately acquainted with the Komarr Revolt than the Security reports seemed to believe," remarked Miles.

"As a drafted apprentice to my father," Galeni confirmed. "Some night forays, other missions of sabotage—I was small for my age. There are places a child, idly playing, can pass where an adult would be stopped. Before my fourteenth birthday I had helped kill men. . . . I have no illusions about the glorious Imperial troops during the Komarr Revolt. I saw men wearing this uniform," he waved a hand down the piped length of his green trousers, "do shameful things. In anger or fear, in frustration or desperation, sometimes just in idle viciousness. But I could not see that it made any practical difference to the corpses, ordinary people caught in the cross fire, whether they were burned down by evil invader plasma fire, or blown to bits by good patriotic gravitic implosions. Freedom? We can scarcely pretend that Komarr was a democracy even before the Barrayarans came. My father cried that Barrayar had destroyed Komarr, but when I looked around, Komarr was still there."

"You can't tax a wasteland," Miles murmured.

"I saw a little girl once—" He stopped, bit his lip, plunged on. "What makes a practical difference is that there not be war. I mean—I meant—to make that practical difference. A Service career, an honorable retirement, leverage to a ministerial appointment— then up through the ranks on the civil side, then . . ."

"The viceroyalty of Komarr?" suggested Miles.

"That hope would be slightly megalomanic," said Galeni. "An appointment on his staff, though, certainly." His vision faded, palpably, as he glanced around their cell-room, and his lips puffed on a silent, self-derisive laugh. "My father, on the other hand, wants revenge. Foreign domination of Komarr being not merely prone to abuse, but intrinsically evil by first principle. Trying to make it un-foreign by integration is not compromise, it's collaboration, capitulation. Komarran revolutionaries died for my sins. And so on. And on."

"He's still attempting to persuade you to come over to his side, then."

"Oh, yes. I believe he will keep talking till he pulls the trigger."

"Not that I'm asking you to, um, compromise your principles or anything, but I really don't see that it would be any extra skin off my nose if you were to, say, plead for your own life," Miles mentioned diffidently. " 'He who fights and runs away lives to fight another day,' and all that."

Galeni shook his head. "For precisely that logic, I cannot surrender. Not will not—*can* not. He can't trust me. If I reversed, he would too, and be compelled to argue himself into killing me as hard as he now feigns to be arguing himself out. He's already sacrificed my brother. In a sense, my mother's death came ultimately from that loss, and others he inflicted on her in the name of the cause." He added in a flash of self-consciousness, "I suppose that makes this all seem very oedipal. But—the anguish of making the hard choices has always appealed to the romance in his soul."

Miles shook his head. "I'll allow you know the man better than I do. And yet . . . well, people do get hypnotized by the hard choices. And stop looking for alternatives. The will to be stupid is a very powerful force—"

This surprised a brief laugh from Galeni, and a thoughtful look.

"—but there are always alternatives. Surely it's more important to be loyal to a person than a principle."

Galeni raised his eyebrows. "I suppose that shouldn't surprise me, coming from a Barrayaran. From a society that traditionally organizes itself by internal oaths of fealty instead of an external framework of abstract law—is that your father's politics showing?"

Miles cleared his throat. "My mother's theology, actually. From two completely different starting points they arrive at this odd intersection in their views. Her theory is that principles come and go, but that human souls are immortal, and you should therefore throw in your lot with the greater part. My mother tends to be extremely logical. Betan, y'know."

Galeni sat forward in interest, his hands loosely clasped between his knees. "It surprises me more that your mother had anything to do with your upbringing at all. Barrayaran society tends to be so, er, aggressively patriarchal. And Countess Vorkosigan has the reputation of being the most invisible of political wives."

"Yeah, invisible," Miles agreed cheerfully, "like air. If it disappeared you'd hardly miss it. Till the next time you came to inhale." He suppressed a twinge of homesickness, and a fiercer fear—*If I don't make it back this time. . . .*

Galeni smiled polite disbelief. "It's hard to imagine that Great Admiral yielding to, ah, uxorial blandishments."

Miles shrugged. "He yields to logic. My mother is one of the few people I know who has almost completely conquered the will to be stupid." Miles frowned introspectively. "Your father's a fairly bright man, is he not? I mean, given his premises. He's eluded Security, he's been able to put together at least temporarily effective courses of action, he's got follow-through, he's certainly persistent. . . ."

"Yes, I suppose so," said Galeni.

"Hm."

"What?"

"Well . . . there's something about this whole plot that bothers me."

"I should think there's a great deal!"

"Not personally. Logically. In the abstract. As a plot, *qua* plot, there's something that doesn't quite add up even from his point of view. Of course it's a scramble—chances must be taken, it's always like that when you try to convert any plan into action—but over and above the practical problems. Something intrinsically screwy."

"It's daring. But if he succeeds, he'll have it all. If your clone takes the Imperium, he'll stand in the center of Barrayar's power structure. He'll control it all. Absolute power."

"Bullshit," said Miles.

Galeni's brows rose.

"Just because Barrayar's system of checks and balances is unwritten doesn't mean it's not there. You must know the Emperor's power consists of no more than the cooperation he is able to extract, from the military, from the counts, from the ministries, from the people generally. Terrible things happen to emperors who fail to perform their function to the satisfaction of all these groups. The Dismemberment of Mad Emperor Yuri wasn't so very long ago. My father was actually present for that remarkably gory execution, as a boy. And yet people still wonder why he's never tried to take the Imperium for himself!

"So here we have a picture of this imitation me, grabbing for the throne in a bloody coup, followed by a rapid transfer of power and privilege to Komarr, say even granting its independence. Results?"

"Go on," said Galeni, fascinated.

"The military will be offended, because I'm throwing away their hard-won victories. The counts will be offended, because I'll have promoted myself above them. The ministries will be offended, because the loss of Komarr as a tax farm and trade nexus will reduce their power. The people will be offended for all these reasons plus the fact that I am in their eyes a mutant, physically unclean in Barrayaran tradition. Infanticide for obvious birth defects is still going on secretly in the back country, do you know, despite its being outlawed for four decades? If you can think of any fate nastier than being dismembered alive, well, that poor clone is headed straight for it. I'm not sure even I could ride the Imperium and survive, even without the Komarran complications. And that kid's only—what—seventeen, eighteen years old?" Miles subsided. "It's a stupid plot. Or . . ."

"Or?"

"Or it's some other plot."

"Hm."

"Besides," said Miles more slowly, "why should Ser Galen, who if I'm reading him right hates my father more than he loves—anybody, be going to all this trouble to put Vorkosigan blood on the Barrayaran Imperial throne? It's a most obscure revenge. And how, if by some miracle he succeeds in getting the boy Imperial power, does he then propose to control him?"

"Conditioning?" suggested Galeni. "Threats to expose him?"

"Mm, maybe." At this impasse, Miles fell silent. After long moments he spoke again.

"I think the real plot is much simpler and smarter. He means to drop the clone into the middle of a power struggle just to create chaos on Barrayar. The results of that struggle are irrelevant. The clone is merely a pawn. A revolt on Komarr is timed to rise during the point of maximum uproar, the bloodier the better, back on Barrayar. He must have an ally in the woodwork prepared to step in with enough military force to block Barrayar's wormhole exit. God, I hope he hasn't made a devil's deal with the Cetagandans for that."

"Trading a Barrayaran occupation for a Cetagandan one strikes me as a zero-sum move in the extreme— surely he's not that mad. But what happens to your rather expensive clone?" said Galeni, puzzling out the threads.

Miles smiled crookedly. "Ser Galen doesn't care. He's just a means to an end." His mouth opened, closed, opened again. "Except that—I keep hearing my mother's voice, in my head. That's where I picked up that perfect Betan accent, y'know, that I use for Admiral Naismith. I can hear her now."

"And what does she say?" Galeni's brows twitched in amusement.

"*Miles*—she says—*what have you done with your baby brother?!*"

"Your clone is hardly that!" choked Galeni.

"On the contrary, by Betan law my clone is *exactly* that."

"Madness." Galeni paused. "Your mother could not possibly expect you to look out for this creature."

"Oh, yes she could." Miles sighed glumly. A knot of unspoken panic made a lump in his chest. Complex, too complex . . .

"And this is the woman that—you claim—is behind the man who's behind the Barrayaran Imperium? I don't see it. Count Vorkosigan is the most pragmatic of politicians. Look at the entire Komarr integration scheme."

"Yes," said Miles cordially. "Look at it."

Galeni shot him a suspicious glance. "Persons before principles, eh?" he said slowly at last.

"Yep."

Galeni subsided wearily on his bench. After a time one corner of his mouth twitched up. "My father," he murmured, "was always a man of great—principles."

Chapter Ten

With every passing minute, the chances of rescue seemed bleaker. In time another breakfast-type meal was delivered, making this, if such a clock was to be relied upon, the third day of Miles's incarceration. The clone, it appeared, had not made any immediate and obvious mistake to reveal his true nature to Ivan or Elli. And if he could pass Ivan and Elli, he could pass anywhere. Miles shivered.

He inhaled deeply, swung from his bench, and put himself through a series of calisthenics, trying to clear the residual mush of drug from his body and brain. Galeni, sunk this morning in an unpleasant mixture of drug hangover, depression, and helpless rage, sprawled on his bench and watched without comment.

Wheezing, sweating, and dizzy, Miles paced the cell to cool down. The place was beginning to stink, and this wasn't helping. Not too hopefully, he went to the washroom and tried the sock-down-the-drain trick. As he had suspected, the same sensor system that turned on the water with a pass of his hand turned it off prior to overflow. The toilet worked fail-safe the same way. And even if by some miracle he managed to get their captors to open the door, Galeni had demonstrated how poor the chance was of fighting their way out against stunners.

No. His sole point of contact with the enemy lay in the flow of information they hoped to squeeze from him. It was after all the only reason he was still alive. As levers went it was potentially very powerful. Informational sabotage. If the clone wasn't going to make mistakes on his own, perhaps he needed a little push. But how could Miles work it, tanked on fast-penta? He could stand in the center of the cell and make spurious confidences to the light fixture, a la Captain Galeni, but could hardly expect to be taken seriously.

He was sitting on his bench frowning at his cold toes—the clammy wet socks were laid out to dry—when the door clicked open. Two guards with stunners. One covered Galeni, who sneered back without moving. The guard's finger twitched tensely on the trigger; no hesitation there. They did not need Galeni conscious today. The other one gestured Miles out. If Captain Galeni was to be stunned instantly, there was not a great deal of point in Miles tackling the guards unilaterally; he sighed and obeyed, stepping into the corridor.

Miles exhaled in startlement. The clone stood waiting, staring at him with devouring eyes.

The alter-Miles was dressed in his Dendarii admiral's uniform. It fit perfectly, right down to the combat boots.

Rather breathlessly, the clone directed the guards to escort Miles to the study. This time he was tied firmly to a chair in the middle of the room. Interestingly, Galen was not there.

"Wait outside the door," the clone told the guards. They looked at each other, shrugged, and obeyed, hauling a couple of padded chairs with them for comfort.

The silence when the door closed was profound. His duplicate walked slowly around Miles at the safe distance of a meter, as though Miles were a snake that might suddenly strike. He fetched up to face him a good meter and a half away, leaning hip-slung against the comconsole desk, one booted foot swinging. Miles recognized the posture as his own. He would never be able to use it again without being painfully self-aware—a little piece of himself the clone had stolen from him. One of many little pieces. He felt suddenly perforated, frayed, tattered. And afraid.

"How, ah," Miles began, and had to pause and clear his thick, dry throat, "however did you manage to escape the embassy?"

"I've just spent the morning attending to Admiral Naismith's duties," the clone told him. Smugly, Miles fancied. "Your bodyguard thought she was handing me back to Barrayaran embassy security. The Barrayarans will think my Komarran guard is a Dendarii. And I win myself a little slice of unaccounted time. Neat, no?"

"Risky," remarked Miles. "What do you hope to gain that's worth it? Fast-penta doesn't exactly work on me, y'know." In fact, Miles noticed, the hypospray was nowhere in sight. Missing, like Ser Galen. Curious.

"It doesn't matter." The clone made a sharp throwaway gesture, another piece torn from Miles, *twang*. "I don't care if you talk truth or lies. I just want to hear you talk. To see you, just once. You, you,

you—" the clone's voice dropped to a whisper, *twang*, "how I've come to hate you."

Miles cleared his throat again. "I might point out that, in point of fact, we met for the very first time three nights ago. Whatever was done to you was not done by me."

"You," said the clone, "screwed me over just by existing. It hurts me that you breathe." He spread a hand across his chest. "However, that will be cured very shortly. But Galen promised me an interview first." He wheeled off the desk and began to pace; Miles's feet twitched. "He promised me."

"And where is Ser Galen this morning, by the way?" Miles inquired mildly.

"Out." The clone favored him with a sour grin. "For a little slice of time."

Miles's brows rose. "This conversation is unauthorized?"

"He promised me. But then he reneged. Wouldn't say why."

"Ah—hm. Since yesterday?"

"Yes." The clone paused in his pacing to regard Miles through narrowed eyes. "Why?"

"I think it may have been something I said. Thinking out loud," Miles said. "I'm afraid I figured out one too many things about his plot. Something even you weren't supposed to know. He was afraid I'd spill it under fast-penta. That suited me. The less you were able to pump from me, the more likely you'd be to make a mistake." Miles waited, barely breathing, to see which way this bait would be taken. A whiff of the exhilarated hyperconsciousness of combat thrilled along his nerves.

"I'll bite," said the clone agreeably. His eyes gleamed, sardonic. "Spill it, then."

When he was seventeen, this clone's age, he'd

been—inventing the Dendarii Mercenaries, Miles recalled. Perhaps it would be better not to underestimate him. What would it be like to be a clone? How far under the skin did their similarity end? "You're a sacrifice," Miles stated bluntly. "He does not intend for you to make it alive to the Barrayaran Imperium."

"Do you think I haven't figured that out?" the clone scoffed. "I know he doesn't think I can make it. Nobody thinks I can make it—"

Miles's breath caught as from a blow. This *twang* bit bone-deep.

"But I'll show them. Ser Galen," the clone's eyes glittered, "is going to be very surprised at what happens when I come to power."

"So will you," Miles predicted morosely.

"D'you think I'm stupid?" the clone demanded.

Miles shook his head. "I know *exactly* how stupid you are, I'm afraid."

The clone smiled tightly. "Galen and his friends spent a month farting around London, chasing you, just trying to set up for the switch. It was I who told them to have you kidnap yourself. I've studied you longer than any of them, harder than all of them. I knew you couldn't resist. I can outthink you."

Demonstrably true, alas, at least in this instance. Miles fought off a wave of despair. The kid was good, too good—he had it all, right down to the screaming tension radiating from every muscle in his body. *Twang.* Or was that home-grown? Could different pressures produce the same warps? What would it be like, behind those eyes . . . ?

Miles's eye fell on the Dendarii uniform. His own insignia winked back at him malevolently as the clone paced. "But you can outthink Admiral Naismith?"

The clone smiled proudly. "I got your soldiers

released from jail this morning. Something you hadn't been able to do, evidently."

"Danio?" Miles croaked, fascinated. *No, no, say it isn't so. . . .*

"He's back on duty." The clone nodded incisively.

Miles suppressed a small moan.

The clone paused, glanced at Miles intently, some of his decisiveness falling away. "Speaking of Admiral Naismith—are you sleeping with that woman?"

What kind of life had this kid led? Miles wondered anew. Secret—always watched, constantly force-tutored, allowed contact with only a few selected persons—almost cloistered. Had the Komarrans thought to include *that* in his training, or was he a seventeen-year-old virgin? In which case he must be obsessed with sex . . . "Quinn," said Miles, "is six years older than *me*. Extremely experienced. And demanding. Accustomed to a high degree of finesse in her chosen partner. Are you an initiate in the variant practices of the Deeva Tau love cults as practiced on Kline Station?" A safe challenge, Miles judged, as he'd just this minute invented them. "Are you familiar with the Seven Secret Roads of Female Pleasure? After she's climaxed four or five times, though, she'll usually let you up—"

The clone circled him, looking distinctly unsettled. "You're lying. I think."

"Maybe." Miles smiled toothily, only wishing the improvised fantasy were true. "Consider what you'd risk, finding out."

The clone glowered at him. He glowered back.

"Do your bones break like mine?" Miles asked suddenly. Horrible thought. Suppose, for every blow Miles had suffered, they had broken this one's bones to match. Suppose for every miscalculated foolish risk of Miles's, the clone had paid full measure—reason indeed to hate. . . .

"No."

Miles breathed concealed relief. So, their med-sensor readings wouldn't exactly match. "It must be a short-term plot, eh?"

"I mean to be on top in six months."

"So I'd understood. And whose space fleet will bottle all the chaos on Barrayar, behind its wormhole exit, while Komarr rises again?" Miles made his voice light, trying to appear only casually interested in this vital bit of intelligence.

"We were going to call in the Cetagandans. That's been broken off."

His worst fears . . . "Broken off? I'm delighted, but why, in an escapade singularly lacking in sanity, should you have come to your senses on that one?"

"We found something better, ready to hand." The clone smirked strangely. "An independent military force, highly experienced in space blockade duties, with no unfortunate ties to other planetary neighbors who might be tempted to muscle in on the action. And personally and fiercely loyal, it appears, to my slightest whim. The Dendarii Mercenaries."

Miles tried to lunge for the clone's throat. The clone recoiled. Being still firmly tied to the chair, Miles and it toppled forward, mashing his face painfully into the carpet. "No, no, no!" he gibbered, bucking, trying to kick loose. "You moron! It'd be a slaughter—!"

The two Komarran guards tumbled through the door. "What, what happened?"

"Nothing." The clone, pale, ventured out from behind the comconsole desk where he'd retreated. "He fell over. Straighten him back, will you?"

"Fell or was pushed," muttered one of the Komarrans

as the pair of them yanked the chair back upright. Miles perforce came with it. The guard stared with interest at his face. A warm wetness, rapidly cooling, trickled itchily down Miles's upper lip and three-day moustache stubble. Bloody nose? He glanced down cross-eyed, and licked at it. Calm. Calm. The clone could never get that far with the Dendarii. His future failure would be little consolation to a dead Miles, though.

"Do you, ah, need some help for this part?" the older of the two Komarrans asked the clone. "There is a kind of science in torture, you know. To get the maximum pain for the minimum damage. I had an uncle who told me what the Barrayaran Security goons used to do. . . . Given that the fast-penta is useless."

"He doesn't need help," snapped Miles, at the same moment that the clone began, "I don't want help—" then both paused to stare at each other, Miles self-possessed again, regaining his wind, the clone taken slightly aback.

But for the outward and visible marker of the damn beard, now would be the perfect time to begin screaming that Vorkosigan had overpowered and changed clothes with him, he was the clone, couldn't they tell the difference and untie me you cretins! A non-opportunity, alas.

The clone straightened, trying to regain some dignity. "Leave us, please. When I want you, I'll call you."

"Or maybe I will," remarked Miles sunnily. The clone glared. The two Komarrans exited with doubtful backward glances.

"It's a stupid idea," Miles began immediately they were alone. "You've got to grasp, the Dendarii are an elite bunch—largely—but by planetary standards they are a small force. *Small,* you understand *small?* Small is for covert operations, hit and run, intelligence gathering. Not all-out slogging matches for a fixed spatial field with a whole developed planet's resources and will backing the enemy. You've got no sense of the economics of war! I swear to God, you're not thinking past that first six months. Not that you need to—you'll be dead before the end of the year, I expect. . . ."

The clone's smile was razor-thin. "The Dendarii, like myself, are intended as a sacrifice. Dead mercenaries, after all, don't need to be paid." He paused, and looked at Miles curiously. "How far ahead do you think?"

"These days, about twenty years," Miles admitted glumly. And a fat lot of good it did him. Consider Captain Galeni. In his mind Miles already saw him as the best viceroy Komarr was ever likely to get—his death, not the loss of a minor Imperial officer of dubious origins, but of the first link in a chain of thousands of lives striving for a less tormented future. A future when Lieutenant Miles Vorkosigan would surely be subsumed by Count Miles Vorkosigan, and need sane friends in high places. If he could bring Galeni through this mess alive, and sane . . . "I admit," Miles added, "when I was your age I got through about one quarter hour at a time."

The clone snorted. "A century ago, was it?"

"Seems like it. I've always had the sense that I'd better live fast, if I'm to fit it all in."

"Prescient of you. See how much you can fit into the next twenty-four hours. That's when I have my orders to ship out. At which point you will become— redundant."

So soon. . . . No time left for experiments. No time left for anything but to be right, once.

Miles swallowed. "The prime minister's death must be planned, or the destabilization of the Barrayaran government will not occur, even if Emperor Gregor is assassinated. So tell me," he said carefully, "what fate do you and Galen have planned for our father?"

The clone's head jerked back. "Oh, no you don't. You are not my brother, and the Butcher of Komarr was never a father to me."

"How about your mother?"

"I have none. I came out of a replicator."

"So did I," Miles remarked, "before the medics were done. It never made any difference to her that I could see. Being Betan, she's quite free of anti-birth technology prejudices. It doesn't matter to her how you got here, but only what you do after you arrive. I'm afraid having a mother is a fate you can't avoid, from the moment she discovers your existence."

The clone waved the phantom Countess Vorkosigan away. "A null factor. She is nothing in Barrayaran politics."

"Is that so?" Miles muttered, then controlled his tongue. No time. "And yet you'd continue, knowing Ser Galen means to betray you to your death?"

"When I am Emperor of Barrayar—then we shall see about Ser Galen."

"If you mean to betray him anyway, why wait?"

The clone cocked his head, eyes narrowing. "Ha?"

"There's another alternative for you." Miles made his voice calm, persuasive. "Let me go now. And come with me. Back to Barrayar. You are my brother—like it or not; it's a biological fact, and it won't ever go away. Nobody gets to choose their relatives anyway, clone or no. I mean, given a choice, would you pick Ivan Vorpatril for your cousin?"

The clone choked slightly, but did not interrupt. He was beginning to look faintly fascinated.

"But there he is. And he's exactly as much your cousin as mine. Did you realize you have a name?" Miles demanded suddenly. "That's another thing you don't get to choose on Barrayar. Second son—that's you, my twin-six-years-delayed—gets the second names of his maternal and paternal grandfathers, just as the first son gets stuck with their first names. That makes you Mark Pierre. Sorry about the Pierre. Grandfather always hated it. You are Lord Mark Pierre Vorkosigan, in your own right, on Barrayar." He spoke faster and faster, inspired by the clone's arrested eyes.

"What have you ever dreamed of being? Any education you want, Mother will see that you get. Betans are very big on education. Have you dreamed of escape—how about Licensed Star Pilot Mark Vorkosigan? Commerce? Farming? We have a family wine business, from grape vines to export crates—does science interest you? You could go live with your Grandmother Naismith on Beta Colony, study at the best research academies. You have an aunt and uncle there too, do you realize? Two cousins and a second cousin. If backward benighted Barrayar doesn't appeal to you, there's a whole 'nother life waiting on Beta Colony, to which Barrayar and all its troubles is scarcely a wrinkle on the event horizon. Your cloned origin wouldn't be novel enough to be worth mentioning, there. Any life you want. The galaxy at your fingertips. Choice— freedom—ask, and it's yours." He had to stop for breath.

The clone's face was white. "You lie," he hissed. "Barrayaran Security would never let me live."

Not, alas, a fear without force. "But imagine for one minute it is, it could be real. It could be yours. My word as Vorkosigan. My protection as Lord Vorkosigan, against all comers up to and including

Imperial Security." Miles gulped a little as he made this promise. "Galen offers you death on a silver platter. I can get you life. I can get it for you wholesale, for God's sake."

Was this informational sabotage? He'd meant to set the clone up for a fall, if he could . . . *what have you done with your baby brother?*

The clone threw back his head and laughed, a sharp hysterical bark. "My God, look at yourself! A prisoner, tied to a chair, hours from death—" He swept Miles a huge, ironic bow. "Oh noble lord, I am overwhelmed by your generosity. But somehow, I don't think your protection is worth spit, just now." He strode up to Miles, the closest he had yet ventured. "Flaming megalomaniac. You can't even protect yourself—" impulsively, he slapped Miles across the face, across yesterday's bruises, *"can* you?" He stepped back, startled by the force of his own experiment, and unconsciously held his stinging hand to his mouth a moment. Miles's bleeding lips peeled back in a grin, and the clone dropped his hand hastily.

So. This one has never struck a man for real before. Nor killed either, I wager. Oh, little virgin, are you ever in for a bloody deflowering.

"Can you?" the clone finished.

Gah! He takes my truth for lies, when I meant to have him take my lies for truth—some saboteur I am. Why am I compelled to speak the truth to him?

Because he is my brother, and we have failed him. Failed to discover him earlier—failed to mount a rescue—"Did you ever dream of rescue?" Miles asked suddenly. "After you knew who you were—or even before? What kind of childhood did you have, anyway? Orphans are supposed to dream of golden parents, riding to their rescue—for you, it could have been true."

The clone snorted bitter contempt. "Hardly. I always knew the score. I knew what I was from the beginning. The clones of Jackson's Whole are farmed out, y'see, to paid foster parents, to raise them to maturity. Vat-raised clones tend to have unpleasant health problems—susceptibility to infection, bad cardio-vascular conditioning—the people who are paying to have their brains transplanted expect to wake up in a healthy body.

"I had a kind of foster-brother once—a little older than me—" the clone paused, took a deep breath, "raised with me. But not educated with me. I taught him to read, a little. . . . Shortly before the Komarrans came and got me, the laboratory people took him away. It was sheer chance that I saw him again afterwards. I'd been sent on an errand to pick up a package at the shuttleport, though I wasn't supposed to go into town. I saw him across the concourse, entering the first-class passenger lounge. Ran up to him. Only it wasn't him any more. There was some horrible rich old man, sitting in his head. His body-guard shoved me back. . . ."

The clone wheeled, and snarled at Miles. "Oh, I knew the score. But once, once, just this once, a Jackson's Whole clone is turning it around. Instead of you cannibalizing my life, I shall have yours."

"Then where will your life be?" asked Miles desperately. "Buried in an imitation of Miles, where will Mark be then? Are you sure it will be only me, lying in my grave?"

The clone flinched. "When I am emperor of Barrayar," he said through his teeth, "no one will be able to get at me. Power is safety."

"Let me give you a hint," said Miles. "There is no

safety. Only varying states of risk. And failure." And was he letting his old only-child loneliness betray him, at this late date? Was there anybody home, behind those too-familiar grey eyes staring back at him so fiercely? What snare would hook him? Beginnings, the clone clearly understood beginnings; it was endings he lacked experience of. . . .

"I always knew," said Miles softly—the clone leaned closer—"why my parents never had another child. Besides the tissue damage from the soltoxin gas. But they could have had another child, with the technologies then available on Beta Colony. My father always pretended it was because he didn't dare leave Barrayar, but my mother could have taken his genetic sample and gone alone.

"The reason was me. These deformities. If a whole son had existed, there would have been horrendous social pressure put on them to disinherit me and put him in my place as heir. You think I'm exaggerating, the horror Barrayar has of mutation? My own grandfather tried to force the issue by smothering me in my cradle, when I was an infant, after he lost the abortion argument. Sergeant Bothari—I had a bodyguard from birth—who stood about two meters tall, didn't dare draw a weapon on the Great General. So the sergeant just picked him up, and held him over his head, quite apologetically—on a third-story balcony— until General Piotr asked, equally politely, to be let down. After that, they had an understanding. I had this story from my grandfather, much later; the sergeant didn't talk much.

"Later, my grandfather taught me to ride. And gave me that dagger you have stuck in your shirt. And willed me half his lands, most of which still glow in the dark from Cetagandan nuclears. And stood behind me in a hundred excruciating, peculiarly

Barrayaran social situations, and wouldn't let me run away, till I was forced to learn to handle them or die. I did consider death.

"My parents, on the other hand, were so *kind*, and *careful*—their absolute lack of suggestion spoke louder than shouting. Overprotected me even as they let me risk my bones in every sport, in the military career—because they let me stifle my siblings before they could even be born. Lest I think, for one moment, that I wasn't good enough to please them. . . ." Miles ran down abruptly, then added, "Perhaps you're lucky not to have a family. They only drive you crazy after all."

And how am I to rescue this brother I never knew I had? Not to mention survive, escape, foil the Komarran plot, rescue Captain Galeni from his father, save the emperor and my father from assassination, and prevent the Dendarii Mercenaries from being put through a meat grinder . . . ?

No. If only I can save my brother, all the rest must follow. I'm right. Here, now, is the place to push, to fight, before the first weapon is ever drawn. Snap the first link, and the whole chain comes loose.

"I know exactly what I am," said the clone. "You won't make a dead fool of me."

"You are what you do. Choose again, and change."

The clone hesitated, meeting Miles's eyes directly for almost the first time. "What guarantee could you possibly give me, that I could trust?"

"My word as Vorkosigan?"

"Bah!"

Miles considered this problem seriously, from the clone's— Mark's—point of view. "Your entire life to date has been centered on betrayal, on one level or another. Since you've had zero experience with unbroken trust, naturally you cannot judge with confidence. Suppose you tell *me* what guarantee you would believe?"

The clone opened his mouth, closed it, and stood silent, reddening slightly.

Miles almost smiled. "You see the little fork, eh?" he said softly. "The logical flaw? The man who assumes everything is a lie is at least as mistaken as the one who assumes everything is true. If no guarantee can suit you, perhaps the flaw is not in the guarantee, but in you. And you're the only one who can do anything about that."

"What can I do?" muttered the clone. For a moment, anguished doubt flickered in his eyes.

"Test it," breathed Miles.

The clone stood locked. Miles's nostrils flared. He was so close—so close—he almost had him—

The door burst open. Galen, dusky with fury, stormed in, flanked by the startled Komarran guards.

"Damn, the time . . . !" the clone hissed. He straightened guiltily, his chin jerking up.

Damn the timing! Miles screamed silently in his head. If he had had just a few more minutes—

"What the hell do you think you're doing?" demanded Galen. His voice blurred with rage, like a sled over gravel.

"Improving my chances of survival past the first five minutes I set foot on Barrayar, I trust," said the clone coolly. "You do need me to survive a little while, even to serve your purposes, no?"

"I told you, it was too damn dangerous!" Galen was almost, but not quite, shouting. "I've had a lifetime of experience fighting the Vorkosigans. They are the most insidious propagandists ever to cloak self-serving greed with pseudo-patriotism. And this one is stamped from the same mold. His lies will trip you, trap you—he's a subtle little bastard, and he never takes his eye off the main chance."

"But his choice of lies was very interesting." The clone moved about like a nervous horse, kicking at the carpet, half-defiant, half-placating. "You've had me study how he moves, talks, writes. But I've never been really clear on how he thinks."

"And now?" purred Galen dangerously.

The clone shrugged. "He's looney. I think he really believes his own propaganda."

"The question is, do you?"

Do you, do you? thought Miles frantically.

"Of course not." The clone sniffed, jerked up his chin, *twang*.

Galen jerked his head toward Miles, gathering in the guards by eye. "Take him back and lock him up."

He followed on untrustingly as Miles was untied and dragged out. Miles saw his clone, beyond Galen's shoulder, staring at the floor, still scuffing one booted foot across the carpet.

"Your name is Mark!" Miles shouted back to him as the door shut. "Mark!"

Galen gritted his teeth and swung on Miles, a sincere, unscientific, roundhouse blow. Miles, held by the guards, could not dodge, but did flinch far enough that Galen's fist landed glancingly and did not shatter his jaw. Fortunately, Galen shook out his fist and did not strike again, regaining a thin crust of control.

"Was that for me, or him?" Miles inquired sweetly through an expanding bubble of pain.

"Lock him up," growled Galen to the guards, "and don't let him out again until I, personally, tell you to." He pivoted and swung away up the hall, back to the study.

Two on two, thought Miles sharply as the guards

prodded him down the lift tube to the next level. *Or at any rate, two on one and a half. The odds will never be better, and the time margin can only get worse.*

As the door to his cell-room swung open, Miles saw Galeni—asleep on his bench, the sodden, sullen, despairing ploy of a man shutting out inescapable pain in the only way left to him. He'd spent most of last night pacing the cell silently, restless to the point of being frantic—the sleep that had eluded him then was now captured. Wonderful. *Now,* just when Miles needed him on his feet and primed like an overtightened spring.

Try anyway. "Galeni!" Miles yelled. "Now, Galeni! Come on!"

Simultaneously, he plunged backward into the nearest guard, going for a nerve-pinching grip on the hand that held the stunner. A joint snapped in one of Miles's fingers, but he shook the stunner loose and kicked it across the floor toward Galeni, who was lumbering bewilderedly up off his bench like a warthog out of the mud. Despite his half-conscious state, he reacted fast and accurately, lunging for the stunner, scooping it up, and rolling across the floor out of the line of fire from the door.

Miles's guard wrapped an arm around Miles's neck and lifted him off his feet, lurching around to face the second guard. The little grey rectangle of the business end of the second guard's weapon was so close Miles almost had to cross his eyes to bring it into focus. As the Komarran's finger tightened on the trigger the stunner's buzz fragmented, and Miles's head seemed to explode in a burst of pain and colored lights.

Chapter Eleven

He woke in a hospital bed, an unwelcome but familiar environment. In the distance, out his window, the towers of the skyline of Vorbarr Sultana, capital city of Barrayar, glowed strangely green in the darkness. Imp Mil, then, the Imperial Military Hospital. This room was undecorated in the same severe style he had known as a child, when he'd been in and out of its clinical laboratories and surgeries for painful therapies so often Imp Mil had seemed his home away from home.

A doctor entered. He appeared to be about sixty: clipped greying hair, pale lined face, body thickening with age. DR. GALEN, his name badge read. Hyposprays clanked together in his pockets. Copulating and breeding more, perhaps. Miles had always wondered where hyposprays came from.

"Ah, you're awake," said the doctor gladly. "You're not going to go away on us again this time, now, are you?"

"Go away?" He was tied down with tubes and sensor wires, drips and control leads. It hardly seemed he was going anywhere.

"Catatonia. Cloud-cuckoo-land. Ga-ga. In short, insane. In short is the only way you can go, I suppose, eh? It runs in the family. Blood will tell."

Miles could hear the susurration of his red blood cells, in his ears, whispering thousands of military secrets to each other, cavorting drunkenly in a country dance with molecules of fast-penta which were flipping their hydroxyl groups at him like petticoats. He blinked away the image.

Galen's hand rummaged in his pocket; then his face changed. "Ow!" He yanked his hand out, shook off a hypospray, and sucked at his bleeding thumb. "The little bugger *bit* me." He glanced down, where the young hypospray skittered about uncertainly on its spindly metal legs, and crunched it underfoot. It died with a tiny squeak.

"This sort of mental slippage is not at all unusual in a revived cryo-corpse, of course. You'll get over it," Dr. Galen reassured him.

"Was I dead?"

"Killed outright, on Earth. You spent a year in cryogenic suspension."

Oddly enough, Miles could remember that part. Lying in a glass coffin like a fairy-tale princess under a cruel spell, while figures flitted silent and ghostlike beyond the frosted panels.

"And you revived me?"

"Oh, no. You spoiled. Worst case of freezer-burn you ever saw."

"Oh," Miles paused, nonplussed, and added in a small voice, "Am I still dead, then? Can I have horses at my funeral, like Grandfather?"

'No, no, no, of course not." Dr. Galen clucked like

a mother hen. "You aren't allowed to die, your parents would never permit it. We transplanted your brain into a replacement body. Fortunately, there was one ready to hand. Pre-owned, but hardly used. Congratulations, you're a virgin again. Was it not clever of me, to get your clone all ready for you?"

"My cl— my brother? Mark?" Miles sat bolt upright, tubes falling away from him. Shivering, he pulled out his tray table and stared into the mirror of its polished metal surface. A dotted line of big black stitches ran across his forehead. He stared at his hands, turning them over in horror. "My God. I'm wearing a *corpse*."

He looked up at Galen. "If I'm in here, what have you done with Mark? Where did you put the brain that used to be in this head?"

Galen pointed.

On the table at Miles's bedside squatted a large glass jar. In it a whole brain, like a mushroom on a stem, floated rubbery, dead, and malevolent. The pickling liquid was thick and greenish.

"No, no, no!" cried Miles. "No, no, no!" He struggled out of bed and clutched up the jar. The liquid sloshed cold down over his hands. He ran out into the hall, barefoot, his patient gown flapping open behind him. There had to be spare bodies around here; this was Imp Mil. Suddenly, he remembered where he'd left one.

He burst through another door and found himself in the combat drop shuttle over Dagoola IV. The shuttle hatch was jammed open; black clouds shot with yellow dendrites of lightning boiled beyond. The shuttle lurched, and muddy, wounded men and women in scorched Dendarii combat gear slid and screamed and swore. Miles skidded to the open hatch, still clutching the jar, and stepped out.

Part of the time he floated, part of the time he fell. A crying woman plummeted past him, arms reaching for help, but he couldn't let go of the jar. Her body burst on impact with the ground.

Miles landed feet first on rubbery legs, and almost dropped the jar. The mud was thick and black and sucked at his knees.

Lieutenant Murka's body, and Lieutenant Murka's head, lay just where he'd left them on the battleground. His hands cold and shaking, Miles pulled the brain from the jar and tried to shove the brainstem down the plasma-bolt-cauterized neck. It stubbornly refused to hook in.

"He doesn't have a face anyway," criticized Lieutenant Murka's head from where it lay a few meters off. "He's going to look ugly as sin, walking around on my body with that thing sticking up."

"Shut up, you don't get a vote, you're dead," snarled Miles. The slippery brain slithered through his fingers into the mud. He picked it back out and tried clumsily to rub the black goop off on the sleeve of his Dendarii Admiral's uniform, but the harsh cloth scrubbed up the convoluted surface of Mark's brain, damaging it. Miles patted the tissue surreptitiously back into place, hoping no one would notice, and kept trying to shove the brain stem back in the neck.

Miles's eyes flipped open and stared wide. His breath caught. He was shaking and damp with sweat. The light fixture burned steadily in the unwavering ceiling of the cell, the bench was hard and cold on his back. "God. Thank God," he breathed.

Galeni loomed over him worriedly, one arm supporting himself against the wall. "You all right?"

Miles swallowed, breathed deeply. "You know it's a bad dream when waking up *here* is an improvement."

One of his hands caressed the cool, reassuring solidity of the bench. The other found no stitches across his forehead, though his head did feel like somebody had been doing amateur surgery on it. He blinked, squeezed his eyes shut, opened them again, and with an effort made it up on his right elbow. His left hand was swollen and throbbing. "What happened?"

"It was a draw. One of the guards and I stunned each other. Unfortunately, that left one guard still on his feet. I woke up maybe an hour ago. It was max stun. I don't know how much time we've lost."

"Too much. It was a good try, though. *Dammit.*" He stopped just short of pounding his bad hand on the bench in frustration. "I was so close. I almost had him."

"The guard? It looked like he had you."

"No, my clone. My brother. Whatever he is." Flashes of his dream came back to him, and he shuddered. "Skittish fellow. I think he's afraid he's going to end up in a jar."

"Eh?"

"Eugh." Miles attempted to sit up. The stun had left him feeling nauseous. Muscles spasmed jerkily in his arms and legs. Galeni, clearly in no better shape, tottered back to his own bench and sat.

Some time later the door opened. *Dinner,* thought Miles.

The guard jerked his stunner at them. "Both of you. Out." The second guard backed him up from behind, several meters beyond hope of reach, with another stunner. Miles did not like the looks on their faces, one solemn and pale, the other smiling nervously.

"Captain Galeni," Miles suggested in a voice rather higher in pitch than he'd meant it to come out as they exited, "I think it might be a good time for you to talk to your father, now."

A variety of expressions chased across Galeni's face: anger, mulish stubbornness, thoughtful appraisal, doubt.

"That way." The guard gestured them toward the lift tube. They dropped down, toward the garage level.

"You can do this, I can't," Miles coaxed Galeni in a *sotto voce* singsong out of the corner of his mouth.

Galeni hissed through his teeth: frustration, acquiescence, resolve. As they entered the garage, he turned abruptly to the closer guard and jerked out unwillingly, "I wish to speak to my father."

"You can't."

"I think you had better let me." Galeni's voice was dangerous, edged, at last, with fear.

"It's not up to me. He gave us our orders and left. He's not here."

"Call him."

"He didn't tell me where he would be." The guard's voice was tight and irritated. "And if he had, I wouldn't anyway. Stand over there by that lightflyer."

"How are you going to do it?" asked Miles suddenly. "I really am curious to know. Think of it as my last request." He sidled over toward the lightflyer, his eyes shifting in search of cover, any cover. If he could vault over or dodge around the vehicle before they fired . . .

"Stun you, fly you out over the south coast, drop you in the water," the guard recited. "If the weights work loose and you wash ashore, the autopsy would show only that you'd drowned."

"Not exactly a hands-on murder," Miles observed. "Easier for you that way, I expect." These men were not professional killers, if Miles read them right. Still, there was a first time for everything. That pillar over there was not wide enough to stop a stun bolt.

The array of tools on the far wall presented possibilities . . . his legs were cramping furiously. . . .

"And so the Butcher of Komarr gets his at last," the solemn guard observed in a detached voice. "Indirectly." He raised his stunner.

"Wait!" squeaked Miles.

"What for?"

Miles was still groping for a reply when the garage doors slid open.

"Me!" yelled Elli Quinn. "Freeze!"

A Dendarii patrol streamed past her. In the instant it took the Komarran guard to shift his aim, a Dendarii marksman dropped him. The second guard panicked and bolted for the lift tube. A sprinting Dendarii tackled him from behind, and had him laid out face down on the floor with his hands locked behind him within seconds.

Elli strolled up to Miles and Galeni, pulling a sonic eavesdropper-sensor from her ear. "Gods, Miles, I couldn't believe it was your voice. How did you *do* that?" As she took in his appearance, an expression of extreme disquiet stole over her face.

Miles captured her hands and kissed them. A salute might have been more proper, but his adrenalin was still pumping and this was more heartfelt. Besides, he wasn't in uniform. "Elli, you genius! I should have known the clone couldn't fool you!"

She stared at him, almost recoiling, her voice circling upward in pitch. "What clone?"

"What do you mean, what clone? That's why you're here, isn't it? He blew it—and you came to rescue me—didn't you?"

"Rescue you from what? Miles, you ordered me a week ago to find Captain Galeni, remember?"

"Oh," said Miles. "Yes. So I did."

"So we did. We've been sitting outside this block

of housing units all night, waiting to pick up a positive voiceprint analysis on him, so we could notify the local authorities. They don't appreciate false alarms. But what finally came over the sensors suggested we'd better not wait for the local authorities, so we took a chance—visions of us being arrested en masse for breaking and entering dancing in my head—"

A Dendarii sergeant drifted up and saluted. "Damn, sir, how'd you do that?" He trotted on waving a scanner without waiting for reply.

"Only to find you'd beaten us to it."

"Well, in a sense, yes . . ." Miles massaged his throbbing forehead. Galeni stood scratching his beard and taking it all in without comment. Galeni could say nothing at noticeable volume.

"Remember, three or four nights ago when you took me to be kidnapped so's I could penetrate the opposition and find out who they were and what they wanted?"

"Yeah . . ."

"Well," Miles took a deep breath, "it worked. Congratulations. You have just converted an absolute disaster into a major intelligence coup. Thank you, Commander Quinn. By the way, the guy you walked out of that empty house with—wasn't me."

Elli's eyes widened; her hand went to her mouth. Then the dark glints narrowed in furious thought. "Sonofabitch," she breathed. "But Miles—I thought the clone story was something you'd made up!"

"So did I. It's thrown everyone off, I expect."

"There was—he is—a real clone?"

"So he claims. Fingerprints—retina—voiceprint—all the same. There is, thank God, one objective difference. You radiograph my bones, you'll find a crazy-quilt pattern of old breaks, except for the synthetics in my legs. His bones have none. Or so he says." Miles cradled his throbbing left hand. "I think I'll leave the beard on for the moment, just in case."

Miles turned to Captain Galeni. "How shall we—Imperial Security—handle this, sir?" he said deferentially. "Do we really want to call in the local authorities?"

"Oh, so I'm 'sir' again, am I?" muttered Galeni. "Of course we want the police. We can't extradite these people. But now that they're guilty of a crime right here on Earth, the Eurolaw authorities will hold them for us. It'll break up this whole radical splinter group."

Miles tamped down his personal urgency, trying to make his voice cool and logical. "But a public trial would bring out the whole clone story. In all its details. It would attract a lot of undesirable attention to me, from a Security viewpoint. Including, you may be sure, Cetagandan attention."

"It's too late to put a lid on this."

"I'm not so sure. Yes, rumors will float, but a few sufficiently confused rumors might actually be useful. Those two," Miles gestured to the captured guards, "are small fry. My clone knows more than they do, and he's already back at the embassy. Which is, legally, Barrayaran soil. What do we need them for? Now that we have you back, and have the clone, the plot is void. Put this group under surveillance like the rest of the Komarran expatriates here on Earth, and they're no further danger to us."

Galeni met his eyes, then looked away, pale profile tense with the unspoken corollary: *and your career will be uncompromised by a splashy public scandal. And you won't have to confront your father.* "I . . . don't know."

"I do," said Miles confidently. He gestured a waiting Dendarii over. "Sergeant. Take a couple of techs upstairs and suck out these people's comconsole files. Take a fast scan around for secret files. And while you're about it, search the house for a couple of anti-personnel-scan devices on belts, should be stored somewhere. Take them to Commodore Jesek and tell him I want him to find the manufacturer. As soon as you call the all-clear, we decamp."

"Now, that *is* illegal," Elli remarked.

"What are they going to do, go to the police and complain? I think not. Ah—you want to leave any messages on the comconsole, Captain?"

"No," said Galeni softly after a moment. "No messages."

"Right."

A Dendarii rendered first aid to Miles's broken finger and numbed his hand. The sergeant was back down in less than half an hour, anti-scan belts hung over his shoulder, and flipped a data disc at Miles. "You got it, sir."

"Thank you."

Galen had not yet returned. All things considered, Miles counted that as a plus.

Miles knelt by the still-conscious Komarran, and held a stunner to his temple.

"What are you going to do?" croaked the man.

Miles's lips peeled back in a grin, cracking to bleed. "Why—stun you, of course, fly you out over the south coast, and drop you in. What else? Nighty-night." The stunner buzzed, and the struggling Komarran jerked and slumped. The Dendarii soldier retrieved his restraints, and Miles left the two Komarrans lying side by side on the garage floor. They let themselves out and keyed the garage doors closed carefully.

"Back to the embassy, then, and nail the little

bastard," said Elli Quinn grimly, calling up the route to their destination from her rented car's console. The rest of the patrol withdrew to covert observation positions.

Miles and Galeni settled back. Galeni looked as exhausted as Miles felt.

"Bastard?" sighed Miles. "No. That's the one thing he is not, I'm afraid."

"Nail him first," Galeni murmured. "Define him later."

"Agreed," said Miles.

"How shall we go in?" asked Galeni as they approached the embassy in the late-morning light.

"Only one way," said Miles. "Through the front door. Marching. Pull up at the front, Elli."

Miles and Galeni looked at each other and snickered. Miles's beard was well behind Galeni's in development—Galeni's after all had a four-day head start—but his split lips, bruises, and the dried blood on his shirt made up for it, Miles figured, in augmenting his general air of seedy degradation. Besides, Galeni had found his boots and uniform jacket back at the Komarrans' house, and Miles had not. Carried off by the clone, perhaps. Miles was not sure which of them smelled worse—Galeni had been incarcerated longer, but Miles fancied he'd sweated harder—and he wasn't going to ask Elli Quinn to sniff and rate them. From Galeni's twitching lips and crinkling eyes Miles thought he might be undergoing the same delayed reaction of lunatic relief that was presently bubbling up through his own chest. They were alive, and it was a miracle and a wonderment.

They matched steps, going up the ramp. Elli sauntered behind, watching the performance with interest.

The guard at the entrance saluted by reflex even

as astonishment spread over his face. "Captain Galeni! You're back! And, er . . ." he glanced at Miles, opened and closed his mouth, "you. Sir."

Galeni returned the salute blandly. "Call Lieutenant Vorpatril up here for me, will you? Vorpatril only."

"Yes, sir." The embassy guard spoke into his wrist comm, not taking his eyes off them; he kept looking sideways at Miles with a very puzzled expression. "Er—glad to have you back, Captain."

"Glad to be back, Corporal."

In a moment, Ivan popped out of a lift tube and came running across the marble-paved foyer.

"My God, sir, where have you been?" he cried, grabbing Galeni by the shoulders. He remembered himself belatedly, and saluted.

"My absence wasn't voluntary, I assure you." Galeni tugged on one earlobe, blinking, and ran the hand through his beard stubble, clearly a little touched by Ivan's enthusiasm. "As I shall explain in detail, later. Right now—Lieutenant Vorkosigan? It is perhaps time to surprise your, er, other relative."

Ivan glanced at Miles. "They let you out, then?" He looked more closely, then stared. "Miles . . ."

Miles bared his teeth, and moved them out of earshot of the mesmerized corporal. "All shall be revealed when we arrest the other me. Where am I, by the way?"

Ivan's lips wrinkled in dawning dismay. "Miles . . . are you trying to diddle my head? It's not very funny. . . ."

"No diddle. And not funny. The individual you've been rooming with for the last four days—wasn't me. I've been rooming with Captain Galeni, here. A Komarran revolutionary group tried to plant a ringer on you, Ivan. The sucker is my clone, for real. Don't tell me you never noticed anything!"

"Well . . ." said Ivan. Belief, and growing embarrassment, began to suffuse his features. "You did seem sort of, um, off your feed, the last couple of days."

Elli nodded thoughtfully, highly sympathetic to Ivan's embarrassment.

"In what way?" asked Miles.

"Well . . . I've seen you manic. And I've seen you depressive. But I've never seen you—well—*neutral.*"

"I had to ask. And yet you never suspected anything? He was that good?"

"Oh, I wondered about it the very first night!"

"And what?" yelped Miles. He felt like tearing his hair.

"And I decided it couldn't be. After all, you'd made that clone story up yourself a few days ago."

"I shall now demonstrate my amazing prescience. Where is he?"

"Well, that's why I was so surprised to see you, see."

Galeni was now standing with his arms crossed, and his hand to his forehead, supportingly; Miles could not read his lips, though they were moving slightly—counting to ten, perhaps. "Why, Ivan?" said Galeni, and waited.

"My God, he hasn't left for Barrayar already, has he?" said Miles urgently. "We've got to stop him—"

"No, no," said Ivan. "It was the locals. That's why we're all in such a flap, here."

"*Where is he?*" snarled Miles, going for a grip on Ivan's green uniform jacket with his good hand.

"Calm down, that's what I'm trying to tell you!" Ivan glanced down at Miles's white-knuckled fist. "Yeah, it's you all right, isn't it? The local police came through here a couple of hours ago and arrested you—him—whatever. Well, not arrested, exactly, but they had a detention order, forbidding you to leave this legal jurisdiction. You—he—was frantic. 'cause it meant you'd miss your ship. You were shipping out tonight. They subpoenaed you for questioning, before the municipal bench's investigator, to ascertain if there was enough evidence to file formal charges."

"Charges for *what*, what are you babbling about, *Ivan!*"

"Well, that's it, why it's such a mess. Somewhere, they got this short circuit in their brains about embassies—they came and arrested you, Lieutenant Vorkosigan, for suspicion of conspiracy to commit murder. To wit, you are suspected of hiring those two goons who tried to assassinate Admiral Naismith at the shuttleport last week."

Miles stamped in a circle. "Ah. Ah. Agh!"

"The ambassador is filing protests all over the place. Naturally, we couldn't tell them why we thought they were mistaken."

Miles clutched Quinn's elbow. "Don't panic."

"I'm not panicking," Quinn observed, "I'm watching you panic. It's more entertaining."

Miles pressed his forehead. "Right. Right. Let us begin by assuming all is not lost. Let us assume the kid hasn't panicked—hasn't broken. Yet. Suppose he has climbed up on an aristocratic high horse and is sneering a lot of no-comments at them. He'd do that well, it's how he thinks Vor are supposed to act. Little schmuck. Assume he's holding out."

"Assume away," remarked Ivan. "So what?"

"If we hurry, we can save—"

"Your reputation?" said Ivan.

"Your . . . brother?" ventured Galeni.

"Our asses?" said Elli.

"Admiral Naismith," Miles finished. "He's the one at risk, now." Miles's gaze crossed Elli's; her eyebrows arched in dawning worry. "The key word is *cover*, as in *blown*—or, just possibly, permanently assured.

"You and I," he nodded to Galeni, "have to get cleaned up. Meet me back here in fifteen minutes. Ivan, bring a sandwich. Two sandwiches. We'll take you along for muscle." Ivan was well endowed in that resource. "Elli, you drive."

"Drive where?" asked Quinn.

"The Assizes. We go to the rescue of poor, misunderstood Lieutenant Vorkosigan. Who will return with us gratefully, whether he wants to or not. Ivan, better bring a hypospray with two cc's of tholizone, in addition to those sandwiches."

"Hold it, Miles," said Ivan. "If the ambassador couldn't get him sprung, how do you expect us to?"

Miles grinned. "Not us. Admiral Naismith."

The London Municipal Assizes was a big black crystal of a building some two centuries old. A slash of similar architecture erupted unevenly through a district of even older styles, representing the bombings and fires of the Fifth Civil Disturbance. Urban renewal here seemed to wait on disaster. London was so filled up, a cramped jigsaw of juxtaposed eras, with Londoners stubbornly hanging on to bits of their past; there was even a committee to save the singularly ugly disintegrating remnants of the late twentieth century. Miles wondered if Vorbarr Sultana, presently expanding madly, would look like this in a thousand years, or whether it would obliterate its history in the rush to modernize.

Miles paused in the Assizes's soaring foyer to adjust his Dendarii admiral's uniform. "Do I look respectable?" he asked Quinn.

"The beard makes you look, um . . ."

Miles had hastily trimmed the edges. "Distinguished? Older?"

"Hung over."

"Ha."

The four of them took the lift tube to the ninety-seventh level.

"Chamber W," the reception panel directed them after accessing its files. "Cubicle 19."

Cubicle 19 proved to contain a secured Euronet JusticeComp terminal and a live human being, a serious young man.

"Ah, Investigator Reed." Elli smiled winningly at him as they entered. "We meet again."

The briefest glance showed Investigator Reed to be alone. Miles cleared a twinge of panic from his throat.

"Investigator Reed is in charge of looking into that unpleasant incident at the shuttleport, sir," Elli explained, mistaking his choke for a request for an introduction and slipping back into professional mode. "Investigator Reed, Admiral Naismith. We had a long talk on my last trip here."

"I see," said Miles. He kept his face blandly polite.

Reed was frankly staring at him. "Uncanny. So you really are Vorkosigan's clone!"

"I prefer to think of him as my twin brother," Miles flung off, "once removed. We generally prefer to stay as far removed from each other as possible. So you've spoken to him."

"At some length. I did not find him very cooperative." Reed glanced back and forth uncertainly from Miles and Elli to the two uniformed Barrayarans. "Obstructive. Indeed, rather unpleasant."

"So I would imagine. You were treading on his toes. He's quite sensitive about me. Prefers not to be reminded of my embarrassing existence."

"Ah? Why?"

"Sibling rivalry," Miles extemporized. "I've gotten farther in my military career than he has in his. He takes it as a reproach, a slur on his own perfectly reasonable achievements . . ." *God, somebody, give me another straight line*—Reed's stare was becoming piercing.

"To the point, please, Admiral Naismith," Captain Galeni rumbled.

Thank you. "Quite. Investigator Reed—I do not pretend that Vorkosigan and I are friends, but how did you come by this curious misapprehension that he tried to arrange my rather messy death?"

"Your case has not been easy. The two would-be killers," Reed glanced at Elli, "were a dead end. So we went to other leads."

"Not Lise Vallerie, was it? I'm afraid I've been guilty of leading her slightly astray. An untimely sense of humor, I fear. It's an affliction . . ."

". . . we all must bear," murmured Elli.

"I found Vallerie's suggestions interesting, not conclusive," said Reed. "In the past I've found her to be a careful investigator in her own right, unimpeded by certain rules of order that hamper, say, me. And most helpful in passing on items of interest."

"What's she investigating these days?" inquired Miles.

Reed gave him a bland look. "Illegal cloning. Perhaps you might give her some tips."

"Ah—I fear my experiences are some two decades out of date for your purposes."

"Well, that's neither here nor there. In this case the lead was quite objective. An aircar was seen leaving the shuttleport at the time of the attack, passing illegally through a traffic control space. We traced it to the Barrayaran embassy."

Sergeant Barth. Galeni looked like he wanted to spit; Ivan was acquiring that pleasant, slightly moronic expression he'd found so useful in the past for evading any accusation of responsibility.

"Oh, that," said Miles airily. "That was merely Barrayar's usual tedious surveillance of me. Frankly, the embassy I would suspect of having a hand in this is the Cetagandan. Recent Dendarii operations in their area of influence—far outside your jurisdiction—displeased them exceedingly. But it was not a charge in my power to prove, which was why I was content to leave it to your people."

"Ah, the remarkable rescue at Dagoola. I'd heard of it. A compelling motive."

"More compelling, I would suggest, than the ancient history I confided to Lise Vallerie. Does that straighten out the contratemps?"

"And are you getting something in return for this charitable service to the Barrayaran embassy, Admiral?"

"My good deed for the day? No, you're right, I warned you about my sense of humor. Let's just say, my reward is sufficient."

"Nothing that could be construed as an obstruction of justice, I trust?" Reed's eyebrows rose dryly.

"I'm the *victim,* remember?" Miles bit his tongue. "My reward has nothing to do with London's criminal code, I assure you. In the meantime, can I ask you to return poor Lieutenant Vorkosigan to the custody, say, of his commanding officer, Captain Galeni, here?"

Reed's face was a study in suspicion, his alertness multiplied. *What's wrong, dammit?* wondered Miles. *This is supposed to be lulling him. . . .*

Reed steepled his hands, leaned back, and cocked his head. "Lieutenant Vorkosigan left with a man who introduced himself as Captain Galeni an hour ago."

"Aaah . . ." said Miles. "An older man in civilian dress? Greying hair, heavyset?"

"Yes . . ."

Miles inhaled, smiling fixedly. "Thank you, Investigator Reed. We won't take any more of your valuable time."

Back in the foyer Ivan said, "Now what?"

"I think," said Captain Galeni, "it is time to return to the embassy. And send a full report to HQ."

The urge to confess, eh? "No, no, never send interim reports," said Miles. "Only final ones. Interim reports tend to elicit orders. Which you must then either obey, or spend valuable time and energy evading, which you could be using to solve the problem."

"An interesting command philosophy; I must keep it in mind. Do you share it, Commander Quinn?"

"Oh, yes."

"The Dendarii Mercenaries must be a *fascinating* outfit to work for."

Quinn smirked. "I find it so."

Chapter Twelve

They returned to the embassy nonetheless, Galeni to galvanize his staff into an all-out investigation of the now highly-suspect courier officer, Miles to change back into his Barrayaran dress greens and visit the embassy physician to have his hand properly set. If there was a lull in his life after this mess was cleared up, Miles reflected, perhaps he'd better take the time to go get the bones and joints in his arms and hands, not just the long bones of his legs, replaced with synthetics. Getting the legs done had been painful and tedious, but putting off the arms wasn't going to make it any better. And he certainly couldn't pretend he was going to do any more growing.

Somewhat morose with these thoughts, he left the embassy clinic and wandered down to Security's office sub-level. He found Galeni sitting alone at his comconsole desk, having generated a flurry of orders that dispatched subordinates in all directions. The lights in the office were dimmed. Galeni was leaning back with his feet on the desk, crossed at the ankles, and Miles had the impression that he would have preferred a bottle of something potently alcoholic in his hand to the light pen he now turned over and over.

Galeni smiled bleakly, sat up, and took to tapping the pen on the desk as Miles entered. "I've been thinking it over, Vorkosigan. I'm afraid we may not be able to avoid calling in the local authorities in this."

"I wish you wouldn't do that, sir." Miles pulled up a chair and sat astride it, arms athwart its back. "Involve them, and the consequences pass beyond our control."

"It will take a small army, to find those two on Earth now."

"I have a small army," Miles reminded him, "which had just demonstrated its effectiveness for this sort of thing, I think."

"Ha. True."

"Let the embassy hire the Dendarii Mercenaries to find our . . . missing persons."

"Hire? I thought Barrayar was already paying for them!"

Miles blinked innocently. "But sir, it's part of their covert status that that relationship is unknown even to the Dendarii themselves. If the embassy hires them in a formal contract for this job, it—covers the cover, so to speak."

Galeni raised his brows sardonically. "I see. And how do you propose to explain your clone to them?"

"If necessary, as a clone—of Admiral Naismith."

"Three of you, now?" said Galeni dubiously.

"Just set them to find your—find Ser Galen. Where he is, the clone will be too. It worked once."

"Hm," said Galeni.

"There's just one thing," Miles added. He ran one finger thoughtfully along the top of the chair back. "If we do succeed in catching them—just what is it that we plan to do with 'em?"

The light pen tapped. "There are," said Galeni, "only two or three possibilities. One, they can be arrested, tried, and incarcerated for the crimes committed here on Earth."

"During the course of which," Miles observed seri-ously, "Admiral Naismith's cover as a supposedly independent operator will almost certainly be compromised, his true identity publicly revealed. I can't pretend the Barrayaran Empire will stand or fall on the Dendarii Mercenaries, but Security has found us useful in the past. Command may—I hope may—regard this as a poor trade. Besides, has my clone in fact committed any crimes he can be held for? I think he may even be a minor, by Eurolaw rules."

"Second alternative," Galeni recited. "Kidnap them and returned them secretly to Barrayar for trial, evading Earth's non-extradition status. If we had an order from on high, my guess is this would be it, the minimum proper paranoid Security response."

"For trial," said Miles, "or to be held indefinitely in some oubliette . . . For my—brother, that might not turn out as bad as he'd at first think. He has a friend in a very high place. If he can escape being secretly murdered by some—overexcited underling first, en route." Galeni and Miles exchanged glances. "But nobody's going to intercede for your father. Barrayar has always taken the killings in the Komarr Revolt to be civil crimes, not acts of war, and he never submitted to the loyalty oath and amnesty. He'll be up on capital charges. His execution will inevitably follow."

"Inevitably." Galeni pursed his lips, staring down at the toes of his boots. "The third possibility being—as you said—an order coming down for their secret assassination."

"Criminal orders can be successfully resisted," Miles observed, "if you have a strong enough stomach for it. High command isn't as free with that sort of thing as they were back in Emperor Ezar's day, fortunately. I submit a fourth possibility. It might be better not to catch these—awkward relatives—in the first place."

"Bluntly, Miles, if I fail to produce Ser Galen, my career will be smoke. I must already be suspect, for having failed to turn him up any time these last two years. Your suggestion skirts—not insubordination, that seems to be your normal mode of operation—but something worse."

"What about your predecessor here, who failed to discover him in five years? And if you do produce him now, will your career be any better off? You'll be suspect anyway, in the minds of those who are determined to be suspicious."

"I wish," Galeni's face had an inward look, deathly calm, his voice a reflective murmur, "I wish he had stayed dead in the first place. His first death was a much better one, glorious in the heat of battle. He had his place in history, and I was alone, past pain, without mother or father to torment me. How fortunate that science hasn't cracked human immortality. It's a great blessing that we can outlive old wars. And old warriors."

Miles mulled over the dilemma. In jail on Earth, Galen destroyed both Galeni's career and Admiral Naismith's, but lived. Shipped to Barrayar, he died; Galeni's career would be a little better off, but Galeni himself—would not be quite sane, Miles rather thought. The patricide would not have the rooted serenity to serve Komarr's complex future needs, certainly. *But Naismith would live*, his thought whispered temptingly. Left loose, the persistent Galen and Mark remained a threat of unknown, and so intolerable, proportion; if Miles and Galeni did nothing, high command would most certainly take the choice from them, issuing who-knew-what orders sealing the fate of their perceived enemies.

Miles loathed the thought of sacrificing Galeni's promising career to this crabbed old revolutionary who refused to give up. Yet Galen's destruction would also damage Galeni, just as certainly. Dammit, why couldn't the old man have pensioned himself off to some tropical paradise, instead of hanging around making trouble for the younger generation on the grounds, no doubt, that it was good for 'em? Mandatory retirement for revolutionaries, that's what they needed now.

What do you choose when all choices are bad?

"This choice is mine," said Galeni. "We have to go after them."

They stared at each other, both very tired.

"Compromise," suggested Miles. "Send the Dendarii Mercenaries out to locate, track, and monitor them. Don't attempt to pick them up yet. This will permit you to put all the embassy's resources to work on the problem of the courier, a purely Barrayaran-internal matter on any scale."

There was a silence. "Agreed," Galeni said at last. "But whatever finally happens—I want to get it over with quickly."

"Agreed," said Miles.

*   *   *

Miles found Elli sitting alone in the embassy cafeteria, leaning tired and a little blank over the remains of her dinner, ignoring the covert stares and hesitant smiles of various embassy personnel. He grabbed a snack and tea and slid into the seat across from her. Their hands gripped briefly across the table, then she rested her chin on her cupped palms again, elbows propped.

"So, what's next?" she asked.

"What's the traditional reward for a job well done in this man's army?"

Her dark eyes crinkled. "Another job."

"You got it. I've persuaded Captain Galeni to let the Dendarii mercenaries find Galen, just as you found us. How did you find us, by the way?"

"Lotta damn work, that's how. We started by crunching through that awful pile of data you beamed up from the embassy files about Komarrans. We eliminated the well-documented ones, the young children, and so on. Then we put the Intelligence computer team downside to break into the economic net and pull out credit files, and into the Eurolaw net— *that* was tricky—and pull out criminal files, and started looking for anomalies. That's where we found the break. About a year ago, the Earth-born son of a Komarran expatriate was picked up by the Eurolaw cops on some minor misdemeanor and found to have an unregistered stunner in his possession. Not being a deadly weapon, it merely cost him a fine, and as far as Eurolaw was concerned, that was that. But the stunner wasn't of Earth manufacture. It was old Barrayaran military issue.

"We began following him, both physically and through the computer net, finding out who his friends were, people who weren't in the embassy's computer. We were following up several other leads at the same time that failed to pan out. But this is where I got a compelling hunch. One of this kid's frequent contacts, a man named Van der Poole, was registered as an immigrant to Earth from the planet Frost IV. Now, during that investigation I did a couple of years back involving the stolen genes, I passed through Jackson's Whole—"

Miles nodded in memory.

"So I knew you could buy documented pasts there—one of the little high-profit-margin services certain laboratories sell to go along with the new faces and voices and finger- and retina-prints they offer. One of the planets they frequently use for this is Frost IV, on account of the tectonic disaster having wrecked their computer net—not to mention the rest of the place—twenty-eight years ago. A lot of perfectly legitimate people who left Frost IV then have uncheckable documentation. If you're over twenty-eight years old, Jackson's Whole can fit you right in. So whenever I see somebody above a certain age who claims to be from Frost IV, I'm automatically suspicious. Van der Poole was Galen, of course."

"Of course. My clone was another fine product of Jackson's Whole, by the way."

"Ah. It all fits, how nice."

"My congratulations to you and the whole Intelligence department. Remind me to make that an official commendation, when I next make it back to the *Triumph*."

"Which is when?" She crunched a piece of ice from the bottom of her glass and swirled the remainder around, trying to look only professionally interested.

Her mouth would taste cool, and tangy. . . . Miles blinked back into professional mode himself, conscious of the curious eyes of embassy personnel upon them. "Dunno. We're sure not done here yet. We should certainly transfer all the new data the Dendarii collected back to embassy files. Ivan's working now on what we pulled from Galen's comconsole. It's going to be harder this time. Galen—Van der Poole— will be hiding. And he's had a lot of experience at serious disappearing. But if and when you do turn him up—ah—report directly to me. I'll report to the embassy."

"Report what to the embassy?" Elli inquired, alert to his undertones.

Miles shook his head. "I'm not sure yet. I may be too tired to think straight, I'll see if it seems to make any more sense in the morning."

Elli nodded and rose.

"Where are you going?" asked Miles in alarm.

"Back to the *Triumph,* to put the mass in motion, of course."

"But you can tight-beam— Who's on duty up there right now?"

"Bel Thorne."

"Right, all right. Let's go find Ivan, we can tight-beam the data swap right from here, and the orders as well." He studied the dark circles under her luminous eyes. "And how long have you been on your feet, anyway?"

"Oh, about the last, um," she glanced at her chrono, "thirty hours."

"Who has trouble delegating work, Commander Quinn? Send the orders, not yourself. And take a sleep shift before you start making mistakes too. I'll find you a place to bunk here at the embassy—" she met his eyes, suddenly grinning, "if you like," Miles added hastily.

"Will you, now?" she said softly. "I'd like that fine."

They paid a visit to Ivan, harried at his comconsole, and made the secured data link to the *Triumph*. Ivan, Miles noted happily, had lots and lots of work left to do. He escorted Elli up the lift tubes to his quarters.

Elli dove for the bathroom by right of first dibs. While hanging up his uniform Miles found his cat blanket bunged lumpily into a dark corner of his closet, doubtless where his terrified clone had thrown it his first night. The black fur broke into ecstatic rumbling when he picked it up. He spread it out carefully on his bed, patting it into place. "There."

Elli emerged from the shower in remarkably few minutes, fluffing her short wet curls out with her fingers, a towel slung attractively around her hips. She spotted the cat blanket, smiled, and hopped up and wriggled her bare toes in it. It shivered and purred louder.

"Ah," sighed Miles, contemplating them both in perfect contentment. Then doubt snaked through his garden of delight. Elli was looking around his room with interest. He swallowed. "Is this, ah, the first time you've been up here?" he asked in what he hoped was a casual tone.

"Uh-huh. I don't know why I was expecting something medieval. Looks more like an ordinary hotel room than what I would have expected of Barrayar."

"This is Earth," Miles pointed out, "and the Time of Isolation has been over for a hundred years. You have some odd ideas about Barrayar. But I just wondered, if my clone had, uh . . . are you sure you never sensed any difference at *all* during the four days? He was that good?" He smiled wretchedly, hanging on her answer. What if she'd noticed nothing? Was he really so transparent and simple that anyone could play him? Worse, what if she had noticed a difference—and liked the clone better . . . ?

Elli looked embarrassed. "Noticed, yes. But to jump from sensing there was something wrong with you, to realizing it *wasn't* you . . . maybe if we'd had more time together. We only talked by comm link, except for one two-hour trip downtown to spring Danio and his merry men from the locals, during which I thought you'd lost your mind. Then I decided you must have something up your sleeve, and just weren't telling me 'cause I'd . . ." her voice went suddenly smaller, "fallen out of favor, somehow."

Miles calculated, and breathed relief. So the clone hadn't had time to . . . ahem. He smiled wryly up at her.

"You see, when you look at me," she went on to explain, "it makes me feel—well—good. Not in the warm and fuzzy sense, though there's that too—"

"Warm and fuzzy," sighed Miles happily, leaning on her.

"Stop it, you goof, I'm serious." But she slipped her arms around him. Firmly, as if prepared to do immediate battle with any wight who might attempt to snatch him away again. "Good, like—I can do. Competent. You make me un-afraid. Unafraid to try, unafraid of what others might think. Your—clone, good gods what a relief to know that—made me start wondering what was wrong with me. Though when I think how easily they took you, that night in the empty house, I could—"

"Sh, sh," Miles stopped her lips with one finger. "There is nothing wrong with you, Elli," he said, pleasantly muffled. "You are most perfectly Quinn." *His* Quinn . . .

"See what I mean? I suppose it saved your life. I'd been meaning to keep you—him—up to date on the hunt for Galeni, even it if was just an interim no-progress report. Which would have been *his* first tip-off that there was a hunt going on."

"Which he would have ordered stopped."

"Precisely. But then, when the break in the case came, I—thought I'd better be sure. Save it up, surprise you with the final result all wrapped up in a big bow—win back your regard, to be frank. In a way, he kept me from reporting to him."

"If it's any consolation, it wasn't dislike. You terrified him. Your face—not to mention the rest of you—has that effect on some men."

"Yes, the face . . ." Her hand touched one cheek, half-consciously, then fell more tenderly to ruffle his hair, "I think you've put your finger on it, what felt so wrong. You knew me when I had my old face, and no face, and the now face, and for you alone, it was all the same face."

His unbandaged hand traced over the arch of her brows, perfect nose, paused at her lips to collect a kiss, then down the ideal angle of her chin and velvet skin of her throat. "Yes, the face . . . I was young and dumb then. It seemed like a good idea at the time. It was only later that I realized it could be a handicap for you."

"Me, too," sighed Elli. "For the first six months, I was delighted. But the second time a soldier made a pass at me instead of following an order, I knew I definitely had a problem. I had to discover and teach myself all kinds of tricks, to get people to respond to the inside of me, and not the outside."

"I understand," said Miles.

"By the gods, you would." She looked at him for a moment as if seeing him for the very first time, then dropped a kiss on his forehead. "I just now realized how many of those tricks I learned from you. How I love you!"

When they came up for air from the kiss that followed, Elli offered, "Rub you?"

"You're a drunkard's dream, Quinn." Miles flopped down with his face in the fur and let her have her way with him. Five minutes at her strong hands parted him from all ambitions but two. Those satisfied, they both slept like stones, untroubled by any vile dream that Miles could later remember.

Miles woke muzzily to the sound of knocking at the door.

"Go *way*, Ivan," Miles moaned into the flesh and fur he clutched. "Go sleep on a bench somewhere, hunh . . . ?"

The flesh shook him loose decisively. Elli hit the light, swung out of bed, slipping into her black T-shirt and grey uniform trousers, and padded to the door, ignoring Miles's mumbled "No, no, doan' let 'im in . . ." The knocking grew louder and more insistent.

"Miles!" Ivan fell through the door. "Oh, hi, Elli. Miles!" Ivan shook him by the shoulder.

Miles tried to burrow underneath his fur. "All right, y'can have your bed," he muttered. "Y'don't need me to tuck you in . . ."

"Get *up*, Miles!"

Miles stuck his head out, eyes scrunched against the light. "Why? What time is it?"

"About midnight."

"Ergh." He went back under. Three hours sleep hardly counted, after what he'd been through the last four days. Displaying a cruel and ruthless streak Miles would never have suspected, Ivan pulled the live fur from his twitching hands and tossed it aside.

"You have to get up," Ivan insisted. "Dressed. Peel off the face fungus. I hope you've got a clean uniform in here somewhere—" Ivan was rooting through his closet. "Here!"

Miles clutched numbly at the green cloth Ivan flung at him. "Embassy on fire?" he inquired.

"Damn near. Elena Bothari-Jesek just blew in from Tau Ceti. I didn't even know you'd sent her!"

"Oh!" Miles came awake. Quinn was by now fully dressed, including boots, and checking her stunner in its holster. "Yes. Gotta get dressed, sure. She won't mind the beard, though."

"Not being subject to beard burn," Elli muttered under her breath, scratching a thigh absently. Miles suppressed a grin; one of her eyelids shivered at him.

"Maybe not," said Ivan grimly, "but I don't think Commodore Destang will be too thrilled by it."

"Destang's *here*?" Miles came fully awake. He still had a little adrenalin left, apparently. "Why?" Then he thought back over some of the suspicions he'd included in his report sent with Elena, and realized why the Sector Two Security chief might have been inspired to investigate in person. "Oh, God . . . gotta get him straightened out before he shoots poor Galeni on sight—"

He ran the shower on cold, needle-spray; Elli shoved a cup of coffee into his working hand as he exited, and inspected the effect when he was dressed.

"Everything's fine but the face," she informed him, "and you can't do anything about that."

He ran a hand over his now-naked chin. "Did I miss a patch with the depilator?"

"No, I was admiring the bruises. And the eyes. I've seen brighter eyes on a strung-out juba freak three days after the supplies ran out."

"Thanks."

"You asked."

Miles considered what he knew of Destang, as they descended the lift tubes. His previous contacts with the commodore had been brief, official, and as far as Miles knew, satisfactory to both sides. The Sector Two Security commander was an experienced officer, accustomed to carrying out his varied duties—coordinating intelligence-gathering, overseeing the security of Barrayaran embassies, consulates, and visiting VIP's, rescuing the occasional Barrayaran subject in trouble—with little direct supervision from distant Barrayar. During the two or three operations the Dendarii had conducted in Sector Two areas, orders and money had flowed down, and Miles's final reports back up, through his command without impediment.

Commodore Destang was seated centrally in Galeni's office chair at Galeni's lit-up comconsole as Miles, Ivan, and Elli entered. Captain Galeni was standing, though extra chairs were available by the wall; his stiff posture worn like armor, his eyes hooded and face blank as a visor. Elena Bothari-Jesek hovered uncertainly in the background, with the worried look of one witnessing a chain of events they had started but no longer controlled. Her eyes lit with relief as she saw Miles, and she saluted—improperly, as he was not in Dendarii uniform; it was more an unstated transfer of responsibility, like someone ridding herself of a bag of live snakes, *Here, this one's all yours.* . . . He returned her a nod, *All right.*

"Sir." Miles saluted.

Destang returned the salute and glowered at him, reminding Miles in a faint twinge of nostalgia of the early Galeni. Another harried commander. Destang was a man of about sixty, lean, with grey hair, shorter than what was middle height for a Barrayaran. Doubtless born just after the end of the Cetagandan occupation, when widespread malnutrition had robbed many of their full growth potential. He would have been a young officer at the time of the Conquest of Komarr, of middle rank during its later Revolt; combat-experienced, like all who had lived through that war-torn past.

"Has anyone brought you up to date yet, sir?" Miles began anxiously. "My original memo is extremely obsolete."

"I've just read Captain Galeni's version." Destang nodded at the comconsole.

Galeni would insist on writing reports. Miles sighed inwardly. It was an old academic reflex, no doubt. He restrained himself from craning his neck to try and see.

"You don't seem to have made one yet," Destang noted.

Miles waved his bandaged left hand vaguely. "I've been in the infirmary, sir. But have you realized yet the Komarrans must have had control of the embassy's courier officer?"

"We arrested the courier six days ago on Tau Ceti," Destang said.

Miles exhaled in relief. "And was he—?"

"It was the usual sordid story." Destang frowned. "He committed a little sin; it gave them leverage to extract larger and larger ones, until there was no going back."

A curious mental judo, that sort of blackmail, reflected Miles. In the final analysis, it was fear of his own side, not fear of the Komarrans, that had delivered the courier into the enemy's hands. So a system meant to enforce loyalty ended by destroying it—some flaw, there . . .

"He's been owned by them for at least three years," continued Destang. "Anything that's gone in or out of the embassy since then may have passed before their eyes."

"Ouch." Miles suppressed a grin, substituting, he hoped, an expression of proper horror. So the subversion of the courier clearly predated the arrival of Galeni on Earth. Good.

"Yeah," said Ivan, "I just found copies of some of our stuff a little while ago in that mass data dump you pulled from Ser Galen's comconsole, Miles. It was quite a shock."

"I thought it might be there," said Miles. "There weren't too many other possibilities, once I realized we were being diddled. I trust the interrogation of the courier has cleared Captain Galeni of all suspicion?"

"If he was involved with the Komarran expatriates on Earth," said Destang neutrally, "the courier didn't know of it."

Not exactly an affirmation of heartfelt trust, that. "It was quite clear," Miles said, "that the captain was a card Ser Galen thought he was holding in reserve. But the card refused to play. At the risk of his life. It was chance, after all, that assigned Captain Galeni to Earth—" Galeni was shaking his head, lips compressed, "wasn't it?"

"No," said Galeni, still at parade rest. "I requested Earth."

"Oh. Well, it was certainly chance that brought me here," Miles scrambled over the gap, "chance and my wounded and cryo-corpses who needed the attention of a major medical center as soon as possible. Speaking of the Dendarii Mercenaries, Commodore, did the courier divert the eighteen million marks Barrayar owes them?"

"It was never sent," said Destang. "Until Captain Bothari-Jesek here arrived at my office, our last contact with your mercenaries was the report you sent from Mahata Solaris wrapping up the Dagoola affair. Then you vanished. From the viewpoint of Sector Two Headquarters, you've been missing for over two months. To our consternation. Particularly when the weekly requests for updates on your status from Imperial Security Chief Illyan turned into daily ones."

"I—see, sir. Then you never received our urgent requests for funds? —Then I was never actually assigned to the embassy!"

A very small noise, as of deep and muffled pain, escaped the otherwise deadpan Galeni.

Destang said, "Only by the Komarrans. Apparently it was a ploy to keep you immobilized until they could make their attempted switch."

"I'd guessed as much. Ah—you wouldn't by chance happen to have brought my eighteen million marks with you now, have you? That part hasn't changed. I did mention it in my memo."

"Several times," said Destang dryly. "Yes, Lieutenant, we will fund your irregulars. As usual."

"Ah." Miles melted within, and smiled blindingly. "Thank you, sir. That is a very great relief."

Destang cocked his head curiously. "What have they been living on, the past month?"

"It's—been a bit complicated, sir."

Destang opened his mouth as if to ask more, then apparently thought better of it. "I see. Well, Lieutenant, you may return to your outfit. Your part here is done. You should never have appeared on Earth as Lord Vorkosigan in the first place."

"To which outfit—to the Dendarii Mercenaries, you mean, sir?"

"I doubt Simon Illyan was sending out urgent inquiries for them because he was lonely. It's a safe assumption that new orders will be following on as soon as your location is known to HQ. You should be ready to move out."

Elli and Elena, who had been conferring in very low tones in the corner during all this, looked up brightly at this news; Ivan looked more stricken.

"Yes, sir," said Miles. "What's going to happen here?"

"Since you have not, thank God, involved the Earth authorities, we're free to clear up this aborted bit of treason ourselves. I brought a team from Tau Ceti—"

The team was a cleanup crew, Miles guessed, Intelligence commandos ready, at Destang's order, to restore order to a treason-raddled embassy with whatever force or guile might be required.

"Ser Galen would have been on our most-wanted list long before this if we hadn't believed him already dead. Galen!" Destang shook his head as though he still couldn't believe it himself. "Here on Earth, all this time. You know, I served during the Komarr Revolt—it's where I got my start in Security. I was on the team that dug through the rubble of the Halomar Barracks, after the bastards blew it up in the middle of the night—looking for survivors and evidence, finding bodies and damn few clues . . . There were a lot of new openings for posts in Security that morning. Damn. How it all comes back. If we can find Galen again, after you let him slip through your hands," Destang's eyes fell without favor on Galeni, "accidentally or otherwise, we'll take him back to Barrayar to answer for that bloody morning if nothing else. I wish he could be made to answer for it all, but there's not enough of him to go around. Rather like Mad Emperor Yuri."

"A laudable plan, sir," said Miles carefully. Galeni had his jaw clamped shut, no help there. "But there are a dozen Komarran ex-rebels on Earth with pasts just as bloody as Ser Galen's. Now that he's been exposed, he's no more threat to us than they are."

"They've been inactive for years," said Destang. "Galen, clearly, has been quite the reverse."

"But if you're contemplating an illegal kidnapping, it could damage our diplomatic relations with Earth. Is it worth it?"

"Permanent justice is well worth a temporary offended protest, I can assure you, Lieutenant."

Galen was dead meat to Destang. Well, and so. "On what grounds would you kidnap my—clone, then, sir? He's never committed a crime on Barrayar. He's never even been to Barrayar."

Shut up, Miles! Ivan, with a look of increasing alarm on his face, mouthed silently from behind Destang. *You don't argue with a commodore!* Miles ignored him.

"The fate of my clone concerns me closely, sir."

"I can imagine. I hope we can eliminate the danger of further confusion between you soon."

Miles hoped that didn't mean what he thought it did. If he had to derail Destang . . . "There's no danger of confusion, sir. A simple medical scan can tell the difference between us. His bones are normal, mine are not. By what charge or claim do we have any further interest in him?"

"Treason, of course. Conspiracy against the Imperium."

The second part being demonstrably true, Miles

concentrated on the first part. "Treason? He was born on Jackson's Whole. He's not an Imperial subject by conquest or place of birth. To charge him with treason," Miles took a breath, "you must allow him to be an Imperial subject by blood. And if he's that, he's that all the way, a lord of the Vor with all the rights of his rank including trial by his peers— the Council of Counts in full session."

Destang's brows rose. "Would he think to attempt such an outre defense?"

If he didn't, I'd point it out to him. "Why not?"

"Thank you, Lieutenant. That's a complication I had not considered." Destang looked thoughtful indeed, and increasingly steely.

Miles's plan to convince Destang that letting the clone go was his own idea seemed to be slipping dangerously retrograde. He had to know— "Do you see assassination as an option, sir?"

"A compelling one." Destang's spine straightened decisively.

"There could be a legal problem, here, sir. Either he's not an Imperial subject, and we have no claim on him in the first place, or he is, and the full protection of Imperial law should apply to him. In either case, his murder would—" Miles moistened his lips; Galeni, who alone knew where he was heading, shut his eyes like a man watching an accident about to happen, "be a criminal order. Sir."

Destang looked rather impatient. "I had not planned to give *you* the order, Lieutenant."

He thinks I want to keep my hands clean. . . . If Miles pushed the confrontation with Destang to its logical conclusion, with two Imperial officers witnessing, there was a chance the commodore would back down; there was at least an equal chance Miles would find himself in very deep—deepness. If the confrontation went all the way to a messy court-martial, neither of them would emerge undamaged. Even if Miles won, Barrayar would not be well served, and Destang's forty years of Imperial service did not deserve such an ignoble end. And if he got himself confined to quarters now, all alternate courses of action (and what was he contemplating, for God's sake?) would be closed to him. He did not want to be locked up in another room. Meanwhile, Destang's team would carry out any order he gave them without hesitation. . . .

He bared his teeth in a smile, of sorts, and said only, "Thank you, sir." Ivan looked relieved.

Destang paused. "Legality is an unusual concern for a covert operations specialist, at this late date, isn't it?"

"We all have our illogical moments."

Quinn's attention was now riveted upon him; a slight twitch of her eyebrow asked, *What the hell . . . ?*

"Try not to have too many of them, Lieutenant Vorkosigan," said Destang dryly. "My aide has the nontraceable credit chit for your eighteen million marks. See him on your way out. Take all these women with you." He waved at the two uniformed Dendarii.

Ivan, reminded, smiled at them. *They're my officers, dammit, not my harem,* Miles's thought snarled silently. But no Barrayaran officer of Destang's age would see it that way. Some attitudes couldn't be changed; they just had to be outlived.

Destang's words were a clear dismissal. Miles ignored them at his peril. Yet Destang had not mentioned—

"Yes, Lieutenant, run along." Captain Galeni's voice was utmost-bland. "I never finished writing my report. I'll give you one Mark, against the commodore's eighteen million, if you take the Dendarii off with you now."

Miles's eyes widened just slightly, hearing the capital M. *Galeni hasn't told Destang yet that the Dendarii are on the case. Therefore, he can't order them off, can he?* A head start—if he could find Galen and Mark before Destang's team did— "That's a bargain, Captain," Miles heard his own voice saying. "It's amazing, how much one Mark can weigh."

Galeni nodded once, and turned back to Destang. Miles fled.

Chapter Thirteen

Ivan trailed along, as Miles returned to their quarters to change clothes for the last time back into the Dendarii admiral's uniform in which he'd arrived, a lifetime and a half ago.

"I don't think I really want to watch, downstairs," Ivan explained. "Destang's well launched into a bloody reaming. Bet he'll keep Galeni on his feet all night, trying to break him if he can."

"Damn it!" Miles bundled his green Barrayaran jacket into a wad and flung it against the far wall, but it didn't carry enough momentum to begin to vent his frustration. He flopped down on a bed, pulled off a boot, hefted it, then shook his head and dropped it in disgust. "It burns me. Galeni deserves a medal, not a load of grief. Well—if Ser Galen couldn't break him, I don't suppose Destang will either. But it's not right, not right . . ." He brooded. "And I helped set him up for it, too. Damn, damn, damn . . ."

Elli handed him his grey uniform without comment. Ivan was not so wise.

"Yeah, nice going, Miles. I'll think of you, safely up in orbit, while Destang's headquarters crew are cleaning house down here. Suspicious as hell—they wouldn't trust their own grandmothers. We're all in for it. Scrubbed, rinsed, and hung out to dry in the cold, cold wind." He wandered over to his own bed and regarded it with longing. "No use turning in; they'll be after me before morning for something." He sat down on it glumly.

Miles looked up at Ivan in sudden speculation. "Huh. Yeah, you are going to be rather in the middle of things for the next few days, aren't you?"

Ivan, alert to the change in his tone, eyed him suspiciously. "Too right. So what?"

Miles shook out his trousers. His half of the secured comm link fell onto the bed. He pulled on his Dendarii greys. "Suppose I remember to turn in my comm link before I leave. And suppose Elli forgets to turn in hers." Miles held up a restraining finger, and Elli stopped fishing in her jacket. "And suppose you stick it in your pocket, meaning to turn it back in to Sergeant Barth as soon as you get the other half." He tossed the comm link to Ivan, who caught it automatically, but then held it away from himself between thumb and forefingers as if it were something he'd found writhing under a rock.

"And suppose I remember what happened to me the last time I helped you sub-rosa?" said Ivan truculently. "That little sleight of hand I pulled to get you back in the embassy the night you tried to burn down London is on my record, now. Destang's birddogs will have spasms as soon as they turn that up, in light of the present circumstances. Suppose I stick it up your—" his eyes fell on Elli, "ear, instead?"

Miles thrust his head and arms up through his black T-shirt and pulled it down, grinning slightly. He began stuffing his feet into his Dendarii-issue combat boots. "It's only a precaution. May never use it. Just in case I need a private line into the embassy in an emergency."

"I cannot imagine," said Ivan primly, "any emergency that a loyal junior officer can't confide to his very own sector security commander." His voice grew stern. "Neither would Destang. Just what are you hatching in the back of your twisty little mind, Coz?"

Miles sealed his boots and paused seriously. "I'm not sure. But I may yet see a chance to save . . . something, from this mess."

Elli, listening intently, remarked, "I thought we had saved something. We uncovered a traitor, plugged a security leak, foiled a kidnapping, and broke up a major plot against the Barrayaran Imperium. And we got paid. What more do you want for one week?"

"Well, it would have been nice if any of that had been on purpose, instead of by accident," Miles mused.

Ivan and Elli looked at each other across the top of Miles's head, their faces beginning to mirror a similar unease. "What more do you want to save, Miles?" Ivan echoed.

Miles's frown, directed to his boots, deepened. "Something. A future. A second chance. A . . . possibility."

"It's the clone, isn't it?" said Ivan, his mouth hardening, "You've gone and let yourself get obsessed with that goddamn clone."

"Flesh of my flesh, Ivan." Miles turned his hands over, staring at them. "On some planets, he would be called my brother. On others he might even be called my son, depending on the laws regarding cloning."

"One cell! On Barrayar," said Ivan, "they call it your enemy when it's shooting at you. You having a little short-term memory trouble? Those people just tried to kill you! This—yesterday morning!"

Miles smiled briefly up at Ivan without replying.

"You know," Elli said cautiously, "if you decided you really wanted a clone, you could have one made. Without the, ah, problems of the present one. You have trillions of cells . . ."

"I don't want a clone," said Miles. *I want a brother.* "But I seem to have been . . . issued this one."

"I thought Ser Galen bought and paid for him," complained Elli. "The only thing that Komarran meant to issue you was death. By Jackson's Whole law, the planet of his origin, the clone clearly belongs to Galen."

Jockey of Norfolk, be not bold, the old quote whispered through Miles's memory, *for Dickon thy master is bought and sold. . . .* "Even on Barrayar," he said mildly, "no human being can own another. Galen descended far, in pursuit of his . . . principle of liberty."

"In any case," said Ivan, "you're out of the picture now. High command has taken over. I heard your marching orders."

"Did you also hear Destang say he meant to kill my—the clone, if he can?"

"Yeah, so?" Ivan was looking mulish indeed, an almost panicked stubbornness. "I didn't like him anyway. Surly little sneak."

"Destang has mastered the art of the final report too," said Miles. "Even if I went AWOL right now, it would be physically impossible for me to get back to Barrayar, beg the clone's life from my father, have him lean on Simon Illyan for a countermand, and get the order back here to Earth before the deed was done."

Ivan looked shocked. "Miles—I always figured to be embarrassed to ask Uncle Aral for a career favor, but I thought you'd let yourself be peeled and boiled before you'd cry to your Dad for anything! And you want to start by hopscotching a commodore? No C.O. in the service would want you after that!"

"I would rather die," agreed Miles tonelessly, "but I can't ask another to die for me. But it's irrelevant. It couldn't succeed."

"Thank God." Ivan stared at him, thoroughly unsettled.

If I cannot convince two of my best friends I'm right, thought Miles, *maybe I'm wrong.*

Or maybe I have to do this one alone.

"I just want to keep a line open, Ivan," he said. "I'm not asking you to do anything—"

"Yet," came Ivan's glum interpolation.

"I'd give the comm link to Captain Galeni, but he will certainly be closely watched. They'd just take it away from him, and it would look . . . ambiguous."

"So on me it looks good?" asked Ivan plaintively.

"Do it." Miles finished fastening his jacket, stood, and held out his hand to Ivan for the return of the comm link. "Or don't."

"Argh." Ivan broke off his gaze, and shoved the comm link disconsolately into his trouser pocket. "I'll think about it."

Miles tilted his head in thanks.

They caught a Dendarii shuttle just about to lift from the London shuttleport, returning personnel from leave. Actually, Elli called ahead and had it held for them; Miles rather relished the sensation of not having to rush for it, and might have outright sauntered if the pressures of Admiral Naismith's duties, now boiling up in his head, hadn't automatically quickened his steps.

Their delay was another's gain. A last duffle-swinging Dendarii sprinted across the tarmac as the engines revved, and just made it up the retracting ramp. The alert guard at the door put up his weapon as he recognized the sprinter, and gave him a hand in as the shuttle began to roll.

Miles, Elli Quinn, and Elena Bothari-Jesek held seats in the rear. The running soldier, pausing to catch his breath, spotted Miles, grinned, and saluted.

Miles returned both. "Ah, Sergeant Siembieda." Ryann Siembieda was a conscientious tech sergeant from Engineering, in charge of maintenance and repair of battle armor and other light equipment. "You're thawed out."

"Yes, sir."

"They told me your prognosis was good."

"They threw me out of the hospital two weeks ago. I've been on leave. You too, sir?" Siembieda nodded toward the silver shopping bag at Miles's feet containing the live fur.

Miles shoved it unobtrusively under his seat with his boot heel. "Yes and no. Actually, while you were playing, I was working. As a result, we will all be working again soon. It's good you got your leave while you could."

"Earth was great," sighed Siembieda. "It was quite a surprise to wake up here. Did you see the Unicorn Park? It's right here on this island. I was there yesterday."

"I didn't see much, I'm afraid," said Miles regretfully.

Siembieda dug a holocube out of his pocket and handed it over.

The Unicorn and Wild Animal Park (a division of GalacTech Bioengineering) occupied the grounds of the great and historical estate of Wooton, Surrey, the guide cube informed him. In the vid display, a shining white beast that looked like a cross between a horse and a deer, and probably was, bounded across the greensward into the topiary.

"They let you feed the tame lions," Siembieda informed him.

Miles blinked at an unbidden mental image of Ivan in a toga being tossed out the back of a float truck to a herd of hungry, tawny cats galloping excitedly along behind. He'd been reading too much Earth history. "What do they eat?"

"Protein cubes, same as us."

"Ah," said Miles, trying not to sound disappointed. He handed the cube back.

The sergeant hovered on, however. "Sir . . ." he began hesitantly.

"Yes?" Miles let his tone be encouraging.

"I've reviewed my procedures—been tested and cleared for light duties—but . . . I haven't been able to remember anything at all about the day I was killed. And the medics wouldn't tell me. It . . . bothers me a bit, sir."

Siembieda's hazel eyes were strange and wary; it bothered him a lot, Miles judged. "I see. Well, the medics couldn't tell you much anyway; they weren't there."

"But you were, sir," said Siembieda suggestively.

Of course, thought Miles. *And if I hadn't been, you wouldn't have died the death intended for me.* "Do you remember our arriving at Mahata Solaris?"

"Yes, sir. Some things, right up to the night before. But that whole day is gone, not just the fight."

"Ah. Well, there's no mystery. Commodore Jesek, myself, you, and your tech team paid a visit to a warehouse for a quality-control check of our resupplies—there'd been a problem with the first shipment—"

"I remember that," nodded Siembieda. "Cracked power cells leaking radiation."

"Right, very good. You spotted the defect, by the way, unloading them into inventory. There are those who might simply have stored them."

"Not on *my* team," muttered Siembieda.

"We were jumped by a Cetagandan hit squad at the warehouse. We never did find out if there was any collusion, though we suspected some in high places when our orbital permits were revoked and we were invited to leave Mahata Solaris local space by the authorities. Or maybe they just didn't like the excitement we'd brought with us. Anyway, a gravitic grenade went off and blew out the end of the warehouse. You were hit in the neck by a freak fragment of something metal, ricocheting from the explosion. You bled to death in seconds." Quite incredible quantities of blood from such a lean young man, once it was spread out and smeared around in the fight—the smell of it, and the burning, came back to Miles as he spoke, but he kept his voice calm and steady. "We had you back to the *Triumph* and iced down in an hour. The surgeon was very optimistic, as you didn't have gross tissue damage." Not like one of the techs, who'd been blown most grossly to bits in that same moment.

"I'd . . . wondered what I'd done. Or not done."

"You scarcely had time to do anything. You were practically the first casualty."

Siembieda looked faintly relieved. And what goes on in the head of a walking dead man? Miles wondered. What personal failure could he possibly fear more than death itself?

"If it's any consolation," put in Elli, "that sort of memory loss is common in trauma victims of all kinds, not just cryo-revivals. You ask around, you'll find you're not the only one."

"Better strap down," said Miles, as the craft yawed around for takeoff.

Siembieda nodded, looking a little more cheerful, and swung forward to find a seat.

"Do you remember your burn?" Miles asked Elli curiously. "Or is it all a merciful blank?"

Elli's hand drifted across her cheek. "I never quite lost consciousness."

The shuttle shot forward and up. Lieutenant Ptarmigan's hands at the controls, Miles judged dryly. Some hooted commentary from forward passengers confirmed his guess. Miles's hand hesitated over, and fell away from, the control in his seat-arm that would comm link him to the pilot; he would not brass-harass Ptarmigan unless he started flying upside down. Fortunately for Ptarmigan, the craft steadied.

Miles craned his neck for a look out the window as the glittering lights of Greater London and its island fell away beneath them. In another moment he could see the river mouth, with its great dykes and locks running for forty kilometers, defining the coastline to human design, shutting out the sea and protecting the historical treasures and several million souls of the lower Thames watershed. One of the huge channel-spanning bridges gleamed against the leaden dawn water beyond. And so men organized themselves for the sake of their technology as they never had for their principles. The sea's politics were unarguable.

The shuttle wheeled, gaining altitude rapidly, giving Miles a last glimpse of the shrinking maze of London. Somewhere down there in that monstrous city Galen and Mark hid, or ran, or plotted, while Destang's intelligence team quartered and re-quartered Galen's old haunts and the comconsole net looking for traces of them, in a deadly game of hide and seek. Surely Galen had the sense to avoid his friends and stay off the net at all costs. If he cut his losses and ran now, he had a chance of eluding Barrayaran vengeance for another half-lifetime.

But if Galen were running, why had he doubled back to pick up Mark? What possible use was the clone to him now? Did Galen have some dim paternal sense of responsibility to his creation? Somehow, Miles doubted it was love that bound those two together. Could the clone be used—servant, slave, soldier? Could the clone be sold—to the Cetagandans, to a medical laboratory, to a sideshow?

Could the clone be sold to Miles?

Now, there was a proposition that even the hyper-suspicious Galen would buy. Let him believe Miles wanted a new body, without the bone dyscrasias that had plagued him since birth . . . let him believe Miles would pay a high price to have the clone for this vile purpose . . . and Miles might gain possession of Mark and slip Galen enough cover and funds to finance his escape without Galen ever realizing he was the object of charity for his son's sake. The idea had only two flaws; one, until he made contact with Galen he couldn't do any deal at all; two, if Galen would make such a diabolical bargain Miles was not so sure he cared to see him elude Barrayar's time-cold vengeance after all. A curious dilemma.

* * *

It was like coming home, to step aboard the *Triumph* again. Knots Miles had not been conscious of undid themselves in the back of his neck as he inhaled the familiar recycled air, and soaked the small subliminal chirps and vibrations of the properly functioning, live ship in through his bones. Things were looking in rather better repair all over than at any time since Dagoola, and Miles made a mental note to find out which aggressive engineering sergeants he had to thank for it. It would be good to be just Naismith again, with no problem more complex than what could be laid out in plain military language by HQ, finite and unambiguous.

He issued orders. Cancel further work contracts by individual Dendarii or their groups. All personnel presently scattered downside on work or leave to go on a six hour recall alert. All ships to begin their twenty-four hour preflight checks. Send Lieutenant Bone to me. It gave him a pleasantly megalomanic sense of drawing all things toward a center, himself, though that humor cooled when he contemplated the unsolved problem waiting for him in his Intelligence division.

Quinn in tow, Miles went to pay Intelligence a visit. He found Bel Thorne manning the security comconsole. If manning was the right term; Thorne was one of Beta Colony's hermaphrodite minority, hapless heirs of a century-past genetic project of dubious merit. It had been one of the lunatic fringe's loonier experiments, in Miles's estimation. Most of the men/women stuck to their own comfortable little subculture on tolerant Beta Colony; that Thorne had ventured out into the wider galactic world bespoke either courage, terminal boredom, or most probably if you knew Thorne, a low taste for unsettling people. Captain Thorne kept soft brown hair cut in a deliberately ambiguous style, but wore hard-earned Dendarii uniform and rank with crisp definition.

"Hi, Bel." Miles pulled up a station chair and hooked it into its clamps; Thorne greeted him with a friendly semi-salute. "Play me back everything the surveillance team picked up from Galen's house after Quinn and I rescued the Barrayaran military attache and left to deliver him back to their embassy." Quinn kept her face quite straight through this bit of revisionist history.

Thorne obediently fast-forwarded through a half hour of silence, then slowed through the disjointed conversation of the two unhappy Komarran guards awakening from stun. Then the chime of the comconsole; a somewhat degraded image resynthesized from the vid beam; the slow toneless voice and face of Galen himself, requesting a report on the guard's murderous assignment; the sharp rise in tone, as he heard of the dramatic rescue instead—"Fools!" A pause. "Don't attempt to contact me again." Cut.

"We traced the source of the call, I trust," said Miles.

"Public comconsole at a tube station," said Thorne. "By the time we got someone there, the potential search radius had widened to about a hundred kilometers. Good tube system, that."

"Right. And he never returned to the house after that?"

"Abandoned everything, apparently. He's had previous experience evading security, I take it."

"He was an expert before I was born," sighed Miles. "What about the two guards?"

"They were still at the house when the surveillance guys from the Barrayaran embassy arrived and took over and we packed our kit and went home. Have the Barrayarans paid us for this little job yet, by the way?"

"Handsomely."

"Oh, good. I was afraid they'd hold it up till after we'd delivered Van der Poole too."

"About Van der Poole—Galen," said Miles. "Ah— we're no longer working for the Barrayarans on that one. They've brought in their own team from their Sector headquarters on Tau Ceti."

Throne frowned puzzlement. "But we're still working?"

"For the time being. But you'd better pass the word along to our downside people. From this point on, contact with the Barrayarans is to be avoided."

Thorne's brows rose. "Who are we working for, then?"

"For me."

Thorne paused. "Aren't you playing this one a tad close to your chest, sir?"

"Much too close, if my own Intelligence people are to remain effective." Miles sighed. "All right. An odd and unexpected personal wrinkle has turned up in the middle of this case. Have you ever wondered why I never speak of my family background, or my past?"

"Well—there are a lot of Dendarii who don't. Sir."

"Quite. I was born a clone, Bel."

Thorne looked only mildly sympathetic. "Some of my best friends are clones."

"Perhaps I should say, I was created a clone. In the military laboratory of a galactic power that shall remain nameless. I was created for a covert substitution plot against the son of a certain important man, key of another galactic power—you can figure out who with a very little research, I'm sure—but about seven years ago I declined the honor. I escaped, fled, and set up on my own, creating the Dendarii Mercenaries from, er, materials found ready to hand."

Thorne grinned. "A memorable event."

"But this is where Galen comes in. The galactic power abandoned their plot, and I thought I was free of my unhappy past. But several clones had been run off, so to speak, in the attempt to generate an exact physical duplicate, with certain mental refinements, before the lab finally came up with me. I thought they were all long dead, callously murdered, disposed of. But apparently, one of the earlier, less-successful efforts had been put into cryo-suspension. And somehow, he has fallen into Ser Galen's hands. My sole surviving clone-brother, Bel." Miles's hand closed in a fist. "Enslaved by a fanatic. I want to rescue him." His hand opened pleadingly. "Can you understand why?"

Thorne blinked. "Knowing you . . . I guess I do. Is it very important to you, sir?"

"Very."

Thorne straightened slightly. "Then it will be done."

"Thank you." Miles hesitated. "Better have all our downside patrol leaders issued a small medical scanner. Keep it on themselves at all times. As you know, I had my leg bones replaced with synthetics a bit over a year ago. His are normal bone. It's the quickest way to tell the difference between us."

"Your appearance is that close?" said Thorne.

"Our appearances are identical, apparently."

"They are," confirmed Quinn to Thorne. "I've seen him."

"I . . . see. Interesting possibilities for confusion there, sir." Thorne glanced at Quinn, who nodded ruefully.

"Too right. I trust the dissemination of the medical scanners will help keep things dull. Carry on—call me at once if you get a break in the case."

"Right, sir."

In the corridor, Quinn remarked, "Nice save, sir."

Miles sighed. "I had to find some way to warn the Dendarii about Mark. Can't have him playing Admiral Naismith again unimpeded."

"Mark?" said Elli. "Who's Mark, or dare I guess? Miles Mark Two?"

"Lord Mark Pierre Vorkosigan," said Miles calmly. Anyway, he hoped he appeared calm. "My brother."

Elli, alive to the significances of Barrayaran clan claims, frowned. "Is Ivan right, Miles? Has that little sucker hypnotized you?"

"I don't know," said Miles slowly. "If I'm the only one who sees him that way, then maybe, just maybe—"

Elli made an encouraging noise.

A slight smile turned one corner of Miles's mouth. "Then maybe everybody's wrong but me."

Elli snorted.

Miles turned serious again. "I truly don't know. In seven years, I never abused the powers of Admiral Naismith for personal purposes. That's not a record I'm anxious to break. Well, perhaps we'll fail to turn them up, and the question will become moot."

"Wishful thinking," said Elli disapprovingly. "If you don't want to turn them up, maybe you'd better stop looking for them."

"Compelling logic."

"So why aren't you compelled? And what do you plan to do with them if you do catch 'em?"

"As for what," said Miles, "it's not too complicated. I want to find Galen and my clone before

Destang does, and separate them. And then make sure Destang doesn't find them until I can send a private report home. Eventually, if I vouch for him, I believe a cease-and-desist order will come through countermanding my clone's assassination, without my having to appear directly connected with it."

"What about Galen?" asked Elli skeptically. "No way are you going to get a cease-and-desist order on him."

"Probably not. Galen is—a problem I have not solved."

Miles returned to his cabin, where his fleet accountant caught up with him.

Lieutenant Bone fell on the eighteen-million-mark credit chit with heartfelt and unmilitary glee. "Saved!"

"Disburse it as needed," Miles said. "And get the *Triumph* out of hock. We need to be able to move out at a moment's notice without having to argue about grand theft with the Solar Navy. Ah—hm. D'you think you can create a credit chit, out of petty cash or wherever, in galactic funds, that couldn't in any way be traced back to us?"

A gleam lit her eye. "An interesting challenge, sir. Does this have anything to do with our upcoming contract?"

"Security, Lieutenant," Miles said blandly. "I can't discuss it even with you."

"Security," she sniffed, "doesn't hide as much from Accounting as they think they do."

"Perhaps I should combine your departments. No?" He grinned at her horrified look. "Well, maybe not."

"Who does this chit go to?"

"To the bearer."

Her brows rose. "Very good, sir. How much?"

Miles hesitated. "Half a million marks. However that translates into local credit."

"Half a million marks," she noted wryly, "is not petty."

"Just so long as it's cash."

"I'll do my best, sir."

He sat alone in his cabin after she left, frowning deeply. The impasse was clear. Galen could not be expected to initiate contact unless he saw some way, not to mention some reason, to control the situation or achieve surprise. Letting Galen choreograph his moves seemed fatal, and Miles did not care for the idea of wandering around till Galen chose to surprise him. Still, some sort of feint to create an opening might be better than no move at all, in view of the shrinking time limit. Get off the damn defensive disadvantage, act instead of react . . . A high resolve, but for the minor flaw that until Galen was spotted Miles had no object to act upon. He growled frustration and went wearily to bed.

He woke on his own in the dark of his cabin some twelve hours later, noted the time on the glowing digits of his wall clock, and lay a while luxuriating in the remarkable sensation of finally having gotten enough sleep. His greedy body was just suggesting, in the leaden slowness of his limbs, that *more* would be nice, when his cabin comconsole chimed. Saved from the sin of sloth, he staggered out of bed and answered it.

"Sir." The face of one of the *Triumph*'s comm officers appeared. "You have a tight-beam call from the Barrayaran Embassy downside in London. They're asking for you personally, scrambled."

Miles trusted that this was not literally true. It couldn't be Ivan; he would have called on the private comm link. It had to be an official communique. "Unscramble and pipe it in here, then."

"Should I record?"

"Ah—no."

Could the new orders from HQ for the Dendarii fleet have arrived already? Miles swore silently. If they were forced to break orbit before his Dendarii Intelligence people found Galen and Mark . . .

Destang's grim face appeared over the vid plate. " 'Admiral Naismith.' " Miles could hear the quote marks dropping in around his name. "Are we alone?"

"Entirely, sir."

Destang's face relaxed slightly. "Very well. I have an order for you—Lieutenant Vorkosigan. You are to remain aboard your ship in orbit until I, personally, call again and notify you otherwise."

"Why, sir?" said Miles, though he could damn well guess.

"For my peace of mind. When a simple precaution will prevent the slightest possibility of an accident, it's foolish not to take it. Do you understand?"

"Fully, sir."

"Very well. That's all. Destang out." The commodore's face dissolved in air.

Miles cursed out loud, with feeling. Destang's "precaution" could only mean that his Sector goons had spotted Mark already, before Miles's Dendarii had— and were moving in for the kill. How fast? Was there still a chance . . . ?"

Miles slipped on his grey trousers, hung ready to hand, and dug the secured comm link from his pocket and keyed it on. "Ivan?" he spoke into it quietly. "You there?"

"Miles?" It was not Ivan's voice; it was Galeni's.

"Captain Galeni? I found the other half of the comm link . . . ah, are you alone?"

"At present." Galeni's voice was dry, conveying

through no more than the tone his opinion of both the misplaced comm link story and those who invented it. "Why?"

"How'd you come by the comm link?"

"Your cousin handed it to me just before he departed on his duties."

"Left for where? What duties?" Was Ivan swept up for Destang's man-hunt? If so, Miles could happily throttle him for divesting Miles's ear on the proceedings just when it might have done the most good—skittish idiot!—if only—

"He's escorting the ambassador's lady to the World Botanical Exhibition and Ornamental Flower Show at the University of London's Horticulture Hall. She goes every year, to glad-hand the local social set. Admittedly, she is also interested in the topic."

Miles's voice rose slightly. "In the middle of a security crisis, you sent Ivan to a *flower show?*"

"Not I," denied Galeni. "Commodore Destang. I, ah—believe he felt Ivan could be most easily spared. He's not thrilled with Ivan."

"What about you?"

"He's not thrilled with me either."

"No, I mean, what are you doing? Are you directly involved with the . . . current operation?"

"Hardly."

"Ah. I'm relieved. I was a little afraid—somebody— might have gotten a short circuit in his head about requiring it of you as proof of loyalty or some damn thing."

"Commodore Destang is neither a sadist nor a fool." Galeni paused. "He's careful, however. I'm confined to quarters."

"You have no direct access to the operation, then. Like where they are, and how close, and when they plan to . . . make a move."

Galeni's voice was carefully neutral, neither offering nor denying help. "Not readily."

"Hm. He just ordered me confined to quarters too. I think he's had some sort of break, and things are coming to a head."

There was a brief silence. Galeni's words drifted out on a sigh. "Sorry to hear that . . ." His voice cracked. "It's so damned useless! The dead hand of the past goes on jerking the strings by galvanic reflex, and we poor puppets dance—nothing is served, not us, not him, not Komarr . . ."

"If I could make contact with your father," began Miles.

"It would be useless. He'll fight, and keep on fighting."

"But he has nothing, now. He blew his last chance. He's an old man, he's tired—he could be ready to change, to quit at last," Miles argued.

"I wish . . . no. He can't quit. Above life itself, he has to prove himself right. To be right redeems his every crime. To have done all that he's done, and be wrong—unbearable!"

"I . . . see. Well, I'll contact you again if I . . . have anything useful to say. There's, ah, no point in turning in the comm link till you have both halves, eh?"

"As you wish." Galeni's tone was not exactly fired with hope.

Miles shut down the comm link.

He called Thorne, who reported no visible progress.

"In the meantime," said Miles, "here's another lead for you. An unfortunate one. The team from the Barrayarans has evidently spotted our target within the last hour or so."

"Ha! Maybe we can follow them, and let them lead us to Galen."

"Afraid not. We have to get ahead of them, without treading on their toes. Their hunt is a lethal one."

"Armed and dangerous, eh? I'll pass the word." Thorne whistled thoughtfully. "Your creche-mate sure is popular."

Miles washed, dressed, ate, made ready: boot knife, scanners, stunners both hip-holstered and concealed, comm links, a wide assortment of tools and toys one might carry through London's shuttleport security checks. It was a far cry from combat gear, alas, though his jacket nearly clanked when he walked. He called the duty officer, made sure a personnel shuttle was fueled, pilot at the ready. He waited without patience.

What was Galen up to? If he wasn't just running—and the fact that the Barrayaran security team had nearly caught up with him suggested he was still hanging around for some reason—why? Mere revenge? Something more arcane? Was Miles's analysis of him too simple, too subtle—what was he missing? What was left in life for the man who had to be right?

His cabin comconsole chimed. Miles sent up a short inarticulate prayer—let it be some break, some chink, some handle—

The comm officer's face appeared. "Sir, I have a call originating from the downside commercial comconsole net. A man who refuses to identify himself says you want to talk to him."

Miles jerked electrically upright. "Trace the call and cut a copy to Captain Thorne in Intelligence. Put it through here."

"Do you want your visual to go out, or just audio?"

"Both."

The comm officer's face faded as another man's appeared, giving an unsettling illusion of transmutation.

"Vorkosigan?" said Galen.

"So?" said Miles.

"I will not repeat myself." Galen spoke low and fast. "I don't give a damn if you're recording or tracing. It's irrelevant. You will meet me in seventy minutes exactly. You will come to the Thames Tidal Barrier, halfway between Towers Six and Seven. You will walk out on the seaward side to the lower lookout. Alone. Then we'll talk. If any condition is not met, we will simply not be there when you arrive. And Ivan Vorpatril will die at 0207."

"You are two. I must be two," Miles began. *Ivan?*

"Your pretty bodyguard? Very well. Two." The vid blinked blank.

"No—"

Silence.

Miles keyed to Thorne. "Did you get that, Bel?"

"Sure did. Sounded threatening. Who's Ivan?"

"A very important person. Where'd this originate?"

"A tubeway nexus, public comconsole. I have a man on the way who can make it in six minutes. Unfortunately—"

"I know. Six minutes gives a search radius of several million people. I think we'll play it his way. Up to a point. Put a patrol in the air over the Tidal Barrier, file a flight plan for my shuttle downside, have an aircar and Dendarii driver and guard meet it. Tell Bone I want that credit chit now. Tell Quinn to meet me in the shuttle hatch corridor, and bring a couple of med scanners. And stand by. I want to check something."

He took a deep breath, and keyed open the comm link. "Galeni?"

A pause. "Yes?"

"You still confined to quarters?"

"Yes."

"I have an urgent request for information. Where's Ivan, really?"

"As far as I know, he's still at—"

"Check it. Check it fast."

There was a long, long pause, which Miles utilized to recheck his gear, find Lieutenant Bone, and walk to the shuttle hatch corridor. Quinn was waiting, intensely curious.

"What's up now?"

"We have our break. Of sorts. Galen wants a meeting, but—"

"Miles?" Galeni's voice came back at last. It sounded rather strained.

"Yo."

"The private we'd sent to be driver/guard called in about ten minutes ago. He'd spelled Ivan, attending on Milady, while Ivan went to piss. When Ivan didn't come back in twenty minutes, the driver went to look for him. Spent thirty minutes hunting—the Horticulture Hall is huge, and mobbed tonight—before he reported back to us. How did you know?"

"I think I've got hold of the other end. Do you recognize whose style of doing business this is?"

Galeni swore.

"Quite. Look. I don't care how you do it, but I want you to meet me in fifty minutes at the Thames Tidal Barrier, Section Six. Pack at least a stunner, and get away preferably without alerting Destang. We have an appointment with your father and my brother."

"If he has Ivan—"

"He had to bring some card to the table, or he wouldn't come play. We've got one last chance to make it come out right. Not a good chance, just the last one. Are you with me?"

A slight pause. "Yes." The tone was decisive.

"See you there."

Pocketing the link, Miles turned to Elli. "Now we move."

They swung through the shuttle hatch. For once, Miles had no objection to Ptarmigan's habit of taking all downside flights at combat-drop speed.

Chapter Fourteen

The Thames Tidal Barrier, known to local wags as the King Canute Memorial, was a vastly more impressive structure seen from a hundred meters up than it had seemed from the kilometers-high view from the shuttle. The aircar banked, circling. The synthacrete mountain ran away in both directions farther than Miles's eye could follow, whitened into an illusion of marble by the spotlights that knifed through the faintly misty midnight blackness.

Watchtowers every kilometer housed not soldiers guarding the wall but the night shift of engineers and technicians watching over the sluices and pumping stations. To be sure, if the sea ever broke through, it would raze the city more mercilessly than any army.

But the sea was calm this summer night, dotted with colored navigation lights, red, green, white, and the distant moving twinkle of ships' running lights. The eastern horizon glowed faintly, false dawn from the radiant cities of Europe beyond the waters.

On the other side of the white barrier toward ancient London, all the dirt and grime and broken places were swallowed by the night, leaving only the jewelled illusion of something magic, unmarred and immortal.

Miles pressed his face to the aircar's bubble canopy for a last strategic view of the arena they were about to enter before the car dropped toward the near-empty parking area behind the Barrier. Section Six was peripheral to the main channel sections with their enormous navigation locks busy around the clock; it was just dyke and auxiliary pumping stations, nearly deserted at this hour. That suited Miles. If the situation devolved into some sort of shooting war, the fewer civilian bystanders wandering through the better. Catwalks and ladders ran to access ports in the structure, geometric black accents on the whiteness; spidery railings marked walkways, some broad and public, some narrow, reserved no doubt to Authorized Personnel. At present they all appeared deserted, no sign of Galen or Mark. No sign of Ivan.

"What's significant about 0207?" Miles wondered aloud. "I have the feeling it should be obvious. It's such an exact time."

Elli the space-born shook her head, but the Dendarii soldier piloting the aircar volunteered, "It's high tide, sir."

"Ah!" said Miles. He sat back, thinking furiously. "How interesting. It suggests two things. They've concealed Ivan around here someplace—and we might do best to concentrate our search below the high waterline. Could they have chained him to a railing down by the rocks or some damn thing?"

"The air patrol could make a pass and check," said Quinn.

"Yes, have them do that."

The aircar settled into a painted circle on the pavement.

Quinn and the second soldier exited first, cautiously, and ran a fast perimeter scan around the area. "There's somebody approaching on foot," the soldier reported.

"Pray it's Captain Galeni," Miles muttered, with a glance at his chrono. Seven minutes remained of his time limit.

It was a man jogging with his dog. The pair stared at the four uniformed Dendarii, and arced nervously around them to the far side of the parking lot before disappearing through the bushes softening the north end. Everybody took their hands off their stunners. Civilized town, thought Miles. You wouldn't do that at this hour in some parts of Vorbarr Sultana, unless you had a much bigger dog.

The soldier checked his infra-red. "Here comes another one."

Not the soft pad of running shoes this time, but the quick ring of boots. Miles recognized the sound of the boots before he could make out the face in the splash of light and shadow. Galeni's uniform turned from dark grey to green as he entered the lot's zone of brighter illumination, walking fast.

"All right," said Miles to Elli, "this is where we split off. Stay back and out of sight at all costs, but if you can find a vantage, good. Wrist comm open?"

Elli keyed her wrist comm. Miles pulled his boot knife and used the point to disengage and extinguish the tiny transmit-indicator light in his own wrist comm, then blew into it; the hiss of it whispered from Elli's wrist. "Sending fine," she confirmed.

"Got your med scanner?"

She displayed it.

"Take a baseline."

She pointed it at him, waved it up and down. "Recorded and ready for auto-comparison."

"Can you think of anything else?"

She shook her head, but still didn't look happy. "What do I do if *he* comes walking back and you don't?"

"Grab him, fast-penta him—got your interrogation kit?"

She flashed open her jacket; a small brown case peeped from an inner pocket.

"Rescue Ivan if you can. Then," Miles took a deep breath, "you can blow the clone's head off or whatever you choose."

"What happened to 'my brother right or wrong'?" said Elli.

Galeni, coming up in the middle of this, cocked his head with interest to hear the answer to that one, but Miles only shook his head. He couldn't think of a simple answer.

"Three minutes left," said Miles to Galeni. "We better move."

They headed up a walk that led to a set of stairs, stepping over the chain that marked them as closed for the night to law-abiding citizens. The stairs climbed the back side of the tidal barrier to a public promanade that ran along the top to allow sightseers a view of the ocean in the daytime. Galeni, who had evidently been moving at speed, was breathing deeply even as they began their climb.

"Have any trouble getting out of the embassy?" asked Miles.

"Not really," said Galeni. "As you know, the trick is getting back in. I think you demonstrated simplest is best. I just walked out the side entrance and took the nearest tubeway. Fortunately, the duty guard had no orders to shoot me."

"Did you know that in advance?"

"No."

"Then Destang knows you left."

"He will know, certainly."

"Think you were followed?" Miles glanced involuntarily over his shoulder. He could see the parking lot and aircar below; Elli and the two soldiers had vanished from view, seeking their vantage no doubt.

"Not immediately. Embassy security," Galeni's teeth flashed in the shadows, "is undermanned at present. I left my wristcomm, and bought cash tokens for the tubeway instead of using my passcard, so they have nothing quick to trace me by."

They panted to the top; the damp air moved cool against Miles's face, smelling of river slime and sea salt, a faintly decayed estuarial tang. Miles crossed the wide promenade and peered down over the railing at the synthacrete outer face of the dyke. A narrow railed ledge ran along some twenty meters below, vanishing away out of sight to the right along an outcurving bulge in the Barrier. Not part of the public area, it was reached by keyed extension ladders at intervals along the railing, all folded up and locked for the night of course. They could fuss with trying to break open and decode one of the locked ladder controls—time-consuming, and likely to light up the alarm board of some night-shift supervisor in one of the distant watchtowers—or go down the fast way.

Miles sighed under his breath. Rappelling high over rock-hard surfaces was one of his all-time least-favorite activities. He fished the drop-wire spool from its own little pocket on his Dendarii jacket, attached the gravitic grappler carefully and firmly to the railing, and doublechecked it. At a touch, handles telescoped out from the sides of the spool and released the wide ribbon-harness that always looked horribly flimsy despite its phenomenal tensile strength. Miles threaded it round himself, clipped it tight, hopped over the rail and danced down the wall backwards, not looking down. By the time he reached the bottom his adrenalin was pumping nicely, thank you.

He sent the spool winding itself back up to Galeni, who repeated Miles's performance. Galeni offered no comment about his feelings about heights as he handed back the device, so neither did Miles. Miles touched the control that released the grappler and rewound and pocketed the spool.

"We go right," Miles nodded. He drew his holstered stunner. "What did you bring?"

"I could only get one stunner." Galeni pulled it from his pocket, checked its charge and setting. "And you?"

"Two. And a few other toys. There are severe limits to what you can carry through shuttleport security."

"Considering how crowded this place is, I think they're wise," remarked Galeni.

Stunners in hand, they walked single file along the ledge, Miles first. Sea water swirled and gurgled just below their feet, green-brown transluscence frosted with streaks of foam within the circles of light, silky black beyond. Judging from the discoloration, this walkway was inundated at high tide.

Miles motioned Galeni to pause, and slipped forward. Just beyond the outcurve the walkway widened to a four-meter circle and dead-ended, the railing arcing around to meet the wall. In the wall was a doorway, a sturdy watertight oval hatch.

Standing in front of the hatch were Galen and Mark, stunners in their hands. Mark wore black T-shirt and Dendarii grey trousers and boots, minus the pocketed jacket—his own clothes, pilfered, Miles wondered, or duplicates? His nostrils flared as he spotted his grandfather's dagger in its lizard-skin sheath at the clone's waist.

"A stand-off," remarked Galen conversationally as Miles halted, with a glance at Miles's stunner and his own. "If we all fire at once, it leaves either me or my Miles on his feet, and the game is mine. But if by some miracle you dropped us both, we could not tell you where your oxlike cousin is. He'd die before you could find him. His death has been automated. I need not get back to him to carry it out. Quite the reverse. Your pretty bodyguard may as well join us."

Galeni stepped around the bend. "Some stand-offs are more curious than others," he said.

Galen's face flickered from its hard irony, lips parting in a breath of deep dismay, then tightening again even as his hand tightened on his weapon. "You were to bring the woman," he hissed.

Miles smiled slightly. "She's around. But you said two, and we are two. Now all the interested parties are here. Now what?"

Galen's eyes shifted, counting weapons, calculating distances, muscle, odds no doubt; Miles was doing the same.

"The stand-off remains," said Galen. "If you're both stunned you lose; if we're both stunned you lose again. It's absurd."

"What would you suggest?" asked Miles.

"I propose we all lay our weapons in the center of the deck. Then we can talk without distraction."

He's got another one concealed, thought Miles. *Same as me.* "An interesting proposition. Who puts his down last?"

Galen's face was a study in unhappy calculation.

He opened his mouth and closed it again, and shook his head slightly.

"I too would like to talk without distraction," said Miles carefully. "I propose this schedule. I'll lay mine down first. Then M— the clone. Then yourself. Captain Galeni last."

"What guarantee . . . ?" Galen glanced sharply at his son. The tension between them was near-sickening, a strange and silent compound of rage, despair, and anguish.

"He'll give you his word," said Miles. He looked for confirmation to Galeni, who nodded slowly.

Silence fell for the space of three breaths, then Galen said, "All right."

Miles stepped forward, knelt, laid his stunner in the center of the deck, stepped back. Mark repeated his performance, staring at him the while. Galen hesitated a long, agonized moment, eyes still full of shifting calculation, then put his weapon down with the others. Galeni followed suit without hesitation. His smile was like a sword-cut. His eyes were unreadable, but for the baseline of dull pain that had lurked in them ever since his father had resurrected himself.

"Your proposition first, then," Galen said to Miles. "If you have one."

"Life," said Miles. "I have concealed—in a place only I know of, and if you'd stunned me you'd never have discovered it in time—a cash-credit chit for a hundred thousand Betan dollars—that's half a million Imperial marks, friends—payable to the bearer. I can give it to you, plus a head start, useful information on how to evade Barrayaran security—which is very close behind you, by the way—"

The clone was looking extremely interested; his eyes had widened when the sum was named, and widened still further at the mention of Barrayaran security.

"—in exchange for my cousin," Miles took a slight breath, "my brother, and your promise to—retire, and refrain from further plots against the Barrayaran Imperium. Which can only result in useless bloodshed and unnecessary pain to your few surviving relations. The war's over, Ser Galen. It's time for someone else to try something else. A different way, maybe a better way—it could scarcely be a worse way, after all."

"The revolt," breathed Galen almost to himself, "must not die."

"Even if everybody in it dies? 'It didn't work, so let's do it some more'? In my line of work they call that military stupidity. I don't know what they call it in civilian life."

"My older sister once surrendered on a Barrayaran's word," Galen remarked. His face was very cold. "Admiral Vorkosigan too was full of soft and logical persuasion, promising peace."

"My father's word was betrayed by an underling," said Miles, "who couldn't recognize when the war was over and it was time to quit. He paid for the error with his life, executed for his crime. My father gave you your revenge then. It was all he could give you; he couldn't bring those dead to life. Neither can I. I can only try to prevent more dying."

Galen smiled sourly. "And you, David. What bribe would you offer me to betray Komarr, to lay alongside your Barrayaran master's money?"

Galeni was regarding his fingernails, a peculiar fey smile playing around his lips as he listened. He buffed them briefly on his trouser seam, crossed his arms, blinked. "Grandchildren?"

Galen seemed taken aback for a bare instant. "You're not even bonded!"

"I might be, someday. Only if I live, of course."

"And they would all be good little Imperial subjects," sneered Galen, recovering his initial balance with an effort.

Galeni shrugged. "Seems to fit in with Vorkosigan's offer of life. I can't give you anything else you want of me."

"You two are more alike than either of you realize, I think," Miles murmured. "So what's your proposition, Ser Galen? Why have you called us all here?"

Galen's right hand went to his jacket, then slowed. He smiled, tilted his head as if asking permission, disarmingly. *Here comes the second stunner,* thought Miles. *Coyly, pretending to the last minute that it's not really a weapon.* Miles didn't flinch, but an involuntary calculation did flash through his mind as to just how fast he could vault the railing, and how far he could swim underwater holding his breath in a strong surf. Wearing boots. Galeni, cool as ever, didn't move either.

Even when the weapon Ser Galen abruptly displayed turned out to be a lethal nerve disruptor.

"Some stand-offs," said Galen, "are more equal than others." His smile tightened to a parody of itself. "Pick up those stunners," he added to the clone, who stooped and gathered them up and stuck them in his belt.

"Now what are you going to do with that?" said Miles lightly, trying not to let his eye be hypnotized, nor his mind paralyzed, by the silver bell-muzzle. Shiny beads, bells and whistles.

"Kill you," Galen explained. His eyes flicked to his son, and away, toward and away; he focused on Miles as if to steady his high resolve.

So why are you still talking instead of firing? Miles didn't speak that thought aloud, lest Galen be struck by its good sense. Keep him talking, he wants to say more, is driven to say more. "Why? I don't see how that will serve Komarr at this late hour, except maybe to relieve your feelings. Mere revenge?"

"Nothing mere about it. Complete. My Miles will walk out of here as the only one."

"Oh, come on!" Miles didn't have to call on his acting ability to lend outrage to his tone; it came quite naturally. "You're not still stuck on the bloody substitution plot! Barrayaran Security is all warned, they'll spot you at once now. Can't be done." He glanced at the clone. "You going to let him run you head first into a flash disposer? You're dead meat the moment you present yourself. It's useless. And it's not *necessary*."

The clone looked distinctly uneasy, but jerked up his chin and managed a proud smile. "I'm not going to be Lord Vorkosigan. I'm going to be Admiral Naismith. I did it once, so I know I can. Your Dendarii are going to give us a ride out of here—and a new power base."

"Nghl!" Miles made a hair-tearing gesture. "D'you think I'd have walked in here if that were even remotely possible? The Dendarii are warned too. Every patrol leader out there—and you'd better believe I have patrols out there—is carrying a med scanner. First order you give, you'll be scanned. If they find leg bone where my synthetics should be, they'll blow your head off. End plot."

"But my leg bones *are* synthetics," said the clone in a puzzled tone.

Miles froze. "What? You told me your bones didn't break—"

Galen swivelled his head round at the clone. "When did you tell him that . . . ?"

"They don't," the clone answered Miles. "But after yours were replaced, so were mine. Otherwise the first cursory med scan I got would have given it all away."

"But you still don't have the pattern of old breaks in your other bones . . . ?"

"No, but that would take a much closer scan. And once the three are eliminated I should be able to avoid that. I'll study your logs—"

"The three what?"

"The three Dendarii who know you are Vorkosigan."

"Your pretty bodyguard, and the other couple," Galen explained vindictively to Miles's look of horror. "I'm sorry you didn't bring her. Now we shall have to hunt her down."

Was that a fleeting queasy look on Mark's face? Galen caught it too, and frowned faintly.

"You still couldn't bring it off," argued Miles. "There are five thousand Dendarii. I know hundreds of them by name, on sight. We've been in combat together. I know things about them their own mothers don't, not in any log. And they've seen me under every kind of stress. You wouldn't even know the right jokes to make. And even if you succeed for a time, become Admiral Naismith as you once planned to become Emperor—where is Mark then? Maybe Mark doesn't want to be a space mercenary. Maybe he wants to be a, a textile designer. Or a doctor—"

"Oh," breathed the clone, with a glance down his twisted body, *"not* a doctor . . ."

"—or a holovid programmer, or a star pilot, or an engineer. Or very far away from *him*." Miles jerked his head at Galen; for a moment the clone's eyes filled with a passionate longing, as quickly masked. "How will you ever find out?"

"It's true," said Galen, looking at the clone through suddenly narrowed eyes, "you must pass for an experienced soldier. And you've never killed."

The clone shifted uneasily, looking sideways, at his mentor.

Galen's voice had softened. "You must learn to kill if you expect to survive."

"No, you don't," Miles put in. "Most people go through their whole lives without killing anybody. False argument."

The nerve disruptor's aim steadied on Miles. "You talk too much." Galen's eyes fell one last time on his silent, witnessing son, who raised his chin in defiance, then flicked away as if the sight burned. "It's time to go."

Galen, face hardening decisively, turned to the clone. "Here." He handed him the nerve disruptor. "It's time to complete your education. Shoot them, and let's go."

"What about Ivan?" asked Captain Galeni softly.

"I have as little use for Vorkosigan's nephew as I have for his son," said Galen. "They can skip down to hell hand in hand." His head turned to the clone and he added, "Begin!"

Mark swallowed, and raised the weapon in a two-handed firing stance. "But—what about the credit chit?"

"There is no credit chit. Can't you spot a lie when you hear it, fool?"

Miles raised his wrist comm, and spoke distinctly into it. "Elli, do you have all this?"

"Recorded and transmitted to Captain Thorne in I.Q.," Quinn's voice came back cheerily, thin in the damp air. "D'you want company yet?"

"Not yet." He let his hand fall, stood straight, met Galen's furious eyes and clenched teeth; "As I said. End plot. Let's discuss alternatives."

Mark had lowered the nerve disruptor, his face dismayed.

"Alternatives? Revenge will do!" hissed Galen. "Fire!"

"But—" said the clone, agitated.

"As of this moment, you're a free man." Miles spoke low and fast. "He bought and paid for you, but he doesn't own you. But if you kill for him, he'll own you forever. Forever and ever."

Not necessarily, spoke Galeni's silent quirk of the lips, but he did not interfere with Miles's pitch.

"You must kill your enemies," snarled Galen.

Mark's hand and aim sagged, his mouth opening in protest.

"Now, dammit!" yelled Galen, and made to grab back the nerve disruptor.

Galeni stepped in front of Miles. Miles scrabbled in his jacket for his second stunner. The nerve disruptor crackled. Miles drew, too late, too goddamn late—Captain Galeni gasped—*he's dead for my slowness, my one-last-chance stupidity*—face harrowed, mouth open in a silent yell, Miles sprang from behind Galeni and aimed his stunner—

To see Galen crumple, convulsing, back arching in a bone-cracking twist, face writhing—and slump in death.

"Kill your enemies," breathed Mark, his face white as paper. "Right. Ah!" he added, raising the weapon again as Miles started forward, "Stop right there!"

A hiss at Miles's feet—he glanced down to see a thin layer of foam wash past his boots, lose momentum, and recede. In a moment, another. The tide was rising over the ledge. The tide was rising—

"Where's Ivan?" Miles demanded, his hand clenching on his stunner.

"If you fire that you'll never know," said Mark.

His eye hurried nervously, from Miles to Galeni, from Galen's body at his feet to the weapon in his own hand, as if they all added up to some impossibly incorrect sum. His breath was shallow and panicky, his knuckles, wrapped around the nerve disruptor, bone-pale. Galeni was standing very, very still, head cocked, looking down at what lay there, or inward; he did not seem to be conscious of the weapon or its wielder at all.

"Fine," said Miles. "You help us and we'll help you. Take us to Ivan."

Mark backed toward the wall, not lowering the nerve disruptor. "I don't believe you."

"Where are you going to run to? You can't go back to the Komarrans. There's a Barayaran hit squad with murder on its collective mind breathing down your neck. You can't go to the local authorities for protection; you have a body to explain. I'm your only chance."

Mark looked at the body, at the nerve disruptor, at Miles.

The soft whirr of a rappel spool unwinding was barely audible over the hiss of the sea foam underfoot. Miles glanced up. Quinn was flying down in one long swoop, like a falcon stooping, weapon in one hand and rappeling spool controlled by the other.

Mark kicked open the hatch and stumbled backwards into it. "You hunt for Ivan. He's not far. I don't have a body to explain—*you* do. The murder weapon has your fingerprints on it!" He flung down the nerve disruptor and slammed the hatch closed.

Miles leapt for the door, fingers scrabbling, but it was already sealed—he came close to snapping some more finger bones. The slide and clank of a locking mechanism designed to defy the force of the sea itself came muffled through the hatch. Miles hissed through his teeth.

"Should I blow it open?" gasped Quinn, landing.

"Y— good God, no!" The discoloration on the wall marking high water was a good two meters higher than the top of the hatch. "We might drown London. Try to get it open without damaging it. Captain Galeni!" Miles turned. Galeni had not moved. "You in shock?"

"Hm? No . . . no, I don't think so." Galeni came out of himself with an effort. He added in a strangely calm, reflective tone, "Later, perhaps."

Quinn was bent to the hatchway, pulling devices from her pockets and slapping them to the vertical surface, checking readouts. "Electromechanical with a manual override . . . if I use a magnetic . . ."

Miles reached around and pulled the rappeling harness off Quinn. "Go up," he said to Galeni, "and see if you can find another entrance on the other side. We've got to catch that little sucker!"

Galeni nodded and hooked up the rappeling harness.

Miles held out stunner and boot knife. "Want a weapon?" Mark had taken off with all the spare stunners still stuck in his belt.

"Stunner's useless," Galeni noted. "You'd better keep the knife. If I catch up with him I'll use my bare hands."

With pleasure, Miles added for him silently. He nodded. They had both been through Barrayaran basic unarmed combat school. Three fourths of the moves were barred to Miles in a real fight at full force due to the secret weakness of his bones; the same was not true of Galeni. Galeni ascended into the night air, bounding up the wall on the almost-invisible thread as readily as a spider.

"Got it!" cried Quinn. The thick hatch swung wide on a deep, dark hole.

Miles yanked his handlight out of his belt and hopped through. He glanced back at Galen's grey-faced body, lapped by foam, released from obsession and pain. There was no mistaking the stillness of death for the stillness of sleep or anything else; it was the absolute. The nerve-disruptor beam must have hit his head square on. Quinn dragged the hatch shut again behind them, and paused to stuff equipment back into her pockets as the door's mechanism twinkled and beeped, slid and clanked, rendering the lower Thames watershed safe again.

They both scrambled up the corridor. A mere five meters farther on they came to their first check, a T-intersection. This main corridor was lighted, and curved away out of sight in both directions.

"You go left, I'll go right," said Miles.

"You shouldn't be alone," Quinn objected.

"Maybe I should be twins, eh? Go, dammit!"

Quinn threw up her hands in exasperation and ran.

Miles sprinted in the other direction. His footsteps echoed eerily in the corridor, deep in the synthacrete mountain. He paused a moment, listened; heard only Quinn's light fading scuff. He ran on, past hundreds of meters of blank synthacrete, past dark and silent pumping stations, past pumping stations lit up and humming quietly. He was just wondering whether he could have missed an exit—an overhead access port?—when he spotted an object on the corridor floor. One of the stunners, fallen from Mark's belt as he ran in panic. Miles swooped it up with a quick *ah-ha!* of bared teeth, and holstered it as he ran on.

He keyed open his wrist comm. "Quinn?" The corridor curved suddenly into a sort of stark foyer with lift tube. He must be under one of the watch-towers. Beware Authorized Personnel about. "Quinn?"

He stepped into the lift tube and rose. Oh, God, which level had Mark got off at? The third floor he passed opened out onto a glass-walled, lobby-looking area, with doors and the night beyond. Clearly an exit. Miles swung out of the lift tube.

A total stranger, wearing civilian jacket and pants, whirled at the sound of his footstep and dropped to one knee. The silver flash of a parabolic mirror twinkled in his raised hands, a nerve-disruptor muzzle. "There he is!" the man cried, and fired.

Miles recoiled back into the lift tube so fast he rebounded off the far wall. He grabbed for the safety ladder at the side of the tube and began slapping up the rungs faster than the anti-grav field could lift him. He wriggled his facial muscles, shot with pins and needles from the nimbus of the disruptor beam. The man's shoes, Miles realized, gleaming out from the bottom of his trousers, had been Barrayaran regulation Service boots. "Quinn!" he yelped into his wrist comm again.

The next level up opened onto a corridor without gunmen in it. The first three doors Miles tried were locked. The fourth swished open onto a brightly lit office, apparently deserted. On a quick jog around it Miles's eye was caught by a slight movement in the shadows under a console. He bent down to face two women in blue Tidal Authority tech coveralls cowering beneath. One squeaked and covered her eyes; the second hugged her and glared defiantly at Miles.

Miles tried a friendly smile. "Ah . . . hello."

"Who *are* you people?" said the second woman in rising tones.

"Oh, I'm not with them. They're, um . . . hired killers." A just description, after all. "Don't worry, they're not after you. Have you called the police yet?"

She shook her head mutely.

"I suggest you do so immediately. Ah—have you seen me before?"

She nodded.

"Which way did I go?"

She cringed back, clearly terrorized at being cornered by a psychotic. Miles spread his hands in silent apology, and made for the door. "Call the police!" he called back over his shoulder. The faint beep of comconsole keys being pressed drifted down the corridor after him.

Mark was nowhere on this level. The lift tube grav field had now been turned off by someone; the auto safety bar was extended across the opening and the red glow of the warning light filled the corridor. Miles stuck his head cautiously into the lift tube, to spy another head on the level below looking up; he jerked his head back as a nerve disruptor crackled.

A balcony ran right around the outside of the tower. Miles slipped through the door at the seaward end of the corridor and looked around, and up. Only one more floor above. Its balcony was readily reachable by the toss of a grappler. Miles grimaced, pulled out his spool, and made the toss; got a firm hook around the railing above on the first try. A swallow, a brief heart-stopping dangle over the tower, dyke, and growling sea forty meters below, and he was clambering onto the next balcony.

He tiptoed to the glass doorway and checked down the corridor. Mark was crouched, silhouetted by the red light, near the entrance to the lift tube, stunner drawn. The—unconscious, Miles trusted—form of a man in tech coveralls lay sprawled on the corridor floor.

"Mark?" Miles called softly, and jerked back. Mark snapped around and let off a stunner burst in his direction. Miles put his back against the wall and called, "Cooperate with me, and I'll get you out of this alive. Where's Ivan?"

This reminder that Mark still held a trump card had the expected calming effect. He did not fire again. "Get me out of this and I'll tell you where he is," he countered.

Miles grinned into the darkness. "All right. I'm coming in." He slipped round the door and joined his image, pausing only to check for a pulse in the neck of the sprawled man. He had one, happily.

"*How* are you going to get me out of this?" demanded Mark.

"Well, now, that's the tricky part," Miles admitted. He paused to listen intently. Someone was on the ladder in the lift tube, trying to climb quietly; not near their level yet. "The police are on their way, and when they arrive I expect the Barrayarans will decamp in a hurry. They won't want to be caught in an embarrassing interplanetary incident which the ambassador would have to explain to the local authorities. This night's operation is already way out of control in that anybody saw 'em at all. Destang will have their blood on the carpet in the morning."

"The police?" Mark's grip tightened on his stunner; competing fears struggled for ascendancy in his face.

"Yes. We could try and play hide and seek in this tower till the police finally get here—whenever. Or we could go up to the roof and have a Dendarii aircar pick us off right now. I know which I'd prefer. How about you?"

"Then I would be your prisoner." Mark's whispering voice blurred with a fear-fueled anger. "Dead now, dead later, what's the difference? I finally figured out what use you had for a clone."

Mark was seeing himself as a walking body-parts bank again, Miles could tell. Miles sighed. He glanced at his chrono. "By Galen's timetable, I have eleven minutes left to find Ivan."

A shifty look stole over Mark's face. "Ivan's not up. He's down. Back the way we came."

"Ah?" Miles risked a flash-peek into the lift tube. The climber had exited at another floor. The hunters were being thorough in their search. By the time they worked their way up here they'd be quite certain of their quarry.

Miles was still wearing the rappelling harness. Very quietly, careful not to clank, he reached out and fastened the grappler to the safety bar, and tested it. "So you want to go down, do you? I can arrange that. But you'd better be right about Ivan. Because if he dies I'll dissect you personally. Heart and liver, steaks and chops."

Miles stooped, checked his connections, set the spool's rate of spin and stop-point, and positioned himself under the bar, ready for launch. "Climb on."

"Don't I get straps?"

Miles glanced over his shoulder and grinned. "You bounce better than I do."

Looking extremely dubious, Mark stuffed his stunner back in his belt, sidled up to Miles, and gingerly wrapped his arms and legs around Miles's body.

"You'd better hang on tighter than that. The deceleration at the bottom is going to be severe. And don't scream going down. It would draw attention."

Mark's grip tightened convulsively. Miles checked once more for unwanted company—the tube was still empty—and thrust over the side.

Their doubled weight gathered momentum terrifyingly. They fell unimpeded in near-silence for four stories—Miles's stomach was floating near his back teeth, and the sides of the lift tube were a smear of color—then the rappelling spool began to whine, resisting its blurring spin. The straps bit, and Mark's grip hand-to-hand across Miles's collarbone began to pull apart. Miles's right hand flashed up to clamp around Mark's wrist. They braked to a demure stop a centimeter or two above the lift tube's bottom floor, back in the belly of the synthacrete mountain. Miles's ears popped.

The noise of their descent had seemed thunderous to Miles's exacerbated senses, but no startled heads appeared in the openings above, no weapons crackled. Miles and Mark both nipped back out of the line of sight of the tube, into the little foyer off the tidal barrier's internal access corridor. Miles pressed the control to release his grappler and let the spool rewind; the falling thread made no noise, but the grappler unit clinked hitting bottom, and Miles flinched.

"Back that way," said Mark, pointing right. They jogged down the corridor side by side. A deep, growling vibration began to drown lighter sounds. The pumping station that had been blinking and humming when Miles had first passed that way was now at work, lifting Thames water to high-tide sea level through hidden pipes. The next station down, previously dark and silent, was now lit, preparing to go into action.

Mark stopped. "Here."

"Where?"

Mark pointed, "Each pumping chamber has an access hatch, for cleaning and repairs. We put him in there."

Miles swore.

The pumping chamber was about the size of a large closet. Sealed, it would be dark, cold, slimy, stinking, and utterly silent. Until the rush of rising water, thrumming with immense force, gushed in to turn it into a death chamber. Rushed in to fill the ears, the nose, the dark-staring eyes; rushed in to fill the chamber up, up, not even one little pocket of air for a frantic mouth; rushed through to batter and twist the body ceaselessly, roiling against the thick unyielding walls until the face was pulped beyond recognition, until, with the tide, the dank waters at last receded, leaving—nothing of value. A clog in the line.

"You . . ." breathed Miles, glaring at Mark, "lent yourself to *this* . . . ?"

Mark wiped his palms together nervously, stepping back. "You're here—I brought you here," he began plaintively. "I said I would. . . ."

"Isn't this a rather severe punishment for a man who never did you more harm than to snore and keep you awake? Agh!" Miles turned, his back rigid with disgust, and began punching at the hatch lock controls. The last step was manual, turning the bar that undogged the hatch. As Miles pushed the heavy beveled door inward, an alarm began to beep.

"Ivan?"

"Ah!" The cry from within was nearly voiceless.

Miles thrust his shoulders through, flashed his handlight. The hatch was near the top of the chamber; he found himself looking down at the white smudge of Ivan's face half a meter below, looking up.

"You!" Ivan cried in a voice of loathing, staggering back and slipping in the slime.

"No, not him," Miles corrected. "Me."

"Ah?" Ivan's face was lined, exhausted, almost beyond coherent thought; Miles had seen the same look on men who had been in combat too long.

Miles tossed down his handy-dandy rappelling harness—he shuddered, recalling that he'd almost decided not to include it when he'd been kitting up back in the *Triumph*—and braced the spool. "Ready to come up?"

Ivan's lips moved in a mumble, but he wrapped the harness sufficiently around his arms. Miles hit the spool control, and Ivan lifted. Miles helped him slither through the hatch. Ivan stood, boots planted apart, hands on knees supporting himself, breathing heavily. His green dress uniform was damp, crumpled and beslimed. His hands looked like dog meat. He must have pounded and scratched, scrabbled and screamed in the dark, muffled and unheard . . .

Miles swung the hatch back. It clicked firmly. He twirled the manual locking bar. The alarm stopped beeping. Safety circuits reconnected, the pump immediately began to thrum. No greater noise penetrated from the pumping chamber than a monstrous subliminal hiss. Ivan sat down heavily, and pressed his face to his knees.

Miles knelt beside him in worry. Ivan turned his head and managed a sickly grin. "I think," he gulped, "I'm going to take up claustrophobia for a hobby now. . . ."

Miles grinned back, and clapped him on the shoulder. He rose and turned. Mark was nowhere in sight.

Miles spat, and lifted his wrist comm to his lips. "Quinn? Quinn!" He stepped out into the corridor, looked up and down it, listened intently. The faintest echo of running footsteps was fading in the distance, in the direction opposite the Barrayaran-infested watchtower. "Little shit," Miles muttered. "To hell with him." He re-keyed his comm for the air patrol. "Sergeant Nim? Naismith here."

"Yo, sir."

"I've lost contact with Commander Quinn. See if

you can raise her. If you can't, start looking for her. I last saw her on foot inside the tidal barrier, halfway between Towers Six and Seven, heading south."

"Yes, sir."

Miles turned back and helped pull Ivan to his feet. "Can you walk?" he asked anxiously.

"Yeah . . . sure," said Ivan. He blinked. "I'm just a little . . ." They started down the corridor. Ivan stumbled a bit, leaning on Miles, then steadied. "I never knew my body could pump that much adrenalin. Or for so long. Hours and hours . . . how long was I in there?"

"About," Miles glanced at his chrono, "less than two hours."

"Huh. Seemed longer." Ivan appeared to be regaining his equilibrium somewhat. "Where are we going? Why are you wearing your Naismith-suit? Is M'lady all right? They didn't get her, did they?"

"No, Galen just snatched you. This is an independent Dendarii operation at present. I'm not supposed to be downside just now. Destang ordered me to stay aboard the *Triumph* while his goons were trying to dispose of my double. To prevent confusion."

"Yeah, well, makes sense. That way, any little guy they see they know they can fire at." Ivan blinked again. "*Miles* . . ."

"Right," said Miles. "That's why we're going this way instead of that way."

"Should I walk faster?"

"That would be nice, if you can."

They picked up the pace.

"Why did you come downside?" asked Ivan after a minute or two. "Don't tell me you're still trying to save that graceless little copy's worthless hide."

"Galen sent me an invitation engraved on *your* hide. I don't have too many relatives, Ivan. They're of surprising value to me. If only for their rarity, eh?"

They exchanged a glance; Ivan cleared his throat. "Well. So. But you're on shaky ground, trying to undercut Destang. Say—if his hit squad is that close— where's Galen?" Alarm suffused his face.

"Galen's dead," Miles reported shortly. They were in fact just passing the dark cross corridor to the outer ledge where that body lay.

"Ah? Glad to hear it. Who did the honors? I want to kiss his hand. Or hers."

"I think you'll have the chance in just a moment." The quick tap of running footsteps, as of a person with short legs, was just audible from ahead around the curve of the corridor. Miles drew his stunner. "And this time, I don't have to keep him arguing. Maybe Quinn's spooked him back this way," he added hopefully. He was getting extremely worried about Quinn.

Mark rounded the curve and skidded to a halt before them with a hopeless cry. He turned, stepped, stopped, turned again like an animal in a trap. The right side of his face was streaked red, his ear was edged with oozing yellow-white blisters, and the stench of burnt hair crept faintly through the air.

"*Now* what?" asked Miles.

Mark's voice was high and stretched. "There's some painted lunatic back there after me with a plasma gun! They've taken over the next watchtower—"

"Did you see Quinn anywhere?"

"No."

"Miles," said Ivan in puzzlement, "our guys wouldn't carry plasma arcs on an antipersonnel mission like this, would they? Not in the middle of a critical facility like this—they'd not want to risk damaging the machinery—"

"Painted?" said Miles urgently. "Like how? Not—not face paint like a Chinese opera mask, by chance?"

"I don't know—what a Chinese opera mask looks like," panted Mark, "But they—well, one—had colors solid from ear to ear."

"The ghem-commander, no doubt," Miles breathed. "On formal hunt. They've upped the bid, it seems."

"Cetagandans?" said Ivan sharply.

"Their reinforcements must have finally arrived. They must have picked up my trail at the shuttleport. Oh, God—and Quinn went that way . . . !" Miles too turned in a circle, and swallowed panic back to the pit of his stomach where it belonged. It must not be permitted to rise to the level of his brain. "But you can relax, Mark. They don't want to kill you."

"The hell they don't! He shouted, 'There he is, men!' and tried to blow my head off!"

Miles's lips peeled back on a dirty grin. "No, no," he carolled soothingly. "Merely a case of mistaken identity. Those people want to kill me—Admiral Naismith. It's just the ones on the other end of the tunnel who want to kill you. Of course," he added jovially, "neither of them can tell us apart."

Ivan made a derisive sputter.

"Back this way," said Miles decisively, and led on at a run. He swung into the transverse corridor and skidded to a halt before the outside access hatch. Ivan and Mark galloped up behind.

Miles stood on tiptoe, and gritted his teeth. According to the control readout, the tide had now risen higher than the top of the hatch. This exit was sealed by the sea.

Chapter Fifteen

Miles slapped his wrist comm channel open. "Nim!" he called.

"Sir!"

"There's a Cetagandan covert ops squad in Tower Seven. Strength unknown, but they have plasma arcs."

"Yes, sir," came Nim's breathless voice. "We just found them."

"Where are you and what can you see?"

"I have a pair of soldiers outside each of the three tower entrances, with a backup in the bushes in the parking area. The—Cetagandans, you say, sir?—just pumped some plasma blasts out the main corridor as we tried to enter."

"Anybody hit?"

"Not yet. We're flat."

"Any sign of Commander Quinn yet?"

"No, sir."

"Can you get a fix on her wrist comm?"

298

"It's somewhere in the lower levels of this tower. She doesn't respond and it's not moving."

Stunned? Dead? Was her wrist even still in her wrist comm? No telling.

"All right," Miles took a breath, "put in an anonymous call to the local police. Tell them there's armed men in Tower Seven—maybe saboteurs trying to blow up the Barrier. Make it convincing—try to sound scared."

"No problem, sir," said Nim earnestly.

Miles wondered how nearly the plasma beam had parted Nim's hair. "Until the constables arrive, keep the Cetagandans sealed in the tower. Stun anyone who tries to exit. The locals can sort them out later. Put a couple of point men down in Tower Eight to seal that end, have them work north and drive the Cetagandans back if they try to exit south. But I think they'll head north." He put his hand over the comm and added to Mark, "Chasing you." He lifted his palm and continued to Nim, "As the police arrive, pull back. Avoid contact with 'em. But if you do get cornered, go meekly. We're the good guys. It's those nasty strangers inside the tower with the illegal plasma arcs they should be after. We're just tourists who spotted something peculiar while out for an evening stroll. You copy?"

There was a strained grin in Nim's voice. "Copy, sir."

"Keep an observer in sight of Tower Six. Report when the police arrive. Naismith out."

"Copy, sir. Nim out."

Mark emitted a muffled moan, and surged forward to grab Miles by his jacket. "You idiot, what are you doing? Call the Dendarii back—order them to clear the Cetagandans out of Tower Seven! Or I will—"

He made to grab at Miles's wrist; Miles held him off and put his left hand behind his back.

"Ah-ah! Calm yourself. There's nothing I'd like more than a game of stunner tag with the Cetagandans, since we outnumber them—but they have plasma arcs. Plasma arcs have more than three times the range of a stunner. I don't ask my people to face that kind of tactical disadvantage without dire need."

"If those bastards catch you they'll kill you. How much more dire does it have to be?"

"But Miles," said Ivan, looking up and down the corridor doubtfully, "didn't you just trap us in the center of a pincers movement?"

"No," Miles grinned, exhilarated, "I did not. Not while we own a cloak of invisibility. Come on!" He trotted back to the T intersection and turned right, back toward the Barrayaran-held Tower Six.

"No!" Mark balked. "The Barrayarans might kill you by accident, but they'll kill me on purpose!"

"The ones back there," Miles jerked his head over his shoulder, "would kill us both just to make sure. The Dagoola operation left the Cetagandans more peeved with Admiral Naismith than I think you have grasped. Come on."

Reluctantly, Mark followed, Ivan bringing up the rear.

Miles's heart pounded. He wished he felt half as confident as his grin to Ivan had suggested. But Mark must not be permitted to sense his doubt. A couple of hundred meters of blank syntacrete jerked past as he ran on tiptoe, trying to make as little noise as possible. If the Barrayarans had already worked their way this far down the tunnel—

They came to the last pumping station, and still no sign of the lethal trouble ahead. Or behind.

This pumping station was quiescent again. It would

be another twelve hours to the next high tide. If no unexpected surges came downstream, it should stay shut down till then. Still, Miles was disinclined to leave it to chance, and from the way Ivan was shifting from foot to foot, watching him with growing alarm, he'd better be able to offer a guarantee.

He began looking over the control panels, raising one for a look within. Fortunately, it was much simpler than, say, the control nexus for a Jumpship propulsion chamber. A cut here, then there, should disable this pump without lighting up boards in the watchtower. He hoped. Not that anyone in the tower was likely to be paying much attention to their boards just this moment. Miles glanced up at Mark. "I need my knife, please."

Unwillingly, Mark handed the antique dagger over, and, at a look from Miles, its sheath as well. Miles used the point to pop the hair-fine wires. His guess as to which ones were which seemed correct; he tried to look like he'd known it all along. He did not hand the knife back when he was done.

He went to the pumping chamber hatch and opened it. No beeping this time. His gravitic grappler made an instant handle on the smooth inner surface. Last problem was that damn manual locking bar. If some innocent—or not-so-innocent—came along and gave it a twirl—ah, no. The same model of tensor field lever, ally to the gravitic grappler, that Quinn had used to open the hatch to the ledge worked here. Miles blew a breath of relief through pursed lips. He returned to the control panel facing the corridor and slapped on his fisheye scan at the end of a row of dials. It blended in nicely.

He gestured toward the open hatch to the pumping chamber, as inviting as a coffin. "All right. Everybody in."

Ivan went white. "Oh, God, I was afraid that was what you had in mind." Mark did not look much more thrilled than Ivan.

Miles lowered his voice, softly persuasive. "Look, Ivan, I can't force you. You can head on up the corridor and take the chance that your uniform will keep you from getting your brains fried by somebody's nervous reflex. If you survive contact with Destang's hit squad, you'll get arrested by the locals, which probably won't be fatal. But I'd rather you stuck with me." He lowered his voice still further. "And didn't leave me alone with *him*."

"Oh." Ivan blinked.

As Miles expected, this appeal for help had more impact than logic, demands, or cajolery. He added, "Look, it's just like being in a tactics room."

"It's just like being in a trap!"

"Have you ever been in a tactics room when the power's knocked out? They are traps. All that sense of command and control is an illusion. I'd rather be in the field." He smirked, and jerked his head toward his double. "Besides, don't you think Mark ought to get the chance to share your recent experience?"

"When you put it that way," growled Ivan, "it has a certain appeal."

Miles lowered himself into the pumping chamber first. He thought he could just hear distant footsteps scuffing in the corridor. Mark looked like he wanted to bolt, but with Ivan breathing down his neck he had little choice. Finally Ivan, with a gulp, dropped beside them. Miles keyed on his hand light; Ivan, the only one tall enough, shoved the heavy hatch shut. It was profoundly silent for a moment, but for their breathing, as they squatted knee to knee.

Ivan's swollen, empurpled hands clenched and unclenched, sticky with sweat and blood. "At least y'know they can't hear us."

"Cozy," grunted Miles. "Pray our pursuers are as stupid as I was. I ran past this place twice." He opened the scanner case and set the receiver to project the north-and-south view of the still-empty corridor. There was a very faint draft in the chamber, Miles noted. Anything more would foretell a rush of water through the lines, and it would be time to bail out, Cetagandans or no Cetagandans.

"Now what?" said Mark thinly. He looked like he felt trapped indeed, sandwiched between the two Barrayarans.

Miles settled back against the slimy wet wall with a false air of ease. "Now we wait. Just like a tactics room. You spend a lot of time waiting in a tactics room. If you have a good imagination, it's—pure hell." He keyed his wrist comm. "Nim?"

"Yo, sir. I was just about to call you." Nim's uneven voice sounded like he was running, or maybe crawling. "A police aircar just landed at Tower Seven. We're withdrawing through the park strip behind the Barrier. The observer reports the locals just entered Tower Six, too."

"Have you got anything off Quinn's wrist comm?"

"It still hasn't moved, sir."

"Has anyone made contact with Captain Galeni yet?"

"No, sir. Wasn't he with you?"

"He left about the time I lost Quinn. Last seen on the outside of the Tidal Barrier at about the midpoint. I'd sent him to look for another way in. Ah . . . report at once if anyone spots him."

"Yo, sir."

Damn, another worry. Had Galeni run into trouble, Cetagandan, Barrayaran, or local? Had he been betrayed by his own state of mind? Miles now wished he'd kept Galeni by him as heartily as he wished he'd kept Quinn. But they hadn't yet found Ivan then; Miles hardly could have done otherwise. He felt like a man trying to assemble a jigsaw puzzle of live pieces, that moved and changed shape at random intervals with tiny malicious giggles. He unclenched his teeth. Mark was regarding him nervously; Ivan was hunkered down not paying much attention to anything, by the way he was biting his lips locked in an internal struggle with his new-won claustrophobia.

There was a movement in the somewhat distorted 180-degree scanner view of the corridor, a man loping silently around the curvature from the south end. Cetagandan point man, Miles guessed, though he wore civilian clothes. He had a stunner, not a plasma arc in his hand—apparently the Cetagandans were now aware that the locals were on the scene in too great force to silence by a convenient murder, and were now thinking of de-escalating, or at least decapitalizing, the Situation. The Cetagandan scouted up the corridor a few more meters, then vanished back the way he'd come.

A minute later, movement from the north: a pair of men tiptoeing along as quietly as a couple of gorillas of that size could move. One of them was the numbskull who'd managed to appear on a covert op still wearing his regulation Service boots. He too had exchanged his original weapon for a more demure stunner, though his companion still carried a lethal nerve disruptor. It looked like it really could be shaping up for a round of stunner tag. Ah, the stunner, weapon of choice for all uncertain situations, the one weapon with which you really could shoot first and ask questions later.

"Holster your nerve disruptor, *that's* right, good boy!" Miles murmured, as the second man too switched weapons. "Heads up, Ivan; this could be the best show we'll see all year."

Ivan glanced up, his absorbed uncertain smile transmuting into something genuinely sardonic, more like the old Ivan. "Oh, shit, Miles. Destang will have your nuts for engineering this."

"At present, Destang doesn't even know I'm involved. H'sh. Here we go."

The Cetagandan point man had returned. He made a come-on motion, and was leapfrogged by a second Cetagandan. On the other end of the corridor, beyond their view due to the curve, the remaining three Barrayarans came jogging. That accounted for all the Barrayarans that had been in the tower; any outer-perimeter backup was now cut off from them by the cordon of local police. The Barrayarans had apparently given up on their mysteriously vanished quarry and were in pull-out mode, hoping to exit via Tower Seven as quickly as possible without having to explain themselves to a bunch of unsympathetic Earthmen. The Cetagandans, who had actually witnessed the supposed Admiral Naismith run this way, were still in hunting array, though their rear guard was presumably closing up with the pressure from the locals coming on strong behind.

No sign of the rear guard yet; no sign of Quinn being dragged along as a prisoner. Miles didn't know whether to hope for that or not. It would be very nice to know she was still alive, but fiendishly difficult to extract her from the Cetagandans' clutches before the constables closed in. Least-cost scenario called for letting her be stunned/arrested with the mob of them, and reclaiming her from the police at their leisure—but suppose some Cetagandan goon decided in the heat of the final crunch that dead women couldn't talk? Miles jittered like a boiling kettle at the thought.

Perhaps he should have jacked up Ivan and Mark and attacked. The breakable leading the disabled and the unreliable in an assault on the unknown . . . no. But would he have done more, done less, for any other officer in his command? Was he so worried about his command logic being ambushed by his emotions that he was now erring in the opposite direction? That would be a betrayal of both Quinn and the Dendarii. . . .

The lead Cetagandan darted into the line of sight of the lead Barrayaran. They both fired instantly, and dropped each other in a heap.

"Stunner reflexes," muttered Miles. "S' wonderful."

"My God," said Ivan, entranced to the point of wholly forgetting his hermetic enclosure, "it's just like the proton annihilating the anti-proton. Poof!"

The remaining Barrayarans, strung out along the corridor, flattened to the wall. The Cetagandan dropped to the floor and crawled to his downed comrade. A Barrayaran popped out into the corridor and blitzed him, the Cetagandan's return shot going wide. Two of the four Barrayarans hurried to the unconscious bodies of their mystery opponents. One prepared to offer covering fire, the other began checking them out, weapons, pockets, clothing. He naturally turned up no IDs. The baffled Barrayaran was just pulling off a shoe to dissect— Miles felt he would continue on to the body itself momentarily— when a distorted amplified voice began booming down the corridor from their rear. Miles could not quite make out the echo-splintered words, but the sense of it was clearly, "Here! Halt! What's all this, then?' "

One of the Barrayarans helped another load up the

stunned one for a shoulder-carry; it had to have been the biggest man who'd been hit, Boots himself. They were close enough to the fisheye that Miles could make out the carrier's legs shake slightly as he straightened and began staggering south under his burden, two men taking the point before and the remaining one the rear guard behind.

The doomed little army had gone perhaps four steps when another pair of Cetagandans appeared around the south curve. One was firing his stunner back over his shoulder as he ran. His attention was so divided, he did not see his partner go down to the Barrayaran point men's stunner fire until he tripped over the sprawling body and fell headlong. He kept his clutch on his own stunner, turned his fall into a controlled roll, and snapped off return fire. One of the Barrayaran point men went down.

The Barrayaran rear guard leapfrogged forward around the burdened middle man and helped his partner zap the rolling Cetagandan, then ran forward with him, hugging the wall. Unfortunately, they overshot the arc of concealment at the same moment as a blast of massed, unaimed stunner fire from beyond the curvature was clearing the corridor for some forward push from the unknowns—police combat team, Miles deduced both from the tactic and the fact that the Cetagandan had been firing in that direction. Men met energy wave with predictable results.

The remaining Barrayaran stood in the corridor bending under the weight of his unconscious comrade and cursing steadily, his eyes squeezed shut as if to shut out the sheer overwhelming embarrassment of it all. When the police appeared behind him he clumped in a circle to face them and raised his hands in surrender as best he could, flipping his empty palms out and letting his stunner clatter to the floor.

Ivan's voice was suffused. "I can just see the vid call to Commodore Destang now. 'Uh, sir? We ran into this little problem. Will you come get me . . . ?' "

"He may prefer to desert," commented Miles.

The two converging police squads came within a breath of repeating the mutual annihilation of their fleeing suspects, but managed to get their true identities communicated just in time. Miles was almost disappointed. Still, nothing could go on forever; at some point the corridor would have become impassable due to the piles of bodies, and the havoc trail off according to the typical senescence curve of a biological system choked on its own waste. It was probably too much to ask that the police clear themselves, as well as the nine assassins, out of the path to escape. Miles was clearly in for another wait. Blast it.

Creaking, Miles stood, stretched, and leaned against the wall with folded arms. It had better not be too long a wait. As soon as the police combat squad called the all-clear, the bomb squad and Tidal Authority techs would appear and start going over every centimeter of the place. The discovery of Miles's little company was inevitable. But not lethal, as long as—Miles glanced down at Mark, hunkering at his feet—no one panicked.

Miles followed Mark's gaze to the scanner display, where the police were checking over the stunned bodies and scratching their heads. The captured Barrayaran was being properly surly and uninformative. As a covert ops agent he was conditioned to withstand torture and fast-penta too; there was little the London constables were likely to get out of him with the methods at their disposal, and he obviously knew it.

Mark shook his head, watching the chaos in the corridor. "Whose side are you on, anyway?"

"Haven't you been paying attention?" asked Miles. "This is all for you."

Mark looked up at him sharply, scowling. "Why?"

Why, indeed. Miles eyed the object of his fascination. He could see how a clone could get to be an obsession, and vice versa. He jerked up his chin in the habitual tic; apparently unconsciously, Mark did the same. Miles had heard weird tales of strange relationships between people and their clones. But then, anyone who deliberately went out and had a clone made must be kinky to start with. Far more interesting to have a child, preferably with a woman who was smarter, faster, and better-looking than oneself; then there was at least a chance for a bit of evolution in the clan. Miles scratched his wrist. Mark, after a moment, scratched his arm. Miles refrained from deliberately yawning. Better not start anything he couldn't stop.

So. He knew what Mark was. Maybe it was more important to realize what he was not. Mark was not a duplicate of Miles himself, despite Galen's best efforts. Was not even the brother of an only-child's dreams; Ivan, with whom Miles shared clan, friends, Barrayar, private memories of the ever-receding past, was a hundred times more his brother than Mark could ever be. It was just possible he had underappreciated Ivan's merits. Botched beginnings could never be replayed, though they could be—Miles glanced down at his legs, seeing in his mind's eye the artificial bones within—repaired. Sometimes.

"Yeah, why?" Ivan put in at Miles's lengthening silence.

"What," piped Miles, "don't you like your new cousin? Where's your family feeling?"

"One of you is more than enough, thanks. Your Evil Twin here," Ivan made a horned-finger gesture, "is more than I can take. Besides, you both keep locking me in closets."

"Ah, but at least I called for volunteers."

"Yeah, I know that one. 'I want three volunteers, you, you, and you.' You used to bully me and your bodyguard's daughter around that way even before you were in the military, back when we were little kids. I remember."

"Born to command." Miles grinned briefly. Mark's brows lowered, as the apparently tried to imagine Miles as playground bully to the very large and healthy Ivan. "It's a mental trick," Miles informed him.

He studied Mark, who squatted uncomfortably, drawing his head down into his shoulders like a turtle against his gaze. Was this evil? Confusion, to be sure. Distortion of spirit as well as body—though Galen could have been only a little more awful as a child's mentor than Miles's own grandfather. But to be properly sociopathic one must be self-centered to an extreme degree, which did not seem to describe Mark; he had hardly been permitted to have a self at all. Maybe he was not self-centered enough. "Are you Evil?" Miles asked lightly.

"I'm a murderer, aren't I?" sneered Mark. "What more d'you want?"

"Was that murder? I thought I sensed some element of confusion."

"He grabbed the nerve disruptor. I didn't want to give it up. It went off." Mark's face was pale in memory, white and deeply shadowed in the sharp sideways illumination cast by Miles's handlight stuck to the wall. "I meant it to go off."

Ivan's brows rose, but Miles ruthlessly did not

pause to fill him in. "Unpremeditated, perhaps," suggested Miles.

Mark shrugged.

"If you were free . . ." began Miles slowly.

Mark's lips rippled. "Free? Me? What chance? The police will have found the body by now."

"No. The tide was up over the rail. The sea has taken it. Might be three, four days before it surfaces again. If it surfaces again." And a repellent object it would be by then. Would Captain Galeni wish to reclaim it, have it properly buried? Where *was* Galeni? "Suppose you were free. Free of Barrayar and Komarr, free of me too. Free of Galen and the police. Free of obsession. What would you choose? Who are you? Or are you only reaction, never action?"

Mark twitched visibly. "Suck slime."

One corner of Miles's mouth curved up. He scuffed his boot through the gook on the floor, stopped himself before he began doodling with his toe. "I don't suppose you'll ever know as long as I'm standing over you."

Mark spat the dregs of his hatred. "You're the free one!"

"Me?" Miles was almost genuinely startled. "I'll never be as free as you are right now. You were yoked to Galen by fear. His control only equalled his reach, and both were broken together. I'm yoked by—other things. Waking or sleeping, near or far, makes no difference. Yet . . . Barrayar can be an interesting place, seen through other eyes than Galen's. The man's own son saw the possibilities."

Mark smirked sourly, staring at the wall. "You making another play for my body?"

"For what? It's not like you have the height my— our—genes intended or something. And my bones are all on their way to becoming plastic anyway. No advantage there."

"I'd be in reserve, then. A spare in case of accidents."

Miles threw up his hands. "*You* don't even believe that any more. But my original offer still stands. Come with me back to the Dendarii, and I'll hide you. Smuggle you home. Where you can take your time and figure out how to be real Mark, and not imitation anybody."

"I don't want to meet those people," Mark stated flatly.

By which he meant, his mother and father; Miles caught that without difficulty, though Ivan was clearly losing the thread. "I don't think they would behave inappropriately. After all, they're already in you, on a fundamental level. You, ah, can't run away from yourself." He paused, tried again. "If you could do anything, what would it be?"

Mark's scowl deepened. "Bust up the clone business on Jackson's Whole."

"Hm." Miles considered. "It's pretty entrenched. Still, what d'you expect of the descendants of a colony that started as a hijacker base? Naturally they developed into an aristocracy. I'll have to tell you a couple of stories about your ancestors sometime that aren't in the official histories . . ." So, Mark had picked up that much good from his association with Galen, a thirst for justice that went beyond his own skin even if including it. "As life-goals go, it would certainly keep you occupied. How would you go about it?"

"I don't know." Mark appeared taken aback by this sudden practical turn. "Blow up the labs. Rescue the kids."

"Good tactics, bad strategy. They'd just rebuild.

You need more than one level of attack. If you figured out some way to make the business unprofitable, it would die on its own."

"How?" Mark asked in turn.

"Let's see . . . There's the customer base. Unethical rich people. One could hardly expect to persuade them to choose death over life, I suppose. A medical breakthrough offering some other form of personal life extension might divert them."

"Killing them would divert them, too," growled Mark.

"True, but impractical in the mass. People of that class tend to have bodyguards. Sooner or later one would get you, and it would be all over. Look, there must be forty points of attack. Don't get stuck on the first one to come to mind. For example, suppose you returned with me to Barrayar. As Lord Mark Vorkosigan, you could expect in time to amass a personal and financial power base. Complete your education—really fit yourself out to attack the problem strategically, not just, ah, fling yourself off the first wall you come to and go *splat*."

"I will never," said Mark through his teeth, "go to Barrayar."

Yeah, and it seems like all the upper-percentile women in the galaxy are in complete agreement with you . . . you may be smarter than you know. Miles sighed under his breath. *Quinn, Quinn, Quinn, where are you?* In the corridor, the police were now loading the last unconscious assassins onto a float pallet. The break would come soon, or not at all.

Ivan was staring at him, Miles realized. "You're completely loony," Ivan stated with conviction.

"What, don't you think it's time somebody took those Jackson's Whole bastards on?"

"Sure, but . . ."

"I can't be everywhere. But I could support the project," Miles glanced at Mark, "if you're all done trying to be me, that is. Are you?"

Mark watched the last of the assassins get wafted away. "You can have it. It's a wonder you're not trying to switch identities with *me*." His head swivelled toward Miles in suddenly renewed suspicion.

Miles laughed, painfully. What a temptation. Ditch his uniform, walk into a tubeway, and disappear with a credit chit for half a million marks in his pocket. To be a free man . . . His eye fell on Ivan's grimy Imperial dress greens, symbol of their service. *You are what you do—choose again. . . .* No. Barrayar's ugliest child would choose to be her champion still. Not crawl into a hole and be no one at all.

Speaking of holes, it was high time to crawl out of this one. The last of the police combat team was marching away past the curve of the corridor after the float pallet. Tidal techs would be all over the place shortly. Better move fast.

"Time to go," Miles said, shutting down the scanner and retrieving his handlight.

Ivan grunted relief, and reached up to pull the hatch open. He boosted Miles through. Miles in turn tossed him a line from his rappelling spool as before. Panic flooded Mark's face for a moment, looking up at Miles framed in the exit, as he realized why he might be last; his expression became closed again as Miles lowered the line. Miles plucked his scanner fisheye and returned it to its case, and keyed his wrist comm. "Nim, status report," he whispered.

"We've got both cars back in the air, sir, about a kilometer inland. The police have cordoned off your area. The place is crawling with 'em."

"All right. Anything from Quinn?"

"No change."

"Give me her exact coordinates inside the tower."
Nim did so.

"Very good. I'm inside the Barrier near Tower Six with Lieutenant Vorpatril of the Barrayaran Embassy and my clone. We're going to attempt to exit via Tower Seven and pick up Quinn on the way. Or at least," Miles swallowed past a stupidly tightened throat, "find out what happened to her. Hold your present station. Naismith out."

They pulled off their boots and padded south down the corridor, hugging the wall. Miles could hear voices, but they were behind them. The T intersection was now lit. Miles held up his hand as they approached, oozed to the corner, and peeked around. A man in Tidal Authority coveralls and a uniformed constable were examining the hatch. Their backs were turned. Miles waved Mark and Ivan forward. They all flitted silently past the tunnel mouth.

There was a police guard stationed in the lift tube foyer at the base of Tower Seven. Miles, boots in one hand and stunner in the other, bared his teeth in frustration. So much for his optimistic hope of exiting without leaving a trace.

No help for it. Maybe they could make up in speed what they were going to lack in finesse. Besides, the man now stood between Miles and Quinn, and thus deserved his fate. Miles aimed his stunner and fired. The constable collapsed.

They floated up the tube. *This level*, Miles pointed silently. The corridor was brightly lit, but there were no subtle people-sounds that Miles could hear. He paced off the meters that Nim had read out to him, and stopped before a closed door marked UTILITY. His stomach was turning over. Suppose the Cetagandans had arranged a slow death for her, suppose the minutes Miles had spent so cool and sensible hiding out had made all the difference. . . .

The door was locked. The control had been buggered. Miles ripped it apart, shorted it out, and heaved the door open manually, nearly snapping his splayed fingers.

She lay in a tumbled heap, too pale and still. Miles fell to his knees beside her. Throat pulse, throat pulse—there was one. Her skin was warm, her chest rose and fell. Stunned, only stunned. Only stunned. He looked up at a blurred Ivan hovering anxiously, swallowed, and steadied his ragged breathing. It had, after all, been the most logical possibility.

Chapter Sixteen

They paused at the side entrance of Tower Seven to pull their boots back on. The park strip lay between them and the city, spangled with white sparks and green patches along the illuminated walks, dark and mysterious between. Miles estimated the run to the nearest bushes, and triangulated the police vehicles scattered about the parking areas.

"I don't suppose you have your hip flask with you?" Miles whispered to Ivan.

"If I had I'd have emptied it hours ago. Why?"

"I was just wondering how to explain three guys dragging an unconscious woman through the park at this hour of the night. If we sprinkled Quinn with a little brandy, we could at least pretend to be taking her home from a party or something. Stunner hangover's enough like the real thing, it'd be convincing even if she started to wake up groggy."

"I trust she has a sense of humor. Well, what's a 'ittle character assassination among friends?"

"Better than the real thing."

"Urgh. Anyway, I don't have my flask. Are we ready?"

"I guess. No, hold it—" Another aircar was dropping down. Civilian, but the police guard at the main tower entrance went to meet it. An older man got out, and they hurried back to the tower together. "Now."

Ivan took Quinn's shoulders and Mark took her feet. Miles stepped carefully over the stunned body of the policeman who had been guarding this exit, and they all double-timed it across the pavement toward cover.

"God, Miles," panted Ivan as they paused in the greenery to scan the next leg, "why don't you go in for little petite women? It'd make more sense. . . ."

"Now, now. She only weighs about double a full field pack. You can make it. . . ." No shouting from behind, no hurrying pursuers. The area closest to the tower was actually probably the safest. It would have been scanned and swept before now, and pronounced clean of intruders. Police attention would be concentrated at the park's border. Which they would have to cross, to reach the city and escape.

Miles stared into the shadows. With all the artificial lighting about, his eyes were not dark-adapting as well as he'd like.

Ivan stared too. "I can't spot any coppers in the bushes," he muttered.

"I'm not looking for police," Miles whispered back.

"What, then?"

"Mark said a man wearing face paint fired at him. Have you seen anybody wearing face paint yet?"

"Ah . . . maybe the police nabbed him first, before we saw the others." But Ivan looked over his shoulder.

"Maybe. Mark—what color was the face? What pattern?"

"Mostly blue. With white and yellow and black kind of swirling slashes. A ghem-lord of middle rank, right?"

"A century-captain. If you were supposed to be me you should be able to read ghem-markings forward and backward."

"There was so much to learn. . . ."

"Anyway, Ivan—do you really want to just assume a century-captain, highly trained, sent from headquarters, formally sworn to his hunt, really let some London constable sneak up and stun him? The others were just ordinary soldiers. The Cetagandans will bail 'em out later. A ghem-lord'd die before he'd let himself be so embarrassed. He'll be a persistent bugger, too."

Ivan rolled his eyes. "Wonderful."

They wound through a couple hundred meters of trees, shrubbery and shadows. The hiss and hum of traffic on the main coastal highway came faintly now. The pedestrian underpasses were doubtless guarded. The high-speed highway was fenced and strictly forbidden to foot traffic.

A synthacrete kiosk cloaked with bushes and vines hopeful of concealing its blunt utility squatted near the main path to the pedestrian underpass. At first Miles took it for a public latrine, but a closer look revealed only one blank locked door. The spotlights that should have illuminated that side were knocked out. As Miles watched, the door began to slide slowly aside. A weapon in a pale hand glittered faintly in the blackness. Mile aimed his stunner and held his breath. The dark shape of a man slipped out.

Miles exhaled. "Captain Galeni!" he hissed.

Galeni jerked as though shot, crouched, and scur-

ried toward them, joining them in their concealment
on hands and knees. He swore under his breath,
discovering, as Miles had, that this grouping of ornamental shrubs had thorns. His eyes took instant inventory of the ragged little group, Miles and Mark,
Ivan and Elli. "I'll be damned. You're still alive."

"I'd sort of been wondering about you, too," Miles
admitted.

Galeni looked—Galeni looked bizarre, Miles decided. Gone was the blank witnessing stillness that
had absorbed Ser Galen's death without comment.
He was almost grinning, electric with a slightly off-
center exhilaration, as if he'd overdone some stimu-
lant drug. He was breathing heavily; his face was
bruised, mouth bloody. His swollen hand flexed on
his weapon—last seen weaponless, he was now carrying a Cetagandan military-issue plasma arc. A knife
hilt stuck out of his boot top.

"Have you, ah, run into a guy wearing blue face
paint yet?" Miles inquired.

"Oh yes," said Galeni in a tone of some satisfaction.

"What the hell happened to you? Sir."

Galeni spoke in a rapid whisper. "I couldn't find
an entrance in the Barrier near where I'd left you. I
spotted that utilities access over there," he jerked his
head toward the kiosk, "and thought there might be
some power optic or water line tunnels back to the
Barrier. I was half-right. There are utility tunnels all
under this park. But I got turned around underground, and instead of coming out in the Barrier, I
ended up coming out a port in the pedestrian cross-
ing under the Channel Highway. Where I found
guess who?"

Miles shook his head. "Police? Cetagandans?
Barrayarans?"

"Close. It was my old friend and opposite number

from the Cetagandan Embassy, Ghem-lieutenant Tabor. It actually took me a couple of minutes to realize what he was doing there. Playing outer-perimeter backup to the experts from HQ. Same as I would have been doing if I hadn't been," Galeni snickered, "confined to quarters.

"He was not happy to see me," Galeni went on. "He couldn't figure what the hell I was doing there either. We both pretended to be out viewing the moon, while I got a look at the equipment he had packed in his groundcar. He may have actually believed me; I think he thought I was drunk or drugged."

Miles politely refrained from remarking, *I can see why*.

"But then he started getting signals from his team, and had to get rid of me in a hurry. He pulled a stunner on me—I ducked—he didn't hit me square on, but I lay low pretending to be more disabled than I was, listening to his half of the conversation with the squad in the tower and hoping for a chance to reverse the situation.

"The feeling was just coming back to the left half of my body when your blue friend showed up. His arrival distracted Tabor, and I jumped them both."

Miles's brows rose. "How the devil did you manage that?"

Galeni's hands were flexing as he spoke. "I don't . . . quite know," he admitted. "I remember hitting them. . . ." He glanced at Mark. "It was nice to have a clearly defined enemy for a change."

Upon whom, Miles guessed, Galeni had just unloaded all the accumulated tensions of the last impossible week and this mad night. Miles had witnessed berserkers before. "Are they still alive?"

"Oh yes."

Miles decided he would believe that when he'd

had a chance to check for himself. Galeni's smile was alarming, all those long teeth gleaming in the darkness.

"Their *car*," said Ivan urgently.

"Their car," agreed Miles. "Is it still there? Can we get to it?"

"Maybe," said Galeni. "There is at least one police squad in the tunnels now. I could hear them."

"We'll have to chance it."

"Easy for you to say," muttered Mark truculently. "You have diplomatic immunity."

Miles stared at him, seized by berserker inspiration. His finger traced over an inner pocket in his grey jacket. "Mark," he breathed, "how would you like to *earn* that hundred-thousand Betan dollar credit chit?"

"There isn't any credit chit."

"That's what Ser Galen said. You might reflect on what else he was wrong about tonight." Miles glanced up to check what effect mention of his father's name had on Galeni. A cooling one, apparently; some of the drawn and inward look returned to his eyes even as Miles watched. "Captain Galeni. Are those two Cetagandans conscious, or can they be brought to consciousness?"

"At least one is. They may both be by now. Why?"

"Witnesses. Two witnesses, ideal."

"I thought the whole point of sneaking off instead of surrendering was to avoid witnesses?" said Ivan plaintively.

"I think," Miles overrode him, "I had better be Admiral Naismith. No offense, Mark, but you don't have your Betan accent quite right. You don't hit your terminal *R*'s quite hard enough or something. Besides, you've practiced Lord Vorkosigan more."

Galeni's eyebrows were going up, as he grasped the idea. He nodded thoughtfully, though his face

as he turned his gaze on Mark was unreadable enough
to make Mark flinch. "Indeed. You owe us your
cooperation, I think." He added even more softly,
"You owe me."

This was not the moment to point out how much
Galeni owed Mark in return, though a brief meeting
of their eyes convinced Miles that Galeni, at least,
was perfectly conscious of the two-way flow of that
grim debt. But Galeni would not fumble this opportunity.

Sure of his alliance, Admiral Naismith said, "Into
the tunnel, then. Lead on, Captain."

The Cetagandan groundcar was parked in a shadowy spot under a tree, a few meters to their left as
they rose up out of the lift tube from the pedestrian
subway to the Barrier park. Still no police guard on
this end; the end toward the park, Galeni had informed them, had a two-man squad, though they had
not risked themselves rechecking that fact. The scurry
through the tunnels had been hectic enough, barely
dodging a police bomb squad.

The spreading plane tree shielded the car from
view of most of the (closed, at this hour) shops and
apartments lining the other side of the narrow city
street. No insomniac peeping out an upper window
could have witnessed Galeni's encounter, Miles hoped.
The highway above and behind them was walled and
blind. Miles still felt exposed.

The groundcar bore no embassy identification, nor
any other unusual features to draw attention; bland,
neither old nor new, a little dirty. Definitely covert
ops. Miles raised his brows and whistled silently at
the fresh dents in the side, about the size of a man's
head, and the blood spattered on the pavement. In
the dimness the red color was fortunately subdued.

"Wasn't that a bit noisy?" Miles inquired of Galeni, pointing to the dents.

"Mm? Not really. Dull thumps. Nobody yelled." Galeni, after a quick look up and down the street and a pause for a lone groundcar to whisper past, raised the mirrored bubble canopy.

Two shapes huddled in the back seat, hitched up with their own equipment. Lieutenant Tabor, in civilian clothes, blinked over his gag. The man with the blue face paint sat slumped next to him. Miles checked one eyelid, and found the eye still rolled back. He rummaged in the front for a medkit. Ivan loaded and settled Elli and took the controls. Mark slid in beside Tabor, and Galeni sandwiched their captives from the other side. At a touch from Ivan the canopy sighed down and locked itself, jamming them all in. Seven was a crowd.

Miles leaned over the back of the front seat and pressed a hypospray of synergine, first aid for shock, against the century-captain's neck. It might bring him around, and certainly would not harm him. At this present peculiar moment, Miles's would-be killer's life and continued health was a most precious commodity. As an afterthought, Miles gave Elli a dose too. She emitted a heartening moan.

The groundcar rose on its skirts and hissed forward. Miles exhaled with relief as they put the coast behind them, turning into the maze of the city. He keyed his wrist comm, and said in his flattest Betan accent, "Nim?"

"Yo, sir."

"Take a fix on my comm. Follow along. We're all done here."

"We have you, sir."

"Naismith out."

He settled Elli's head in his lap and turned to

watch Tabor over the seat back. Tabor was staring back and fourth from Miles to Mark, beside him.

"Hello, Tabor," said Mark, carefully coached, in his best Barrayaran Vor tones—did it really sound that snide?—"How's your bonsai?"

Tabor recoiled slightly. The century-captain stirred, staring through slitted but focusing eyes. He tried to move, discovered his bonds, and settled back—not relaxed, but not wasting energy on futile struggle.

Galeni reached over him and loosed Tabor's gag. "Sorry, Tabor. But you can't have Admiral Naismith. Not here on Earth, anyway. You can pass the word up your chain of command. He's under our protection until his fleet leaves orbit. Part of the agreed price for his helping the Barrayaran Embassy find the Komarrans who had lately kidnapped some of our personnel. So back off."

Tabor's eyes shifted, back and forth, as he spat out his gag, worked his jaw, and swallowed. He croaked, "You're working together?"

"Unfortunately," growled Mark.

"A mercenary," carolled Miles, "gets it where he can."

"You made a mistake," hissed the century-captain, focusing on the admiral, "when you took contract against us at Dagoola."

"You can say that again," agreed Miles cheerily. "After we rescued their damned army, the Underground stiffed us. Did us out of half our promised pay. I don't suppose Cetaganda would like to hire us to go after them in turn, eh? No? Unfortunately, I cannot afford personal vengeance. At present, anyway. Or I would not have taken employment with," he bared his teeth in an unfriendly smile at Mark, who sneered back, "these old friends."

"So you really are a clone," breathed Tabor, staring at the legendary mercenary commander. "We thought . . ." he fell silent.

"We thought he was yours, for years," said Mark-as-Lord-Vorkosigan.

Ours! mouthed Tabor in astonishment.

"But the present operation confirmed his Komarran origin," Mark finished.

"We have an agreement," Miles spoke up as if unsettled by Mark's tone, glaring from Mark to Galeni. "You cover me till I leave Earth."

"We have an agreement," said Mark, "as long as you never come any closer to Barrayar."

"You can have bloody Barrayar. I'll take the rest of the galaxy, thanks."

The century-captain was blurring out again, but fighting it, squeezing his eyes shut and breathing in a controlled pattern. Concussion, Miles judged. In his lap, Elli's eyes popped open. He stroked her curls. She emitted a ladylike burp, saved by the synergine from the more usual post-stun vomiting. She sat up, looked around, saw Mark, the Cetagandans, Ivan, and shut her jaw with a snap, concealing her disorientation. Miles squeezed her hand. *I'll explain later*, his smile promised. She lowered her brows at him in exasperation, *You'd better*. She lifted her chin, poised before the enemy even in the teeth of her own bewilderment.

Ivan turned his head, inquiring out of the side of his mouth of Galeni, "So what do we do with these Cetagandans, sir? Drop them off somewhere? From how high up?"

"There is, I think, no need for an interplanetary incident." Galeni was wolfishly cheerful, taking his tone from Miles. "Is there, Lieutenant Tabor? Or do you wish the local authorities to be told what the ghem-comrade was really trying to do in the Barrier last night? No? I thought not. Very well. They both need medical treatment, Ivan. Lieutenant Tabor unfortunately broke his arm, and I believe his, ah, friend has a concussion. Among other things. Your choice, Tabor. Shall we drop you off at a hospital, or would you prefer treatment at your own embassy?"

"Embassy," croaked Tabor, clearly cognizant of possible legal complications. "Unless you want to try and talk your way out of an attempted murder charge," he counter-threatened.

"Only assault, surely." Galeni's eyes glittered.

Tabor smiled most uneasily, looking as if he'd like to edge away if only there was room. "Whatever. Neither of our ambassadors would be pleased."

"Quite."

It was getting near dawn. Traffic was beginning to increase. Ivan circled a couple of streets before spotting a deserted auto-cab stand that did not have a queue of waiting patrons. This seaside suburb was far from the embassy district. Galeni was quite solicitous, helping unload their passengers—but he didn't toss the code-key to the century-captain's hand and foot bonds to Tabor until Ivan began to accelerate back into the street. "I'll have one of my staff return your car this afternoon," Galeni called back as they sped off. He settled in his seat with a snort as Ivan sealed the canopy and added under his breath, "After we go over it."

"Think that charade'll work?" asked Ivan.

"In the short range—convincing the Cetagandans that Barrayar had nothing to do with Dagoola—maybe, maybe not," sighed Miles. "But for the main security issue—there go two loyal officers who will swear under chemohypnotics that Admiral Naismith and Lord Vorkosigan are without question two separate men. That's going to be worth a great deal to us."

"But will Destang think so?" asked Ivan.

"I do not believe," said Galeni distantly, staring out the canopy, "that I give a good goddamn what Destang thinks."

Miles found himself in mental agreement with that sentiment. But then, they were all very tired. But they were all here: he looked around, savoring the faces, Elli and Ivan, Galeni and Mark; all alive, all brought through the night to this moment of survival.

Almost all.

"Where do you want to be dropped off, Mark?" Miles asked. He glanced through his lashes at Galeni, expecting an objection, but Galeni offered none. With the jettisoning of the Cetagandans Galeni had lost the hyper-adrenal edge that had been carrying him; he looked drained. He looked old. Miles did not solicit an objection; *Be careful what you ask for, you might get it.*

"A tube station," said Mark. "Any tube station."

"Very well." Miles called up a map on the car's console. "Up three streets and over two, Ivan."

He got out with Mark as the car settled to the pavement in the drop-off zone. "Back in a minute." They walked together to the entrance to the DOWN lift tube. It was still night-quiet here in this district, only a trickle of people flowing past, but morning rush would be starting soon.

Miles opened his jacket and drew out the coded card. From the tense look on Mark's face he was anticipating a nerve disruptor, in the style of Ser Galen, right to the last. Mark took the card and turned it over in wonder and suspicion.

"There you go," said Miles. "If you, with your background and this bankroll, can't disappear on Earth, it can't be done. Good luck."

"But . . . what do you want of me?"

"Nothing. Nothing at all. You're a free man, for as long as you can keep so. We will certainly not be reporting Galen's, ah, semi-accidental death."

Mark slipped the chit into his trouser pocket. "You wanted more."

"When you can't get what you want, you take what you can get. As you are finding." He nodded toward Mark's pocket; Mark's hand closed over it protectively.

"What is it that you want me to do?" Mark demanded. "What are you setting me up for? Did you really take that Jackson's Whole garbage seriously? What do you expect me to do?"

"You can take it and retire to the pleasure domes of Mars, for as long as it lasts. Or buy an education, or two or three. Or stuff it down the first waste chute you pass. I'm not your owner. I'm not your mentor. I'm not your parents. I have no expectations. I have no desires." *Rebel against that—if you can figure out how—little brother.* . . . Miles held his hands palm-out and stepped back.

Mark swung into the lift tube, never turning his back. "WHY NOT?" he yelled suddenly, baffled and furious.

Miles threw back his head and laughed. "You figure it out!" he called.

The tube field took him, and he vanished, swallowed into the earth.

Miles returned to the friends who waited for him.

"Was that smart?" Elli, breaking off a rapid fill-in from Ivan, worried as he settled in beside her. "Just letting him go like that?"

"I don't know," sighed Miles. " 'If you can't help, don't hinder.' I can't help him; Galen's made him too crazy. I am his obsession. I suspect I'll always be his obsession. I know all about obsessions. The best I can do is get out of his way. In time he may calm down, without me to react against. In time he may—save himself."

His own weariness flooded in. Elli was warm against him, and he was very, very glad of her. Reminded, he keyed his wrist comm and dismissed Nim and his patrol back to the shuttleport.

"Well," Ivan blinked after a full minute of wiped-out silence from all present, "where now? D'you two want to go back to the shuttleport too?"

"Yeah," breathed Miles, "and flee the planet. . . . Desertion is not practical, I'm afraid. Destang would catch up with me sooner or later anyway. We may as well all go back to the embassy and report. The true report. There's nothing left to lie for, is there?" He squinted, trying to think.

"For all of me, there's not," rumbled Galeni. "I do not care for doctored reports anyway. Eventually, they become history. Embedded sin."

"You . . . know I didn't mean it to work out that way," Miles said to him after a silent moment. "The confrontation last night." A damned sorry weak apology that sounded, for getting the man's father blown away. . . .

"Did you imagine you controlled it? Omniscient and omnipotent? Nobody appointed you God, Vorkosigan." Ghostly faint, one corner of his mouth turned up. "I'm sure it was an oversight." He leaned back and closed his eyes.

Miles cleared his throat. "Back to the embassy then, Ivan. Ah . . . no rush. Drive slowly. I wouldn't mind seeing a last bit of London, eh?" He leaned on Elli and watched the early summer dawn creep over the city, time and all times jumbled and juxtaposed like the light and shadow between one street and the next.

*　　*　　*

When they all lined up in a row in Galeni's Security office at the embassy, Miles was put in mind of the set of Chinese monkeys his Dendarii chief of staff Tung kept on a shelf in his quarters. Ivan was unquestionably See-no-evil. From the tight set of Galeni's jaw, as he returned Commodore Destang's glower, he was a prime candidate for Speak-no-evil. That left Hear-no-evil for Miles, standing between them, but putting his hands over his ears probably wouldn't help much.

Miles had expected Destang to be furious, but he looked more disgusted. The commodore returned their salutes and leaned back in Galeni's station chair. When his eye fell on Miles his lips thinned in a particularly dyspeptic line.

"Vorkosigan." Miles's name hung in the air before them like a visible thing. Destang regarded it without favor, and went on, "When I finished dealing with a certain Investigator Reed of the London Municipal Assizes at 0700 this morning, I was determined that only divine intervention could save you from my wrath. Divine intervention arrived at 0900 in the person of a special courier from Imperial HQ." Destang held up a data disk marked with the Imperial seal between his thumb and forefinger. "Here are the new and urgent orders for your Dendarii irregulars."

Since Miles had passed the courier in the cafeteria, this was not wholly unexpected. He suppressed a surge forward. "Yes, sir?" he said encouragingly.

"It appears that a certain free mercenary fleet operating in the far Sector IV area, supposedly under contract to a subplanetary government, has slipped over the line from guerrilla warfare to outright piracy. Their wormhole blockade has degenerated from stopping and searching ships to confiscations. Three weeks ago they hijacked a Tau Cetan registered passenger vessel to convert into a troop transport. So far so good, but then some bright soul among them hit on the idea of augmenting their payroll by holding the passengers for ransom. Several planetary governments whose citizens are being held have fielded a negotiating team, headed by the Tau Cetans."

"And our involvement, sir?" Sector IV was a long way from Barrayar by any measure, but Miles could guess what was coming. Ivan looked wildly curious.

"Among the passengers happened to be eleven Barrayaran subjects—including the wife of Minister for Heavy Industries Lord Vorvane and her three children. As the Barrayarans are a minority of the two hundred sixteen people being held, Barrayar was of course denied control of the negotiating team. And our fleet has been denied permission by their unfriendly governments to cross three of the necessary wormhole nexuses on the shortest route between Barrayar and Sector IV. The next shortest alternate route would take eighteen weeks to traverse. From Earth, your Dendarii can arrive in that local space area in less than two weeks." Destang frowned thoughtfully; Ivan looked fascinated.

"Your orders, of course, are to rescue alive the Emperor's subjects, and as many other planetary citizens as possible, and to deal such punitive measures as you can compatible with the first goal, sufficient to prevent the perpetrators from ever repeating this performance. Since we ourselves are in the midst of critical treaty negotiations with the Tau Cetans, we don't wish them to become aware of the source of this unilateral rescue effort if, ah, anything goes wrong. Your method of achieving these goals appears to be left totally to your discretion. You'll find all the intelligence details HQ had up to eight days ago in here."

He handed the data disk across at last; Miles's hand closed over it itchily. Ivan now looked envious. Destang produced another object, which he handed to Miles with a little of the air of a man having his liver torn out. "The courier also delivered yet another credit chit for eighteen million marks. For your next six month's operating expenses."

"Thank you, sir!"

"Ha. When you're done you're to report to Commodore Rivik at Sector IV headquarters on Orient Station," Destang finished. "With luck, by the time your irregulars next return to Sector II, I will have retired."

"Yes, sir. Thank you, sir."

Destang turned his eye on Ivan. "Lieutenant Vorpatril."

"Sir?" Ivan stood to attention with his best air of eager enthusiasm. Miles prepared to protest Ivan's complete innocence, ignorance, and victimhood, but it turned out not to be necessary; Destang contemplated Ivan for a moment longer, and sighed, "Never mind."

Destang turned to Galeni, who stood stiff-legged— and stiff-necked, Miles guessed. Having beaten Destang back to the embassy that morning, they had all washed, the two embassy officers had changed to clean uniforms, and they had all filed laconic reports, which Destang had just seen. But no one had slept yet. How much more garbage could Galeni absorb before reaching his explosive limit?

"Captain Galeni," said Destang. "On the military side, you stand charged with disobeying an order to remain confined to your quarters. Since this is identical to the charge that Vorkosigan here has managed to so luckily evade, this presents me with a certain problem of justice. There's also the mitigating factor of Vorpatril's kidnapping. His rescue, and the death of an enemy of Barrayar, are the only two tangible results of last night's . . . activities. All else is speculation, unprovable assertions as to your intentions and state of mind. Unless you choose to submit to a fast-penta interrogation to clear up any lingering doubts."

Galeni looked revulsed. "Is that an order, sir?"

Galeni, Miles realized, was about two seconds away from offering to resign his commission—*now*, when so much had been sacrificed—he wanted to kick him, *No, no!* Wild defenses poured through Miles's mind. *Fast-penta is degrading to the dignity of an officer, sir!* or even, *If you dose him you must dose me too—it's all right, Galeni, I abandoned dignity years ago*—except that Miles's idiosyncratic reaction to fast-penta made that a less than useful offer. He bit his tongue and waited.

Destang looked troubled. After a silence he said simply, "No." He looked up and added, "But it does mean that my reports, and yours, Vorkosigan's, and Vorpatril's, will all be bundled up together and sent to Simon Illyan for review. I will refuse to close the case. I didn't arrive at my rank by shying away from military decisions—nor by involving myself gratuitously with political ones. Your . . . loyalty, like the fate of Vorkosigan's clone, has become too ambiguously political a question. I'm not convinced of the long-range viability of the Komarr integration scheme —but I wouldn't care to go down in history as its saboteur.

"While the case is pending, and in the absence of evidence of treason, you'll resume your routine duties here at the embassy. Don't thank me," he added glumly, as Miles grinned, Ivan choked back an out-loud laugh, and Galeni looked fractionally less black, "it was the ambassador's request.

"You are all dismissed to your duties."

Miles squelched the impulse to run before Destang changed his mind; he returned Destang's salute and walked normally with the others toward the door. As they reached it Destang added, "Captain Galeni?"

Galeni paused. "Sir?"

"My condolences." The words might have been pulled out of Destang with pliers, but his discomfort was perhaps a measure of their sincerity.

"Thank you, sir." Galeni's voice was so devoid of inflection as to be deathly, but in the end he managed a small, acknowledging nod.

The locks and corridors of the *Triumph* were noisy with returning personnel, the final placement of equipment and repairs by tech teams, and the loading of the last supplies. Noisy, but not chaotic; purposeful and energetic but not frantic. The absence of frantic was a good sign, considering how long they'd been on station. Tung's tough cadre of non-coms had not permitted routine preparations to slide till the last minute.

Miles, with Elli at his back, was the center of a hurricane of curiosity from the moment he stepped on board—*What's the new contract, sir?* The speed with which the rumor mill cranked out speculation both shrewd and absurd was amazing. He sent the speculators on their way with a repeated, *Yes, we have a contract—yes, we're breaking orbit. Just as soon as you're ready. Are you ready, Mister? Is the rest of your squad ready? Then maybe you'd better go assist 'em. . . .*

"Tung!" Miles hailed his chief of staff. The squat

Eurasian was dressed in civilian gear, carrying luggage. "You just now back?"

"I'm just now leaving. Didn't Auson get hold of you, Admiral? I've been trying to reach you for a week."

"What?" Miles pulled him aside.

"I've turned in my resignation. I'm activating my retirement option."

"*What*? Why?"

Tung grinned. "Congratulate me. I'm getting married."

Stunned, Miles croaked, "Congratulations. Ah— when did this happen?"

"On leave, of course. She's actually my second cousin once removed. A widow. She's been running a tourist boat up the Amazon by herself since her husband died. She's the captain and the cook too. She fries a moo shu pork to kill for. But she's getting a little older—needs some muscle." The bullet-shaped Tung could certainly supply that. "We're going to be partners. Hell," he went on, "when you finish buying out the *Triumph*, we can even afford to dispense with the tourists. You ever want to try water-skiing on the Amazon behind a fifty-meter hoversloop, son, stop by."

And the mutant piranhas could eat what was left, no doubt. The charm of the vision of Tung spending his sunset years watching—sunsets, from a riverboat deck, with a buxom—Miles was sure she was buxom— Eurasian lady on his lap, a drink in one hand and scarfing down moo shu pork with the other, was a little lost on Miles as he contemplated a) what it was going to cost the fleet to buy out Tung's share of the *Triumph*, and b) the huge Tung-shaped hole this was going to leave in his command structure.

Gibbering, hyperventilating, or running around in

small circles were not useful responses. Instead Miles essayed cautiously, "Ah . . . you sure you won't be bored?"

Tung, damn his sharp eyes, lowered his voice and answered the real question. "I wouldn't be leaving if I didn't think you could handle it. You've steadied down a lot, son. Just keep on like you've been." He grinned again and cracked his knuckles. "Besides, you have an advantage not shared by any other mercenary commander in the galaxy."

"What's that?" Miles bit.

Tung lowered his voice still further. "*You* don't have to make a profit."

And that, and his sardonic grin, was as close as cagey Tung was ever likely to admit that he had long ago figured out who their real employer was. He saluted as he left.

Miles swallowed, and turned to Elli, "Well . . . call a meeting of the Intelligence department in half an hour. We'll want to get our pathfinders en route as quickly as possible. Ideally, we want to put a team inside the enemy organization before we arrive."

Miles paused, as he realized he was now looking into the face of the most wily pathfinder in his fleet for people-situations, as versus terrain-situations which called for the talents of a certain Lieutenant Christof. To send her ahead, out of reach, into danger—*No, no!*—was compellingly logical. Quinn's best offensive talents were largely wasted bodyguarding; it was merely an accident of history and security that threw her into that defensive job so often. Miles forced his lips to move on as if never tempted to illogic.

"They're mercenaries; some of our group ought simply to be able to join up. If we can find someone to convincingly simulate the low criminal-psychotic minds of these pirates—"

Private Danio, passing in the corridor, paused to salute. "Thanks for bailing us out, sir. I . . . really wasn't expecting that. You won't regret it, I swear."

Miles and Elli looked at each other as he lumbered on.

"He's all yours," said Miles.

"Right," said Quinn. "Next?"

"Have Thorne pull everything there is off the Earth comm net on this hijacking incident before we quit local space. There might be an odd angle or two not apparent to Imperial HQ." He tapped the data disk in his jacket pocket and sighed, marshalling his concentration for the task ahead. "At least this should be simpler than our late vacation on Earth," he said hopefully. "A purely military operation, no relatives, no politics, no high finance. Straight-up good guys and bad guys."

"Great," said Quinn. "Which are we?"

Miles was still thinking about the answer to that one when the fleet broke orbit.

he clumped in a circle his horse and his and
hands to consider

MILES VORKOSIGAN/NAISMITH:
HIS UNIVERSE AND TIMES

Chronology	Events	Chronicle
Approx. 200 years before Miles's birth	Quaddies are created by genetic engineering.	*Falling Free*
During Beta-Barrayaran War	Cordelia Naismith meets Lord Aral Vorkosigan while on opposite sides of a war. Despite difficulties, they fall in love and are married.	*Shards of Honor*
The Vordarian Pretendship	While Cordelia is pregnant, an attempt to assassinate Aral by poison gas fails, but Cordelia is affected; Miles Vorkosigan is born with bones that will always be brittle and other medical problems. His growth will be stunted.	*Barrayar*
Miles is 17	Miles fails to pass physical test to get into the Service Academy. On a trip, necessities force him to improvise the Free Dendarii Mercenaries into existence; he has unintended but unavoidable adventures for four months. Leaves the Dendarii in Ky Tung's competent hands and takes Elli Quinn to Beta for	*The Warrior's Apprentice*

	rebuilding of her damaged face; returns to Barrayar to thwart plot against his father. Emperor pulls strings to get Miles into the Academy.	
Miles is 20	Ensign Miles graduates and immediately has to take on one of the duties of the Barrayaran nobility and act as detective and judge in a murder case. Shortly afterward, his first military assignment ends with his arrest. Miles has to rejoin the Dendarii to rescue the young Barrayaran emperor. Emperor accepts Dendarii as his personal secret service force.	"The Mountains of Mourning" in *Borders of Infinity* *The Vor Game*
Miles is 22	Miles sends Commander Elli Quinn, who's been given a new face on Beta, on a solo mission to Kline Station.	*Ethan of Athos*
Miles is 23	Now a Barrayaran Lieutenant, Miles goes with the Dendarii to smuggle a scientist out of Jackson's Whole. Miles's fragile leg bones have been replaced by synthetics.	"Labyrinth" in *Borders of Infinity*

Miles is 24	Miles plots from within a Cetagandan prison çamp on Dagoola IV to free the prisoners.	"The Borders of Infinity" in *Borders of Infinity*
	The Dendarii fleet is pursued by the Cetagandans and finally reaches Earth for repairs. Miles has to juggle both his identities at once, raise money for repairs, and defeat a plot to replace him with a double. Ky Tung stays on Earth. Commander Elli Quinn is now Miles's right-hand officer. Miles and the Dendarii depart for Sector IV on a rescue mission.	*Brothers in Arms*
Miles is 25	Hospitalized after previous mission, Miles's broken arms are replaced by synthetic bones. With Simon Illyan, Miles undoes yet another plot against his father while flat on his back.	*Borders of Infinity*

PRAISE FOR
LOIS MCMASTER BUJOLD

What the critics say:

The Warrior's Apprentice: "Now here's a fun romp through the spaceways—not so much a space opera as space ballet.... it has all the 'right stuff.' A lot of thought and thoughtfulness stand behind the all-too-human characters. Enjoy this one, and look forward to the next." —Dean Lambe, *SF Reviews*

"The pace is breathless, the characterization thoughtful and emotionally powerful, and the author's narrative technique and command of language compelling. Highly recommended." —*Booklist*

Brothers in Arms: "... she gives it a geniune depth of character, while reveling in the wild turnings of her tale. ... Bujold is as audacious as her favorite hero, and as brilliantly (if sneakily) successful." —*Locus*

"Miles Vorkosigan is such a great character that I'll read anything Lois wants to write about him. ... a book to re-read on cold rainy days." —Robert Coulson, *Comics Buyer's Guide*

Borders of Infinity. "Bujold's series hero Miles Vorkosigan may be a lord by birth and an admiral by rank, but a bone disease that has left him hobbled and in frequent pain has sensitized him to the suffering of outcasts in his very hierarchical era.... Playing off Miles's reserve and cleverness, Bujold draws outrageous and outlandish foils to color her high-minded adventures." —*Publishers Weekly*

Falling Free: "In *Falling Free* Lois McMaster Bujold has written her fourth straight superb novel. ... How to break down a talent like Bujold's into analyzable components? Best not to try. Best to say 'Read, or you will be missing something extraordinary.'" —Roland Green, *Chicago Sun-Times*

The Vor Game: "The chronicles of Miles Vorkosigan are far too witty to be literary junk food, but they rouse the kind of craving that makes popcorn magically vanish during a double feature." —Faren Miller, *Locus*

MORE PRAISE FOR LOIS MCMASTER BUJOLD

What the readers say:

"My copy of *Shards of Honor* is falling apart I've reread it so often. . . . I'll read whatever you write. You've certainly proved yourself a grand storyteller."
—Liesl Kolbe, Colorado Springs, CO

"I experience the stories of Miles Vorkosigan as almost viscerally uplifting. . . . But certainly, even the weightiest theme would have less impact than a cinder on snow were it not for a rousing good story, and good storytelling with it. This is the second thing I want to thank you for. . . . I suppose if you boiled down all I've said to its simplest expression, it would be that I immensely enjoy and admire your work. I submit that, as literature, your work raises the overall level of the science fiction genre, and spiritually, your work cannot avoid positively influencing all who read it."
—Glen Stonebraker, Gaithersburg, MD

" 'The Mountains of Mourning' [in *Borders of Infinity*] was one of the best-crafted, and simply best, works I'd ever read. When I finished it, I immediately turned back to the beginning and read it again, and I can't remember the last time I did that."   —Betsy Bizot, Lisle, IL

"I can only hope that you will continue to write, so that I can continue to read (and of course buy) your books, for they make me laugh and cry and think . . . rare indeed."   —Steven Knott, Major, USAF

What do you say?

Send me these books!

Shards of Honor • 72087-2 • $4.99 ____
The Warrior's Apprentice • 72066-X • $4.50 ____
Ethan of Athos • 65604-X • $4.99 ____
Falling Free • 65398-9 • $4.99 ____
Brothers in Arms • 69799-4 • $3.95 ____
Borders of Infinity • 69841-9 • $4.99 ____
The Vor Game • 72014-7 • $4.99 ____
Barrayar • 72083-X • $4.99 ____

Lois McMaster Bujold:
Only from Baen Books

If these books are not available at your local bookstore, just check your choices above, fill out this coupon and send a check or money order for the cover price to Baen Books, Dept. BA, P.O. Box 1403, Riverdale, NY 10471.

NAME: _____

ADDRESS: _____

_____

I have enclosed a check or money order in the amount of $ _____.

Anne McCaffrey
vs.
The Planet Pirates